ACKNOWLEDGEMENT

I want to acknowledge the following amazing individuals. From writer friends who helped shape the story, to the enthusiastic beta readers pushing me to publish, to those who became instant Krov fans. An idea has become reality and a dream has been achieved, all because you believed.

Tiffani Burkett
Rachel Hobbs
Eva Bond
Sebastian Vice
Gregory D Stevens
Alexandra Woolf
Suzanna Anderson
Danielle Burreson
Angharad Bentley
Keisha D.
Jen Jungman
Ons Mnajja
Greer Rivers
Bianca White
Kasi Jay

·ONE

TRISTAN

H arder!" Kamilla challenged him as she held onto the heavy steel bed frame above her head. The sun was out now, and they had barely slept, but Tristan was never one to rush things.

Hovering over her, Tristan's mid-length raven hair was doused in sweat, and his lean, muscular body was strained to continue. It was his fourth session with her that night, and he was exhausted. Of all his lovers Kamilla was the most demanding.

He stopped for a moment to catch his breath.

"You *really* need to stop telling me what to do," he warned through shallow breaths.

"I just need it harder."

"I *know* what you need," Tristan said through his teeth.

No matter how many times she begged him to use all his strength on her, Tristan knew Kamilla like the back of his hand. She yearned for the foreplay and the build-up that would cause the tension in her body to be wound up so tight, it had no choice but to snap into intense ripples of pleasure.

"I'm trying not to break the bed again. I just bought it." He said, and then kissed her passionately.

Finally, when her frustration threatened tears, and her body surrendered to its fate, he gave in to her pleas. With every ounce of strength, he pounded into her, repeatedly, with a force that would have hurt the average human. Fortunately, Kamilla wasn't human, she was incredibly powerful, but Tristan didn't know that. When he started dating Obsidian City girls years ago, their occasional use of inhuman strength used to alarm him, but now he'd grown used to it and jaded. For him, city girls were simply tough, both physically and mentally. Still, they needed to stop fucking up his furniture. Lucky, only weeks ago, he had asked his interior decorator to make everything in his bedroom unbreakable, which included bolting the steel bed frame to the floor. He had learned his lesson and was tired of buying furniture.

Kamilla's glistening body arched in pleasure and Tristan's mouth met her breast. Lost in ecstasy, Kamilla's hands clasped the steel bedframe above her head, bending it to her will as if it were made of cheap aluminum.

Tristan, now sated, laid next to Kamilla, regulating his breathing.

"I'm sorry," Kamilla breathed, her eyes closed.

"For what?"

She pointed above her head to the bent bars of the headboard. "I really tried not to—"

"Goddamnit Kam!"

Irritated, Tristan sat up and got out of bed. But, after a few steps, he jolted, suprised by the amount of pain he was in. Curious, he looked down and noticed black and blue marks on his abdomen. The effect of the illicit drugs he'd consumed the night before had worn off, causing his head to pound and his body to reel in sudden pain. He tried to recall what had caused the bruises but couldn't.

When he went into the bathroom to brush his teeth, a clothed Kamilla followed and wrapped her arms around him from behind.

Kamilla was Asian, pale, and almost gothic-looking, wearing a tight black corset and dark make-up. However, her style was quite tame compared to the type of girls he was used to.

"What happened last night?" he asked, his memory in a fog.

"Wow. You don't remember?" Kamilla released her embrace and sat on the sleek chaise inside his luxury-style bathroom. "God, you *really* have to go easy on the Dust."

As he adjusted the temperature in the shower, Kamilla laid back on the chaise to enjoy the view. The glass shower door left nothing to the imagination, but he didn't care.

Tristan was a confident man, and rightfully so. Although his body was a perfect specimen, it was his beautiful face and eyes that entranced most women. His face was chiseled, with a prominent angular jawline, and his eyes, though always tired looking, were a captivating light green. He was also tall, with tattoos and just a few piercings in all the right places.

Kamilla knew Tristan well, having been his constant love interest and, recently, his business confidant.

Kamilla sighed in disappointment as the heat of the water finally fogged the shower door. "So, if you really forgot, I was just leaving the club when a group of guys grabbed me in the alleyway. I had a gun in my boot, but I was forced up against the wall. I screamed for help and then you showed up. I was so scared..."

Kamilla continued to explain her fake damsel in distress story. She didn't need saving, especially not from a fragile human, but she was aware that Tristan had a soft spot for the meeker females, so, pretending to be weak helped her win his affection.

"You really need to be more careful," he said, as he relished the hot water that helped soothe the painful bruises he now had as a result of that fight.

"I know," she admitted with a sigh. "I just don't know why these things keep happening to me."

"Really, Kam?" he scolded sarcastically as he shut the water off, slid the glass door open, and glared at her through dripping wet raven hair. "As if you're that fucking clueless."

She noticed his sudden change of character but simply gave him a blank stare. He grabbed a towel and continued, "You know *exactly* why these things keep happening to you. You intentionally get in those situations because you're desperate for attention. *My* attention." He pointed at his chest.

Shocked and insulted, she spat back, "Are fucking you serious? You think I did that on purpose? You think I try to get beaten, mugged, and nearly raped on purpose!"

Tristan ignored her, put on a pair of jeans and walked out towards the living room.

"Don't you dare walk away!" she called, running after him.

"I didn't say you wanted to be raped!"

"No, but you're insinuating it!"

"No, Kam, I wasn't! You misunderstood. I'm insinuating that you're not an idiot, so *quit* acting like one just to get your way. Did you seriously think I wouldn't notice that you just happen to be in danger every time I'm nearby? This isn't the first time you've done something this. Then I console you, bring you home and we—"

"Oh, so now, not only am I being attacked on purpose, you think I'm manipulating you?"

Tristan rolled his eyes. "Cut the crap, Kam. Why can't you be honest with me? Why don't you talk to me instead of playing these stupid gam—"

"I have!" Kamilla's eyes watered. "I've tried talking to you!"

"When?" Tristan yelled, but his expression softened when he turned and noticed her tears. "I don't know. Weeks ago, days? But you've been pushing me away! You've been pushing everyone away since your mother died! And every time I talk about—about us, you find every excuse to avoid…"

Kamilla rambled on about his lack of commitment to her as he sat on the couch to organize the drugs on his coffee table.

"So, this is what you're going to do again, Trist?" she

complained as he ignored her. "Get high again, go fuck another girl, and then call me all depressed again?"

"Kam, please. Don't do this," he pleaded as he held his aching head. "Not you too. Why has it been the same argument with everyone lately? Seriously, why can't everyone just leave me the fuck alone? I'm never alone!"

Kamilla knew what he meant by 'everyone.' He had meant the women in her clan, in short his friends. After all these years, Tristan still didn't understand why the clan obsessed over him. Kamilla's *kind* required a certain caliber of man, one who wasn't intimidated by their women's god-like strength, among other things, and could satisfy them both sexually and emotionally. It was easy to train a male human, most teenage boys wouldn't object to learn. Yet now, at twenty-five, what made Tristan a hot commodity was his uncanny ability to be physically rough, demanding and punishing in the bedroom, while never losing his protective and compassionate nature. She only wished he was *still* like that.

Ever since his parents' death, Tristan had become bitter, angry and distant. Even though, as a trainee they allowed him to have various women at once, Tristan was admired for staying true to his cardinal rule—one girlfriend, one faithful relationship at a time. Yet, now, to fill the endless void in his life he'd begun to soothe his depression with meaningless sex and drugs.

Tristan lit a cigarette, and when he noticed she had finished arguing he patted the seat next to him. Kamilla stood with her arms crossed but eventually sat down.

"Look, I'm sorry," he said, holding a cigarette and looking at her tenderly. "I'm sorry I've been avoiding this talk. I just can't... I can't give you what you want right now. If I could I—" He stopped, unable to hold her gaze.

"Let's just try it again, Trist." She placed a hand on his leg. "Hey, what do you have to lose? We are basically a couple now anyway. We'd just be exclusive."

"Kami," he sighed. "I've told you before, if I wanted a girlfriend, I'd have one. You're right, I've pushed everyone away and you're… you're my best friend. I don't want to jeopardize that by being a shitty boyfriend. I'm just… not in a good place right now."

And there, he had said it; She would always just be his *best friend*. Kamilla was filled with rage. He wasn't just some charity case to her, and she wasn't the fuzzy, cuddly, human-helping type. Everything she had done, she did with a single goal in mind—him! She had tried being patient, but it had been months since his parents' death, and this path of destruction he was on had to stop.

"Alright!" she cried, frustrated and disillusioned. "You know what? Fuck this, Trist! I'm leaving!" She stood up.

"Come on, Kam. You admit other girls are crazy when they try to force this on me!"

"I am not other girls!" She *hated* being compared to other females. "I've been by your side for years. When you were nothing! When you were a teenager in and out of juvie. Who would bail you out? Me. Who helped you build your businesses? Me! If it wasn't for me, you would've rotted in jail or overdosed on—"

"You know damn well everything I did was to help mom! Plus, you act like I haven't done anything for you." His eyes narrowed. "Last night? This morning? It was *all* about you. All the years we were together? Everything was *always* about you. What else do you want from me? You want me to commit to you again because you run my business? Because you did me favors? That's not how it works, Kam. I've never once asked you to do any of it!"

"You're right." Kamilla paced with her arms crossed. "You're absolutely right Trist. I don't have to do *anything* for you! And it doesn't even matter because you're just going to end up a broke, homeless drug addict on the streets once you go through all of your father's money and your nightclubs go to shit! Don't call me or talk to me ever again!"

"Kam!" He tried to get her attention, but she had grabbed her purse and was already on her way out.

"No. I'm done helping you! I'm worth more than this."

"Kam just listen!"

After she left, he stayed seated, annoyed and alone. He knew she was right, and he knew she deserved better; It was one of the reasons he wouldn't date her again. Kamilla was an amazing woman, and at the moment he was in no position to be the boyfriend she deserved. The truth was, he just wanted to be alone in his darkness, but his female friends were high maintenance.

He looked at the closed door and wondered if she honestly intended to stay out of his life for good. Which wasn't what he wanted. He cared about her, but, for once, he just needed... space.

A few days later, as was his usual evening routine, Tristan went for a walk through the dirty streets of Obsidian City. These walks reminded him of his most recent ex-girlfriend, Sophia. She had a small white Pomeranian, so they would take long walks together. He had hired her as his interior decorator when he bought his upscale city condominium. From the moment they met, he was drawn to her, and when she was done with the renovations, he asked her out. She was a simple but elegant girl, which was a deep contrast to him and most of his exes. There was something very different about Sophia, a vulnerability, and Tristan had never been more attracted to a woman before.

Unfortunately, Sophia mysteriously disappeared from his life. And in the two weeks they dated, they never slept together. His friends never understood why he'd become so obsessed with her. Everyone took one look at him, and they assumed he wanted the wild, darker-type girl, and for reasons he didn't *yet* understand, that was the only kind of girl that ended up in his bed. He believed it was

7

probably because of his work environment. He excelled at partying and organizing musical events, and he turned it into a career.

After his father died, he inherited a decent amount of money and he used part of it to build a few successful ultramodern event venues, bars, and industrial rock clubs.

His phone rang.

"Hey Mack, what's up?"

"We need a few shipments. Our inventory is running low. I'd order them, but we need someone to sign off on payment."

"Okay? Call Kami," Tristan coldly instructed.

"We did. I've been calling her but she won't answer. She hasn't been here in over a week."

"Goddamnit," he whispered. "All right, I'll be right over."

Tristan knew Kamilla was still mad at him. However, she had a stake in these businesses, and it wasn't like her to ignore her job over a personal argument. Clearly, she was doing this to spite him.

As Tristan made his way back to retrieve his car, he passed by a white Gothic-revival style church. It was a magnificent structure linked to many buildings and it took up the whole block. Unlike the dirty, advanced and corrupted surroundings of Obsidian City, the church block was like a rose in the rubble. Its manicured gardens were safely protected by tall, shiny bronze gates.

Obsidian City was a free sector, otherwise known as a 'Dark sector' to outsiders. Dark sectors were cold, dirty, and driven by its focus on technological advancements. Their lack of laws ensured individual freedoms but came with the price of high crime. Light sectors, by contrast, had strict religious laws and were bright, clean, heavily guarded, and full of colorful vegetation. This church was a protected Light sector sanctuary within the city, which is why it looked so out of place.

Tristan heard singing coming from the main cathedral and it reminded him of his mother, Marivel. She died in a car accident on the way to this church. Had he listened to her pleas to come, perhaps she'd still be alive.

Marivel was a single mom who worked hard to put food on the table. His estranged father never helped her financially and it was torture for young Tristan to watch her struggle. He did everything a teenager could do to help, but his wages were never enough. Eventually he resorted to a life of crime. Tristan could still see her tearful face of disappointment when she learned the truth about the money. The guilt still consumed him.

In a cruel twist of fate, only months after inheriting his father's wealth, she died. This beautiful church was a painful reminder of his loss.

Tristan climbed out of his black Tesla roadster as he studied the line outside of his club. Cyberpunks, cybergoths, and others who wore dreadful masks were waiting impatiently to enter. He looked up and noticed that the bright yellow hologram signage advertising his club was flickering. He made a mental note to get it fixed.

When Tristan approached the entrance, the very buff bouncer straightened up and adjusted his tie. Tristan always dressed down, usually in black T-shirt and jeans, but his employees always feared and respected him. He was a fair but uncompromising boss. Those who mistook his kindness for weakness were sent packing.

"Good evening, Mr. Leonhart," the bouncer said, unable to lock his gaze.

"Rez," Tristan said, greeting him.

The bouncer opened the throbbing doors and Tristan was greeted with loud industrial metal music. It was obvious by the crowd that the 800-guest capacity had been reached. The fluorescent painted faces and bodies created waves of color that could rival a Tom Bacher painting. Women holding drink trays, while dressed in skimpy outfits with black bunny masks, greeted him with a smile. The renovation was complete, ultramodern and highly expensive. Glowing colors illuminated the ceiling and walls; even the two bars were lit. Sexy women danced on raised platforms, most of whom instantly noticed his presence. As he made his rounds to the back, a girl grabbed his hand.

"Hey, Trist! It's so good to see you again!" she said with a high-pitched voice. She was pale, with medium-length blonde hair, dark make-up, and a skimpy pink and black cyberpunk outfit. She looked like a corrupt futuristic version of Marilyn Monroe, sexy with a full figure. She threw herself at him with a kiss before he could object. He knew her, of course.

"I'm... sorry, Lea. I'm busy right now," he said tenderly.

She pouted. "Promise you'll come say bye to me before you leave? Pretty please?"

Slightly annoyed, he muttered, "Sure honey." Sporting an overdone smile, she skipped away.

Even though his list was long, Tristan wasn't a player; at least, he didn't think so. He simply didn't want to be attached to anyone at the moment. Yet, his female friends were drawn to him. He felt bad that he couldn't offer himself exclusively to one person, so he'd cater to his girls with affection, clothing, money, and in Kamilla's case, *special* privileges. He also had to be careful how much he led certain girls on. Even before the money, a few girls had gone from obsessed to downright crazy.

After over an hour discussing business with Mack inside the club's office, Tristan came out and was surprised to see Lea still waiting for him. He was slightly annoyed since he just wanted to see and settle things with Kamilla.

"Hey, Trist!" Lea said, as she jumped up to hug him.

"I'm so sorry, Lea, I'm just busy tonight," he said, walking past her, but she grabbed his hand and walked alongside him.

"I can see that. You look like something's got you down," she gave him a cartoonish frown. "Anything I can do to help?"

Lea was special to him. Her voice and her spunkiness always made him smile. She was a sharp contrast to Kamilla who was extremely intelligent, while Lea was just… sweet. Still, she was a girl, and a bisexual, so maybe she could help him figure out how to get Kamilla back on his good side. As they walked outside, Lea held onto his arm proudly, to make other girls understand he was hers for the time being.

As they approached his car, he noticed Lea's excitement, but this wasn't a trip to his house for some *play*. He simply needed a woman's advice. When they got in his car and sat down, he rubbed his forehead.

"Okay, sexy, what's up?" Lea said, "I know something is wrong. You're not—"

"No, I'm fine. I promise," Tristan assured her.

Lea pressed her lips together. He had attempted to end his life more than once recently, and if it weren't for her and Kamilla, this last attempt would have been a sure thing. Lea was aware that Tristan's mother had been the only other human in his life, and when he wanted to end his life, he had mentioned feeling alone, and disconnected. Lea wanted to tell him the truth, that his feelings had merit. That everyone he knew personally was a *Krov*. That he *was* alone, isolated in his humanity. But, it was forbidden to disclose that kind of information to a trainee without the group's permission.

"It's just Kami, she's being impossible," Tristan continued.

Lea rolled her eyes.

"What?" Tristan asked, examining her face for clues.

"Nothing. I just don't like her." She scrunched her face.

"Okay, seriously. Why does everyone hate Kamilla?"

"She's just… not who she is around you."

"How so?" It wasn't the first time he'd heard women express this double life Kamilla seemed to have. He shrugged it off, knowing that

Kamilla was a businesswoman who had a thriving career. She had to be tough in public, but she had a gentle side, sometimes.

Tristan saw Lea contemplate telling him something, but she bit her bottom lip instead.

"Nothing. So, what's the problem Trist?"

"She wants to be exclusive again. You know I haven't been myself lately. I know mom died two months ago. I should be over this by now but… I just don't want to drag Kamilla into problems that I need to solve myself."

"Have you… been sleeping with her?"

"You know she's not exactly the easiest person to say no to. Last night I found her getting assaulted just outside the club. I brought her home, she was crying and begging me to let her stay. One thing led to another…"

"How many times?"

Tristan sighed. "I don't know. Like… four? Maybe five times."

"Tristan! You can't just be friends with a girl, have mind-blowing sex all the time, be the way you are, spend so much time together, and then expect her not to want more."

"So, what am I supposed to do? Blow her off entirely? You know how bad her temper can get."

"No. Do the opposite." Tristan narrowed his eyes. "Look, you can push a girl away, but you have to be nice to her. Buy her something; tell her how much she means to you. Don't mention the word 'friends', some women hate that. She obviously wants to be more than that, but if I were you, I'd leave the sex out of it for a bit. Focus on your friendship."

He lifted an eyebrow suggestively and repeated, "Leave the sex out of it, eh?"

She pushed her head back on the headrest and did her best to look irresistibly cute.

"Well, for her. I'm just satisfied with every little ounce of you I can get."

He smiled, knowing that's what they all say at first. She leaned over to kiss him, and he initially accepted getting lost in the moment, but after a few seconds, he pulled away.

"I'm sorry, sweetie. Not today," he whispered. "But God do you look amazing tonight."

"See, just like that," she sighed in disappointment. "You turned me down gently, *unfortunately*." She got out of his car and leaned into the opened window. "But it won't work forever! See you later, Trist."

"You're the best, Lea!" he called out as she walked away.

TWO

THE PROMISE

There was a knock at Kamilla's front door, and she opened it. Tristan stood there, propped up against the doorway, looking adorable as ever with puppy eyes. In his hand he held up a small gift box.

"Hey, beautiful," he said with a sly smile. "Missed you."

She closed her eyes and rubbed her forehead.

"Stop," she demanded, fighting the smile forming on her face. "Don't start with the cute stuff."

He looked down and chuckled as she walked away, leaving the door open for him to enter.

"Do you have *any* idea how incredibly hard it was to find someone who would sell me jewelry at this time of night?"

"Not as hard as the stuff I do, and the shit I put up with for you," she spat back, mocking his tone.

"Oof. True," he admitted as he set the jewelry box on the kitchen island in front of her and, like an excited child, he placed his elbows on the counter and rested his face in his hands. "Open it."

"Trist, you didn't have to get me anything," she said, putting her hand over her heart.

Kamilla opened the box to find the most beautiful diamond necklace paired with a set of earrings. Each black diamond was encircled with smaller white diamonds that sparkled intensely, even under the soft lights of her kitchen.

"Your favorite color," he said proudly. "Here." He walked behind her and gently put the necklace and earrings on her. The whole situation brought shivers down her spine. Kamilla had dark, almond-shaped eyes and black hair. So, anything black and sparkling looked absolutely stunning on her pale skin.

"Thanks, Trist," she said, in a soft voice, "but… what does this mean?"

Tristan hadn't figured out what to say yet. He needed time to think, so he glanced back looking through the glass window of her liquor cabinet and fetched a bottle of whiskey.

"What does what mean?" he asked, as he grabbed two crystal glasses.

"All this… us?" she said, holding back a smile as he poured the whiskey.

"It means," he cleared his throat, "that you mean a lot to me… that I… care deeply about you." He handed her a glass. "It also means that I've missed you and that I don't like it when you're mad at me."

She took the drink. He gulped down his whiskey and poured himself another. Liquor was all he had to ease his nerves.

"So?" she said while holding back a smile.

Tristan stood there clueless. He knew he had to turn her down gently but struggled to figure out how. Kamilla would surely be upset either way. Still, he had to try.

"Come," he extended his hand to her, "sit with me."

Sighing and rolling her eyes, she placed her hand in his and he led her to the couch. She knew he was stalling, but she hoped this was it, that this was the day he finally realized how much he needed her.

They both sat on her white velvet couch, and he invited her to lay her head on his lap so he could caress her hair. Tristan had always been affectionate with his circle of women. Flirting and sex were, at some point, a part of all his relationships, so he had a difficult time keeping things platonic.

The living room had black floors and stark white furniture. Where there should have been a television, there was a lit fireplace. Knowing he couldn't stall anymore; he took a long swig of whiskey and began to meticulously phrase what he was going to say.

"You know you mean the world to me, right?" he said in a serious tone, and she nodded as he gently ran his fingers through her hair. "And I know you deserve a man who takes care of you and has his shit together… Kami, I'm—I'm a mess right now. I have no drive, no focus, and I simply know you deserve someone who's not in the state I am in. I'm high all the time. I'm angry. I drink often. I'm depressed—"

She got up and turned to face him. "You're all I want, Tristan. And the rest we can work on."

"No Kami," he sighed, "it doesn't work like that. To change I have to want to, but I don't know what I want right now. I can't be anybody's boyfriend because I know I can't treat you the way you deserve. Please understand."

A long silence filled the room.

Irritated, she eventually got up and carried her glass to the kitchen. She stood over the sink and wiped a tear from her cheek.

For Kamilla, the fact that Tristan was the only man capable of making her cry irritated her. She had finally had enough; it was time. Kamilla was a rational woman, but when it came to her love for him, she held on to hope like a child. The truth was, every time he was intimate with someone else, it hurt. Sometimes even physically, and she couldn't bear it any longer. There was also a time constraint, a reason he had to be eliminated.

Because he'd been sexual with her *kind* for so long, Tristan, although still human, was likely infected with a mind-altering virus. Symptoms developed slowly, taking up to ten years to fully develop, but this meant that, unbeknownst to Tristan, every day that passed he'd become more attracted to humans, and eventually violent towards them.

"It's time. Just get it over with," she whispered to herself as she prepared to kill the man she loved.

Tristan saw her carelessly toss her glass into the sink, causing it to shatter. She hit the table with effortless force, and it cracked the marble. He immediately stood up and went to her. He had heard her fist on the counter but he didn't notice the damage.

"Kami… please, stop," he said sweetly, attempting to calm her down before her anger became worse.

After a moment of silence, he wiped the tears from her eyes with the back of his finger. Kamilla wasn't the crying type, so he knew just how much this was hurting her.

"Okay," he hugged her and surrendered. "Please, don't cry. I will… we will be exclusive."

Kamilla shook her head and pushed him away from her. She didn't believe him.

"I will, Kami. Just… just give me time." He held her hands. "Please, I don't like who I am right now and—" Tristan looked away as he tried to control his emotions. "You know, when she passed… I honestly felt like she took everything that was good in me with her… It kills me I can't love you the way you deserve, not now. But I do care about you. And once I figure all this out, on my own," he said, looking up at her, hinting he no longer wanted her help, "I promise I want to try to have a serious relationship with you again. I… don't want to lose you," Tristan held her gaze, meaning every word.

Kamilla was an amazing woman—smart, sexy and successful. He felt like a fool for not loving her the way he should, but he simply wasn't ready emotionally for such a leap.

She rolled her eyes at him and pulled her hands away. "I'm not some stupid girl you can play around with," she said, choking up but still clenching a fist.

17

"Kami, it's not like that. If I say I want you, if I say I look forward to something between us, I mean it. Just… just not now, but soon." He lifted her face gently to look up at him. "I swear it… ok? All I ask is that you give me some space. I need to be alone for a while."

She contemplated for a moment. She knew better, but she desperately wanted to believe him. Eventually, she convinced herself that she had nothing to lose. Tristan would surely pay if he didn't keep his promise.

A few hours after their argument, Kamilla finally loosened up. She had waited patiently over the years to win Tristan's heart, and though she hated waiting, Kamilla was too far gone and emotionally attached to him to refuse.

On her couch, as they cuddled and conversed about old times, Kamilla studied him. There were many reasons she had fallen for him. He was funny, kind and always had a sly and mysterious disposition. He was also cocky and extremely sure of himself; that was the side of him she loved the most.

They both drank the night away, but alcohol didn't affect Kamilla the way it affected him. Alchol and drugs were pushed on trainees, mostly because this way her kind could get away with occasionally letting their speed and powers show. Tristan was known for being exceptionally rough while high or intoxicated, and Kamilla adored him for it.

Not being able to resist him any longer, Kamilla went in for a kiss. He was caught off guard, but gladly accepted. They kissed for a few minutes, and she instinctively straddled him. He pulled away to look at her, and he caressed her face. He wanted her. He *always* wanted her, and over the years he always found himself coming back to her, but Lea's advice echoed in his head, *Keep the sex out of it.* Just then, he stopped. He knew that this was the vicious cycle he needed to end. Kamilla meant a lot to him. She wasn't an occasional fuck or a one-night stand, this was Kamilla, a woman who deserved to be respected, who deserved someone who was faithful to her, and if he couldn't offer her a relationship yet, he wasn't going to sleep with her.

"Kam… let's not do this," he said, cringing and hoping her reaction wasn't a bad one.

"Why?" Her eyes narrowed. She studied his face, attempting to understand what was possibly holding him back.

"I don't know. It's just better this way. For now."

She looked away, trying to understand. She wondered if perhaps he just needed some inspiration. She kissed him again and slowly unbuttoned his shirt.

"Kam… stop," he requested, but she ignored him. She was becoming rough, and he wasn't turned on by it. He tried to be nice as he forcefully pushed her hands away from his body, but Kamilla was strong, and she was able to easily continue. Sex with a human was euphoric for her *kind*. Some were even addicted to the high. Kamilla was one of them.

"Kami, stop it!" He didn't mean to, but he had used all his strength to push her off him, and she had fallen onto the coffee table, crashing objects and glass cups onto the floor.

"Oh shit, Kam… I'm sorry," he said, expressing his concern for her. But he knew from her expression that she was pissed. Unbeknownst to him, he didn't hurt her physically; in fact, his strength was no match for her, and all of this was just another act on her part. She was, however, insulted at the fact that he rejected her. He got up and tried to help her stand, but she refused his help.

"Sorry…" He really didn't know what else to say. Once on her feet he tried to console her, but she pushed him away from her.

"Just… just leave, Trist."

He stood there for a moment trying to find a way to make the situation better, but his vision was blurred, and his speech was slurred. He knew it was best to just wait until he was sober to apologize. So, he walked over to grab his keys from the counter but, knowing he was too drunk to notice her speed, she ran and swiped the keys. She then returned to her position in the blink of an eye. If he was going to die, she wanted to be the one to do it. Currently, he still meant something to her.

Confused at what had just happened he yelled, "What the— Kam! Did you just—? How am I supposed to get home?"

She walked away yelling, "I don't care, but you're not taking your car." She disappeared into the hallway and locked herself in her bedroom. His face was flushed with anger as he approached her bedroom door and knocked on it loudly.

"Kam? Kami! Open the door! I'm serious, open the door now!"

After a long period of no response, he realized he would not get his keys tonight.

"Goddamnit!" he said, pacing and running his hands through his hair.

With all the whiskey gone he grabbed a bottle of wine, took his black trench coat, and decided to walk the two miles to his condo. It wasn't the best idea. Obsidian was a dangerous city, and no one with any sense would walk the streets alone at this hour. He could have called a cab or even a friend, but Tristan often made bad decisions while drunk.

By the time Tristan was halfway home, he had finished the large bottle of wine. Though tired and exhausted, he didn't care if the alcohol killed him, and at this rate, it was probably going to.

Suddenly, Tristan saw movement in the alley from the corner of his eye. A figure emerged, followed by several others. Too many to count in his haze. Before he knew it, they surrounded him, with all his escape routes gone. There was nowhere to go but through them.

"Wallet, jacket and shoes. Now!" said one of the blurry figures. Tristan studied them, searching for a gun but didn't see one. Clearly, they were amateurs or homeless.

"Fuck off," Tristan said as he spat in the figure's face. He didn't have the patience for this, so he did his best to swing at them as they attempted to tackle him.

Somehow, through the haze he got lucky and successfully knocked one man down. Tristan immediately hovered over him and began to pound his fists into the man's face. Remembering he had a knife, Tristan attempted to retrieve it from his back pocket but, before he could pull it out the others pulled him up by his arms.

He stood there, jaw clenched and doing his best to fight them off. Another larger man punched his abdomen repeatedly and Tristan collapsed on the sidewalk, defeated. These kinds of attacks were common in the city. Tristan was angry, but not surprised.

Once the men ripped the jacket, wallet, and shoes from his body, they ran off. Tristan coughed through the pain, and after several minutes, he gathered enough strength to get up again.

"Great. Just fucking great!" he yelled, annoyed as rain came crashing down on him. He was now cold, barefoot and wet as he ran across the street. However, he stepped in a pothole and fell face first onto the curb.

His head had hit the curb, and his forehead was now bleeding.

He got up again and did his best to continue his journey home, but he became lightheaded and disoriented. He quickly found shelter from the rain under a large canopy in front of the church's garden gates and passed out.

Hours later he heard an angelic woman's voice.

"Hello? Sir? Are you okay?"

THREE

THE VIRUS

"Hello? Are you okay?" A woman knelt in front of him as she carefully moved a lock of his hair away from his face. "Sir, please wake up," she pleaded and shook him gently. Tristan had never heard a voice as gentle as hers. He opened his eyes and the sun's brightness blinded him.

"Serene? Serene! Come over here now!" A plump, older woman scolded her as she ran over. Serene ignored the woman's calls and was relieved to see him moving.

"Sir? Are you okay?"

Fuck, he thought to himself when he realized he wasn't dreaming. He rubbed his eyes, before opening them again to look at her. She immediately noticed his bright green eyes as well as the blood on his forehead. Her attraction to his beauty was instantaneous, and she jolted back in surprise.

With her body blocking the sun, she had an ethereal glow about her. Her golden-brown hair beamed around her face. He was instantly captivated by her natural angelic features, as well as her very large and sad hazel-colored eyes that seemed to express genuine worry for him. At first, he wondered if she was a teenager since her simple blue dress looked almost child-like, but when his eyes finally adjusted, he realized she was a woman.

"Get away from that man!" the now heavy-breathing woman demanded with an angry tone as she finally reached them.

"No, I think he's seriously hurt, Aunty," Serene said with concern in her voice. "He's bleeding. He... he needs help!"

"He's not hurt!" the older lady said. "Ugh, and he reeks of alcohol! Probably looking to do God knows what to God knows who! Have you lost your senses?" She grabbed Serene's arm with force and pulled her back behind the garden gates. "You must never pass the gates by yourself! This city is riddled…"

As the woman spoke about the horrors of Obsidian City and the number of people that went missing there, Serene looked back past her shoulders to get one last look at him. He slowly got up and felt embarrassed that a girl like her had even spoken to him. He felt like a mangled-up dog, a trash bag on the side of the road. Yet she seemed honestly concerned for his well-being. He wondered why.

When Tristan got back to his condo, he walked into his bedroom to find clothing so that he could shower.

"Holy shit…" Tristan said when he finally looked at himself in the mirror. His hair was dirty and wet; he had more bruises throughout his body and dry blood on his nose and brow. His shirt even had what looked to be blood or wine on it, he couldn't tell which it was. Tristan tore off his dirty clothes and took a shower.

As the hot water fell over his blood-soaked brow Tristan remembered Serene's face of pity and then fear. He laughed at the irony. Women usually smiled when they looked at him, yet he believed she had to have thought the worst of him. That thought bothered him, and he didn't know why at the time, but it was because he had instantly been attracted to her and he felt... embarrassed.

Suddenly, his heart began to race, and he placed a hand on the wall to keep his balance. He saw a flash and then another, as he began to see warped memories of his encounter with her. It was like a video that would skip, and the order of the memories became distorted. He closed his eyes and tried to shake what he was feeling but couldn't. Serene's gentle voice echoed in his head.

Excuse me, sir? Please wake up. Hello? Tristan covered his ears until finally, the voice went away. It was the same feeling he had felt when he had met Sophia, his ex. Something was wrong.

Around 6 p.m. Tristan was in his office working. He finished inputting some data on spreadsheets and, still feeling unwell, he went to bed.

That night Tristan dreamt:

He's in a room flooded with sunlight... A woman with a tender smile is sitting on a couch. Her hair gleams in the light and her white dress is luminous. He doesn't know who she is, but in this dream, she's his everything. Tristan lies on the couch with his head on her lap, and she caresses his hair. There's a joyful feeling as they talk and share laughter. In this heaven, he feels no worries, no pain. He could rest here for eternity...

Suddenly, the sunlight is gone. The walls turn a gloomy shade of grey, and the room starts to shake. The woman covers her face and sobs. Her cries get louder, and Tristan kneels before her, attempting to calm her. The woman looks up and screams in terror at what she sees in him. Tristan moves back in shock when he notices her familiar face.

"Serene?" he asks, but she stands and moves away from him. Confused, Tristan tries to get closer, but she runs away into the hallway and he finally notices the glowing white feathered wings on her back, they weren't there before.

Unable to make sense of the chaos, he runs after her, yelling, "Come back!" He's afraid to be alone in the darkening rubble. As he chases her through the labyrinth of corridors in the still crumbling building, the hallways lengthen, then become narrow. An eerie ringing gets louder and louder the more he runs after her and eventually, he loses sight of her. "Where is she? I can't find her!" He collapses onto his knees defeated and cries. He wipes his tears then looks down at his palms. They are drenched in blood.

The following morning, Tristan sat on the side of his bed, out of breath and shook-up by his dream. What did it all mean? He wondered. Nothing, it was just a dream after all.

He dressed and then entered his kitchen to make himself some coffee.

Serene's face in the dream suddenly appeared to him in the form of a flash, causing him to drop his coffee cup on the counter. The loud noise echoed through the house. Luckily it didn't break. He put his hands on the counter and closed his eyes.

"What is happening?"

Finally convinced something was wrong, Tristan went to his office and opened his laptop. In the browser he did a symptom search:

[Symptoms: Headaches, flashes of light, distorted memories, chest pain, arousal towards strangers?]

He deleted the last part and scrolled through the possible causes. "Migraines, panic attacks, stress…" he read to himself.

Tristan had felt these things before, but he had kept them to himself. He sat back and attempted to come to terms with the fact that what he was going through was likely related to stress. After all, only months after his father passed, his mother had died as well.

Tristan never saw a pattern before, but now he wondered, why did this happen after meeting Sophia? And why was it happening again after seeing Serene?

He sat back on his chair lost in thought for a moment when the sound of the clock began to annoy him.

Tick, tock, tick, tock.

He looked up at the clock on the wall and felt like every tick was louder than the last. Every second that went by irritated him. He was anxious to get out and had trouble admitting to himself that it was because he wanted to see *her* again. But why?

He couldn't make sense of what he was feeling; it was a deep, desperate desire to satisfy a curiosity. Like an itch he couldn't scratch, the annoyance grew. Serene was pretty, but that didn't justify what he was feeling, or why he kept thinking about her enough to cause flashes and dreams. No, how could a stranger cause such intense feelings?

Bothered and unable to relax, he put on his boots and left. Tristan knew he wasn't going to fulfill his curiosity or alleviate the fact that he still felt like a low-life until he saw her again. Maybe then these symptoms would stop.

Tristan calmly walked through the gates and beyond the flourishing gardens of the church property. He had never walked into a Light sector, so being in such an environment was new to him.

Decades ago, when the country became politically divided, both sector types were created. Laws in both sectors changed so drastically that it began to visually change the terrain. Dark sectors became technologically advanced, dark, and dirty. Light sectors, by contrast, became bright, clean, and reminiscent of 1950s America. They yearned for a simpler time, from the clothing they wore, the food they ate, to the cars they drove. This church was everything Light sectors represented.

On the property, he was stopped by a security officer.

"Do you have a pass sir?"

"No?" Tristan said scratching the back of his head.

"You need a pass. You can get one from the front office." Tristan stood in front of him for a moment and then made his way back out.

"This was stupid," he whispered, and it was obviously a waste of time. Even if he did get in, he wouldn't know where to find her.

As he walked through the gates and turned to make his way back home, he saw people freely entering the large cathedral. He stopped in front of the open doors for a moment debating his decision to go inside. He looked up and made a noise in frustration, annoyed by his inability to stop this ridiculous endeavor.

When Tristan walked inside the church, he was greeted by soft angelic music. He tried not to look down the center of the pews and instead made his way around the large marble pillars. He felt uneasy being there, guilty somehow. He stopped to look up at a large angelic statue staring down at him. It was a beautiful but eerie piece of art that momentarily captured his attention. He continued walking until he came upon a set of double doors and opened them.

Tristan squinted as his eyes adjusted to the change. He never liked the brightness and the pastel colors associated with Light sectors. The door had opened to a courtyard surrounded by buildings that were a blinding white color and at least two stories high.

In the center of the courtyard was a fountain, surrounded by a garden overflowing with color.

He noticed there were windows and doors on the bottom floors, so all the lower rooms were accessible from the outside. As he walked past the many windows, he realized that this was some sort of school. As students walked past him, they began to stare. His attire wasn't exactly up to Light sector code. He wore all black, down to his boots. Today he also wasn't wearing a jacket, just a dark printed t-shirt. His long raven hair, tattoos, and piercings were not favoring him either. It became obvious to him, and to others, how out of place he was.

"Now what?" he whispered to himself as he assessed his surroundings.

He walked to another building and, suddenly, he heard a child's laughter and a familiar voice. When he turned around, he saw a room with an open door. He carefully looked inside, not wanting to be seen.

Simple, and yet beautiful, he saw her again, and he tried to find something special about her, *anything* that would justify his obsession with her. She wore a short black pleated skirt and a short-sleeve light blue polo shirt with a small emblem. It was some sort of uniform. Around her neck was a simple gold cross necklace and he quickly noticed that her breasts seemed slightly larger than what he had remembered.

Everything about her was so innocent and clean. The epitome of a Light sector girl.

Finally, he saw her smile, and something rose up inside of him like a flame. His muscles tightened, and his heart raced. He placed a hand on his chest and his eyes widened. Something was off. What he was feeling wasn't good or normal. She didn't evoke a feeling of peace in him, what he felt was a feeling of lust and possession.

She played with the children and hugged them. Her sweetness became more evident the more he watched her. Though she was beautiful, it was her tender nature that had attracted him more so than her physical attributes.

A loud bell rang, and she began getting the children ready to go home by helping them put on their backpacks.

Once the children began to leave, she grabbed her things and walked outside. He instinctively hid away from view, and then followed her.

Tristan had expected her to go to her car, but instead, she went inside another building and then up a flight of stairs. Although he was fully aware how his actions could be perceived by others, he was so overtaken by this feeling that he couldn't stop.

On the second floor, she stopped at a door, and he quietly walked up behind her as she pulled out a pair of keys from her purse.

"Serene, right?"

She jolted, dropped the keys on the floor and froze, unable to move. He bent down to retrieve them, but he didn't give them back to her. "Sorry. I didn't mean to scare you yesterday. *However,* this time, I did," he said, with a flirtatious grin.

She looked at him for a moment, confused as to who he was, but then remembered him once she noticed his beautiful, bright green eyes.

"That was *you?*" she asked, surprised. He looked very different now.

She remembered how attractive he was, but now he looked clean, and well put together. So much so that it was intimidating. His black t-shirt showed off his large biceps and his arms were decorated with tattoos. And though she immediately noticed his beautiful eyes, she was mostly taken aback by his chiseled facial features and his gorgeous dark hair. Hair that fell around his forehead in a haphazard way, occasionally covering his eyes.

"You... didn't scare me," she said, as she turned red at the mere sight of him.

She tried to look up at him again but couldn't. Looking at his beauty directly felt like looking at the sun, so she kept her gaze low.

"No, I'm pretty sure I did," he said, remembering how startled she was yesterday. He rubbed the back of his neck. "Anyways, I just wanted to come by and prove to you I wasn't a bum or something. Actually, far from it," he stated with a smirk trying to flirt with her. He quickly realized that she wasn't flirting back, instead, she was looking down and away from him.

"Okay. So, you're not a bum. Can I have my keys back now?" Her words were quick and to the point. He pretended to hand her the keys, but just as she tried grabbing them, he pulled his hand away.

"Why won't you look at me?" he asked, confused by her shy demeanor. She was making every effort to look at anything but his face.

She sighed, annoyed. "If I look at you, will you give me my keys?"

"Yes. Maybe… maybe not," he said playfully as he took a step closer.

She instinctively took a step back towards the door. Her heart raced, and her breathing became elevated, and try as she might, she couldn't get herself to look up at him. He noticed her hesitation, so he decided to help her by gently lifting her face with his hand.

"There," he said quietly, and she finally studied his face directly. Suddenly, all her fears were confirmed; he was strikingly handsome, and she was so attracted to him that she felt herself melt. The feelings that arose in her scared her, and her breathing became so elevated that it was now apparent she was shaking.

Tristan noticed anxiety in Serene's eyes. He cocked his head and he went from flirting, to concerned. She didn't react like a normal girl, in fact, he had never seen a woman so terrified of him before. When he saw her in the classroom, she was cheerful, but now her eyes told him a different story, they hid a deep sadness, a fear, something that wasn't immediately evident, but that was obviously consuming her. Her eyes made him want to soothe the agony and fear he found in them, but how?

Still holding her chin, he cautiously went down to kiss her, but she quickly moved her face away from his.

He sighed.

Realizing his presence bothered her, he took a step back, giving her space.

"So, what time do you normally leave this place?" He said, placing his hands in his pockets and studying the building.

"I… live here. These are dorms. I'm here all the time."

"Wait. How old are you?" He asked, wary of her young appearance and desperately trying to find any excuse to stop being attracted to her.

Serene couldn't help but smile at his forwardness, knowing that he was concerned she was underage.

"Twenty? Twenty-one in a few days," she said smiling and

forgetting her own age for a moment.

Just then, a woman carrying books passed by them and stared at him in a self-righteous manner. Serene looked down and played with her hair—nervous about being seen with him.

When the lady finally went down the stairs, Serene motioned for him to hand her the keys by cupping her hand.

"I'm sorry. I'm not allowed to be talking with outsiders. Please... leave," she whispered.

He looked at her confused, not understanding what she meant about not being *allowed*.

"When can I see you again?"

"What? Um, you can't." She paused for a moment then nervously said, "I'm not allowed to see you, or talk to you, period."

"You *can't*? Or you *won't*?" Tristan arched an eyebrow, having trouble believing she wasn't allowed to talk to him. Yet he also had trouble believing she was blowing him off. He was utterly confused by the situation.

"Both," she admitted, since she wasn't allowed, nor did she want to be around someone who made her feel this uncomfortable. She liked him but he was a Dark, and she had never spoken to a Dark sector resident before, other than store employees.

"Well then," he began, then playfully threatened her, "since I know where you live now, I know where to find you. I'll see you around," he said as he handed her the keys and walked away.

"No! Please. Don't ever come here again."

He paused at the top of the stairs, wondering whether she was truly not interested in him, or just scared. It baffled him, since it was something that had never happened to him before, being rejected in such a manner.

Serene quickly realized her choice of words and regretted saying them. She turned away from him to think. The truth was she liked him, regardless of how different he was, and regardless of the fact he terrified her, she still wanted to see him again. She turned to look at him.

"Wait. I'm sorry. I just… we can talk. Just not here."

"Then, where?" he demanded, almost annoyed since this was an awkward situation for him too. He saw her struggling to think of something. The tension in the air grew with every second she remained quiet.

"Serene?"

"The garden?… Northernmost part. Not now."

"When?"

"Midnight?" she asked, embarrassed, unsure, and regretting her words again. "Just please… go!"

He stared at her, then looked away. *God*, he wondered, *why is she so nervous?* He had never seen a woman react that way towards him, and he felt terrible about it. He knew the best thing to do was to leave, but he desperately wanted to comfort her somehow, show her he wasn't a threat. And, though making her feel comfortable was the goal, he also felt a pull to touch her.

Without thinking, he moved up the stairs towards her. Serene took a few steps back in response, her back now almost against the door. Tristan looked away. It was clear he had to leave. She was much too nervous.

"Be there. Okay?" His tone was none threatening, but still a command.

She nodded. "I will."

As soon as he was out of sight, she entered her dorm room, closed the door behind her, pushed her back and head against the door, and let out a loud sigh in relief.

She looked at her hands, and it made her finally realize that she was shaking profusely.

FOUR

THE RING

Serene was in her dorm room, sitting on her window bench trying to study, but it was useless. All she could think about was her mystery man from earlier, and she wished she had at least asked for his name.

A name, what's your name? She wondered.

Serene knew she had set up a meeting with him at midnight, but now she had no intention of going. Asking him to meet her had been a knee jerk reaction because regardless of how different Tristan was to her, she was smitten and curious. Everything about him, including the way he dressed, made him all the more appealing.

Looking out through the small, round window of her dorm room made her feel like a princess in a tower. It wasn't like she was physically locked up. Leaving was an option. If she wanted to. But she would have to ask permission, be asked a million questions or be chaperoned. She felt confined and forced to forbid so many worldly things in her Light sector life. Her parents were extremely religious and protective of her, and so was her aunt, Vivian, who was a teacher at the academy and kept a close eye on her. At least here, her mother couldn't hurt her physically, and she no longer had to worry about hiding the bruises.

However, Serene's parents lived just outside the city, so it wouldn't take much for her mother to come into her dorm room and give her due punishment... if she disobeyed.

In only a few days she would be done with her A.A. in Religious studies and be off to an actual university, far away. The thought brought her some consolation. She knew then, she could get the freedom she craved. She was tired of pretending to be this poised and proper woman.

Oh, to go out dancing or drinking just once. She daydreamed as she stared out the window. It was something she was dying to do. Something that, perhaps, this mystery man could help her with.

"So, he's scary looking and you like him?" Serene's friend Casey laughed in confusion. Casey had natural red hair up in a bun, and a pixie-like face. She had brought her little Yorkie dog and Serene played with him as they talked. Casey was rich and more pious than Serene, and that led to many arguments between them. Yet it was Serene's free-spirited nature that was also alluring to Casey.

"Yes, I mean, you should have seen him. He was so strong... interesting, dangerous!" Serene was lost in thought as she sat on the bed and hugged Casey's dog.

"You keep saying that." Casey rolled her eyes and then half-serious asked, "What, did he look like a psychopathic serial killer or something?"

"No!... He was sleeping by the trash near the gate. I thought for sure he was homeless, or dead! But then as I got closer, his face was so, so beautiful. Like sure he had blood on him, and he smelled like alcohol, but I just knew he didn't belong there. I mean, I know no one belongs on the streets, but it was like finding the most adorable puppy on the sidewalk. And he was hurt, and wet, cold, and dirty." Serene puckered her lips to emphasize her pity. "Then, as I moved the hair from his face, I saw the most beautiful set of bright green eyes. But then ugh, Vivian came out of nowhere and ripped me away from him! I thought I'd never see him again. But he just came back to me today. Like, came straight up to my dorm room. But this time he was clean and well dressed, and... he just had this... magnetism to him. Hands down the hottest guy I've ever seen. I mean no offense to your brother of course." Casey rolled her eyes. "But, there was also darkness in him. Like—like I had something he wanted? He even tried to kiss me Casey, but I chickened out!"

"Wow. Well that sounds dreamy!" Casey spat sarcastically, exaggerating her excitement. "You should totally marry him and live by the dumpsters, happily ever after!" Serene gave her an angry look. Casey was simply never interested in the 'bad boy' type. Actually, she was never interested in a boy period.

Serene picked up the Yorkie to talk to him instead. "Whatever. Wasn't he cute Gizmo? Yes, he was. Casey wasn't there. No, she wasn't..." Casey rolled her eyes again and ignored her. "Anyways, I'm supposed to go see him again. Tonight, at midnight."

"Wait. Okay, what? No! You're going to intentionally see the scary, homeless, drunk guy at midnight... all by yourself?"

"Casey! I already explained. He isn't homeless, at least... I don't think he is, and I think I will go to see him. I have to," she admitted, her eyes open wide realizing now that the situation was just too intriguing. "I just wanted to tell you, just in case."

"In case of what?" Casey snapped back, and then paused to finally understand what Serene had meant; in case anything bad happened to her. "Okay no, you sound absolutely crazy. I am NOT going to get involved in this." Casey had been in trouble before as a result of Serene's shenanigans. Mostly for not telling anyone about it before it happened. Serene's family had done well to tame her curious impulses, but they couldn't change her nature.

"Oh relax! Please understand... I really like him. I know how it sounds, but he's not dangerous."

"Not dangerous? You barely know him! Heck, you don't even

know his name!" Serene stayed silent since she couldn't argue with that logic. Casey sighed, "What about Alex? I thought you loved him?"

Serene's eyes suddenly became sad as she played with the promise ring, he had given her. Alex was her ex, and he was also Casey's brother; both of their families were excited at the prospect of them getting married one day. But he had gone off to medical school and Serene wasn't just going to sit around and wait, especially since he had cut off all communication with her.

"Casey, don't start..." Every time Serene became disillusioned with Alex, Casey would assure her that he was going to come back to marry her, but Serene was losing hope. "He broke up with me, remember? And that was a year ago!"

"He didn't break up with you! He just said that talking to you is a distraction. He wants to focus on his last year of med school so that he can graduate quickly and come back to you."

"Casey!" Serene interrupted her. "He has a girlfriend." Serene had seen tagged photos of him with other girls on social media, and she had shared them with Casey.

"No, he doesn't! I asked him about them. He's just... hanging out or going to a movie with friends. It's innocent."

"Then why am I not allowed to go out if he can?" Serene finally raised her voice, her eyebrows furrowed. Casey sat quietly and listened, "I do love Alex, I do. But I just can't sit around and wait for him. Maybe if he wasn't," she paused, "...sleeping around." Her last words were almost a whisper. She was sheltered but she wasn't that naive.

Serene knew how different things were viewed by both of their families on the matter. Perhaps in Free sectors, women were seen as equal, but things were different in the sectors of Light. Alex was a man, so he was allowed to explore his sexuality, while Serene was to be kept pure until he returned.

"We don't know that! You're jumping to conclusions!" Casey

exclaimed, doubting her brother was sleeping around, but knowing there was no way of proving it. "Listen, he's coming back. Sooner than you think Serene. I promise. Just be patient, please."

"I doubt he'd even want me again."

"Serene, you have to trust me. He loves you." Serene was emotionless as she continued to pet the dog. "Promise you won't go see that man?"

Serene looked away from her unable to hold her stare, "Fine... I won't." Serene said lying. She had made up her mind, she was going, but she was also filled with guilt as she remembered the promise she had made to Alex.

Three years earlier

On a bright summer day, families were setting up a feast on picnic tables in the large backyard, just a few meters from a glistening lake. Casey's parents' house was impressive. It had a modern Victorian style to it and was three stories high.

Serene was in the large upscale kitchen. She was barely seventeen and in a beautiful pale-yellow sundress. Everyone was outside and she was helping to prepare some more lemonade when, suddenly, someone put their arms around her waist. It was Alex, and he kissed her cheek softly.

Alex was tall, handsome, clean-cut, with blue eyes and dirty blond hair in that iconic, all-American, 60's style haircut. He wore expensive, preppy attire, as he came from an extremely conservative family. She was a bit young for him, since he was three years her senior, but their families never had an issue with their age difference.

"Meet me by the tree in five?" he whispered in her ear. She turned around, excited to finally see him. He gave her a suggestive look as he bit his bottom lip, but they kept their distance from each other. He wished he could touch her more here and he was dying to kiss her, but he knew it was out of the question. Serene offered him a shy smile, looked down, and nodded. He gave her a quick peck on the cheek and then walked away.

After Serene finished the lemonade, Alex's mother came and thanked her for it before grabbing it herself.

"You're so welcome Mrs. Elbridge. Let me know if you need anything else."

When she was out of sight, Serene fixed herself in a nearby mirror. Then, being careful not to be seen, she walked outside and through the path that led her to their secret meeting place.

It was a beautiful, sunny and windy day. A big leaning Willow tree stood alone, but Alex was nowhere to be found. Suddenly, he came up behind her, lifting her up above him and spinning her around. She gave him a playful scream in surprise, and just as he was putting her down, he leaned in and kissed her passionately.

Moments later, they were lying under the willow tree; it was where they often met when they had officially started dating two years ago. Since he had started college, she didn't see him very often, so they had to make their time together count.

Alex had always been a smart kid, and now he had grown into a handsome young man. A man who had just graduated from a nearby university in record time and was now off to med school. Lost in each other, they made out under the willow tree as its coverings hid their shame.

"I love you," she whispered softly.

"I love you too," he said, as he hovered on top of her and with yearning kissed down her neck to reach the top of her ample chest. Her breathing was heavy. They both knew what they wanted, but it was forbidden. He slowly unbuttoned the top of her sundress to expose her bra, and he watched her chest rise and fall as her breathing became elevated. She was beautiful, and he knew no better girl to give the privilege of being his wife one day.

However, Alex wasn't ready to get married. He had barely dated, and he didn't want to regret not having slept with other women.

Alex had devised a plan to both have his freedom and keep Serene for himself. After all, he was convinced that only a person like Serene could ever make him the perfect wife. Serene was sweet, intelligent, entirely submissive to him, and religious, with impeccable moral integrity. She also had all the qualities his mother possessed. Lillian was obedient, elegant, loyal and a domesticated housewife, as well as an amazing mother to him. He knew Serene would be all those things one day.

"Don't go," she pleaded with him, emotional at the thought. "Find a school a little closer, we can still be together, or we can get married and we can both move away."

He sighed loudly, frustrated as he watched her get up and button up her dress. He really wanted to enjoy her more before he left.

"We've been through this. It's a great school. It will be better for us in the long run."

"Better for us? Or for you?" Her words came with a side of anger.

He looked down and held her hand, then assured her, "For us."

Just then, out of his pocket, he pulled out a ring box. Serene became excited as she believed he was finally proposing. He opened it and inside was a silver ring with two gems swirled around each other.

"It's a promise ring. It has our birthstones." He took the ring out and placed it on her ring finger.

"A promise for what?" she said as the excitement escaped her body and sadness overcame her again.

"This ring will remind you, every day, that regardless of anything, I solemnly swear that I will come back to marry you." He kissed her hand tenderly, "And..." He stopped for a moment.

"And what?" she asked.

"That you'll promise to remain pure for me, can you promise

me that?"

She was disappointed since she knew it meant a very long time. "For how long?"

"Until I graduate, and possibly start my residency here."

She looked down at the new ring he had put on her and asked, "And all this time, will we still be together?"

He looked into her beautiful hazel eyes. He knew she was getting prettier by the day, the thought of leaving her alone worried him, but he trusted her and her family to keep her safe until he returned. They also understood why he had to do this.

"Yes, but you know long distance relationships never work. If I hope to come back to you quickly, I need to focus on finishing med school. I already spoke to your family about this."

"And they agreed!?" she asked, shocked.

He laughed, "Your mom wasn't too keen about it, but your father agreed that you're too young to get married right now anyways. Trust me, if I don't come back to marry you, your mom has promised to hunt me down."

She laughed, but barely, at the thought of her mother saying that; since it did sound like something she would say and would likely do. Clair, her mother, was absolutely crazy about Alex, and she had every reason to be. Alex had graduated from high school as Valedictorian and was fairly athletic. He had also graduated in less than three years from a nearby university, but most importantly, he was an avid member of the church. According to Clair, Alex was an example to everyone, a beacon of light.

However, Serene felt it was the fact that he came from a wealthy family that had appealed to her mother the most. Her mother constantly reminded her that, even if she tried, she would never find a better suitor. He was also the only boy that her mother had not only allowed her to date, but insisted she do so. However, Clair was still strict regarding Serene's virtuous innocence.

Serene didn't want to agree because she loved Alex and couldn't bear to see him go. She was frustrated and angry at his decision to leave, but she reluctantly agreed because, after all, she couldn't force him to stay.

In the present

By 11:30 p.m., Serene was ready and anxiously waiting for her meeting with the mysterious stranger. She wore tight jeans and a sleeveless button-up white shirt with her cross necklace. Her hair was loose, full of volume and flipped to one side. She wore pink lip-gloss and eye make-up to draw attention to her large hazel eyes. Serene had taken one last look in the mirror. She unbuttoned a few more buttons to reveal just the right amount of cleavage.

"See. I could be sexy if I wanted to. Maybe," she said as she practiced her best mature and sexy pose. She was inexperienced but she didn't want him knowing that.

In case it got cold, she took a blanket and a book, and at 11:45 p.m., began her walk into the garden.

FIVE

THE SECRET MEETING

Tristan was leaving one of his clubs when he looked at his phone to check the time. Serene had been on his mind for most of the day, but he got caught up in business meetings with Kamilla and Mac.

Dave, a good friend of his, had also begged him to stay and watch a famous band perform. He hadn't spoken to anyone about Serene; he didn't see any reason to. Over the years his close group of friends, especially the females, didn't like it when he pursued a girl they didn't know. They all had a clique of sorts, and he remembered how they had behaved when he dated Sophia.

"Shit," he said to himself when he realized it was 12:42 a.m. He got in his car and looked at the time on his dash; He knew it was too late to go see her, and he was angry that he had lost track of time.

After a moment, he shrugged it off and tried his best to just forget about Serene.

A few minutes later he stopped at a red light. As he waited for it to turn green, he became restless and wondered again why this girl continued to flood his thoughts. He lit up a cigarette and opened his window slightly. Girls usually came to him; he rarely pursued a girl. At least it never took much, so this situation was new to him.

"I don't have time to be messing around with naive little girls," he whispered to himself. She wasn't a little girl, she was clearly an attractive woman, but he was doing his best to erase her from his mind.

As he waited for the light to turn green, he tried to think about something else, anything else, but couldn't. Instead, his mind wandered into wondering why he could never get a girl like Serene or Sophia in bed. Since high school, there was *always* a Serene, or a Sophia. The quiet girl he'd try to approach but somehow could never get. Was the world jinxing him? Did he not know how to behave around them? Did he come on too strong? These were questions that had been eating away at him for years.

When he caught himself daydreaming, he looked up and noticed the traffic light was green, but only for half a second before it immediately went back to red. He didn't remember it turning green in the first place. Giving in, he immediately put the car in reverse, turned the car around and drove in the opposite direction towards the church. He hoped she was still there.

After a few minutes of searching the northernmost part of the garden, Tristan noticed something white behind a large bush. When he walked up to her, she was… asleep.

Kneeling in front of her, he carefully moved a lock of hair away from her face, mimicking her actions towards him when they first met. Her hair was long and silky to the touch. Crickets sang loudly and the moon that night was very bright, so he was able to see her face clearly. He now understood why his subconscious had used Serene's ethereal-like appearance in his dream. If he was able to imagine what an angel looked like, she would look like Serene.

Still kneeling, Tristan took a moment to figure out his pull towards her. She was pretty, but that alone wasn't enough to justify his actions, and he knew it. *What the hell am I doing here?* He wondered, finally absorbing where these feelings had led him, again.

This is weird. I should leave.

Tristan felt overpowered, and at the same time, undeserving. She was also young, likely still innocent, and he was obviously no good for her.

Still, now seeing her this way, he wanted someone like her, at least once, if she were willing. He thought for a moment that maybe, making her his, would be the only way to get her off his mind and break the curse of never being able to have such a gracious woman.

"Serene?" he said. His voice a low growl, but she didn't respond. "God, it's *really* not safe for you out here," he whispered, and put a hand through his hair, worried that if he left something or someone could hurt her. He then shook her arm gently.

Serene immediately sat up and screamed.

"Shhhh!" He made the loud sound as he covered her mouth, then whispered, "It's me. It's just me."

Serene looked disoriented and confused. When she finally recognized him, she became disappointed at herself. *Oh great! How did I fall asleep?* She thought as she fixed her hair. When she noticed she had grass in it her cheeks flushed.

"I'm so sorry," she said, apologizing. "I didn't mean to... wait. What time is it?"

"It's like one, one thirty," he said too casually, acting as though he couldn't care less about the fact that he was late.

"One thirty? And you just got here?"

"Yea? And it's a good thing I did," he said sitting next to her, "or else... you would have kept sleeping here." He looked around at the extremely secluded area they were in, "Which can't possibly be safe for you."

"Oh. No, no one else knows I'm here," she assured him. "So... the homeless guy came back and just over an hour late. This is probably why you can't keep a job," she smiled, joking with him.

He smiled brightly, and she melted. He had the most beautiful smile she'd ever seen.

"Well, I accidentally fell asleep behind a dumpster again. It happens more often than not."

She laughed and realized she couldn't hide the fact that she liked him, a lot. Especially the way he dressed tonight. He was wearing a black leather jacket, black jeans, and a printed white t-shirt. She also noticed that, regardless of his constant attempts to comb back his hair, small locks of his raven hair always found themselves back over his face. His voice now was also deeper than she had remembered.

"So, what's your name?" she asked, eager to finally know.

He caught himself looking at her inappropriately. Her cross necklace hovered right above the line of her ample breasts. To avoid looking at it, he played with the grass.

"Tristan."

"Tristan?… I think that means noise, sadness. Or Trinity?"

"My mother was Catholic at one point. I believe it has something to do with that."

As she continued talking, he tried to focus on their conversation, but found it difficult to do since, for whatever reason, he began to contemplate how to start something physical with her. He was sure she wasn't the type to initiate it, which made things difficult.

"I see your cut is looking better," she pointed out. "What happened that night?"

"I fell, it was nothing. What is this place, anyway?" His eyes focused on an eerie cherub-like statue several feet away that was staring at them in a judgmental manner.

"It's a church. It expanded into a private school. An academy. I'm getting my A.A. here… Religious studies."

"Religious studies? God, you are such a typical Light." He chuckled playfully, pointing out the obvious. People from the Light sector were called 'Lights' while his kind were called 'Darks', especially in derogatory terms during political speeches.

"Hey! What's that supposed to mean?"

"Nothing, I just always found Light sectors uncomfortable, fake, and wildly pretentious."

"Okay? But you have to admit there's less crime, marriages last longer, and the scenery is better."

"Well, you're only allowed to marry once in your sector, right? You don't have much of a choice, quite literally actually since you must obey your husbands by law. And crime," he stared at her, "is sometimes a symptom of circumstance. Free sectors have higher poverty rates. Often the homeless are kicked out of Light sectors. Yet, they love to pray for the poor."

"So, you don't think the legalization of drugs, and the lack of religious laws have anything to do with the crime? Or the vast amount of homeless people addicted to drugs?"

Tristan cringed, not wanting to dive into religion or politics. He was also an atheist and didn't want to offend her. "I guess you could say neither sector type is perfect."

"Hmm. I'll give you that." she conceded, noticing his discomfort. She then proceeded to ask him an array of questions. He crossed his legs and continued to play with the grass as he answered them.

"I actually don't live far, but no. But I've never been here. My mother... she used to come here, for Mass."

"Oh? What's her name?" she asked, wondering if her name would ring a bell.

"Maribel, but, she died in a car wreck on her way here about two months ago."

"Oh no. I'm so sorry," she said, with intense empathy.

"It's fine."

"Maribel?... her name does ring a bell. Though unfortunately vaguely. She spoke Spanish, right?"

"Yes."

"Interesting, you don't look Spanish."

He laughed. "My father was Irish American. Everyone says I look like him, but I barely knew him. He... also died five months ago."

"Goodness. Both parents recently? How are you holding up?"

"Not great, if I'm being honest. I've just been drowning my sorrows in..."

"In what?"

He sighed. "You name it, drugs, drinking, partying, constant and meaningless..."

"Meaningless what?"

He gave her a sly grin and when she realized he meant sex her face flushed and they both laughed. Pre-martial sex was illegal in Light sectors.

"Okay, okay. So, tell me, what's a week is like for you? What do you do? Where do you go?"

As he continued talking, he was surprised that she didn't try to preach to him about all the dangers his habits posed, nor did she try convincing him to stop. Instead, she looked up at him wide-eyed in wonder and seemed oddly intrigued by his lifestyle. She even lit up when he mentioned what he believed were some serious faults in his life.

"Your life sounds fascinating," she said hopelessly, and then laid back on the grass to look up at the full moon with her hands behind her head.

"Hardly."

"I wish I could experience the Obsidian nightlife, at least once."

"What? Why haven't you?" He looked over at her for a moment and wished she would not put herself in such a vulnerable position.

"My parents are sort of overprotective. I'm not allowed to do much... and I'm definitely not allowed to do drugs."

"But you're almost twenty-one, right? You're not bound to stay in Light sectors. You should be more independent. Go out and do all the things you want to do."

"Yes. I should," she said, lost in thought and looking out into the sky.

He lay down next to her on the blanket and eventually broke the silence.

"You know, if you want, I can take you out tomorrow. We can go to one of my clubs; you can try a drink or two. We can—"

"I can't tomorrow," she looked over at him, "but Friday night I can… Also, I'm not twenty-one yet," she said, pointing out the fact that she wasn't legally allowed to drink.

He shrugged, "So what. I own the place."

She wanted to go, but she never had the guts to go into the city alone. Tristan looked like he knew how to have fun, and she oddly felt safe with him. Or perhaps her fears were overshadowed by her growing attraction to him. Either way she felt comfortable around him, like she could be herself.

Alex was controlling, and she rarely got to make her own decisions around him. Tristan was the opposite of Alex's uptight, preppy and clean-cut disposition and therefore Tristan's darkness intrigued her.

"Come," Tristan said, ending their long conversation and getting up, "it's almost three." He extended a hand to help her up. She grabbed her book and blanket and then took his hand.

"Would you like me to walk you to your room?" he asked politely as they walked.

"Um, you can walk me out of the garden, but then I have to go into the building on my own. If they see me with a Dark, they might—"

"Sound the alarms?" He joked and they both laughed.

He then led her through the garden with one hand on her lower back.

The way she reacted to his touch, and the fact that she wouldn't hold his stare indicated how nervous she was. Yet, he was no longer confused by it, instead it was endearing. She was gentle, coy, and a strong contrast to what he was used to. Perhaps it was instinct, but he just knew to be extra gentle around her.

"Okay, thank you," she said in a low voice as they reached the side of the building. They were away from any lights, but the moon was bright, and a large tree gave them cover. "So, I'll see you Friday night by the garden gate. Is ten too late?" She hoped he'd agree to the time because she had to pretend to be in her dorm room asleep.

"Ten's fine." He said but knew ten was too late for a proper date. They would have to skip dinner and go straight to the club.

He studied her and noticed she was looking down and holding her blanket and book close to her chest. He wondered why she would constantly avoid eye contact with him.

"Can I ask why you do that?" he asked, smiling.

"Do what?"

"Lower your head that way."

She shrugged and tucked a lock of hair behind her ear. He felt it was a shame she wasn't more confident, since she was stunningly beautiful.

"Okay, spill it. Something's wrong. I can tell." He said, sensing her discomfort.

She sighed. "It's just there's a saying here. Go into Obsidian after dark and chances are you won't come back."

He understood her worry. Obsidian City was notorious for their missing people reports, mostly it was young women that wouldn't come home. "You'll be fine. I promise. I'll be right next to you the whole time." He took a step closer, "If anyone tries to hurt you, they'll have to go through me and I don't go down easily."

Serene laughed but looked away, still weary.

"However, you can't be with someone you don't trust. So, I have to know you trust me." He lifted her face with his hand so she would look at him, "Do you... trust me?" His eyes narrowed studying her and searching for an answer.

She looked at his lips and her heart began to race. Was he testing her? Seeing if she would stay still or run away? Could she *trust* him?

"Yes," she breathed.

Tristan doubted her words but leaned in expecting her to pull away but instead, she closed her eyes submitting to him.

Taking her invitation, he pressed his lips against hers.

Her lips were uniquely soft, and they gave in to the slightest pressure. Serene tilted her head and had barely parted her lips when he slipped his tongue inside. His eyes were closed but once his tongue caressed hers something magical happened and his eyes opened. He tasted something and it was... familiar. Tristan closed his eyes again and went in deeper dominating her mouth wanting to verify that what he was tasting wasn't just in his head.

She tasted like foreign fruit, sweet and fragrant, and he needed more. Whatever he was tasting made him addicted to her touch, her taste, her smell and he was instantly aroused. He had felt something similar with Sophia, but this was stronger.

Needing her more than ever now, he lifted her and placed her back against the wall. He didn't feel he was rough about it, but she had never experienced anything like that before. Her jaw dropped when she felt the impact on her back, and it happened so fast she didn't even notice she had dropped her things to place her arms around his neck and her legs around his waist.

With his lips hovering and breathing heavily over hers, he caressed her face, searching her eyes, studying her, trying desperately to find answers, confused by his overwhelming desire to taste her and be inside her. He looked down at her lips then locked her gaze again, sending her a clear message. *I want you, right here, right now.*

Tristan had been holding back all night and now he worried that his growing need for her would explode the moment he succumbed to his impulses. He regretted touching her. He regretted kissing her. He liked her but something inside of him was growing, fast, tensing up in anticipation to the point that being around her and holding back was becoming painful. His body ached for her, and his muscles tensed up as he struggled within himself to control his actions and remain focused. These intense feelings scared him, but at this point all he could do was slow it down.

Focus!

He kept his position, wanting to make sure she would not scream at what he was about to do, but just as he hoped, she was quiet and inviting, but shaking. With utmost restraint, he gently kissed each lip and eventually led her into an open, passionate kiss again. A moan escaped his lips the moment he tasted her mouth again.

Serene was trembling, but not only did she give into his kiss, she deepened it, letting him know that she also needed him. Serene wanted to enjoy him, but her nerves were so bad that she thought her limbs would give out. She was scared, but she also didn't want him to stop.

Just stop shaking! Her thoughts screamed.

Tristan began to test his limits as he sensually kissed down her neck. The tantalizing taste was absolutely everywhere. Her lips, her cheeks, her neck. He simultaneously caressed up and down the side of her body, lifting her blouse slightly and feeling the soft skin underneath. When she felt his hands on her bare waist she moaned, and the sound of her yearning turned him on further. *Stay focused, control yourself, slow down.* He repeated to himself. It took every bit of self-control on his part not to touch her breasts, or her ass, or anything remotely private. The idea was to get her turned on enough to have her begging him to come upstairs, or to have him take her to his place tonight, but something told him it may not be that easy.

As he kissed her, one of his hands slid under her bra to finally meet her breast.

She gasped, "Stop."

Tristan's body was ready, aching, craving, and stopping irritated him, which was unusual. With a significant amount of self-control, he begrudgingly pulled back, yet kept her caged with both of his hands on the wall, her legs still wrapped around him. He watched her as she attempted to regulate her breathing.

Tristan was now determined to make her his. Yet, he knew Serene would be a challenge. From the moment he met her, he was doing his best to study her, learn her cues and adapt to such a new and unusual creature.

Realizing that pushing her further would only scare her away, he moved back, allowing her feet to fall on solid ground.

"Are you okay?" he asked, noticing her hand was over her heart.

"Yes. No, I'm fine." She shook her head and attempted to regain her composure.

He leaned down to grab her book and handed it to her.

She picked up her blanket and, as she walked away, she turned to say, "Good night, Tristan. I'll... see you Friday."

He simply put a hand through his hair and said, "Be there."

She smiled, and he gave her a mischievous smile in return.

Oh Serene, if only you knew all the things I want to do to you...

SIX

A Date with Corruption

Thursday night Serene couldn't sleep. She had finals the following morning, and her aunt, Vivian, had booked a flight for them to leave Saturday. They were visiting a university out of state, and though the school was still in a Light sector, she hoped the distance from her family would finally allow her some freedom.

Tomorrow night was her date with Tristan, and Serene wished she had met him sooner. Then again, she also wished she had never met him at all since the thought of him kissing her and pinning her up against the wall made her restless.

She touched her lips, remembering the way he kissed her. Tristan was rough, passionate, and carnal. Alex had never once kissed her that way. Alex also never made her feel this rush of adrenaline, passion, and fear.

With her eyes closed she was lost in that moment again, helplessly pinned against the wall. His hard body pressed up against hers. His hot tongue sliding over hers, dominating her mouth in a way that ripped the oxygen from her lungs.

Her eyes opened and she took in deep breaths, forcing her heart back into a normal rhythm.

Tristan excited her. He represented everything she couldn't

have, freedom, fun, excitement and sex. There was also something about him that made her want to please him, regardless of consequence. The fact that this stranger evoked such torrid emotions worried her.

She never planned on giving *it* up before marriage, but Tristan made her feel weak. He knew what strings to pull, what words to say, and how and when to touch her. With a simple gaze he made her feel naked, vulnerable, and yet... safe.

Drunk in his seduction, it was obvious that he could ruin her, have his way and leave, but that thought didn't bother Serene. She wanted to use him probably as much as he wanted to use her.

Tristan was the perfect excuse to make Alex pay for his indifference. She had loved Alex, faithfully, but she had also grown to despise him, not only for leaving her, but for extracting such a promise when he was clearly playing the field.

Well Alex. She thought, *two can play at that game.*

Yet, as much as she played with the fantasies of crossing forbidden barriers, sex with Tristan was something that at her core she hoped she wouldn't do. Regardless of how much she wanted him, she *had* to resist.

"Oh, Tristan," she moaned softly, "What have you done to me?"

Whilst Serene lay restless in the quietness of her dorm room, loud industrial music was beating through Tristan's two-story condo.

Tristan's place was packed, and a few corners had started to resemble the beginnings of an orgy. The coffee table was adorned with an assortment of drugs, needles, and pills and a girl named Raven kept Tristan company on the couch. She was voluptuous, with long black hair, heavy makeup, a black bodice, and a tiny red skirt. Raven wanted him, but all Tristan could think about was Serene, and how she kept him waiting.

On one of his couches, Lea was purposely making out with one of Tristan's male acquaintances, knowing that it would make him jealous. He was jealous, but not because he wanted Lea. He was jealous because he was unable to enjoy the person he wanted at that moment: Serene.

Tristan placed a few pills in his hands and knocked them back while closing his eyes. He had felt frustrated all night was making an effort to get exceptionally high.

Moments later, his world slowed down around him. He exhaled as his body finally relaxed, but Raven was next to him, touching him, pestering him.

Tired of waiting for Tristan to make the first move, Raven took control and began to make out with him. Raven was an amazing kisser, yet he couldn't help but immediately think about Serene, and compare her kiss to Raven's. Raven was strong, and her kiss was punishing, bruising his lips.

There was something about Serene's vulnerability that enticed him. However, not in a good way. With Serene, he felt like a hungry lion maintaining his composure around a gentle lamb. Her gentleness made him want to both protect and destroy her. Even now, her memory haunted him as he saw flashes of her soft innocent face shyly yearning for him while her helpless body trembled against his.

Raven pulled away from their kiss and licked his neck. She then made a sound expressing just how great he tasted. It was something Tristan noticed his lovers enjoyed doing, tasting him.

Eventually, Raven got up and pulled him off the couch. He didn't want to go, but she forcefully lifted him onto his feet.

Raven led him to the bedroom and he strenuously objected, stopping them just short of the bedroom door.

"Wait!" he called out to her, but she continued, pulling him like a rag doll. "Raven. Fucking stop!" he said, pulling himself from her grip. When she came back for him, he pushed her away with every ounce of force he had. It did nothing to her physically, but it *had* pissed her off, and she pushed back with such force that Tristan's body flung back several feet and into a wall.

The loud sound of the crash echoed through the room, causing the chatter around them to stop. Initially, Tristan had no idea what had happened. He bent over as he held his hand over his aching chest. The wall behind him cracked and bits of debris fell to the ground. He was no stranger to blows aimed at his body, yet he was amazed at the sudden level of pain he was in.

"Get out," he growled, his face now red.

All the guests were motionless as they watched them. When he noticed she didn't move, he repeated it, "I said get the hell out of my place!" He coughed and tried to breathe through the pain.

Raven quickly gathered her things. Everyone looked at her and shook their heads as if she had done something wrong, and she had. What she had done was forbidden. Tristan was human, and she had forgotten that detail for a moment. She hadn't meant to push him that hard, but the cracks on the wall and his painful expression proved she had used too much force.

A sense of fear overcame her because everyone knew Tristan was precious to Kamilla. He was her pet, and Raven was relieved she hadn't killed him.

"Tristan, I'm so sorry. I—"

"I said now!" Tristan gathered himself and stood up to walk towards her.

Raven shook her head slowly as her eyes flooded with tears. Tristan eventually lost patience and grabbed her by the arm, opened the front door, and threw her out of his place.

"Why? Why are you acting like this!" Raven screamed at him through sad eyes, trying to understand what she had done previously to make him reject her in such a manner. It wasn't like Tristan to have shoved her the way he had.

The partygoers looked on as he ignored her question and slammed the door. He then grabbed a cigarette from the coffee table and lit it.

"What!" he asked, annoyed at the negative attention he was receiving. "What the fuck is everyone looking at!"

When he finally realized how insane and emotional he looked, he combed a hand through his hair and walked into his bedroom to calm down.

Sitting on the side of his bed he puffed his cigarette. He felt guilty. Guilty for rejecting Raven and so many others so harshly. It's not that he didn't want sex or companionship, he craved it, needed it to feel normal. But, he didn't want sex with Raven, or with Kamilla, or Lea, or anyone else he knew. For reasons he didn't understand, he wanted and pined for Serene. Whenever he pictured her, he felt a pit in his stomach, a pain in his joints, and an ache in his groin. For days he had also been experiencing flashes of light and headaches, similar to a migraine. He knew something was wrong. Terribly wrong. But he didn't know what.

"One more day." He told himself.

The Next Day

A little before 9:30 p.m., Tristan was tapping his fingers on the steering wheel waiting for Serene by the gate. Tristan was early and it had just finished raining. He was hoping that she hadn't forgotten their date, but even if she did, he knew where to find her, so he wasn't worried. He *was* however impatient.

Luckily, she arrived on time and he saw her cautiously walk out through the gate as if she didn't want to be seen leaving. She looked very different this time. She wore the same small gold cross necklace, a short, fitted blood red dress, a long black jacket, and a pair of black high heels. He smirked because what she was wearing was much more his style. She now looked like a normal near twenty-one-year-old woman.

Bringing down his car window, he asked her to "Hop in." Serene stood shocked for a moment when she noticed his car; it looked expensive and clearly a lot of money was put into the bodywork. She then carefully opened the car door and right before she sat down she hesitated.

Tristan perceived her wavering and images of her walking away flashed through his mind. Women like her always slipped through the cracks, but this time he wasn't going to let that happen. Without hesitation, he leaned over, grabbed her wrist and pulled her inside. The instant she sat down, he leaned over, grabbed her seat belt, and buckled her in.

Serene's eyes widened, surprised by his immediate and swift actions.

Ignoring her look of fear, he demanded that she close the door. She did as he asked.

As he drove, Serene felt something was off but it was too late now to turn back. In the awkward silence, he eventually looked over at her. She was quiet and clutching onto her seat while staring straight ahead. She seemed tense, but, if he was being honest so was he.

Eventually, he took a deep breath and remembered the type of girl he was dealing with. It was never his intent to make her feel uncomfortable.

Trying to soothe her, he reached over to stroke her leg. This instantly backfired and she slapped his hand away.

"Don't do that," she demanded.

His eyes widened in confusion. "Sorry. You just looked... tense." Silence filled the air, and they both felt this wasn't going well. The date was already a disaster.

Moments later Tristan tried to break the tension again. "You really don't get out much, do you?" He turned to smile at her and watched as she closed her jacket, covering any exposed cleavage.

"Not really. And I definitely don't get into cars with men I barely know."

"So then why did you?" he asked, honestly curious as to why

someone so scared would put themselves in such an uncomfortable position.

She shrugged, realizing she didn't have a good answer to that. What she *did* know was that this date wasn't going as expected. She was hoping for the gentlemen she had met in the garden, yet now he seemed like a completely different person. He was intimidating, and she worried that she had made a terrible mistake by getting in a car with him.

As every negative possibility ran through her mind, she began to feel nauseous.

He looked over to see her nervously rubbing her arms. It seemed like she wanted to be anywhere but on a date with him.

Sighing, his conscious and soft nature finally took over and he parked the car.

Putting a hand through his hair, he surrendered, giving up on this ridiculous endeavor.

"Hey, listen," he said gently. "If you want, I'll take you back. I don't want you feeling uneasy," he said, genuinely worried.

She nodded as a complete sense of relief came over her. This wasn't her, and what she was wearing was embarrassing. She wasn't even allowed to own such a dress. She felt completely exposed.

"I'm sorry," she said, "I think that would be best. I'm just not..."

"Not what?" he coaxed her softly.

"Not used to this. I know this may come as a shock, but I've never been out on a date with someone I wasn't close to."

"Are you kidding me?" he laughed with a sneer. "It's extremely obvious you've never been on a date. Have you ever even had a boyfriend?" Serene lowered her gaze. "Jesus fucking Christ, I'm taking you back." He put the car in reverse and turned the car around.

As he drove, he tried to understand why he was so frustrated with her. Maybe it was because she had the ability to make him feel ravenous, or maybe it was because he had to put in so much effort into being gentle. Maybe it was the fact that she haunted his dreams. Whatever the reason he was sure of one thing; he had never been with a girl like Serene, and it was... uncomfortable.

Serene had taken offense, but it took her a moment to respond. "I have been out on dates, and I have had boyfriends," she said quietly. He narrowed his eyes looking at her with intense doubt. "Okay fine. One boyfriend. But it lasted years!" she boldly informed him, but knew it wasn't much of a defense.

They were quiet, and she realized that he had completely given up on her. Her anger and anxiety subsided when she realized that he couldn't possibly be that bad if he was willing to take her back.

Sighing, she looked over to study him. Everything about Tristan looked dark and sinister, yet somehow she knew that he was also kind. Behind his tough persona, she hoped he was hiding something much more vulnerable. Anyone could see he was attractive, but there was so much more that had intrigued her. He was sweet, mature, serious, confident and *experienced*. Definitely experienced.

As she admired him, all she wanted to do was touch him, kiss him and melt into him if she could allow herself to. It was frustrating how her nerves always got the best of her.

"I'm sorry." Her words were sweet and apologetic. "Tristan, can you please stop the car?"

"We're almost back," he said, trying to protect her. She was much too young, and from a completely different world. He also knew premarital sex was punishable by law in Light sectors, so even if he had his way with her, she would suffer the consequences. It simply wasn't worth it.

Just then, she touched his arm gently. "Tristan?"

He looked over at the angelic face that was driving him mad, and, unable to help his sudden need to please her, he gave in to her request.

Tristan pulled over, shut off the car, and sighed.

After about a minute he eventually looked over at her. At this point, she wanted to look calm and put together to make up for her childish behavior. She took off her seatbelt, leaned against the door, crossed her legs, and tried to look mature and relaxed. There was more to her than just this scared Light sector girl. She wanted him to see another side of her. The side that could handle a wild Obsidian night and, most of all, the side that could handle *him*. She was leaving tomorrow, and he was her only chance at finally experiencing the Obsidian nightlife.

She smiled. "Okay, you're right. I haven't gone out on many dates, and I haven't even been to a Dark sector at night, but, I want to know what your world is like. I want to experience what it's like to be… someone like you."

He laughed. "Someone like me? You mean a Dark sector resident?" The thought of her at one of his parties, around his friends, was suddenly hilarious to him. "Trust me Halo, you don't stand a chance in my world. You were scared just sitting here. Do you really—"

"I promise! I promise I'll relax from now on." She smiled and put on her seat belt. Tristan stared at her confused. He didn't know if he was attracted to her innocence or completely annoyed at this point. Truth was, he felt a little of both.

He hesitated for a bit as he tried to decide between what was best for her, and what he selfishly wanted from her. But, all it took for him to make a decision was a glance into her sad hazel eyes, and he was hooked again. *Goddamnit you're cute.*

"Fine… just promise me then, that you're not going to freak out on me tonight. I don't need you running off and getting hurt, so stay near me. Obsidian is dangerous at night, but for Christ's sake relax a bit would you?"

"I swear I won't freak out about anything. Bring it on," she said, fully determined to prove herself to him. "What?" She said as he stared at her. "Let's go!" she motioned for him to turn on the car and drive. "I *dare* you to freak me out and I promise you I won't."

"Oh, you're daring me now?" he asked, lifting an eyebrow.

"Yup."

"Alright. You asked for it."

Tristan wasn't going to intentionally freak her out, but he was glad she had finally decided to relax.

Moments later as they reached the center of the city, Tristan had slowed down due to the traffic.

The city was crowded, full of pedestrians and holograms advertising lewd and extreme products. The skyscrapers had black windows that faded into the dark sky. The bottom floors, however, had businesses with open doors and clear windows. There were bars, sex shops, brothels, high-tech consumer goods, and drug shops. Serene noticed the city had a color scheme: Neon against a black backdrop.

When Tristan finally found a parking spot, he opened her door and held her hand as he led her down a dark alleyway in haste.

"Ben." Tristan said as he approached a homeless man by a garbage can that was on fire.

"Tristan! Ooo such a nice lady. She's human!"

"That she is." Tristan said as he pulled out a twenty and placed it in a little can in front of the man. "Offers still open if you want to come work for me."

"I would but there is no point. Soon *they* will take over and kill us all."

Tristan laughed. "Sure thing Ben."

When they walked away Serene asked, "Is he...?"

"Insane? A bit."

Finally, they walked past a long line and a buff bouncer swiftly opened the club's double doors exclusively for them, no questions asked.

Once they made it down a staircase, Tristan led her through the dense crowd. The heavy metal industrial music was deafening, and Serene could feel the bass throbbing through her body. She had never heard music like this before, nor seen people dressed this way. She noticed that their attire was sometimes very bright or black, or digitally enhanced with bright patterns on thin flexible screens. Some were barely clothed, if at all. Couples of all genders were kissing and touching each other inappropriately. In Light sectors they would have gone to jail. Two men were having intercourse in a dark corner as if no one was watching. Their demeanor and attire made no sense to her, bull masks and leather that barely covered their bodies.

Tristan noticed Serene's eyes wandering wildly. She was clearly freaking out. He gripped her hand tightly reassuring her.

Suddenly, Serene latched onto his arm when a group of men ran by them screaming nonsense. Trailing behind was a man with devil-like face paint, who was tripping on acid. He ran into her, grabbed her by the neck and shook her violently as he screamed obscenities into her face.

SEVEN

THE CLUB

Tristan shoved the deranged man off her.

When the man rushed back, Tristan whipped out a large pocketknife and placed it against his neck. "Stay the *fuck* off of her." Tristan roared, his eyes narrow and looking as if he'd kill the man without the slightest bit of hesitation.

Serene eyes widened as she trembled. The man cursed at them in a language she didn't understand and ran off.

Serene leaned against the wall and catch her breath.

"You okay?" Tristan asked softly, as he put away the knife. "Did he hurt you?"

"No, well. No, I'm fine." She shook her head. He lifted her face gently to examine her. "Why—Why did he do that?"

"He... likely can tell you're a Light." Serene looked down at her attire. "It's okay. You're safe now." He hugged her gently until her shaking stopped.

"You ready?" He eventually said pulling away. Serene nodded. Tristan placed an arm around her, and held her tightly against his body as he continued to led her through the club. Eventually, they made it to a secure room in the back where there were large red booths in the shape of half circles.

Serene could tell this room was a VIP section since only a

privileged few were allowed in. On the round table in front of them, she saw an assortment of drinks and various other items. *What do they need needles for?* She wondered. Drugs were outlawed in Light sectors but were legal in Dark sectors as long as the user was twenty-one or older. So regardless, Serene was too young.

As she sat down, Tristan greeted people he knew, and plenty of girls in skimpy outfits came up to hug and greet him with a flirtatious kiss on the lips. Serene looked away and her cheeks became flushed as a feeling of jealousy and embarrassment overwhelmed her. She then watched as those same girls would look down on her with vicious contempt. Even with the loud music, she could clearly hear them gossip.

"Who the hell is she?"

"I'm not sure."

"Oh my god!" One of them said laughing, "The better question is what is she?"

"How did this happen?"

"This is going to be good. Should we tell Kam?"

"No. Fuck Kam! She told us to back off. This is her issue now."

Serene stared at the three ladies, making it clear to them that she could hear them, yet they didn't seem to care.

Serene analyzed Tristan around his friends. He seemed comfortable, happy, and in his element, especially around the other women. He smiled more, flirted more, and she desperately wanted to see him act that way towards her.

As Tristan continued talking to a female friend, he caught a glimpse of Serene as she stood up and confidently took off her jacket. Tristan drank in the view, momentarily entranced. He thought she would always look cute, and innocent-like, but the red dress hugged all her curves and she was actually very sexy. He swiftly ended his conversation and sat next to Serene.

"I forgot to mention, you look amazing," he sensually whispered in her ear.

Trying to remain confident Serene coldly thanked him, then focused her attention on a small tray of pills that was being passed around. She saw Tristan take one, and she reached out to grab one as well. However, Tristan quickly grabbed her hand, almost hurting her.

"Don't," he commanded.

"Why not? You are!" she pointed out in an angry tone.

"Here," he said as he waved at someone, "I'll get something more your speed." When the woman approached him, he requested a few drinks.

"Bring us an Obsidian Fog—sweet, an Amaretto Stone Sour and a Sangria."

"Sure thing boss." The blonde lady with large knockers said sweetly while winking at him.

Serene was now officially upset at how women continued to act around him, but she tried not to show her discomfort.

Moments later the drinks arrived, and he carefully grabbed each of them and placed them on the table in front of her. He then handed her the dark purple one with white fog on top as he put his arm around her and watched her drink it.

"Oh wow. That's good, and also absolutely terrible at the same time," she said as she scrunched her nose. The drink was sweet, but she had never tasted alcohol before.

"You'll get used to it. Here, try this one," he said, handing her another drink. With Tristan's encouragement, she had managed to drink two more.

About an hour later, Serene was buzzed and she loved the way she felt. Tristan, now noticing that she was feeling the alcohol, led her onto the dance floor to get lost in the crowd and indulge in the music.

The music's rhythm made no sense to her, and she realized by watching the people around her that it wasn't about dancing as much as it was about losing yourself in the music.

"What is this genre?" she asked. Music was outlawed in Light sectors unless it was classical or religious.

"Dubstep? Heavy metal dubstep, I think. It's an assortment of songs."

Serene was confused but still enjoyed it. "I like it!" she yelled. "Do you?"

"I prefer heavy metal or rock but, this is fine."

"What?" she yelled, unable to hear him.

He smiled and shook his head, "Nothing."

The drinks helped her shyness melt away, and she finally felt comfortable with him touching her. He wrapped his arms around her from behind. She leaned up against him as they both swayed to the beat.

"You smell amazing!" she yelled in order to be heard over the music. She then turned to bury her face in his chest to smell him. "Like sandalwood, juniper and soap," she looked up at him.

"Thanks? I guess?"

"I need more drinks!"

"Are you sure you can handle it?" Tristan asked, unsure if he should allow her to be drinking so much, since she was a novice.

"Yes! I feel fine!" she assured him.

"How are you feeling right now though?" He wanted her to enjoy herself; however, he didn't want her getting sick.

"I barely feel anything!" she smiled up at him.

"Hm. I don't believe you."

"If I kiss you, will you please get me another drink?"

They both stopped swaying.

He gazed into her eyes and placed his hand under her chin gently.

Suddenly, it was as if time had stopped and no one else was in the building. Serene wrapped her arms around his neck and pulled him down for a kiss. She had intended it to be a fast and passionate kiss, but he slowed her down, savoring her intoxicating taste and gently caressing her tongue. He was lost inside of her and barely able to make sense of what was going on around them. He loved the way she tasted and how soft her lips were. He was used to rough females, so he craved the tenderness Serene's personality and body offered.

With their eyes closed they both kissed slowly for several minutes. As he caressed her tongue, she felt herself aching for him. More importantly, for the first time in her life she was actually having fun.

Serene was free, and she was… happy.

At the bar, Serene tried to down another drink but Tristan stopped her midway by softly putting his hand over hers and taking her drink. He then told the bartender, "No more."

The bartender nodded.

"Not Fair." She frowned.

Tristan quickly changed the subject, "Come. I have something I want to show you."

Grabbing her hand, he pulled her away from the crowd. His eyes were dilated, and he was having trouble concentrating since the pills he had taken were kicking in. The world around him had suddenly turned into smears of bright neon colors. Fortunately, he knew the club like the back of his hand.

Leading her upstairs, he passed a pair of guards and walked into a secluded area. It was a large, empty lounge with soundproof windows that overlooked the crowd.

He stopped in front of a long table that was against the wall and turned to lift her up onto it.

Above the table on the red wall, hung a painting that had two dim candelabra sconces on either side. The music was faint, but the bass was still throbbing. He positioned himself in front of her and placed his hands on the table by her sides. He then closed his eyes and kept his head down, as if trying hard to focus on something.

Serene, now drunk and able to let go of her inhibitions,

instinctively spread her legs so that he could get closer. He followed her lead and gently placed the side of his face against hers. She knew where this was going and her heart was racing. Everything about him made her body ache with desire.

Tristan, however, felt an unfamiliar pain growing in his groin. Mentally he wanted to be patient, but physically he wanted to ravish her, right here, right now, regardless of her possible opposition until he was fully sated and the pain was gone.

He had felt these worrisome and conflicting feelings before, but never this intensely. His desire for her had become a need, and it was taking every muscle in his body to keep himself from kissing her because he *needed* her to initiate it.

It seemed like they were in this position forever; close and barely hugging.

Serene closed her eyes as she took in this moment of dizziness and arousal. She smelled his neck and then his hair. His scent was something she wanted to remember.

With his eyes also closed, Tristan softly nuzzled her face, hovering his lips over hers, tempting her, giving her as clear of a sign as he could. *Want me, Serene. I need you to want me as much as I want you.*

His tactic was working. Serene nuzzled him back. *Just kiss me already*, she tried expressing with her lips parted and her breathing elevated, but *he* wouldn't kiss her. Finally, the yearning inside of her took over and she grabbed his face and kissed him.

Serene's lips, skin, and flesh was incredibly delicate and he always gave only as much pressure as she did. The more vulnerable and gentle she was, the more he wanted her.

Serene deepened their kiss allowing her tongue to caress his. He loved how sweet and gentle their kiss was, barely there, forcing him to focus on all the micro sensations. It was a clear reflection of the type of person she was, and he was turned on by it.

"My Halo," he whispered.

As their kiss deepened, he pressed his body against hers, and she instinctively pushed her dress up with both hands so that he could fully press up against her. Serene wrapped her arms tightly around his neck, in an effort to fully lose herself to him.

She was a natural, nothing about this kiss made him feel like she was inexperienced, but her shaking told him a different story.

For Serene, her actions were unexpected. It was as if her desire had taken over, and her body was on autopilot. If Tristan wasn't so irresistible she would've had more control over her actions, or at least fear would have taken over, but right now her lust was greater than her fear. Tristan had a way of making her yearn for him.

When he pressed harder against her, her eyes widened as she felt his hardness. He watched her expression as he rubbed himself against her.

Serene's face flushed, her lips parted, and her breathing became louder. The sensation of him so close to being inside of her felt amazing.

Tristan took off his jacket and allowed it to fall carelessly on the floor. Serene took the opportunity to slide her hands under his shirt, and up his stomach and chest since she had been eager to touch him there since that night in the garden. Surprised at what she found, she couldn't help but lift up his shirt and look at his upper body firsthand. He was covered in tattoos and was rock hard. This new discovery caused her body to warm up, her joints and muscles to tense up, and her womanhood to tighten and become ready.

Tristan read her expression, and, knowing just how badly she wanted him, he took off his shirt to fully satisfy her curiosity.

Serene slid her hands up his chest and marveled at the dark and evil artwork on his stomach and chest. She gazed up at him, trying to save this memory. Piercing green eyes hungry for her were staring down at her through locks of dark hair. He could have been evil incarnate, and she still couldn't resist. He was everything she was supposed to avoid and fear. Instead, the idea of not having him now felt like torture.

As she continued to touch his chest, Serene noticed the bruises caused by Raven and he flinched when she pressed that area. He gently pushed her hands and no longer holding back, he pulled down on her hair, so that he could kiss down her neck, remembering to be somewhat gentle as he did.

However, Serene wasn't used to his roughness. "Ow." Serene scrunched her eyes as he continued to pull her hair, "Okay, please stop."

Tristan pulled away.

Zap!

A sudden painful pinch and a bright light flashed through his brain. His body tensed and his heart rate sped. Scrunching his eyes, he instinctively kissed her again, and the moment he did the pain completely disapeared.

"Trist... we *need* to stop." She cried, but her voice became distorted.

An unfamiliar heat of anger rose up inside of him. *Stop?* He wondered. She couldn't possibly mean it. Pulling on her hair harder, he gently bit the flesh just above her breast. She moaned, at his roughness and threw her head back.

Taking it as a sign of surrender, his hands met her hips, and he pulled on her underwear. But, just then, only moments away from his goal, he saw an image of her screaming in opposition as he violently claimed her. Terrified that the thought of her agony aroused him, he forced himself away from her.

"Ah." Tristan gasped, holding his aching head. Disconnecting from Serene felt like pulling away from heaven and entering a burning Hell.

Tristan didn't just want her, he *needed* her, but he didn't want to hurt her. He wanted her willing and begging.

"Trist? Are you okay?" Serene's expression softened and she pulled down her dress.

"Yea. Just, the drugs... they sometimes give me a headache."

71

"Oh," she responded.

Ignoring the throbbing pain Tristan tried to act normal. "So, how was it?" he asked through a tortured smile.

"Not bad for my first make-out session in an Obsidian night club. But, I think you can do better," she joked.

"Oof cut me some slack. I am *extremely* high right now." He said, and they both laughed as he helped her off the table.

Heading back Serene could barely walk, both from the alcohol and from swooning. She walked ahead of him and stumbled down the hallway bumping into the walls while he stayed behind putting on his t-shirt and jacket.

Serene walked up to the bar and convinced one of the earlier bartenders to get her another drink. He obliged.

Tristan walked down and saw her sitting at one of the bars talking to the bartender. He kept an eye on her as a few of his female friends approached him. He pretended to mingle not wanting them to notice he was with Serene.

When he had managed to shake them off, he noticed Serene wasn't at the bar anymore.

Tristan's heart began to race as he frantically searched the crowded club for her red dress. He walked up to the bartender and grabbed his shirt.

"Where is she? Serene! The girl with the wavy hair and the red dress. She was sitting at your bar just a moment ago."

"Whoa. Calm down. I think she went down that way." The bartender said pointing to a secluded corner of the club.

Tristan exhaled in relief when he saw her dress in the distance. But she was with another man. A man Tristan barely knew.

Serene was wasted and felt completely unstoppable. The man whispered something in her ear, grabbed her waist and then licked her neck. Tristan became possessive of her and his eyes narrowed. He rushed up to them, grabbed her hand, and pulled her away from the suitor.

"I told you to stay near me," he growled.

Serene laughed, "Sorry. I was just having fun."

Tristan led her out of the club. She was stumbling and needed to lean on his body to stand upright. It was obvious to him that Serene was beyond drunk.

"Whoa Handsome. Where are we going?"

"Leaving."

"Leaving where?"

"Somewhere safe. My place."

Serene giggled. "Yes. Onward. Take me to your castle."

Tristan was too drugged to drive, so when they reached the road he hailed a cab.

Inside the cab, Serene straddled him as they kissed, and her hands were lost in his beautiful raven locks.

"Touch me," she begged, but he became hesitant. Though Tristan had changed for the worse since his mother's death, he was still a gentleman. "Please, I want you," she begged him.

"Are you sure?" he said, lifting her face and searching her eyes for sincerity.

"Yes, please," she said in agony.

He wanted her to mean those words. However, as a Light sector woman, he needed her to be sure. Tristan had a weak understanding of Light sector laws, but he knew Light women were generally chaste until marriage. He'd give her some time to sober up. In the meantime, he limited himself to kissing her soft pristine mouth.

The cab stopped in the dark and desolate area where he lived.

They got out and walked up to the building's entrance. He made sure to walk in front of her in an effort to make her realize that this was clearly her choice.

The stairs creaked and every step higher made the both of them increasingly nervous. Once they arrived on the fourth floor, he swiftly opened the door to the complete darkness of his condo. Serene took a step back then turned around, as if by reflex, ready to run. For a moment he froze as he watched her hesitate. It felt like precious water slipping through his fingers. The thirst filled his chest and it was as if time itself had stopped and the only sound was that of his loudly, beating, heart.

He heard a million voices scream in his head, and just like that he quickly wrapped his arms around her from behind.

He stood there, holding her in silence, not wanting to scare her, but also not wanting to let her go.

After a moment, he finally spoke.

"Stay."

Serene's breathing echoed in the emptiness.

He then softly kissed her neck and ever so gently massaged her arms with his hands. In the darkness, only the moonlight shined on them. And as he stood behind her, he led his hands down to grab both her hands and then held them behind her back, as if his subconscious was expressing his desire to tie her up so that she couldn't run away from the idea.

This position suddenly brought a sense of fear to Serene. He then walked in front of her releasing her arms.

With the back of his index finger he caressed her shoulder. "You're so beautiful," he whispered. His cast was low and his eyes looked sad, "You have no idea how *badly* I want you." His voice, barely a whisper, sounded like a man in pain.

Wanting to soothe him she kissed him and he placed a hand on her lower back to gently push her body against his. She felt the ache building up in her body, and it was torture for her to know that she might run away from the opportunity to enjoy him.

He stepped back. "Please. I'd do anything to have you right now... *anything*." His eyes were gentle and fixated on hers. Begging, praying.

She looked down and wondered how he was able to get her to the point of her wanting to throw all her morals and inhibitions into the wind. Her very life was on the line, she could be penalized or stoned, but Tristan was a master of seduction. Everything about him made her want him; his voice, his touch, his smell, his beautiful face and well-sculpted body beckoning to be explored. His words were also always carefully chosen to be exactly what she wanted to hear. She was a stranger, but somehow, she was an instrument he was very familiar with, and he played her body and mind beautifully. It was the most enchanting symphony she had ever heard.

"Anything?" she whispered.

"Anything." He repeated his eyes narrowed.

Noticing her hesitation, he kissed her and then trailed down her neck. Keeping her aroused and focused on his touch.

Trembling, she managed to whisper a request, "Promise me one thing?"

He stopped and sighed on her neck as he closed his eyes in disappointment. He worried about what she was about to ask; was she going to say something he didn't want to hear? 'Promise me you won't hurt me?' or 'Promise you will stop?' All these were promises he worried tonight he couldn't keep. Yet he desperately wanted to fulfill her request, whatever it was.

"Anything my halo," he said, assuring her as he placed his forehead against hers and took hold of her hands. "Tell me... tell me anything and I swear I'll do it."

She closed her eyes. She wanted him; she wanted her first time to be with someone like him. She wasn't sure if it was her rebelling against her parents, or if this was a way to get back at Alex. All she knew for sure was that she wanted Tristan, regardless of consequence.

"Promise me," she whispered, "no matter what I say... or how scared I get..." she paused, making sure this was what she wanted, "that... you'll make love to me." She lowered her face in surrender.

He exhaled, feeling relieved. Never in a million years could he have hoped to hear something more beautiful come from her lips. "I swear... on my life and yours... I'm going to make you mine tonight, and there isn't anything anyone can do to stop me." Without hesitation, he gave her a deep and passionate kiss. Her eyes widened, shocked at his choice of words, and before she had a chance to process what he had said, he kissed her and pulled her into darkness.

Unfortunately for Serene, there was no way she could have prepared for what was about to happen.

EIGHT

THE MISTAKE

The door to Tristan's apartment closed behind them, and they were both surrounded in complete darkness. He turned on the lights, and like a new scene in a movie, her new life was about to begin.

Serene's eyes widened as she noticed the sheer size of his modern but industrial looking condo. An array of sleek brown leather couches, pricey looking rugs and a dining table that could seat twelve barely filled the large open space. She saw a large spiral staircase just past the dining table, leading her to believe he also owned the upstairs flat.

He took off his jacket and then hers, placing them on the back of a leather couch. He grabbed her hand and with haste led her into a bathroom.

Not once letting go of her hand he opened the medicine cabinet and swallowed a small handful of drugs. For the first time in a long time, he was extremely anxious. It had been a while since a woman had made him feel this way and he was desperate to calm his nerves.

He handed her a pill. "It's not what you think," he assured her. "It'll help you not have a hangover in the morning." He handed her a glass of water and she swallowed the pill.

Still holding her hand, he led her through his spacious condo and as they walked, he gave a voice command to his sound system to play some music. The soft, alternative music filled the air.

Serene stopped at the doorway of his bedroom.

Tristan gently tried to pull her inside, but she stood her ground.

Her eyes were wide and glossy, expressing her nervousness and hesitation, but he wasn't worried. After all, she had given him permission, and he had little to no experience with rejection.

Serene stood frozen, and began to shake in both nervousness and anticipation. His room was intimidating and somehow made everything feel real. *Too* real.

The room had a cold, industrial look with a brick wall. The long white curtains that flowed onto the polished cement floor accentuated the height of the ceiling. Sitting predominantly in the center of the room was a large bed with a metal headboard. On the side table was a set of handcuffs and a vision of him handcuffing her to his headboard made her heart beat so loud it seemed to echo off the walls of her mind. Everything about the room, including the bed's dark red décor, seemed to scream: 'Sex has happened here more than you can imagine.'

Tristan studied Serene. Her breathing was elevated, her skin was pale, and he could almost see her pulse beating through her neck's soft skin. Tristan remembered this look. She had acted this way when she had first entered the club. Usually, this was the point where he'd ravish a woman and take her without hesitation. Yet feeling her anxiety, he approached her with caution.

His arm barely touched hers as he walked past and behind her. A painful ache caused a flash of light. He scrunched his eyes and took a deep breath, fighting back the aching need growing inside him. He then gently gathered her hair to one side to expose the zipper on her red dress. He slid her zipper down, and slowly pulled the top of her dress down.

As he tenderly kissed her shoulder, a chill went down her spine. When he had pushed the dress down far enough, she helped him by releasing her arms and exposing her bra. He placed a hand on her midsection and with a slight force pulled her to him.

Holding her in his embrace, he attempted to suppress her slightly shaking body.

Then, as if they were about to dance, he lifted her arm and spun her around to face him. Dark green eyes full of lust bore into her, punishing her in their intensity. With a shuddering breath her gaze dropped away, lashes lowered, hiding her own appetite. She worried he could see just how much she yearned for him.

With forefinger and thumb he gently held her chin and forced her to meet his gaze. *No, please,* she worried. It was hard to look at him and not melt into him. She bit her bottom lip and tilted her head, subconsciously begging him to kiss her.

He answered her prayers and pressed his lips against hers.

Against all reason she put all her fears aside and deepened their kiss, wanting him to hurry and take her before she had a chance to change her mind.

Their tongues played and circled each other, his clearly dominating hers. He coaxed her backward until her legs touched the bed.

Eventually, Serene sat on the bed and Tristan tore himself away from her intoxicating taste. Serene leaned back on her elbows as he carefully removed his shirt to expose his strong upper body. The view was better than anything she had imagined.

He looked down on her with brooding green eyes that were visible through the raven strands of hair that covered his face. Faint light from the single lamp caused shadows on his body defining every muscle.

Like a curious child, she placed a hand on his stomach and made her way up. She named the colors in her head as she followed the lines of his tattoos, *Deep green, royal blue, crimson red...* Serene stopped when she felt her chest tighten. The fear and consequences of her upcoming actions rushed through her.

"Serene," he whispered, noticing her hesitation. She looked up at him through glossy eyes. He was stunningly handsome, in a very dark and sinful way. Tristan emanated darkness and Serene radiated innocence. It was a stark contrast, like light meeting darkness in secret, yearning to be one.

Tristan bent down to kiss her, then trailed fiery kisses down her arched neck. Serene dug her fingers into his hair, gripping the locks as his lips warmed her skin. Serene positioned herself up further on the bed. She wasn't experienced, but she was eager.

Tristan slid his hand behind so that he could expertly remove her bra. Once he had released the clasp, he held onto the straps and he saw her topless body fall graciously onto his bed.

The pain in his groin intensified, and he moaned at the mere sight of her ample breasts. They were flawless, pale, and her nipples a perfect pink.

An animalistic hunger, and his need to dominate her, claim her, and make her his in every imaginable way, overwhelmed him.

Giving into his hunger, he went down to lick, and gently sucked on her breasts, until her nipples were so hard it shot waves of pain down her body. She arched her back and let out small cries as her body ached, not only in desire but also at his roughness.

"Trist," she whispered as she dug her fingers into his back. His roughness was bordering on too much but, she was lost in the moment and found herself unable to finish a sentence.

His skilled hands explored her body and made their way up the curves of her hips, lifting the dress pooled around her waist. He grabbed the thin material of her underwear and angry that it stood between him and her sex he pulled it down nearly ripping it off of her. Once she was naked with only her dress gathered around her waist, he went up to kiss her.

Please slow down, she thought, wanting to enjoy this moment but unable to.

Eager to finally touch her, he led his open palm down her stomach until it met her womanhood. Serene tensed up, and her breathing became labored. The weight of his body was crushing her small frame.

"Trist… please, stop," she requested, unable to fill her lungs. "Trist I… can't breathe!"

The drugs were kicking in again but he did his best to focus on what the issue was. When he became aware that his weight was on top of her, he adjusted himself to better accommodate. In the heat of the moment, he had forgotten just how fragile she was. He wasn't used to it. In fact, he had never been so patient and gentle with a woman before, and yet somehow he was still hurting her.

Serene covered her breasts with her arm, and with intense sadness whispered, "I'm so sorry. I… I can't."

Hovered above her, he studied her eyes and was devastated when he found sincerity in them. *Is she seriously denying me?* He wondered, *How is this possible?*

"I'm sorry. I'll be more careful," he whispered, attempting to kiss her, but she turned her face away from him and sat up on the bed. She pulled the dress up to cover herself.

"No, *I'm* sorry," she said, feeling guilty as her eyes watered. "I need to go home. I haven't finished packing and I have a flight to catch tomorrow."

"Wait, what? Where?"

"I'm moving," she informed him as she stood up and attempted to fix her dress.

"Moving where?" he asked.

"To a university. Out of state. My flight leaves at two tomorrow, so I have to be there by noon. I need to pack and get some sleep. I'm… so sorry, I must go." She grabbed her bra and got out of bed.

"Wait!" he said, getting out of bed and grabbing her arm to stop her.

In an act of desperation, he held her face close to his and nuzzled her. He clenched his jaw. "Don't leave yet." He breathed onto her lips. "Please stay. I... need you."

Serene dismissed his words as a romantic attempt to seduce her, but he had meant them. Tristan had never been more aroused, and he had never wanted anybody more than he wanted her. At that moment, he felt like he would surely stop breathing if she left.

She lowered her head. "I want to... I do. But, I'm not ready. I thought I was." Stopping was difficult for her as well. She wanted him. She wanted to get lost in his eyes, his kiss, and his embrace. Wanted him buried deep inside of her for eternity. But this was too much too fast for her. The consequences and price too steep. And she had a flight to catch.

She walked away from him when he called out, "Serene!" She turned around. "You made me promise."

Tension filled the air as he coldly reminded her that she made him promise not to let her walk away from this.

"I know. I know what I said... I changed my mind." She gulped. His frustration was clear, and she felt guilty for her own hesitation.

The drugs raced through his head and frustration mixed with arousal built up inside. He saw the flashes of light again, and even though she was right in front of him, images of her skin and body flashed through his mind building his arousal. He paced in front of her and ran his hands through his hair as the pain at his core built. Something was wrong. This feeling was the most powerful thing he had ever felt. He knew he could never hurt her or force her because the guilt would consume him, but at that moment, he felt like his very life depended on her surrender and he didn't have the slightest idea as to why.

"I'll call a cab," she said, realizing he was too high to drive her.

As she walked away Tristan walked up in front of her and instantly blocked her path by putting his arm across the doorframe, cutting off her exit. Serene took a step back, shocked by his actions.

His head was down, and after a moment he spoke again, slowly, attempting to not look at her directly because of the pain she inflicted on him.

"Do you want me, Serene?" he whispered hoarsely.

"What?" Her eyes narrowed.

He put his arm down and stood right in front of her. "Do you, or do you not want me?"

Serene looked towards the doorway. She wanted to say no, and she knew she should. Yet, she wasn't a good liar. There was nothing she wanted more then to enjoy this night with him, but she was scared. Scared of going back to her family after losing her virginity to a stranger. Scared of the stigma and the consequences of the law she was breaking, but she wasn't afraid of *him*. She wanted him.

"I—I do… want you. But I have to go."

"I can't." His voice shook, and his body was trembling.

Serene looked up at him puzzled. "You can't what?"

Tristan held her hands and placed his forehead against hers. He was trying incredibly hard to be tender, to remain calm and collected because all his instincts were telling him to jump her, claim her, and to rush at her with every bit of his being.

"Serene, I can't let you leave. I wish I could." His voice broke, and she sensed the agony in his words, and somehow, understood him. For whatever reason he was in pain.

"I'm sorry, but you don't have a choice," Serene whispered, full of guilt.

Tristan caressed her face and carefully studied her angelic features. In that moment, regardless of the volcano of aching passion burning inside of him, he realized that for as long as he could remember he had always wanted someone like her. She was wholesome, kind, and gentle. Tristan saw other women similar to her disappear from his life without warning. Sophia for one, and he never understood why. But this time it was different, he didn't just need Serene sexually; He wanted her in his life.

"Oh, Serene," he moaned while gazing into her eyes, pitying her sinless and innocent mindset, "but I do have a choice... I do," he warned her through tear-filled eyes.

He kissed her again, and as he did, lifted her up by her waist and brought her back into bed with him.

She fell under his spell for only a moment before panic kicked in, "What are you doing?" she asked as he passionately kissed and licked down her neck with yearning. "No, no, please, Tristan," she begged.

Her fear-filled words broke his heart, but a lust that he couldn't control blinded him. Still, even in this fog of passion caused by his mysterious ailment, he was trying to be gentle in his seduction.

Serene moaned as his hands caressed her, starting from her neck down her stomach and finally her sex. His fingers ever so gently teased her, building up her passion again. She wasn't fighting, and her body was craving his touch, contradicting her words. However, Tristan knew he was crossing a line.

Hovering over her, Tristan shook as a battle in his mind ensued:

What are you doing?

I don't know!

Don't do this. She's scared. Get a hold of yourself.

I'm trying! But I can't!

Why?

Because I want her! Because I... need her. Goddamnit just once... I need someone like her!

"Tristan, *please*," she gasped, out of breath as a tear escaped her eye. Her body was ready, almost to the point of no return. Even in her objection, she held his face tenderly. She wasn't scared of him, but the situation and even her own inability to stop was terrifying her.

In an attempt to have her understand what he was going through, he held her hand against his pounding chest.

She felt his heart.

"I want you Serene... God, if you only knew *how much* I want you," he whispered, his eyes watering from the pain that came from holding back. He closed his eyes, and a tear escaped landing on her chest.

His words and tears moved her. Serene gave in as he kissed her and his hand went down to caress her clit, attempting to stimulate her further and ensuring her readiness.

Serene moaned loudly for him as her body arched at the sensation of his fingers against the most sensitive part of her being.

"Tristan please!" she gasped, no longer able to hide her arousal and she held his face to hers. "Okay," Her words were a cry, a white flag. "You win." She whispers, willing to give anything to have him relieve the tension building in her core. Yet he continued to tease her, driving her to insanity.

"God, you're beautiful, you're so fucking beautiful," he said in reaction to her surrender and the way her facial expressions proved that she also ached for him.

As he continued to stimulate her, he placed his forehead against hers, closing his eyes. He wanted more from her. He wanted her to feel what he was feeling.

"Say you want me... say you want me inside you."

"I... I" She couldn't find the words.

"Please be mine, Serene. I'd do anything. Anything," he said as her breathing quickened.

"I... want you, Tristan?... please." She begged her eyes now flooding with tears.

He stopped caressing her and kissed her roughly, passionately. She returned his kiss with equal vigor. Tristan was crying, not due to emotions nor fear but at the pain. It was taking every single muscle in his body to keep himself from forcefully, and painfully, single thrusting all the way inside of her fragile body. It was as if another force was pushing him to hurt her, and though he couldn't stop it he was doing his best to protect her and lessen the damage.

He kissed her as he slowly melted into her body. He was used to being rough, but he used every ounce of self-control to make his movements into her slow and painless. Regardless, her discomfort was apparent. Serene cried out to him, and he felt waves of regret sink into him, for whatever reason this was hurting her. Eventually, he was in, and he stopped, now inside of her, to immerse himself in the sensation. Tristan moaned loudly in surprise and almost collapsed on top of her when he felt her warmth.

Something was different.

Serene *was* different.

She felt… amazing.

She felt… warm?

Gone was the familiar piercing pain that came with making love. The sharp sting of his manhood entering all of his ex's icy bodies, and the numbness that followed. Sex had always been painful to him and now his body was in blissful agony. He knew it was her first time with a man, but unbeknownst to either of them, it was his first time having sex with his *own* kind.

Once inside her, the yearning intensified. He opened his eyes to admire her, and her glossy golden-brown curls surrounding her shoulders like ocean waves around paradise. Her body was soft, and her breasts were perked and perfect. She arched her back and moaned for him beautifully. The view was too much to bear and all self-control escaped him. What had begun as gentle and shallow thrusts had now become fast and deep. He wanted every inch of his manhood inside of her. The thrusts became stronger, and each time his moans became just as loud as her screams.

He wanted her to come for him, multiple times, but tonight he couldn't hold out and for once he became a selfish lover. Her screams and the noises in the room seemed to become muted in his mind and he saw everything in slow motion. Her warm body was wrapped tightly around him, stretching to accommodate him, filling him with unimaginable pleasure. It was absolute heaven to be inside of her.

Amongst the chaos, he involuntarily whispered a command, "Say you love me." The words barely escaped his mouth. He couldn't believe what he was asking her, he never wanted to hear those words so soon, but he needed Serene to say it, to scream it! Even if it meant nothing. It sounded crazy, but he needed that connection if only momentarily.

"Say you love me," he said louder, but his requests were lost in her temporary discomfort and she had no desire to say it. He tried desperately to stop, realizing her anguish, but he was losing control, "Goddamnit Serene. What have you done to me?" he cried.

Her pain had surpassed pleasure. He was being too rough, "Stop!" she begged loudly, "Stop please. I beg you."

He closed his eyes, attempting to focus on something else, anything else but her. It worked. Tristan stopped.

Still inside her, and able to finally think clearly, he lifted her, hugging her to him. "I'm sorry, I'm so sorry," he whispered, his body trembled as if it were angry that he had slowed down. He studied her face, wiping away her tears. "I'll move slower, I promise." He knew Serene was special and he was trying to adjust. To help her along, while still inside of her, he made circles around her clit with his thumb.

He searched her face for clues, tuning into her needs. He moved slowly in and out her, keeping his strokes shallow, testing her tolerance.

Then, the pain inside of him returned, ignoring it he kept his pace slow. His muscles tensed, his body became hot, his joints ached, and flashes of light caused pins and needles in his brain as arousing memories of Serene filled his brain. He hugged her.

"Can you say you love me, Serene? Please..." he whispered, "Even if you don't mean it." His voice broke.

Somehow, regardless of her animosity towards him, she couldn't refuse his request. At least he had slowed down and she was now lost in the sensation of his fingers on the most sensitive part of her being.

"I love you," she whispered, her eyes closed. His thrusts became deeper, but the pressure was subsiding as her body adjusted to his length. With the sting gone, she felt only intense pleasure, but it was a pleasure that was forced upon her. She also didn't understand why she was tensing up inside.

"Say it again. Please, Halo," he begged softly, removing the hair from her face and gazing into her eyes.

Just then, she began to feel it, the growing tension of an orgasm building up inside her. She fought the feeling, angry at the pain he had inflicted on her earlier, until her body betrayed her and edged a climax. "I love you," she said again with yearning.

Instinctually, she wrapped her arms around his neck, hugging him tightly as an overwhelming tension overcame her. "I love you, Tristan." she exhaled, with a final moan as her body released and pulsated intensely around his length.

He closed his eyes as he finally allowed himself to take what his body needed. He held her tightly as he thrust deeply into her, forcing her to take him head to base. She screamed and he moaned loudly as he released hours, days, weeks, a lifetime of pain and frustration when he came inside her.

Tristan collapsed beside her as they both regulated their breathing. The world around him became fuzzy as he felt an intense high and a ringing in his ears as the virus rewarded him with a chemical reaction that made him dizzy, euphoric, and tired at the same time. The pain in his body subsided, and he felt like himself again, only better. Yet, he caulked it up to the drugs he had taken earlier.

When Serene sat up and he knew something was wrong. It was clear to him that regardless of his attempts at gentleness he had hurt her, and perhaps upset her.

"You're not leaving, are you?" He asked, guilty and worried.

Serene didn't respond.

Serene did not respond.

Tristan's world was getting darker with every blink. He was blacking out, and though he didn't have a plan as to how to fix this now, he needed to be sure she didn't leave while he slept.

He looked at the handcuffs on the nightstand. He wanted to talk to her, apologize, explain himself. But it would have to wait until tomorrow when he had a sober and sound mind. Tristan was high, but he was smart enough to know that letting her go right now, into Obsidian at this hour, while she was upset, would be a careless mistake. As a Light sector resident, her very life could also be at stake. Both because Darks hated Lights in their sector, and because she was returning to her sector no longer a virgin.

Grabbing her wrist, he handcuffed her to him.

"What are you doing?" Her eyes widened. "Tristan, I have to go!" Her voice seemed far away.

"No. You're staying," he commanded as he held the key and threw it as far from the bed as possible. "Go to sleep, we'll talk in the morning." Shutting off the lamp next to him, he got under the covers and attempted to pull her towards him.

"Don't!" She yelled, turning away from him.

"Serene, I'm sorry."

A moment later he heard her crying softly.

"Serene?" he whispered.

When she refused to answer him, he kissed her shoulder tenderly and sighed. He felt absolutely terrible, but couldn't think clearly enough to fix what had gone wrong.

He covered her with a blanket and, though she initially rejected his hug, he pulled her towards him anyways and hugged her as he fell asleep.

Serene was sore, emotional, and devastated. Sex wasn't the gentle experience she once thought it would be. She was full of regret and felt she had been incredibly foolish to have fallen for Tristan. More importantly, she had broken her precious promise to Alex. She could have fought with Tristan, kicked him, bitten him, and eventually convinced him to let her go. But she was emotionally drained, and somehow, she knew it was a useless endeavor. She'd convince him to let her go in the morning and leave the moment she could.

NINE

DAMAGE CONTROL

T he same familiar nightmare, where his angel would run from him in terror, awoke Tristan. His face went pale, and he immediately looked over and exhaled in relief when he saw Serene alive and well.

Tristan had forgotten how beautiful her complexion was in the sun. She had flawless skin, rosy cheeks and soft lips that were slightly parted. Her golden waves glistened in the morning light slipping through the curtains. Tristan didn't want to wake her. If it were his choice, he'd have her sleep next to him for an eternity. Rather that than the anger her face would display the moment he awoke her. But he had to in order to retrieve the key and release the handcuffs.

Tristan carefully hugged her and kissed her head. She gently woke up until she realized where she was. Serene jolted and looked at him as if she had seen a ghost.

"Shh. It's okay," he whispered, but she swiftly turned around and loudly smacked him. "Ow! Okay... I deserve that."

"Take these off me, now!" she spat, her face flushed. She was sober and much braver than last night.

Tristan got up and pulled her with him in order to retrieve the keys. Serene covered herself as much as she could with one arm.

Once he found the key, he released the handcuffs from both of their wrists but quickly grabbed her hand; worried she would run from him.

"Let go!" she blurted.

"I will!" He returned her angry tone as his eyes narrowed. "Just give me a moment."

As he turned away from her, he realized the sheets on the bed had blood on them. It seemed like she had not yet noticed, and he didn't want her to. He opened a drawer and gave her a long white button-up dress shirt. He released her hand momentarily to help her put it on.

Serene put the shirt on in haste. He noticed she would tense up whenever he touched her, and it bothered him that his touch had such a negative effect on her.

Tristan then attempted to grab her hand again, but she swiftly moved her hand away. However, he tricked her by pretending to grab one hand and instead grabbing the other. She gave him a loud grunt in response as he pulled her into the bathroom.

In the bathroom, Serene sat on the chaise couch. Tristan watched her intently from the mirror as he brushed his teeth. Eventually he finished and he grabbed a bunch of small hand towels and ran them through warm water.

Serene did everything she could to avoid staring at his naked body, but it was hard not to. She was ashamed, disgusted and angry with herself for still being attracted to him after what he did to her. Somehow, his arms seemed larger than she had remembered. In the past, this was an aspect of him she was attracted to, but right now it just made her realize how underpowered she was in comparison. Even if she ran or fought him, he'd likely win. She struggled to come up with a strategy. Getting away from people who would hurt her was never her forte. They always caught up to her.

He gathered all the small towels and placed them in a container then began to walk out.

"Don't move," he whispered. "I'll be right back," he said as he stood by the doorway, ashamed and unable to look at her without feeling terribly guilty.

Serene wondered why he'd say that. There was nowhere she could go. The bathroom's only exit was his bedroom.

A few minutes later he came back and extended his hand to her. She stared at him unflinching, but his hand didn't move. Eventually she grabbed it and he led her into the bedroom.

The covers were changed now, but she didn't know why.

"Lie down," he requested.

When she didn't, he asked her again, but nicely. "It's not what you think," he assured her as he kissed her hand. "I won't hurt you again."

She studied his expression. If last night hadn't happened, she would trust this man, but her heart began to race at what might happen again.

"Lie down," he said again, this time with a more commanding tone. Serene pondered whether or not to show her angry. Her only goal in that moment was to leave, but how?

She walked cautiously towards the bed and sat down. As Tristan laid her down, he kept his eyes on hers the whole time, making every effort to be gentle and slow with his movements.

"I don't blame you for not trusting me, but we're not having sex. I promise."

Serene stared at him and was then stuck looking up at the ceiling when she felt him open her legs. Her body tensed up and her heart immediately started pounding, but just then she felt warmth. She sat up slightly, curious as to what he was doing, and it seemed like he was cleaning her? She could tell she had bled since the small towels had a familiar pink color to them. Serene was perplexed and for a moment was embarrassed that he'd put himself in that position.

Trying to somehow personally erase his mistake, Tristan took his time, and was very thorough. The silence around them was extremely awkward, but neither of them spoke a word. When he was finally finished, he went into the bathroom to wash his hands, and he put away any evidence that would remind him of last night.

"I fucked up," Tristan spoke to himself as he gripped the sink tightly. He was extremely angry and disappointed at himself.

What do I do now? He wondered.

Just say you're sorry.

That's not enough.

Then just do what you can and let her go.

That's the thing; I can't let her go.

Why?

"Because I like her. Dammit! I don't know why but I *really* like her."

Tristan came back out, and, relived she was still there, he joined her in bed. She moved away from him but he grabbed her and though she fought him he placed her in front of him, holding her in his embrace until she relaxed.

They sat in silence as he began to piece together what he planned to say to her.

"Serene," he sighed dejectedly. "I'm—"

"You're what?" she said in an angry tone. "Sorry?"

"I am. It's just—"

"I don't care what you are!" she yelled as she attempted to escape his embrace. "Just let me go! My flight is in a few hours and I… I'm going to be in so much trouble. Why don't you understand? I need to go now!" she yelled, attempting to gather whatever authority she could muster, but instead the emotions caused her eyes to water.

"Can you at least let me explain?" he begged her. "I need you to hear me out."

"No! There's nothing you can say. Nothing, you hurt me! You—" Serene put her palms up to her face as she began to cry. Tristan was quiet as she cried. He knew this was progress.

As her cries became deep sobs, she began to express her

emotions. Tristan could barely make out what she was saying, but it was all words to make him understand how terrible his actions had been. His eyes saddened as the weight of his wrongs weighed heavy on his chest. *How could I possibly make things right again?* He worried.

Knowing she was done talking, but still crying, he held her with her back against his chest.

"I… don't know what to say. I'm sorry. I'm so sorry Serene." His words were sincere and empathetic. "And, I know just saying sorry won't make it better but… it's just…" He found it hard to swallow and struggled to find the words that would fully express what this mysterious thing inside of him was causing.

She turned to look at him as he had finally loosened his embrace. Serene began to talk again but he gently covered her mouth.

"Listen, please. I beg you. I've… never wanted anybody or anything the way I wanted you last night." He looked down and ran his hand through his hair. "Ever since the first day I saw you, I couldn't stop thinking about you… Serene, I swear it drove me insane," he looked up at her and noticed her face was emotionless, but at least it wasn't full of scorn now. "I've… never felt something this powerful before, or done this with anybody else. I just couldn't get you out of my head. You're different somehow. Very different. And you're… you're tender, sweet, and beautiful… God damn you're beautiful… and you're far too careless by the way," he said, as he knew the number of rapes, missing people, and murders in Obsidian City had increased dramatically over the past few years, and yet she had not only got in a car with a stranger but she also went her own way at the club. Tristan was convinced had he not found her in time the man she was with would have hurt her, more so than he did.

He continued, "You wanted to experience my world, but lately it's been *nothing* but emptiness, deep depression, and drugs that barely numb the pain. And, the only family I had left Serene… the only person I truly loved," he said, tearing up, "was found murdered a few weeks ago!" Serene was quiet as he became emotional, and she suddenly actually wanted to hear what he had to say. "It wasn't an accident. Someone killed the only person I truly loved, the one person I was supposed to protect and I... I don't know what got into me last night... I just wanted you. This feeling I felt towards you, was more than I could control. I was scared of it. I tried to fight it. Then you made me *promise* that I could have you... I let down my guard, I let the feeling consume me and I just lost all self-control."

"Doesn't matter. You should have stopped."

"You're right! I get it; you changed your mind... I get that I should have just let you go. That even though I was high as fuck, I should have listened to you. And then I should have known I was hurting you. I swear, I wanted to stop. I made a mistake Serene... a terrible mistake. I feel terrible and yet, I want you now... more than before. I don't know why just looking at you makes me feel like I can't breathe unless I have you again. I felt, feel like I'm suffocating." He held her hands and he kept his gaze low, unable to look at her. "But I want to make this right and... I just don't know how, or if I can ever get you to forgive me. I felt that if I didn't... if I didn't make you mine... that you would just... Jesus Christ, Serene, just tell me what I can do to make it up to you?" He bowed and begged as he held her hands. She wished he was crying due to the emotional way he had spoken to her, but his green eyes were simply glossed over with tears. He felt repulsive, mostly because he really liked her, and he didn't want her hating him. The way Serene looked at him and pulled way from him, was something no other woman had done.

There was so much she could have said to him. She had a caring and forgiving heart, but this was unforgivable. What she wanted to say was cruel, but for whatever reason, she couldn't bring herself to say anything that would hurt him. She was never able to hurt people, no matter what they did to her, and she hated herself for that.

After a moment of silence, he spoke again, "Did you want me in the same manner? Did you think about me as much as I thought of you?" The motive of his questions made no sense to her.

She looked away from him, and then whispered, "I did... but I'm not sure if I want you now. I'm not sure if I like you or despise you. I feel like I'm supposed to be afraid of you."

He sighed. "Serene," he tucked a lock of her hair behind her ear, "the moment I set eyes on you I wanted you. I found it hard to resist you when I had you in my arms. I've never felt this kind of connection before. I just thought, hoped, you were feeling the same way. If you found me attractive, if I turned you on so much, how were you able to resist me? Most women can't. Actually... no woman ever has."

Serene squinted her eyes in disbelief. She disliked him for what he was saying, but then, she noticed his expression wasn't that of a conceited man. Nor of a man who thought of himself as a Casanova. Instead, he looked sincerely confused. Had he never been rejected before?

"I, couldn't resist you," she said, realizing that Tristan was incredibly attractive and charming, "but then you became rough and I, I got scared... I am scared!" she reminded him.

"Scared of what though? Of wanting each other?... Serene, sex is normal in our sector. It's—"

"I'm not afraid of sex! I was never scared of sex," she interrupted him angrily. "It was apparent you still don't understand the severity of our actions. Someone like you would *never* understand what all of this means to a Light sector girl like me!"

"Try me Serene! Explain it.... And tell me. Tell me what I can do to make this right." He held her chin lightly as he nuzzled his face against hers. He desperately wanted to kiss her. Feelings inside of him were rising up like last night, but this time, he had a clear head, and more control.

"Tell me... Tell me you don't feel the same way I do right now," he begged, feeling like he'd die if he didn't have her again. He put her hand against his chest again, letting her feel his throbbing heart.

He gazed into her eyes for a moment, and then, he finally kissed her.

"You find me attractive," he kissed her again, "and I turn you on, I *know* it," he said, absolutely sure of it. "You want me... Serene. You want me just as much as I want you." He slowly led her hands up his hard chest and chiseled abdomen, remembering how turned on she looked when she touched his him there last night. "I'll be so gentle this time, I swear. I'll never hurt you again." His tone couldn't be sweeter but his words still alarmed Serene.

Tristan had a different plan this time, regardless of how much it hurt to hold back he was just going to please her.

Serene was shaking, probably more than last night, but she wasn't fighting. She felt tingles all over her body. She closed her eyes as he placed his face next to hers to whisper in her ear, "My Halo. Do you have *any* idea how incredibly sexy you are?" His hands went up under her shirt to meet her breasts, and he slowly caressed them. Sensing her arousal, he then kissed her, in what felt to him like extreme slow motion.

Against her will, she melted the very moment he touched her, and the soft caress on her nipples made her wet and wanting more.

Oh, why aren't you stopping him? The voice in her head screamed as she tried, desperately, to convince herself she didn't want this.

You hate him. You don't want this.

Then why do I want him again?

You're being an idiot. He'll have his way with you and leave you.

I know, but I'm so turned on by him.

He'll hurt you again.

He said he wouldn't.

And you believe him?

No. Yes...

"Last night hurt," she whispered.

"I know. We won't have sex again. I promise. I just want to please you."

Serene closed her eyes. Tristan was so skilled, and adroit in his seduction, it was almost as if he was so good at what he did, that he could possess her body and mind. He continued to circle his fingers around her breasts, and he kissed her as he gently laid her down. Then he looked into her eyes as he slowly unbuttoned her shirt. Serene's mental battle continued:

If you weren't so hot, if you weren't such an amazing kisser,

if you weren't so skilled at turning me on, I would fight you tooth and nail. Oh, how I would fight you! But I can't stop wanting you. How are you able to do this?

Searching her face for clues, and sensing any fear or reluctance from her, Tristan continued cautiously. He was relieved when he found her wanting. Her eyes were gentle, her lips were parted and her body was relaxed now, but her breathing was elevated.

In a trail of a million kisses, Tristan kissed down her neck then her chest, and finally her navel. It killed him to not go crazy, but he was patient. He opened her shirt fully, and looked at her naked body, now completely exposed in the sunlight. She was simple but flawless. He caressed and soothed every part of her body with his hands and then his lips. He slowly positioned himself to kneel in between her legs. He looked up at her giving her ample opportunity to object, but she didn't, so he began to kiss up her leg then eventually, he reached her clit.

With his fingers, he held her open, and gently allowed his tongue to skillfully dance around the most sensitive part of her body. The virus he had made her taste like an unknown fruit. Sweet, like mild nectar. Tristan forced down the mental and physical arousal he was feeling to focus solely on her pleasure. She began to moan, and it was music to his ears. Her body began to tense up, and beg for more of him. More than just his tongue. She wanted him inside her again.

Still, slow, and gentle, his tongue massaged every inch of her opening. He wanted to drive her crazy, so he took his time, and finally, he heard her moans peak. She covered her face completely ashamed of herself as he flicked her clit with his tongue while periodically licking into her opening. Her body arched in pleasure. She was amazed at how good this felt. It was gentle and non-threatening. However, suddenly she tried to remember how horrible last night was in an effort to keep her from enjoying his actions and gain the strength to stop him, but the thoughts melted away and all she could do was focus on the pleasure. Her virginity was gone, there was no way she'd get that back, and in a way that thought gave her an excuse, although a bad one, to indulge in the sensation.

Serene dug her fingers into the bed sheets, her knuckles white as she ached for him. When her body approached its peak, he began to finger her with one digit and then two. He closed his eyes as he envied the inviting warmth that wrapped his fingers. He kept the pain he was feeling to himself as he focused on putting all his years of practice into slowly driving her to the brink of insanity.

Giving in, Serene surrendered to his touch and her body relaxed. He felt her tighten up and about to orgasm, and with his fingers still inside of her, and his thumb still massaging her clit, he came back up to kiss her. This time it was her that sunk deep into his kiss as if overtaken by blinding passion. As she kissed him, she buried her hands into his soft hair. She then gasped loudly as she opened herself up, giving into his massage. He loved seeing her so turned on and unchaste. "God, I want you Serene," he whispered, through glossy eyes as he continued to kiss her, "You're so fucking hot."

His massage finally caused the tension in her to build up so much it had nowhere else to go but to release into intense ripples of pleasure. Serene exhaled in relief, having finally reached heaven. As she released, he continued to kiss her, and slowed down the rhythm of his fingers allowing the orgasm to continue and slowly come to a halt.

Moments later, he carefully pulled out from inside her and hugged her tightly. The pleasure was unlike anything she'd ever experienced. It was more than she had ever imagined an orgasm to be like. She just wished last night had never happened, but then she knew if it hadn't, she wouldn't be enjoying herself now. Within one day, Tristan had become her worst nightmare and her best dream.

In the silence, no words were necessary.

He wiped away a tear that had escaped from her eye, and he eventually whispered,

"Un angel encontre,

Y sus alas corté,

Asi nunca me dejes,

Mi querida mujer."

"Pft what does that mean?" She laughed.

"It means you're *my* angel now," he said with a smile, omitting certain parts. And just like that, she laughed at his cheesy line.

"What?" He laughed. "It's a song... I think?"

It was still early, about 10 a.m., and they lay together and conversed. Mostly about how little Spanish his mother had actually taught him.

"Did they ever find who did it?" Serene asked about his mother as he played with her hand.

"No, but they know it wasn't an accident."

"Oh... Can I... ask you something?"

"Sure."

"What happened to your ear?" Serene noticed his hair length wasn't a style choice. Sometimes she was able to catch a glimpse of his semi-deformed ear.

"It's a long story. I don't ever talk about it."

"You wondered what you can do to make it up to me. Can I pick knowing that story?"

Tristan sighed and scratched his head, "I've... never told anyone." He gazed at Serene hoping she would pull away, but she didn't. "My father... When I was very young... well, he wanted a typical Light sector wife. Obedient, domesticated. My mother grew up in Light sectors but, little by little she began to disobey him. One day, he came home drunk and angry that food wasn't ready. It was my fault, and he went to hit her with a cast iron pan. I jumped in to protect her."

"So, he hurt your ear?"

"Yes, and more than that. She blamed herself for the damage, but… it was never her fault. She was a saint."

"I'm sure. I can tell you really miss her."

"Every day. When she left him, and he left her penniless, I promised myself I'd take care of her one day. She did so much for me…"

Tristan continued to open up to Serene. Including how her death had led him to overdose a few times. Serene was a good listener and she never judged him. Her body, mind and soul felt therapeutic to him. Perhaps, it also helped that he finally had someone near him that was also a human and vulnerable, even though he didn't know it.

Tristan tried to continue their conversation, especially because they had moved on to more carefree subjects, but every time she smiled it triggered the growing need inside of him.

While under the covers his hand began to make his way up her leg. Serene gasped.

"Go on. You were saying?" he said, instructing her to continue to talk about her college plans. And how happy she was to be moving away from her parents.

As she spoke, he reached his goal and massaged her gently. She was so sensitive she twitched and playfully tried to move away.

He grabbed her as she giggled and turned her back towards him, spooning her as he caressed between her legs. He wanted to get her to orgasm again, but this time, with him inside of her.

He finally gave into her request to stop teasing, and lifted her to positioned her on top of him. Tristan wanted to put her in a position of power this time. This way he couldn't hurt her.

"What do you want me to do?" she asked shyly as she straddled him.

"Whatever you want," he said with a sly smirk.

"I have to leave soon."

"I know…"

"Like, really soon." She reminded him.

Tristan's expression softened, and she felt him yearn for her. He caressed her arms and legs softly, begging her, but Serene wouldn't move.

Eventually, Tristan began to unbutton the shirt she was wearing but Serene moved his hands off of her and instead leaned down to kiss him.

Tristan took some control momentarily, since he was determined to be inside her and feel her warmth again. He lifted her by her waist and led her to position his shaft near her opening.

Tristan closed his eyes as he felt her slide down his length. Her body was heaven and through her, Tristan reached the purest of pleasures.

"God, you feel amazing," he whispered. "You're so warm. Why are you so warm?" His voice was full of lust, and his thrusts were slow and deep. He wanted her just like this, open and inviting. He wanted his angel, in his bed, with him inside her, until he was completely sated, and he wanted her around so that he could have her wherever and whenever he wanted. This feeling of wanting her didn't seem to be going away anytime soon, and instead of alarming him he gave into it, feeding his body what it was craving.

He watched her move on top of him. And he was glad she hadn't allowed him to remove her shirt because this way he was able to fully focus on her angelic face.

Tristan gently cupped her face. Her eyes were fixated on him as the tension in her body grew. "You're mine Serene… mine," he said, kissing her and thrusting slowly but deeply inside of her. He felt he was being as gentle as possible, but Serene was in blissful agony. His thrusts became more intense, but this time instead of cries she moaned loudly for him.

Tristan had finally found something good in his life again, someone to live for; pure, kind, virtuous, untouched and clean. Like a shiny new toy, she was all his, and he never wanted to share her.

This kind of sex was a different kind of pain for Serene, she was in control, wet and stimulated, and all she wanted to do was come again and experience the pleasure that brought her peace earlier.

With each painful thrust he claimed her, and he spoke a line as if making it clear to her that she was his now. "I'm your first. Your last. No other man will ever touch you. Do you understand?"

She couldn't think, and she collapsed on top of him as the painful tension rose up inside of her. She wondered if sex was always going to be this deliciously rough and agonizing. He hugged her as he continued to push himself deep inside of her.

"Tell me your mine, Serene." he demanded.

Her eyes were closed, and she was straining to listen. Eventually, she tearfully gasped, "Yes. Yes!" she screamed as she exploded in intense ecstasy, screaming loudly for him until eventually, she was begging him to stop.

Soon after, he released deeply inside of her.

I did better this time. God I hope I did better.

TEN

Stay

11:21 a.m.

Serene noticed how Tristan's demeanor always changed drastically after sex. During sex, he was controlling, passionate, rough, and demanding. Once he was sated, however, he was quite the opposite—gentle, selfless and caring. It was as if he had two contrasting personalities, and one was difficult to control, for the both of them.

Tristan was shirtless but had put on a pair of black jeans. He then handed Serene one of his white T-shirts and a pair of red cotton shorts that could be tightened by a drawstring.

She was no longer a virgin, but her shy personality hadn't changed. As she dressed, she turned away from him to put on her bra and shirt, not allowing him a single glimpse. She was also cautious about bending down to put on her shorts since she could feel his eyes on her.

He smiled at what he wanted to say, but wouldn't dare. *I've already seen every inch of you, my dear.*

Serene turned around and extended her arms, then placed them on her hips. "How do I look?"

He snickered, as he grabbed his shoes and sat on the bed.

"What?" she asked, pretending to be angry.

"Nothing. You clearly look sexy in anything."

She shook her head and walked out into the living room. "Sure, and now you will drop me off and forget about me."

Tristan's heart sank when he heard those words; it seemed as though she hadn't heard a word of what he had said earlier. He finished putting on his shoes and walked out into the living room but stopped dead in his tracks when he saw her hang up the phone. His face pale with worry.

"I called a cab," she said.

Tristan exhaled, having not realized he was holding his breath. He was worried she had called the cops on him. "Serene, listen... This wasn't a fling. I like you, I..." He stopped talking since he noticed she was walking away from him. He went up to her and grabbed her wrist, pulling her towards him.

"Ow!"

"Sorry. Sorry! I forgot," he said, releasing her swiftly. He reminded himself to remember her frail disposition. She scowled at him for a moment, then turned to grab her coat. "Can we just talk for a minute?"

"No!" She screamed.

Tristan's eyes widened in surprise.

"That's enough! I am leaving now... Goodbye Tristan."

Serene grabbed her purse and walked towards the door but he rushed in front of her, blocking her from leaving.

"Is this about the flight? It's about the flight isn't it?" he asked playfully. "I'll buy you a ticket on a later flight. Or even a ticket for—"

"Why don't you understand? I have to go! My aunt will be waiting. They're going to kill me if I don—"

"Damnit, Serene! Just one fucking minute!" Tristan moved away, covered his mouth, paced and ran a hand through his hair. He immediately felt guilty for snapping at her. "Sorry. Just one minute. That's all I'm asking." He said softly. Holding back his frustration.

The one girl he wanted more than anything in the world to stay, didn't want to. He tried to understand, wondering if it was solely because of his mistake last night, or if it was really about the flight, or if perhaps she honestly wasn't that into him. He found the latter a bit too far-fetched. After all he'd never been rejected before. He had made plenty of mistakes with women in the past but he always knew how to turn things around. He just needed time.

"Fine! ONE minute," she said with a rigid expression, throwing her coat and purse on the couch before sitting down. "And *only* because my cab's not here yet."

Relieved, he exhaled and sat next to her, but then opted to kneel in front of her instead.

Serene scrunched her eyebrows, confused by his actions.

"Listen. I know how this is going to sound," he whispered, putting his hands on her legs "I don't know how to explain what I'm feeling. I know it's soon and crazy but I think I've... fallen for you." He stopped himself, looked away and laughed. "God, I must sound like a complete lunatic right now," he whispered as he rubbed his forehead.

"Yeah, you do," she agreed, partly convinced he was indeed clinically insane.

"I know. I know how it sounds... and I don't expect you to understand this but just... stay. There are plenty of good colleges here, and they're not in Light sectors. I could pay for it all. Your school, your car—"

She laughed at him, and he looked up at her, flustered.

"What?" he asked, sincerely.

"I'm sorry, Tristan; I can't."

"Why?" He waited for her to respond, but she didn't. "Damnit, Serene. Talk to me. I'm pouring my heart out here. Why can't you stay for a bit?"

"Because!" she snapped at him. "I don't want to be someone's sex toy!"

He leaned back, shocked by her words. "I don't want to fall into this trap, so that when you're done having your fun with me, you move on to the next. Isn't that what Dark sector men do?"

"No. We don't. Are you even listening?"

"Yes! You're saying for a while—how long? A week? A month? How long do your lovers stay?"

"Jesus Christ," he whispered under his breath. "Do I need to spell it out? I want something serious with you. I want to get to know you. I want us to be a couple." Tristan knew how impulsive he was being, but he was sincere about his feelings, no matter how fast his feelings were growing or how confusing they were. He was curious about Serene, and even behind the fog of his sexual need to have her, he was aware that there was something else there—a genuine connection to her that wasn't just physical and something that made Serene special.

She rolled her eyes.

"Stop doing that! Why don't you believe me?" He stared at her furrowed brow.

She placed her hands over her face, wondering when this madness would end.

"Look at me Halo… Why don't you believe me?"

"What am I supposed to believe, Trist?" She yelled as she looked down at him, teary-eyed. "Huh?… That you met me and, in a few days, you just fell for me? Look at you! You can have any girl you want! All those girls at the club," she said, remembering how the girls couldn't keep their hands or lips off him. "So why me? Is it because I said no? Or is it because you enjoy finding and seducing virgins from Light sectors, then playing with their emotions? Is this some sort of screwed-up game to you?" she exclaimed in anger. Her heart wanted to believe that he was, in fact, *that* into her. She didn't understand what someone as attractive as Tristan saw in her. What would make him fall in love so quickly?

He stood up and walked away from her. She was asking

questions he himself couldn't answer.

"Serene. I don't know," he said, maintaining his voice low and not feeding off her energy. "I don't know why I'm feeling this way. You're beautiful, no doubt, but it's something more…" He looked out his window, lost in thought. "What I do knowis that this isn't a game to me.. I already told you I've never done… *that* before. Maybe…" He sighed loudly. "Maybe it's… some sort of connection, or an obsession? Maybe it was love at first sight—what fucking difference does it make?" He looked at her, "All I know is I want you. It's like—" He looked away as he suddenly had a realization; Serene reminded him of someone he missed dearly, his mother. Her gentleness and vulnerability had filled a void he had been trying to fill for months.

However, Tristan knew he was losing her and, short of handcuffing her to his wrist again, he was left with no choice. He also feared for her well-being, since his obsession with her wasn't healthy and his need to be sexual with her was overbearing.

"Serene, I can't express how much I want to take back last night." He closed his eyes and scrunched his face. Trying hard to force the words out. "I can't—I can't control myself around you. So, it's probably not safe for you to stay." The words were difficult to say because he didn't want her to leave, but the impulse to keep her safe was as strong, or stronger, than his sexual need. "If you must go, go."

He went into his bedroom before he did something he would later regret.

Moments later he heard a car horn, and the front door opened and closed. Even though he had told her to leave, he'd never had a girl walk out on him before. Not when he wanted them to stay.

He walked out into the living room and the room echoed with her absence. A warming pain rose up in his chest and for a moment he couldn't breathe. He looked at the door and tried to control his urge to chase after her.

Let her go. If she doesn't want to stay, you can't make her.

I know. I know! But why does this hurt?

His heart started pounding and the muscles in his chest tensed up. He gave in and bolted out to chase after her.

When he finally made it outside, she was nowhere to be found. He watched as a cab disappeared into the distance.

Back in his bathroom, he looked in the mirror of his medicine cabinet, trying to cope with the withdrawal symptoms he was feeling. He knew he was attractive, smart, great in bed, and now he even had money. But none of that mattered. He was so angry at himself for last night, and at the mess of a man he had become. Inheriting his father's money couldn't have come at a worse time. Money just gave him more ways to destroy himself physically and as a person.

Agonized, and unable to look at himself any longer, he punched the mirror. His fist went through the glass, past the cabinet, and into the wall. The pill bottles fell into the sink and onto the floor as bits of shattered glass showered the floor. He grabbed one bottle at random and put a few pills in his mouth. He chewed them and didn't even wash them down with water. He knew he had hurt his hand and that he was bleeding, but he didn't care. He was back to his reality, to his darkness, to women that for whatever reason would never fill the entombing loneliness inside.

Tristan collapsed in his bathroom and his eyes began to water. He didn't know what connected Serene to his mother and why they felt so similar, but losing her made him relive the day he learned of his mother's death. An everlasting non-relenting void consumed him. Losing Serene reminded him of the type of person and the type of love he could never have again… A love he felt he no longer deserved.

3:28 p.m.

Tristan awoke on his couch. He looked at the clock on his phone.

Serene was officially gone. He placed a hand on his stomach feeling sick from the massive dose of drugs he had taken without food, but he was in no mood to eat, so he simply fell back to sleep.

He dreamt of her, his angel, caressing him as he laid his head on her lap again. "Serene, will you stay?"

"I love you, Tristan, of course," she said, smiling brightly at him.

As the virus progressed, the dreams became longer.

He saw a moment where they argued and she forced him to get rid of the drugs, and then she stood by his side through his withdrawals.

"Stay with me Tristan. I know you can do this," his angel whispered as she held his shaking body. He then dreamt of her body being his release for all the pain in this world. Suddenly Tristan felt a sharp pain and it woke him up. He blinked and the fogginess of the drugs faded.

Clear headed, he gazed up.

"Shhh relax," Serene whispered as she pulled out a piece of glass from his wounded hand, and then used wet cloths to wipe the blood off his knuckles.

"You... you came back?... your flight?" he asked, perplexed. He looked around, wondering if he was still dreaming. Serene was quiet and didn't respond to his question as she carefully cleaned and disinfected his cuts. She had found some wrap bandages in the bathroom to dress his knuckles. He wondered why, even in an innocent situation like this, it was so hard for him to sit still and control his need to touch her.

"Thank you... for this... and for... coming back."

Only the very corner of her lips curled up. "You're welcome," she whispered as she finished bandaging his hand. She placed the wet cloths, alcohol and other items on the coffee table and sat on the floor.

Tristan looked at his hand and flexed it. After a brief moment of silence, she finally spoke.

"I took some time… to think, but it didn't help… I'm still confused as to how I feel about you."

"What are you confused about?" he asked her softly.

"Everything. I'm confused as to why I still want you after you hurt me. Confused as to why you're like this with me. I finished packing and knew leaving was the right decision. But, I couldn't—I couldn't leave… and I'm not sure why. I couldn't get on the plane, go on with my life, and erase you."

A silence crept up between them.

"So, are you moving in?" he asked, hiding his eagerness and noticing her luggage by the door.

She stood up and sighed, "Tristan… We barely know each other. I don't even know why I came back."

He sighed, then stood up, feeling drained and tired of this ongoing conversation. He went into the kitchen to get himself something to drink.

"You thirsty? Hungry?" he asked, calling out to her as he prepared himself a drink while massaging his forehead. *No more drugs today.*

She walked up to him and he offered her a cup, but she motioned that she didn't want anything.

"By the way… that's not entirely true. I actually know a lot about you."

She shook her head. "Trust me, you don't know *anything* about me."

He drank his drink quickly, then confidently said, "Want to bet?"

She crossed her arms as he approached her. "Fine… Enlighten me."

"Well," he placed his empty cup behind her on the dining table. "For one, I know you live a completely sheltered life, but you desperately want to experience everything." She looked at him un-amused. "You've also never cursed a day in your life, until last night," he said, arching an eyebrow at her.

112

"Why do you say that?" she said, squinting her eyes.

"Because I saw you cuss by accident at the club and you caught yourself. Never seen anybody look so guilty." She opened her mouth to say something but decided to let him finish, "I also know you love kids."

She did love kids, but wondered how he knew.

He then slowly caressed her face with the back of his hand, "I know you're sweet... and you wear your heart on your sleeve." His touch instantly made her nervous again. "You also have no idea how beautiful you are." She got lost in his eyes, but then looked away.

"Okay, no. You're just being smooth. All those things are obvious. You'll have to do better than that."

He smiled. "I know people may be fooled into thinking you're pious and prude, but you're the complete opposite. You're just forced to be like that, probably because of your strict parents." Serene was unamused as he continued. "You're open-minded... because you never looked at me or any of my friends any differently, even though you obviously come from a wealthy, conservative family deep in a sector of Light," he said, touching her cross necklace and then gently trailing his hand down her shirt to the center of her chest. "I know you have a big heart... you didn't even know me and yet you were genuinely worried about me when I was passed out on the sidewalk. That's saying a lot considering how dangerous the city has been lately. Not many people would take that risk. I bet you're involved in a lot of local charities. Is that why you chose the Academy in the heart of the city?"

He was close, she was part of a group that visited shelters in Obsidian and she would provide, toys, clothing and food to the children there.

He moved his hands and gently brushed over her nipple. He saw her tense up and she moved back slightly. "I know... I'm the first man to ever touch you there..." He moved his hand to make a line just under her navel "or here..." She began to shake and he slowly moved his hand up and under her shirt to caress her, but she turned around. "I also know every time I touch you, you play with that ring of yours and immediately feel guilty." She looked down and she noticed she was currently messing with the ring Alex had given her.

Tristan then placed both hands on her shoulders, then kissed the back of her head and whispered, "I knew you Serene. I just didn't know your name… until recently." Serene turned to look at him. His eyes were looking down at her lips with intense yearning. He went down to kiss her, but stopped short. "I also know *one* more thing about you… there is something you're not telling me. Something you try really hard to hide."

"Like what?" she asked nervously as she looked up at him.

He studied her eyes as he tried to express what he saw there. "There is a sadness. Pain, fear, you cry, often… Your back had… scars." He mentally began to put the pieces together, and it broke his heart, "You're afraid!" he said, finally realizing someone at home was hurting her. "You're afraid… you aren't scared of me, you are scared of going back, or else… you wouldn't have returned to me." Her eyes watered and Tristan was overwhelmed with empathy for her. He put his hands on her shoulders, "Serene. Who hurt you?"

Serene couldn't believe he was able to read her so easily. Tristan had been right about everything. She then began to understand his feelings for her, because she was beginning to feel the same way about him. Yet, even though she liked him she was still worried, and after last night she didn't trust him. She also still had morals and felt that what they had done recently was wrong.

Serene pulled away from him and wiped a few tears from her eyes.

"No one. Not anymore." She sniffed, "And I do want to move in, but only under one condition," Serene said, very seriously.

"Anything Halo."

"I'll move in… if we don't have sex, at least for a few months."

"What? Why?"

"Because that's the only way I can know that you're serious about me. And that you respect me."

"Serene… come on." he said, knowing the idea was ridiculous. "You can't be serious." He locked her gaze, searching for sincerity. "Fuck, you are serious."

"I am! If you try anything, anything at all, I'll leave again."

"Serene… I'm sorry but you're being unreasonable."

"I'm being unreasonable?" she raised her voice. "You hurt me last night—and me knowing you can control yourself to refrain from sex is unreasonable?"

Tristan was quiet and he lowered his head. She was right; he knew she was right. However, he was also aware that this feeling building up inside of him wasn't going to make holding back easy. Holding back only led to hurting her. It was insane but the only time he felt sane around her was after sex, and that was always short lived.

"Serene, I have yet to lie to you, and I'm not going to start." He lowered his voice but made his stance clear, "The answer is no. I already told you how I feel around you and…" He placed his hands on the back of a dining chair and gripped it. A single flash of her naked body flashed through his mind causing a sharp pain. Tristan closed his eyes. He wanted her again, he wanted to get lost in her warm body, and the sooner the better, but he didn't want to scare her away again. He cared about her well-being and therefore he needed to warn her about the consequences of being around him. If he couldn't hold back, it was best she knew now.

He approached her. "I want to promise you that I won't touch you halo… but I can't. And even if I did, it wouldn't last. It's taking everything inside me to not bend you over this table and fuck you— right here, right now. I won't last a month." His voice broke. "Goddamnit Serene, I won't last a day." He lifted her by her waist and pinned her back against the wall, holding her tightly and securely against it as he tasted the sweetness of her mouth. Serene attempted to push him away but then gave into his kiss.

It wasn't easy, but Tristan forced himself to stop kissing her.

They both caught their breath. "I want you Serene, all of you, without restraints... You're right; I can't control this need to have you, but allow me to show you what comes with being mine." He begged, gazing deep into her eyes. His voice demanding but soft, "I told you I was serious about what I said earlier. Call me what you want; crazy, addicted, obsessed. I obsessed over having you for days. You're all I ever thought about, and I didn't stop until I made you mine. But Serene, I need you to understand that I will treat you right. I will make you laugh, take you out to extravagant dinners and stupid dates. I want to spoil you day in and day out, but then I also want to come home and *Fuc—*" He placed his forehead against hers and clenched his jaw as he attempted to control the rising pain, "—make love to you for hours. But... I want the feeling to be mutual. To know you enjoy me taking you, to forgive me when I want to make you cum and cry in pleasure... and I want to do this to you over and over again until we're completely sated. I want your full surrender Serene. And in turn, I'll surrender to you."

She looked up at him and was shocked by his words. Her breathing was just as loud and as heavy as his. She wanted him. She just couldn't get herself to admit it or to allow it, but she also couldn't see a person like Tristan getting anything less than his way with any woman.

He whispered, "Just try it Serene... give into me." He nuzzled his face against hers, and she melted into him. He had given her a taste of his world, but he had so many more things in mind to show her, and he was dying to get started.

Finally, she closed her eyes and nervously whispered, "You promise?... You promise me you'll do all those things? And that you'll be only mine as well?" He lifted her face and looked into her large, sad hazel eyes as he processed what she had just said.

"Yes. I'm yours. And I'll do all those things, Serene, all of it." He swept in quickly, kissing her passionately, taking off her shirt, as she removed his. They wanted each other desperately, but Tristan wasn't finished with his conversation. "Serene, if I ever treat you wrong, if I ever fail to be the man you need, I swear I'll let you go, but I need you to promise me that you won't deny me, that I can have you, and that you won't hold it against me or leave because of it."

"What if I say no? What if I need you to stop?" she said, eyes widened.

He knew she was worried, and Tristan was also worried for her. What he felt was stronger than lust, and he knew that once he reached a certain point, he could lose control again. But he also noticed that once he was sated, he was able to handle being around her. It was holding back that was the issue.

"Serene, whatever *this* is, I can only control it until a certain point. It's painful. I've never felt anything like it."

She looked at him but he was staring down at the floor. His beautiful hair partially covered his face. His breathing was loud and heavy. His strong arms were on the wall on either side of her. His fingers were pressed firmly into the wall, and, he was shaking. "I don't want to have to hold this back anymore," he said, trembling in pain and on the brink of tears.

Serene couldn't possibly understand how much effort it was taking Tristan to hold back. Nor could she comprehend the level of torture and strain his body was under. Yet, somehow she understood that living beside her in this state of agony would be too much for him. She knew he needed reassurance, that she would not hate him if he lost control again and she ached for him as well, but he had been too rough.

"What if you become rough again? What if you hurt m—"

"I swear I won't. Please believe that I will do my best to never hurt you like I did last night. I swear it. I will never let whatever *this is* hurt you again… But I need you. I need to be able to have you. *Please.*"

Serene was confused by his feelings and the way he spoke about them. She also knew she couldn't possibly agree. There would surely be moments where she would need him to restrain himself. Yet, as her own need for him grew, she reluctantly answered, "Okay." The word was barely a whisper.

"Okay what?" he asked her, still looking at the ground and needing reassurance. "I need an answer."

He saw her tense up by closing her fists and bracing herself for what was to come.

She closed her eyes and whispered, "I can't believe I'm agreeing to this." She tried to understand how she had gotten to this point. Yet right now, against her will, she found herself yearning to be his, always.

Tristan saw her body surrender, ready for him to take her, but he needed more. "I need to hear you say it Serene… Say that you won't hold it against me if I take you."

A battle was raging in her head. Millions of reasons as to why she shouldn't agree, and why she shouldn't be doing this, ran through her head. And although she was nervous, she was completely unable to resist him. He had her, he had her the moment they met.

Finally, she whispered, "You can have me, Tristan…"

In the emptiness only their heavy breathing could be heard.

Without warning, he spun her around and pinned her against the wall.

ELEVEN

THE GIRLFRIEND

S erene sat on the side of the bed in just her underwear. She was on Tristan's phone, talking with her mother. Her wrists were bruised, and her body was beginning to be filled with light red and blue reminders of Tristan's roughness. She was exhausted and ached all over.

"Your father and I have been worried sick! Where are you?" Clair berated her daughter through the phone. Serene didn't want to speak to her parents, but thought it a good idea to call since she had been gone for two days. She didn't know when she would be able to face them, if ever.

"I'm at a friend's house. I'll be back in a few days."

"In a few days? What's gotten into you, Serene! Haven't you seen the news? All these missing people! A girl like you is surely a prime target! You can't just leave without telling anyone! What do you think the congregation—"

"Mom! I'm twenty-one-years-old now! I'm allowed to do whatever I want."

There was a deep silence. Serene feared her mother and therefore always obeyed her, but she wanted to be free for a moment, while she still had the chance. Although she barely knew Tristan, she felt safe and protected.

Irritated at her, Clair passed the phone to Serene's father.

"Hey pumpkin, why didn't you go to the airport?"

"I'm sorry Dad, I just wanted to spend some time with a friend of mine before I left—"

"Serene, I understand, but you could have called. It's not safe nowadays and you know how your mother gets. Which friend is this anyways? Do we know her?"

"No, but we met at the Academy. Look, I'll call you guys later."

"Wait. Everyone was planning on—" Her mother got on the phone quickly before he could finish. Serene hung up.

Both of her parents stood in their own living room, shocked by Serene's actions.

Clair was an elegant lady with bleach blonde hair. Peter was a simple man with brown hair and hazel eyes, like Serene's. He was usually very gentle with Serene and it irritated Clair that she always felt alone when it came to reprimanding their daughter.

"I don't like this at all, Peter. How dare she not call and be gone for days without even telling Vivian! What if something had happened to her?" Clair exclaimed, pacing in their living room.

"She is not a child anymore Clair. It's not like we can call the police anyways. She'll come back when she's ready."

Serene was still sitting on the bed when she hung up the phone. A naked Tristan came up behind her to kiss her shoulder. He noticed a bruise on her arm and gently caressed it.

"You bruise so easily," he whispered sweetly. His voice lower than usual since he had just woken up.

"Yeah? I never noticed."

"Why'd you get dressed?" he asked, disappointed. Serene realized that he must have forgotten what it meant to keep clothes on if he considered her in her underwear, "dressed."

"Hmm, maybe because it's my birthday, and we've been cooped up in your apartment for days! Let's go do something."

He kissed her lips, and as he did he laid her down in bed. "I am doing something. I'm doing you."

She rolled her eyes, "Trist, I'm sorry but I'm extremely sore. So, no! No more sex. That's an order!"

He lifted an eyebrow at her and laughed at her new-found attitude. Making a salute gesture with his hand he said, "Yes ma'am!"

He then grabbed her hand and ripped her away from bed.

Tristan took Serene shopping in the city as a birthday gift.

The city looked different in the morning. The skyscrapers blocked the sun and had black windows that hid the people inside. The bottom floors always had businesses with open doors and clear windows. Light sectors depended on greenery and florals for color, Obsidian City had neon holographic Ad's that turned pastel in the daytime. They walked past open bars, brothels, high-tech consumer goods, and drug shops.

In public, Tristan and Serene were an odd couple; his raw dark and serious disposition was juxtaposed with her startlingly bright and cheerful nature. Even the way they dressed was a walking contrast. He wore Dark sector style clothing; blacks, decorated with silver accents and she wore common Light sector attire— a white vintage cocktail dress with a matching headband. They were an epitomic Light and Dark sector couple.

"Oh my God," he said in disbelief as she walked out of the dressing room wearing nearly the same outfit as him. Black pants, a studded belt, big black boots, and a highly-decorated black shirt with cutouts.

"What? You don't like it? I thought you liked this sort of thing," she joked sarcastically as she mimicked his serious debonair stance.

His eyes narrowed as she continued to impersonate him perfectly. "I just need some tattoos, make-up, some piercings and I'll be good! Think we can do that today?"

"Wow. Okay, slow down. First of all, take that off. You're freaking me out." It wasn't that she looked bad, he thought she looked amazing, it just wasn't her.

She laughed. "Okay, maybe not this, but I would like to buy something more appropriate since I'm going to be living here."

"We don't have a dress code, Halo. Just be yourself. That's the point of free sectors."

Serene looked at herself in the mirror and agreed. This just wasn't her, but she was happy to finally be on this journey to find herself. *Free sectors*, she smiled in the mirror at the thought, *I finally live in a free sector. What would I wear if I could wear anything I want?* She wasn't sure.

As they shopped, Serene was curious about the way people dressed. Instead of everyone being unique in their attire, the population did seem to group into one style or another. She pointed at people and asked Tristan to explain what their clothing indicated.

"He's a metalhead—just likes Heavy rock music," Tristan whispered to her as they walked.

"What about that?" she pointed at a woman walking towards them with a shaved head, nose piercings, and a see-through mesh shirt that in no way hid her perky breasts.

"Uh, I haven't the slightest clue," he said, not being able to pinpoint a style other than racy and vulgar.

"What are you looking at? Light sector brat." The woman looked straight at Serene in a judgmental manner. "Aren't you supposed to be on your fucking knees somewhere?"

Serene's heart raced as they walked past her. Tristan put his arm around her, knowing she could be attacked for no other reason than the way she was dressed.

Tristan attempted to take Serene's mind off the uncomfortable moment by continuing their previous conversation.

"She's a Cyber-punk," he said, pointing at another girl in a spunky neon outfit, "but she's just into the club scene. That girl across the street," he said looking at a woman with high-tech goggles and a black leather bodysuit with blue neon stripes on the side. She was getting on a very interesting and modified motorcycle. "She's an actual Cyber-punk."

Serene continued to question him about the people in the city as she insisted on going into every tattoo, bar, and drug shop. These were all things that didn't exist in Light sectors and she was fascinated by them.

Tristan grabbed Serene's hand and brought her down an alley and up to a secluded sex shop that advertised live shows.

Serene blushed in embarrassment, "No. No way," she said, turning back and letting go of his hand.

"So, you'll walk in every store except this one?" he asked, confused by her sudden lack of interest.

"It's weird." She said hiding a smile with her hand.

"Fine," He continued walking with her when suddenly he picked her up and took her inside the shop as she laughed and playfully fought him.

><

After buying her a cell phone, and a few other *personal* electronics, Serene suggested some ice cream. They had shopped all day, and they sat around an outdoor table to eat, surrounded by shopping bags. He looked at his phone as it rang for what felt like the hundredth time that day. He hung up and placed it on the table.

"Who keeps calling? Is it still my parents?"

"No, not anymore. It's just a... friend of mine."

"Girl?"

He sat back, slightly nervous. "Yup."

"Oh. You're not married, are you? And that's your wife calling?" she joked.

"Maybe. Maybe not," he said, putting on his best poker face.

It rung again, and this time she snatched the phone and answered it for him.

"Hello?" she asked, grinning at him. Tristan tried to grab it from her but she got up and ran out of his reach.

"Hello? Who's this?" The woman on the other line asked.

"Tristan's girlfriend. Who's this?"

Irritated, Tristan grabbed Serene's wrist and forcefully yanked the phone from her hands.

"Ow!" Serene yelled in pain, rubbing the spot on her arm he had just grabbed. "That hurt!"

"Hey, what's up?" he said into the phone, then he mouthed 'sorry' to Serene for hurting her. Kamilla was silent as she made sense of what she had just heard.

"... I need to see you. It's about the entertainment hall's renovation."

"Just... go ahead without me. I trust you'll do well with it. I'm just dealing with some... stuff," he said, clearly not interested in talking.

"Well, can we go out tonight? I could use a drink," Kamilla asked.

"Uh... now's not a good time. Maybe next week?"

"Who was that girl?... Do we know her?"

He looked nervously at Serene, who was holding a cherry and twirling her tongue around it in an attempt to arouse or distract him, but he was intensely focused on his conversation with Kamilla.

"Her name is Serene."

"Oh? Okay. Well, I'll talk to you later then. You seem... *preoccupied.*"

"Yeah, um. I'll see you later."

He hung up the phone, looking at it for a moment, knowing he was in deep shit.

He glanced up at Serene, who was still playing with her food like a child. He lifted an eyebrow, confused. *God you're weird.*

"Hey Lea, do we know of a 'Serene'?" Kamilla asked Lea over the phone while pacing in her kitchen. Kamilla was aware that Lea was just as obsessed with Tristan's life as she was.

"Serene?" Lea thought for a moment. "No, why?"

Kamilla sighed loudly, "Because I think we have a problem. It's Trist. Fuck! I left him alone for a week! There are no 'Serenes' registered in the database. I think she's human!"

"Relax Kami. Are you sure you have her name right? Either way, he'd have told at least one of us about it. Or someone would have said something. Though you did insist on being the one to watch him from now on, after you got on our case for letting Sophia slip by us. So, we pulled back."

"Shit! Shit! Shit!" Kamilla whispered to herself while continuing to pace nervously.

"Did he hurt her? I knew it! It's been years Kam! You know he's likely infected by now and will for sure end up hurting her, or even killing—"

"No, No! I heard her when I called. He didn't seem worried. I don't think he's infected. I basically interrogated him after Sophia and I've not seen any symptoms but I think he slept with this one!"

"Well, he was bound to sleep with a human sooner or later. Sophia was a close call. We can only do our best to keep him within the circle for so long... do you think he noticed anything yet?"

"More than likely!" Kamilla said in an obvious tone. "But I don't know yet. I have to talk to him."

"Why don't you just turn him already?" Lea mentioned, hoping Kamilla would turn around on her decision not to.

"No! Not yet! And don't any of you dare!"

"We aren't doing anything..." Lea said, knowing no one would even dare defy her. "But you know what's happened in the past. If you wait too long, he *will* hurt someone. And if you're not quick he'll end up in jail, and that's a whole lot of legal trouble," Lea explained.

Kamilla knew that even if Serene was just a fling, Tristan had only been with her kind since his first time, and as long as it stayed that way, he'd be none the wiser; not being able to differentiate human from Krov. However, for the past few months, she had let her guard down because she was busy working and managing his endeavors. He had also promised to come back to her so long as she gave him space. Tristan had always been trustworthy, and never broke a promise.

Kamilla knew that if she bothered him now, and went into her usual jealous rage, he'd be turned off by her actions. But if Serene was human, and he hadn't slept with her yet, she had to find a way to end that relationship quickly. It wasn't the first time her kind had intervened in Tristan's relationships. Kamilla felt Lea was right; it had been long enough, and she had to turn him now... or kill him.

Kamilla had meant to install cameras in his condo after the renovations, but never got around to it. As silly as it was, she had to spy on him the old-fashioned way, through his bedroom window that night. She was filled with jealousy as she watched them be intimate. Tristan having lovers and girlfriends throughout the years was nothing new to her, she was used to it. But Serene was in fact human, which meant Tristan was enjoying sex more than usual. She was angry, but she wasn't threatened by Serene in the slightest. Serene looked too young, immature and naive for Tristan. Kamilla was certain that he couldn't possibly take her seriously, so she would allow him his fun for the time being. As soon as they were apart, she'd confront him and if that didn't work, she'd deal with Serene later.

Tristan's place was beginning to feel like home. Serene didn't know when or how she planned on explaining this to her friends or her parents. All she knew was that right now, she was the happiest she had ever been. The way Tristan treated her was liberating. She could do anything she wanted around him—sleep till noon, stay up late, let the dishes pile up, walk around in just her underwear—he actually insisted on that one. When they went out, he'd buy her whatever she wanted. He was dominant only during sex. Otherwise, he treated her like a princess, coddling her and even preparing her food whenever she was even slightly hungry. Men rarely cooked or cleaned in Light sectors.

Tristan got up from the couch and Serene laid herself sideways. She wore only a tight white T-shirt and a racy black underwear. It was amazing to her how comfortable she felt in her own skin now. Tristan eventually came back into the living room and placed a variety of objects on the coffee table. Drugs in free sectors were very complex and some required a certain level of chemistry.

Tristan put on some music and lit a cigarette.

"Can I try some tonight?" Serene asked, referring to the drugs on the table. She had been asking for days, but he always refused.

"Umm, actually… No. I told you I'm done with drugs, but unfortunately I have to wean myself off first."

She touched him with her feet playfully. "Pleeeease?" she begged him sweetly.

He sighed. "What do you want to try and I'll think about it."

She sat up and her eyes widened. "Everything."

He laughed. "Um, yeah that would kill you…"

"Well how about something small?"

"Do you like to smoke?"

"I'd rather not."

He thought about it. He didn't want her on a pill she could later find and take, but also nothing she could get addicted to.

"Okay. I'll get you something. It may make you sleepy."

He gathered a few things from a different room and came back to her. He then carefully prepared her arm and began looking for a vein.

"You have tiny veins…" he whispered, flirting with her. "You have tiny everything."

"So do you," she joked.

"Ouch! We both know that's not true… Okay, actually not everything on you is tiny," he looked at her breasts. "So, I take that back." She blushed. "Alright, I diluted this so you can see how it feels first. Remember to breathe because your heart will slow down—"

"It's not going to freak me out is it?" she said, excited but nervous.

"No… it's going to relax you. This first dose is diluted, so you won't feel much… Okay, found one," he said having located the vein he planned on using. He prepared the needle and she turned her head away as he injected the drug into her.

She closed her eyes and her mind became slightly numb as her heart slowed down. It felt good but she had to focus to feel anything at all.

"You feel it?" Tristan asked.

"Yeah… it feels nice, but it almost feels like nothing now."

"Good. Now I'm going to give you more. It's going to feel that way, but more intense. When your heart slows down, remember to breathe."

She closed her eyes and shortly after quickly opened them. "Whoa," she said, grabbing his arm to keep herself from falling backwards.

He smiled. "Nice. Isn't it?"

She sat there with her eyes closed and her head down. He quickly gave himself a small dose of the drugs he was weaning himself off and got up to turn off the lights and close the curtains. He then laid down on the couch, grabbed her, and positioned her so that she was lying on top of him.

She was quiet as he caressed her hair.

"You okay?" he asked, concerned.

"Yes… Just… enjoying it. It feels like I'm on a cloud."

"Oh Yeah?" He laughed slightly.

She was overwhelmed with happiness and felt a peace she had never experienced before.

"So, tell me, Serene. How did a vixen like you manage to stay in the dark this long? Or at least not experiment with oral sex, alcohol, drugs, or dating. I mean, I originally thought it was because you were a typical Light, but you're always so curious. So, I know neither religion nor Light sector laws were stopping you."

She was quiet for a bit as she absorbed the serenity the drugs provided her.

"I was… home-schooled before the Academy. My parents are very strict Lights. I… wasn't allowed to do anything. And by anything, I mean *anything*. I would get punished for even talking to a guy in my own sector. I hated the way my parents were…"

As she spoke, he began to feel intense sadness for the sheltered life she had lived.

She paused, listening to what Tristan had chosen for background music. "What's the name of this song?" she asked.

"This? It's actually two songs: Vermilion part one and two. This is part two playing now. Why? Do you like it?"

"Yes… I like both songs," she said softly as they both enjoyed the calmness. "Can you make me a playlist on my phone. I enjoy all of your music."

"Okay. I promise. What's the point of making music illegal in your sectors anyways? What are they afraid of?"

"It's what the music promotes."

"What? Love, hate, anger?"

"—drugs, sex, violence. We try to keep those things out of our sectors."

"You mean normal human wants and emotions?" Serene was silent for a moment. "Serene?" he whispered trying to get her attention.

She made a small noise and it was obvious to him that she was falling asleep in his arms. He got up carefully and took her to bed with him.

He held her.

After a few moments, he whispered, "Thank you, Serene."

"For?" Her eyes were closed and her words were barely a whisper.

"For the way you are."

"… and how am I right now?" she whispered right before she passed out.

"… Perfect."

TWELVE

KAMILLA

A sound in the living room awoke Serene. She got out of bed to investigate the source but couldn't see anything. When she walked back into the bedroom, she noticed the pair of handcuffs lying on the floor.

Serene grabbed them and quietly handcuffed one of Tristan's wrists to a pole on the metal headboard, being careful not to wake him as she did.

Yesterday, Serene noticed Tristan had deleted several voicemails from her phone, and that he was acting… unusual and nonsensical. As if something in the voicemails had worried him or made him jealous.

When she confronted him about it, he'd change the subject or tell her it was nothing, that the voicemails were just robocalls. She later tried to call her family or her friend Casey, but Tristan had blocked their numbers from her phone. How he did that, she wasn't sure, but something wasn't right, and it was a clear red flag that either Tristan was crazy or there was something else going on. Something he didn't want her knowing. If he refused to talk, she had no choice but to go home and find out for herself. However, she knew Tristan would not make leaving easy.

Tristan blinked as he awoke, and when he noticed the

handcuffs, he had hoped it had meant sex but was disappointed when he saw Serene fully dressed.

"Um, where are you going?" he asked her.

"I have to get back to my family or they might start thinking something absolutely terrible has happened to me."

"Or something amazing," he said with a smirk and a wink. Serene smiled. "So, you think you can run away from me by simply handcuffing me to the bed? How am I going to remove the cuffs once you leave?"

"I'll leave you the key. I'll be back in a day or so."

"You're taking my car?"

"No. I called a cab."

When she had put on her shoes, she grabbed her purse and threw the key just out of his reach on the bed before running out of the condo as fast as she could.

When she got into the cab her phone rang. It was Tristan. Serene rolled her eyes.

"Hey?" she said answering it.

"Yea, the key just broke. I hope you aren't planning on leaving me cuffed to my bed until you return."

"Maybe I will. I guess that could work to make sure that you're there when I return."

"Yes, except I need to pee," She could hear the smile in his voice.

Serene hung up but her phone rang again. She answered.

"Sorry Trist, I guess you'll just have to figure it out!"

"Come on. Just come uncuff me and you can go. I know where the spare is." He knew Serene wouldn't leave him there, but he played along.

"Do you love me?" she asked, smiling as she waited for him to respond.

"We barely know each other." His voice was tight.

"And yet, you tell me those words during sex. Why?" She silently instructed the cab driver to turn back.

"I don't know. Lost in the moment maybe?" She was silent. "...
Fine. I love you," he mumbled, fighting back a smile.

"Hmm, that doesn't seem good enough."

"Fuck, Serene, I'm not kidding! I have to piss."

"Hey! If you really had to pee, you'd do better than that!"

"Ugh. Fine... how about an I really *really* like you?"

"Keep going..." she said sweetly.

"I like you and... you are the sweetest woman I've ever met.
Also... I... would like you to marry me..." he paused for dramatic
effect, "someday."

She laughed. "Has anyone ever told you you're obsessive and
crazy?" She walked out of the cab smiling from ear to ear and debated
whether or not she should enter the building.

"Obsessive? Never. Possessive? Maybe. I take care of what's
mine. By the way, that wasn't a question."

"What wasn't a question?" she asked, confused.

"When I said I wanted you to marry me. Maybe not today, or
tomorrow, but you will."

She scoffed, "What makes you think I'd say yes?"

"I have my ways of persuasion... haven't I done pretty well so
far?"

She smiled and covered her eyes with her hand. Tristan was
indeed crazy—crazy about her, and it made her feel powerful to
know she could get a guy like him to think about marriage so quickly.
He couldn't possibly mean it... or maybe he did? Either way, it still
felt good.

Still smiling to herself, she walked up the steps and into the
condo. When she closed the door she let out a quick scream. He had
grabbed her from behind and quickly landed a kiss on her neck. He
had tricked her into coming back, but that fact only surprised Serene
for a second.

Tristan *always* got his way.

"You're not getting away that easy," he said as he took off her blouse. She knew he was role-playing, and she wasn't threatened. "You have something that belongs to me." He growled and she placed her hands on the wall.

"And what's that?" She held her head down and closed her eyes as he unclipped her bra.

"You."

"Ahem!" Someone behind them made themselves known.

Tristan turned and saw Kamilla sitting on a chair in the living room with her legs crossed.

"Kami?" he asked, surprised and wondered how long she'd been there. Serene's face became flushed and she scooped up her blouse and put it on.

"What the hell are you doing here?" Tristan snarled.

"Hmm, I don't know Tristan," she replied, bitterly. "Did you forget you gave me the keys to your condo a long time ago? I haven't heard from you in days. And you're not answering my calls. I sent you a text that I was coming over and you told me you were out of town. But you lied because you've been here all week!"

He analyzed Kamilla's confident glare, realizing she knew more than he wanted her to. Tristan's lip twitched with anger. "Kamilla you can't just barge in h—!"

"Why not? I practically used to live here! Didn't you tell her about *us*?" Kamilla glared at Serene. "By the way sweetie, *I'm* his girlfriend."

Serene stared at Tristan but his blank stare did very little to reassure her. She believed Kamilla's every word, because she dressed and looked exactly like the type of girl Tristan would date. A typical Dark sector goth.

"Oh my God," Serene put her hand up to her mouth. "I got to go," she said making her way out the door.

"By the way dear, he says 'I love you' to all his lovers!" Kamilla called after her, sounding gleeful.

As Serene ran out the front door, Tristan opened his mouth to argue with Kamilla, but bolted after Serene instead.

"Serene!" he called out to her as he leaned over the wood railing, but she continued to run down the stairs without looking back. He sprinted to catch up with her and grabbed her arm, remembering to be gentle.

"Let me go!" she demanded, and he did, not wanting to hurt her.

"It's not what you think, she's not... she's a friend."

"A friend? You mean girlfriend? Like I am? How many are there?" she yelled, her mind racing as she began to realize she should have followed her instincts—all this had been too good to be true.

"Just you! And no, she's not a girlfriend she's—she's just— Goddammit, Kam!" he whispered the last part to himself. He was at a loss for words because he didn't want to lie to her, but this was also something that couldn't be resolved quickly. So, he grabbed Serene by the waist and, regardless of her objections, lifted her over his shoulder.

"Stop! Put me down! I'm serious! Agh!" Serene screamed and struggled as he climbed back up.

On the way up they passed an older man leaving his condo. Serene saw him and yelled out, "Please sir. Help me! Call the cops!"

Tristan turned around to face the white bearded man. "Sorry Mr. Sower, we're just having a lovers' quarrel. Please excuse us."

"Another one?" The old man put on his glasses and looked at Serene. He shook his head in disappointment, "Goodness boy! For once can you keep it in your pants?" The old man turned around, locked his door, then, as he made his way down the stairs he muttered, "It's a new girl every week with you."

Serene's eyes widened in shock and anger. Tristan sighed; this wasn't helping his case. Serene was now fighting him harder.

"Every weekend! You have a new girl every weekend? Ugh! Put me down! I knew—" She continued to argue with him all the way up into his condo.

He plopped Serene onto his couch and stood between her and the doorway while he caught his breath. He then looked straight at Kamilla.

"You! I need to speak with you in the hallway RIGHT FUCKING NOW!" He pointed at the door with his eyes narrow, his face red and the veins on his neck clearly visible.

Kamilla, however, was calm and collected as if Tristan had always spoken to her in that tone. She walked past Serene but stopped right in front of her and, like a cat, hissed in her face startling Serene. Tristan rolled his eyes and pushed Kamilla out the door.

Holding the door open, he looked back at Serene. "I swear to god Serene if you fucking move—!" He didn't finish his threat.

Serene's eyes widened; he had never yelled at her in such a vulgar manner before.

Tristan walked into the hallway and slammed the door behind them. Serene could hear them arguing but couldn't make out their words. She began to realize she had, just as she suspected, probably been a game to him. The thought angered her, but then again it all made sense now. To Serene, Tristan was just a skilled player. One who unsuccessfully tried to juggle multiple women at once. She had never felt more naïve.

They stood near the staircase.

"Listen! I know what I told you, Kamilla, but I *really* like this girl."

"Whatever Tristan, she's what... sixteen?" Kamilla spat back at him.

"Twenty-one!"

"Yeah, and I sure hope you don't believe that! Tristan, if you want to play around that's fine, but I heard you on the phone with her... Telling a young girl like her that you love her? That you want to marry her? What the fucks gotten into you?"

Tristan sighed and nervously put his hands through his hair. He knew he had a lot of explaining to do.

She continued, "You can't just say things like that to a young girl like her. They take it seriously! And you know the type of crazies you've gotten yourself involved with before. Do you want another obsessive episode? Remember Tia? Scarlette? You even had to warn Lea!"

He studied her closely as she spoke; her buzzing energy, her desperation. He realized that Kamilla had just become one of *those* girls.

"I'm not fucking playing around with her! I like her; she's different. She's gentle, kind, and I am crazy about her. Please understand. I've never wanted something to work out as much as—"

"Do you love her?" she asked nonchalantly, firmly believing he'd say no.

Tristan was silent for a moment. "It's complicated."

"Complicated? If you don't love her why are you telling h—"

"—Yes! Yes okay? I love her. I wasn't lying when I told her that." Kamilla rolled her eyes. "Unfuckingbelivable."

"Listen. I don't expect you to understand. I know it's fast but, I swear I've never felt this way before."

Kamilla's expression darkened and her bad temper came spewing out. "If that's true why did you promise yourself to me? Were you just playing around with *me* then? Keeping me on the shelf until you found someone better?" Kamilla's heart sank as she finally realized she was never going to have his heart. She knew love was something that couldn't be forced, but he had lied to her, led her on, played with her emotions. The thought infuriated her.

"Kam. I met her after I said that. I never expe—"

"You said you needed space!" Her eyes became glossy with tears as her anger grew. "You told me—"

"I didn't mean for this to fucking happ—!"

"No! Don't! I fucking warned you! I told you I wasn't one of those stupid girls you can play around with! I..." She continued as she paced struggling to contain her powers. "I fucking warned you Tri—!"

"Oh, grow up!" Tristan spat tired of this game with her, "We are done! Okay? Officially and forever. Thanks for every goddamn thing you've done for me, but there will *never* be anything between us!" He then grabbed her arm, stopping her nervous pace and pulled her close. "I need you to get that through your fucking skull."

Tristan didn't mean to be cruel, but it seemed to be the only way to get her to understand once and for all that he was done. He had tolerated Kamilla and her jealousy for years, and after meeting Serene, he was relieved he didn't end up with her. She always tried to force something that wasn't there.

There was a brief silence. She was seething and on the verge of losing control.

"Now... leave." He held her gaze and watched as the determination in her eyes turned to realization. When he was satisfied that she had gotten the message, he released her and turned to head back.

Whack!!!!

The loud sound vibrated through the building.

Dust and debris filled the air.

Tristan's back had hit a concrete wall, and the impact caused a depressed hole that cradled his body. Something powerful had struck him, sending him flying through the air. The sound of plaster falling to the ground echoed around him.

Kamilla stood several feet away from him, her hands still by her side.

Tristan was stunned and motionless for a moment as the air was taken from his lungs. He gasped loudly and fell to his knees in immense pain.

As he moaned and coughed Kamilla walked up to him. She knew no one else lived on this floor but she didn't care who saw or heard them. She was furious and just wanted him dead.

"We could have been so fucking happy together!" Her voice was a ground-shaking growl. Tristan struggled to move but made an effort to look up at her. A red circle around her iris began to glow as if she was wearing contacts to conceal their true color. She bent down to whisper to him, "You could have been a powerful Krov had you not been SO FUCKING STUPID!"

Suddenly, Tristan was lifted into the air by an invisible strangling force around his neck. Kamilla was several paces away and simply held her arm out to guide her powers.

"Kami," he gasped, unable to breathe. His desperation was mixed with confusion as he struggled to free himself. "I'm... sorry..."

She stared at him in furious loathing as a red aura began to appear around her. The red mist slowly thickened and her hair flowed as if it was blowing in a wind that wasn't there. She guided his body through the air and hovered him over the center of the staircase. He felt his limbs lose their strength when he looked down at the distance beneath his feet. The force around his neck tightened until it was unbearable, and then, she dropped him.

Kamilla's intention was to drop him down the center of the staircase so that he could fall to his death, but he fell short. His body had crashed into the wood railing only one floor down, and the right side of his mid-section was pierced by a large, sharp piece of broken wood from the railing.

The force and wind around her suddenly stopped and she peered over the ledge to see what she had done.

She watched with remorse as he writhed in pain, blood creeping along the railing and dripping down to the distant floor. Her anger subsided, and now, all she saw was the man she loved.

"Tristan!" she cried out, running to his aid.

When she reached him she lifted him up into her arms effortlessly removing his body from the wood that had pierced him.

"Tristan!" She shook him, but he didn't respond. Through

tearful eyes, she searched his body for movement, but there was none. She closed her eyes and focused so that she could attempt to hear his heart beating. Her hearing was incredibly advanced, and she gasped with relief when she found it was still beating.

Kamilla groaned with despair, holding his face against her chest tenderly. She loved him with every bit of her being and hated him with the exact same intensity.

It was against all reason, but she didn't waste any time in saving him. She couldn't let him die!

Kamilla looked at a piece of broken wood that was a few feet away from her and made it levitate to her. She then exposed the wound in Tristan's midsection and took the strong, sharp piece of wood and stabbed her inner arm repeatedly but the wood didn't even cause a scratch. Her skin was too hard to penetrate.

"Ugh! Why did I think that would work!" Kamilla threw away the piece of wood in frustration. "Fucking useless."

Unable to find another solution, she bit her arm, tearing off her own flesh. She screamed in agony but knew there was little time. Swiftly she drained her blood into his wound before her own injuries had a chance to heal. When she was sure enough blood was inside of him, she covered his wound with her hand, adding pressure. Her blood had to reach his heart at the precise moment for anything to happen.

Kamilla looked over as she continued to apply pressure to his abdomen. She was already flooded with regret because if this worked, it meant Tristan would be as powerful as her, or more so. She got up, annoyed at herself and paced the floor, unable to make up her mind. To kill him or to let him become her equal.

After a moment she placed her hands around his neck determined to kill him. But, when she was unable to apply pressure she collapsed, sobbing over his body instead like a heartbroken little girl.

"I can't do it," She sobbed and held him, "Why can't I do it? I hate you! I swear to god I hate you!" She yelled at him, resenting just how much she cared for him.

Serene had heard the noises in the hallway but was too terrified to go out there. She paced in the center of the living room and called the cops. Serene knew they had physically fought, but there was no way she could have known just how bad things had escalated.

Suddenly, the door flung open and she watched in horror as Kamilla threw Tristan at her feet.

"Here. He's yours!" Kamilla screamed, with blood all over her mouth and body. Serene's jaw dropped and the color left her face. She looked down in horror as Tristan lay, bloody and dying, at her feet. When she looked up again, Kamilla had vanished.

Confounded, Serene knelt down to tend to him, ignoring the police on the cellphone.

"Tristan? Tristan, can you hear me?" She shook him softly her hands shaking. "Tristan. Please, please answer me." She checked his pulse and knew he was at least alive. She saw the mass amount of blood around his waist and instantly grabbed her cell phone to talk to them again. Her adrenaline kicked in and she was shaking but focused. As she spoke to them on the phone, she took off her blouse and used it to apply pressure on his wound. She then gave them directions and became increasingly irritated when they asked her questions she couldn't answer.

"I said I don't know! Just hurry! Send an ambulance. There's… there's so much blood!"

She checked his pulse again but couldn't feel anything. "Trist!" she screamed as she dropped the phone. She checked his wrist, his neck, any part of him that would give her hopes of a pulse… but Tristan was gone.

Serene's world stopped and she shook him as she screamed. She tried to hold him but his lifeless body had become heavy. Serene began to sob. Her world spun as she couldn't believe that Tristan had just died in her arms. *This can't be real,* she tried to convince herself, *there is no way. There is no way you're gone!* She laid him down and put her head on his chest, shaking and sobbing hysterically.

"Don't leave me. Don't you dare leave me!"

Moments later, regretting having not said it earlier, she lay her head on his chest and whispered "I love you." she sobbed, "I didn't even get to tell you I loved you."

Serene had known him for only a short period of time, but the past two weeks had been heaven to her. She had never laughed so much or smiled as much as she had while at his side. She saw memories of them together flash through her mind. Tristan made her feel loved and free, and she finally knew how it felt to be loved for who she was, but most importantly she had experienced a love so pure nothing else would ever compare. In the past two weeks, she had learned a lot about herself, about what she wanted in life, and what truly made her happy. However, regardless of how she felt, because of Kamilla, she believed that Tristan had never truly loved her.

It was dark out. The phone was still on the floor and Serene could hear the operator trying to get her attention, but Serene was too overwhelmed to do or say anything. She hugged him tight as her tears continuously fell on his lifeless body.

After several minutes, she suddenly felt him move.

"Trist?" Her eyes opened in shock. As much as she wanted him alive, his movement was alarming. Tristan forcefully pushed her away from him and began to get up. "Tristan, please. Answer me. Are you okay?"

Serene's voice echoed loudly in his ears. His head was aching and felt like it was about to explode. He got up and accidentally stepped on her phone, causing it to shatter. Then, what began as a headache quickly turned into incapacitating pain. He held his hands to his head and screamed loudly in complete agony.

The sound was so loud that Serene immediately covered her ears and scooted herself back on the floor as far as she could.

The pain was growing and migrating to his jaw. Tristan continued to give gut-wrenching screams as blood, and every single tooth began to fall from his mouth. He placed his hands over his mouth as all his teeth were painfully being replaced by rows of long sharp fangs. He looked down at his hands, now drenched in his own blood. His nails had grown in size and strength. The pain offered no mercy as it migrated to the rest of his body. Tristan gave an inhuman ground-shaking growl, causing everything in the large room to vibrate. Serene continued to cover her ears since she couldn't handle the sounds that were coming out of him.

"Tristan!" she yelled as she continued to cover her ears. "Tristan! What's going on?"

Finally, all of the noise stopped.

His pain was subsiding, and the wound at his midsection was healing rapidly. Relieved, a crying Tristan collapsed onto his knees.

Serene cautiously walked up behind him.

After hesitating for a moment, she touched his shoulder, wanting desperately to console him. But he flinched at her touch and spun around faster than he could control, hitting Serene in the process. His powerful swing threw Serene into the corner of the marble dining table with such force that her rib cracked in the process.

Serene was speechless and unable to breathe as the impact forced the air out of her lungs. The intense pain she felt caused her to collapse onto the floor. She finally looked up at Tristan, now transformed.

His skin was pale and slightly grey, with dark circles under his eyes making him appear dead. His body grew in size and strength, and his eyes were no longer green, but instead, a bright yellow color. She gasped in horror when she also saw that his mouth had two rows of bloodied sharp fangs.

This wasn't Tristan. It couldn't be Tristan. This was a demon!

Demons lurked in Dark sectors. She had learned about them growing up—demons that preyed on innocent women. Is that what he was? Is that what he had been all along? She screamed at the sight of him and got up off the ground and ran!

Serene had barely reached the front door when his hand grabbed her shoulder. His nails dug deep into her thin flesh and knocked her back, causing her body to hit the ground with a loud thud. She screamed in agony as she squirmed on the floor, holding her bloody shoulder where his nails had exposed her collar bone. Her adrenaline kicked in harder than before and she turned around attempting to get on her knees so that she could get up again, but just as she did, he grabbed her by the neck and lifted her up above him.

He growled that intense, ground-shaking low guttural sound into her face. He saw her blood pulsating through her veins and could now hear her pulse throbbing loudly in his ears. All his senses were elevated to extreme proportions: Sight, sound, smell, taste. He could see everything about her in extreme detail, and he instinctively knew just how delicious she was. Tristan felt an unbearable hunger and his mind convinced him that unless he ate her he would surely die! As he held her up, her abdomen was exposed, revealing blood-filled flesh. He opened his mouth to bite into her, but just then, another sense became apparent. He sniffed her. There was a familiar smell, a paternal instinct, Serene was pregnant.

Tristan's eyes instantly saddened, and he shook his head many times trying desperately to control the painful hunger in his gut. He yelled and moaned as he stumbled back, but the hunger controlling him was too powerful to hold back. Tristan needed to eat and he needed to eat now! Gathering all his strength and what little self-control he had left, he then threw her away from him like a rag doll, causing her to hit her head on the coffee table. Then, Tristan vanished.

Serene went in and out of consciousness for several minutes and she knew she was dying. Unable to breathe properly, she was petrified, cold, bleeding, and shaking in both fear and pain. She tried desperately to stay awake, knowing she had hit her head but was quickly losing the battle. A few moments later she heard the sounds of paramedics talking to her, but all she wanted to do was sleep and soon everything faded into darkness.

THIRTEEN

KROVS

L ea was asleep when her phone rang. She looked at the clock on her dresser and it was two in the morning. She would have been alarmed if not for the fact that Tristan had called her around this time before.

"Hey Trist," she answered the phone through a yawn, her blonde hair full of fake platinum dreads was messier than usual.

Tristan didn't immediately answer, and all she heard for a moment was his intense breathing. When he finally did speak his voice was shaky.

"I don't know what to do… or who to call," he said, distressed. He was lucky his phone and keys were in his jacket the whole time.

"Okay? Calm down Tristan. What happened?" she asked him as if this was a routine call. When he didn't answer she continued, "Damn it Trist, did you overdose again?"

Tristan was sitting in his car soaked in blood from head to toe, and there was blood smeared everywhere. He needed her to understand how serious this was.

"No! I—" He debated telling her anything, but he needed to talk to someone he trusted before he lost his mind. "I think I killed… No, I *know* I killed—"

"Tristan. Where are you?" she demanded and instantly

wondered if Kamilla had finally turned him. If that was the case, she needed to get to him, fast!

"I just need to ask you about Kamilla."

"Tristan, where the hell are you?" she repeated, louder this time. "I'm coming right now," she said, getting out of bed.

"It's too dangerous. Damnit Lea just listen! Something happened. Kamilla, she attacked me and I just killed, and I don't know consumed... two or three people... I—" Regardless of his attempts to explain, he became flustered that he couldn't put into words what had happened. But what Tristan had said was enough for Lea to realize that Kamilla had turned him.

"Okay Trist, just breathe. Relax," she said, trying her best to comfort him over the phone. "I know what has happened to you, but I need to see you."

"What do you mean *you know*? What the fuck is going on?!"

She wanted to tell him over the phone but needed to see him first. If he wasn't turned yet, she wasn't allowed to explain anything.

She rushed to get dressed and made her way out the door. "I'll explain once I get there. Stay away from humans. Just tell me where you are already!"

Tristan was exhausted and just gave in by answering her questions. "I'm in my car." He exhaled, "If you come, I'm worried I'll kill you too."

"No, you won't. I promise! I'll explain everything once I get there."

"I'm in an empty parking lot. The grocery store on my block."

Half an hour later, Lea approached his black sports car and knocked on the driver's side window. Tristan cracked open the window just enough to hear her and put a hand up over his eyes expressing that he couldn't look at her.

"I need you to stay outside of the car," he said, worried for her safety.

"Tristan. look at me. You're *not* going to hurt me."

With the deepest hesitation, he turned to look at her. It shocked Lea when she saw his yellow eyes. She then walked over to the passenger side.

"Open the door!" she demanded.

"No! It's for your own safety."

Not wanting to waste any more time trying to reason with him, Lea punched the back window and once it shattered, she slid her hand in to unlock the front door. He stared at her, perplexed, as she got inside the car and sat next to him.

"See!" She motioned with her unharmed hands. "You're *not* going to attack me. It's *fine*."

Tristan sighed and put his head back, relieved. Lea placed her hand over his in an effort to relax him.

"It's okay Tristan," she whispered, consoling him. "How—how bad was the pain? When you turned?" Lea didn't wish that kind of pain on her worse enemy, let alone someone she cared deeply about.

He sat there stoic, staring out into the darkness.

"Bad." He laughed through tears knowing that was an understatement. "It was more than bad. It was hell."

"I know. I'm so sorry… Well, the good news is: It's over," she reminded him, trying to make light of the situation. "And you're a *Golden*. I never would have seen that coming."

Tristan scrunched his eyebrows and Lea decided to explain things by showing him. She went inside her pocket to pull out a contact lens holder and then took out her lenses. Once she did, she looked at him and her eyes were a golden color, like his. He wasn't amused; in fact, he was angry that she was so calm and didn't understand the severity of what had just happened.

"Can you just fucking tell me what the *hell* is going on?"

Lea realized she needed to cut to the chase and began to speak extremely fast, which was something she normally did, and it usually annoyed Tristan.

"Okay. So, we are called Krovs. It's actually a long story. Basically, it comes from our original Russian name кровь Воин (Krov' Voins)." Lea pronounced the name correctly in Russian. "It roughly translates to Blood Warriors. Blood Warriors were genetically enhanced super-soldiers created for the purpose of war back in the 1940's. But you're actually a golden eye and Goldens are rare and *much* weaker than Reds. About ninety-two percent of all those who get the virus become Reds. That's sort of what you want to be because they are stronger and have powers. We are sort of a mistake. Oh my god, when they realize you're a golden—" Tristan was annoyed that she was talking *way* too fast.

"Crows!?" he asked her, not understanding the name. She then continued to talk quickly, mentioning scientific terms that he didn't understand.

"—so then they engineered a new strain of the tribe's virus and genetically modified their genotype —"

"Fucking English Lea! I don't understand a goddamn word you're saying!"

"Okay!" Lea expected him to be confused and upset, but not this hostile. "I'll explain later, I promise. But right now, there are only a few facts that take precedence. First, you will attack any human you see, but you won't have the urge to attack your own kind. Second, the cops are probably looking for you right now and we need to do a few things." She got out of the car and then waved asking him to follow her. "Well come on! They might be looking for your car."

Tristan climbed out of his car and followed her. As he approached her white SUV, she told him to lie down in the back, which he did. She turned on the car and drove.

"Okay. Stay down, breathe out your mouth. Your senses are enhancing so you will smell humans from a distance. Doing so would trigger the urges. You will have to disappear out of society and liquidate your assets asap. Unfortunately, fucking Kamilla didn't plan this properly and now you're likely a wanted man."

As he lay, he rubbed his forehead. All of this information was making his head spin. Suddenly, he remembered what he did to Serene, and he was panic-stricken.

"We need to go to my place!" he commanded her, as he sprung up. "Serene, I attacked her! She might be... dead!"

"Who? You can't... I'm sorry."

"Then, I need you to go! Please Lea just drive by; someone needs to help her!"

She contemplated for a moment, knowing Tristan was obviously worried about this girl, but now wasn't the time. "It's too risky. There will probably be cops there. Plus, I'm trying to avoid going deeper into the city with you. Too many humans around."

"Argh!" Tristan grunted in disappointment. "Then just drop me off somewhere. Fuck, I don't know. Can't you just go—we'll be careful about it. Lea, I need to know if I killed her! Please understand."

"What difference does it make? She's human. Plus, it will be a long time before you can even get close to her."

He didn't want to believe it, but it was undeniable; he'd become some sort of monster. He thought he might eventually come to terms with the fact that he'd killed three strangers—but if he'd killed Serene and his unborn child? That fact would be more than he could *ever* handle.

Tristan punched the back of the passenger seat in frustration, but his hand drove a hole right through the seat with ease. She immediately brought the car to a screeching halt.

"Really?!" she glared back at him.

"I'm sorry. I didn't realize I hit it that hard," he said, pulling out of the hole, and then looking at his fist trying to understand how it had happened.

She rolled her eyes at him. "Alright. Fine! I'll go see if she's there and pick up some clothes for you. But right now, I need you to stay at my house just outside the city. I promise, as soon as I drop you off, I'll go to your place."

While Tristan waited for Lea to return, he took a shower and did his best to stay hopeful that Serene was alive. He paced nervously for several minutes with a towel around his waist as he continued to text Lea.

> Tristan: *Please let me know as soon as you know anything.*
> Lea: *I'm almost there.*
> Tristan:... *Okay? You should be there by now.*
> Tristan combed his hair with his hand. The anticipation was killing him. "Come on Lea hurry," Tristan said to himself.
> Lea: *There is no one in your condo. I searched well.*
> Tristan: *Ask a neighbor, people on the streets, anyone you see! Don't stop until you find out something. I'll start calling the hospitals.*
> Lea: *DO NOT CALL THE HOSPITALS. Talking to the downstairs neighbor now.*
> Tristan:... ;.;
> Lea: *Okay. From what he said he believes she was alive when they took her. He is almost certain.*

"Mr. Sower," Tristan sighed in relief. He was a blunt man who wouldn't have sugar-coated the details. Yet he knew this didn't mean she was *still* alive, but there was hope.

Lea arrived back at her house with a trash bag full of clothes for him. She sat next to him on the couch.

"There was a suitcase in my closet," Tristan explained looking up at her. His eyes were sad and tired.

"Yeah well, I was in a rush. At least you know Serene is alive."

"I need to be sure. Which hospital do you think she'd be in?" he asked, worried.

"We'll worry about that later. Try to get some rest."

"Are you serious?" His golden eyes shot towards her. It bothered him that she was so calm. "I can't sleep right now. I need to see her," he said, leaning forward and covering his face with his hands.

"No! You'll kill her! Get dressed so we can talk."

The towel around his waist was distracting and Lea had always been attracted to him. There was no way she could focus on explaining things while he was almost naked on her couch. Tristan reluctantly got dressed in her bathroom then went to her kitchen, grabbed a beer and then sat on the couch again, polishing off the bottle in barely more than a minute.

"It's not going to do anything to you," Lea pointed out looking at the beer in his hand and at the four other empty bottles on the table. He slammed the beer down and looked at her furrow-browed. She continued. "The beer, alcohol, drugs. It will take a lot more than before to do anything to you now."

He scratched his head. "Fuck, Lea. Do you have *any* good news?" She sat quietly, knowing he was irritated. He continued, "So what? I learn to eat animals now?"

Lea laughed but quickly stopped knowing this was a very serious moment in Tristan's life.

"No. No, unfortunately, you're made to be like this. Animal blood and flesh won't nourish you."

"Well, obviously you controlled yourself." he was convinced there was no way sweet Lea ate humans. She got up to fix a snack for the both of them and she spoke to him from the kitchen.

"Sorry to disappoint you further Trist, but none of this is going to be easy. Your body needs human DNA, flesh, bones, and blood to survive now. Your body is dying every day and you will become weak otherwise."

She came back and laid down some cold square meat cuts on a plate and two glasses of blood. He rubbed his head as he saw what he would have to consider food now.

152

"So, where do you buy this stuff?"

"You *can* buy it, but why would you want to?" she asked, then grabbed a piece of meat and ate it with ardor. "Food is right outside." She motioned with her hand to suggest how easy it was. "You just go get it!" She then took a brief moment to examine the piece of meat she was holding, "This one is actually very good. It's Chinese." She handed him a piece then smiled at him. "Here try it."

Tristan always found it odd that Lea was always so cheerful at the most inappropriate times, yet he figured he should probably keep himself fed.

As he carefully ate it, he was surprised at how much he was enjoying it. It almost felt euphoric.

"This is insane. You actually kill people?"

"Do we have a choice?"

Lea finished her food and sat on the couch facing him.

"I blacked out. I barely remember the people I killed. Why is that?"

"You probably went into a feeding frenzy. Especially if your body was wounded and it had to use its resources to heal you. Do you want to know the story?"

"Of?"

"Of why there are Krovs, silly!" Lea laughed at him.

Tristan had just experienced the roughest night of his life, and the only thing on his mind was Serene. But, as he tried to process what he had done, he realized he needed to listen. If he could understand what was going on, perhaps he could find a way to stop it. He took one more bite and sat back ready to focus, but found himself gritting his teeth when Lea began telling the story with too much enthusiasm and gesturing wildly, as though she was telling a children's story.

"A long, *long* time ago there was a tribe of mystical cannibals deep inside the enchanted forests. They hunted humans—"

"Lea! Stop. Jesus, no! Just tell me!" Right now, his patience for her over-the-top personality was limited. Even at the best of times it was just too much for him.

Lea pouted and became serious again.

"Okay. *Sorry…* So, as I was saying…" She then continued the story in a normal tone of voice. "… originally, there was a specific tribe of cannibals. They were cannibals because some of them carried a rabies-like virus that made them bloodthirsty and strong. When a family member was sick and dying, they would use this virus to keep them alive.

However, it came at a cost. When they awoke, they would attack and eat other tribe members. Eventually, the tribe began to hunt humans outside of their closed society. Stealing men, women and children to keep their family members alive. Because of their threat to ordinary society, when a tribe member was captured, they were burned at the stake, accused of being demons.

For this reason, the tribe's members became very rare. But, in the 1940's a group of German Scientists were given the task to create a superior race. Their first task was to create a genetically-enhanced super-soldier. Yet, after many failures, scientists tried to save their lives by convincing their superiors that a race of stronger, faster humans was simply not possible.

It was during this time that a tribal member revealed her superhuman strength while trying to protect her child who had stolen some food. She fought off many guards but was eventually captured and taken to the scientists as proof that such a race was possible. Fearing for their lives, the scientists took the original virus's genetic code and mutated it, creating a new super virus."

"A superior race? I see—create an unbeatable army and you can conquer the world."

"Yes, but they didn't stop at stronger and faster soldiers. They wanted something *more.*"

"So, what happened next?"

"Well, they had nearly completed the virus and began

experimenting on test subjects. The subjects hungered for human flesh and were extremely bloodthirsty, but they wouldn't attack each other. The scientists learned that the subjects couldn't live off each other's DNA, nor that of any species other than humans. With a lot of painful discipline and regular feedings, the test subjects were able to control their appetite and become functional soldiers. Except, the new virus had a serious problem, sometimes it would turn subjects into superhumans with ten times the strength and speed, and other times, the virus simply didn't work properly."

"Red Eyes and Golden Eyes," he said, trying to piece together what he knew.

"Yes. The virus gave erratic results. The scientists were stumped as to why this kept happening. They studied the strain of the virus carefully and found nothing that would cause these results. However, one day, a Russian scientist's young child saw the subjects. He asked his father why some had red eyes and others yellow eyes. He wasn't able to give his child an answer, and simply told him, 'That's what we're trying to figure out.' The child stared at the subjects in wonder for several days. Later, he came up to his father saying he knew why some had red eyes and others yellow eyes. His father initially ignored him but eventually decided to listen to his child. The child then said, 'Yellow eyes have a pure heart and the red eyes have a dark heart.'"

"But you said Golden Eyes are rare."

"They are. They managed to modify the virus, based on this theory, but a specific caliber of soldier was still needed to minimize the occurrence of Goldens. The more aggressive and cold-hearted a warrior was, the better the odds of producing Reds. Still, like I said, their superiors wanted more than faster and stronger soldiers, and just as they were getting close to the results they initially wanted, the empire fell, and the labs were destroyed. Only a few Krov survived and made their way back into society. They eventually learned how the virus could be transferred. Since then we have grown in numbers and now, there a few thousand Krovs in at least three major cities."

"How does it transfer?" he asked.

"Well, if the right amount of blood enters the bloodstream and reaches the heart just as the human dies, the virus takes over—restarting the heart. So technically—"

"I died," he finished her sentence as she began to falter.

"Yes. And you are no longer human."

Tristan rubbed his face with his hands and took a moment to absorb the information. He then looked at his palms and at his pale and slightly off-colored skin and he knew what he was; he was dead, or rather undead. He noticed Lea's skin was normal yet pale. He wanted to ask her why his skin was gray, but he had a more serious question jump into his mind.

"So, Kami, is she a Red Eye?"

"Mmm hmm," Lea said, nodding as she played with her hair nervously. She didn't want to get into depth with this particular part of the conversation. "A very powerful Red Eye actually."

There was so much Tristan still didn't know, but Lea thought it was best if he took it one day at a time. He got up and paced. His thoughts swung between acceptance and denial. He considered the possibility he'd simply hit his head *really* hard, and that this was all some sort of nightmare. He wondered how it was possible that both Kamilla and Lea were undead, or Krovs, or whatever it was they called themselves. How could he not have noticed? How did they hide it so well? He began to question everyone he knew.

"Who else is one?" he asked her, his fierce stare demanding the truth.

"Krov? Umm..." She fidgeted with her hands nervously. "Basically, every woman you've ever dated?" she said without meeting his gaze.

He looked at her and the corners of his mouth slightly curled, he was about to laugh, but when she didn't look up his smile faded. She was serious.

"How many of them?" he asked, worried about the answer.

"All of them." She shrugged trying to make light of the situation. He looked at her confused and she decided to elaborate.

"Seriously, who was your first? If you even remember."

"I remember. Rebecca. I was fifteen. She was older."

"Yup Krov. Then her friend wanted you, and so on… You became pretty popular with us, so we made sure you stayed within the circle. The fact that you would only sleep with and date one of us at a time was frustrating for all of us."

"Wait. Lea, that was like… eleven years ago!" he said, then arched an eyebrow at her. "And I'm not bragging but I've slept with a lot of women since then."

She rolled her eyes. "Don't flatter yourself. You were cute but our choices were also limited, and you were being trained."

"Trained to do what? Have sex?"

"No… Yes. I mean—" She stopped for a second as she tried to figure out a way to explain everything. "Male Krovs… they *only* like female humans because they both hunger and lust over them. The more attracted a Krov is to a human, the better they taste and the better the sex. A Krov also feels sexual desire much stronger than a human does. They often hunt, rape, and kill women. Sometimes simultaneously. In fact, there is some sort of chemical reaction that gives us Krovs a mind-blowing euphoric high when they lay with a human. So unfortunately, for us female Krovs, it's hard for us to find a sexual partner. We can't just…" She stopped and played with her hands.

"You… can't just force yourselves on a male." Tristan finished her sentence.

Glad that he understood, Lea continued. "We can seduce them and then kill them, but there are a lot of Krov laws we must abide by, so usually we end up looking for young human candidates and train them. Another problem is, we can't just train any human, they have to be inexperienced because we also *feel*… different to humans." She looked away, not wanting to get into detail.

"You're extremely cold inside. Also, humans are softer," he said understanding. "Serene... she was warm, soft. She wasn't a Krov."

"No, she slipped through. We tried to keep you away from humans because of your training. You were trained to be *very* rough; you were trained to pleasure only Krovs, especially Reds. Since you didn't know this, sleeping with a human would have been dangerous."

"Dangerous, how?"

"If you treated a human girl the way you treat us in role play, you'd probably end up severely hurting her or even killing her. We didn't want you ending up in jail for the murder. We needed you."

"You needed me? You mean you all manipulated me. Lied to me, and used me!" Tristan snarled and got up doing his best to control his anger.

He needed Lea's support at the moment, but he was furious. "How many humans did you all push away from me? Did you all– No I don't even want to know."

"I'm... sorry. I promise I had little control over the order of things. And also..." Lea hesitated, looking at her hands again.

"What?"

"Nothing... it's just, by being sexual with us, some trainees eventually contract a virus. It may take years to appear and strengthen, but it mimics Krov-like symptoms. Had you been human much longer, you might have begun to have symptoms."

"What kind of symptoms?"

"Heightened appetite, usually sexually but eventually a real hunger for humans you're attracted to. It's why there is a time limit to either turn you or kill you. You would become violent, but only towards humans." Tristan squinted his eyes at her, "Okay, have you ever seen an animal or a baby so *adorable* that you wanted to bite it's toes? It's hard to explain but it's like that, times a thousand. An attractive human's touch or kiss, it becomes addicting, and it builds until eventually you feel this force to destroy it, be inside it, and eventually consume it..."

As she went on, he began to have flashbacks of everything she was explaining. He had felt it with Sophia, but especially with Serene. It was similar to an addiction. It was painful, and the arousal was so intense he was willing to do anything to relieve it, including hurting the source.

"Jesus Christ. That explains it… I felt that with Serene. I became obsessed with her. I even forced myself onto—You mean I could have killed her?"

"I don't know… maybe. Eventually. But you didn't… I don't think," Lea said trying to console him. "Why didn't you tell us?"

"About?"

"About the symptoms?"

Tristan shrugged, "I thought the symptoms were caused by fucking stress after my parents' deaths. Plus, after the way you all freaked out about Sophia, I didn't want to alarm anyone about Serene."

Lea nodded.

Even with this new understanding, Tristan still felt guilty that he'd forced himself on Serene and, even though he had tried to be gentle, he realized by her bruises that he was too rough on her. For a moment he was glad he never gave her the "usual" treatment… yet it wasn't for lack of wanting. Every minute he was with her his symptoms increased. Had it not been for all this, he would have eventually hurt her. The thought made his stomach turn.

He sat back and groaned, closing his eyes, hoping to wake from his nightmare.

"What is it?" Lea asked.

Tristan sat forward.

"Serene… she's pregnant. When I almost bit— I just knew," Tristan shook his head unable to explain it himself. "I never got a woman pregnant before." Everything was making more sense than he wanted it to. Over the years he thought perhaps he was the problem. "Krovs must not be fertile," he whispered, realizing that now, his only chance at a child, at a family, was with Serene.

"Unfortunately." Lea sighed, keeping her head low.

"I need to find her. She's pregnant and hurt. I can't just sit here!" He grabbed Lea's car keys from the coffee table and made his way towards the door.

"Trist! Seriously, you'll kill her!" She stood. "It's not like before. You're a Krov now. Anything you felt before... it's child's play compared to now. It's so much worse. You have to train!"

Tristan stopped at the door. "I won't hurt her. I won't allow it!"

"Yes. You. Will! You're attracted to her aren't you? And even if you weren't——"

"Well then, hurry up and train me!" he scolded, losing patience. "It can't be that hard."

"It is! It's *extremely* hard! And it may be especially hard for you!" she yelled back at him, but then calmed down. "This is worse than a drug addiction. This is... This is what you're genetically programmed to do."

"How long did it take you?" he asked, worried about the answer. When she didn't answer he approached her. "How long?" He asked sternly.

"Four... maybe five months," Tristan shook his head and walked away from her. "But I'm a female. It seems to be easier for us since physical aspects alone don't always trigger the intense urges."

His eyes widened. There was NO way it took that long.

"There HAS to be a better way."

"There is. Or, was a way, but it's painful. Shock therapy, various excruciating training exercises. Even then... how much do you desire Serene?"

"What?"

"Ugh, just... How aroused do you get when you're around her?"

Tristan gave her a blank stare, but then sat back down on the couch to think. He officially had a migraine now. He rubbed his face as images of Serene, naked and screaming for him in ecstasy, raced through his mind, causing his chest to tighten. He clenched his fists and closed his eyes as he remembered her face, her smell, and her fragile warm body wrapped tightly around his. Remembering made his heart pound, and his joints ache. He wanted her, needed her. What frightened him the most was that he also felt a compulsion to consume her, tear into her and live inside of her if he could. He shook the terrifying thought away.

"I want her… but more than that I care about her… more than I can explain. She's perfect, in a simple way."

Lea saw that Tristan was infatuated with even the thought of Serene. She wouldn't admit it to Tristan, but she expected Serene to be dead or more than likely dying. There was just no way he'd turned and didn't consume her, at least partially.

They sat in silence as they both realized this meant he couldn't go anywhere near her anytime soon, if ever.

Lea picked up the plates and glass cups and walked into the kitchen as she continued talking to him.

"I'll check the hospitals tomorrow. I'll find her, Trist, but right now you need to get some rest. You can have the guest room," she said as she shut off the lights and walked towards her bedroom.

Tristan called out to her, "Wait." She turned around as he approached her. "I am still royally pissed off and I'm sure you understand why but… Thanks… for tonight."

Lea put a hand on his arm, "It's going to be okay Tristan. You'll see."

"I *highly* doubt that," he said, his eyes on the brink of tears. "Just please, find her. For me."

Lea hugged him and his eyes finally released the tears he'd been holding back all night.

"I will. I promise." She walked away from him and went into her bedroom closing the door behind her.

Tristan was left with more questions than answers, and sleep was impossible for him, but he tried to empty his mind, hoping that maybe, if he fell asleep, he would awake next to Serene.

FOURTEEN

SERENE

"Look, she's awake!" Casey exclaimed.

Serene awoke on a hospital bed surrounded by her parents, Peter and Clair, as well as Casey and her mother, Lillian.

Lillian was the epitome of class and sophistication; thin, poised, and always wore her hazelnut hair in a stylish bun.

"Honey, what happened? Tell us." Serene's mother demanded.

Serene couldn't answer. All she could do was focus on the intense pain in her chest, and the growing ache inside of her head.

"She's up. Hurry." Casey whispered into the phone.

"How are you feeling, pumpkin?" Peter asked, worried.

"Bad… Like—like I was hit by a bus," Serene placed a hand on her forehead and rubbed the bandages there.

When memories began to rush through her brain like a runaway train, she became nauseous, dizzy, and felt like her head was about to explode.

"Everything hurts, Dad," she cried. "Please, something isn't right."

"They will come with drugs for the pain soon," her mother said, trying to comfort her. "Oh, we were so worried, sweetie. Who did this to you? Whose apartment were you in?"

Her mother's words merged together, and Serene's mind was still too foggy to answer.

A doctor strode into the room.

For a moment Serene could have sworn she was seeing things. He came up to her with a cup of water and some medication.

"A—Alex?" Serene asked, confused as she grabbed the medication from him.

"Alex started his residency here last week! Isn't that great?" Casey informed her in a cheerful tone. "He's asked to *personally* look after you."

Serene knew from everyone's bright expression that they were expecting a reaction from her, but currently she couldn't care less that Alex had returned, she just wanted the pain gone and for everyone to leave the room.

Alex watched her swallow the pills, and then crouched down to talk to her. "How's the pain?" His words were sweet and genuine.

"It's…" Serene paused. It felt so weird to see him dressed this way. "It's hard to breathe… My head… it hurts, really bad. I'm dizzy, nauseous."

"Well, it's going hurt for a while. You hit your head pretty hard, but I can help you with the dizziness and nausea." He placed a hand on her face, gently lifting it to check her eyes with his penlight. "You also fractured two ribs and you're bruised, so that's why it hurts to breathe, but you have to remember to breathe in deeply and through the pain to avoid complications. Any memory loss? Do you know what day it is?…" He continued asking questions while examining her reflexes.

Serene studied him as she answered his questions. He was different, mature beyond his years, and it was evident that he took his job very seriously. He had always been handsome, but more so now; his hair was a lush brown instead of the golden sun-kissed color she was used to, and it was shorter. His blue eyes were bright, but tired-looking, as though he'd been working long hours. He also seemed taller and leaner than she remembered. Alex was a man now and his professional appearance intimidated Serene.

Peter asked Alex a few questions about her health, and her mother took the opportunity to ask Serene some more questions about what had happened, but Serene didn't know what to say.

"Clair," Alex interrupted her, "right now Serene needs to rest. Don't ask her too many questions." Alex placed a hand on Clair's shoulder. "Please, give her some space. We can ask questions later."

Clair nodded.

Serene wasn't sure why, but regardless of Alex's kindness she was angry at him. Maybe it was because, although nice, he was acting indifferent. He had somehow successfully made her feel like a stranger. Serene glared at Casey wondering why she hadn't told her he was coming back so quickly. Casey simply lowered her head; she was definitely hiding something.

A nurse came in and handed Alex a clipboard. He looked it over.

"Clair, can I speak to you in the hallway for a moment?" Alex asked, and they disappeared into the hallway.

Casey and Lillian got up to say their goodbyes.

"We're so glad you're going to be okay," Lillian said, gently hugging her. "We'll be praying for your recovery, sweetie."

Casey hugged her immediately after. "I was worried sick about you." she whispered, "I kept texting you and leaving you messages about Alex."

"I know, I wasn't able to— I'll explain later." Serene said hugging them goodbye.

Once they left Alex walked back in without Clair and asked Peter if he could speak to Serene in private. Her father agreed.

Being alone together was suddenly awkward for the both of them. Serene noticed he was nervous because he just stood there, unable to say a word and was avoiding eye contact. He grabbed a chair and brought it close to the bed so that he could sit next to her. Up close she could see the stubble on his face and those crystal blue eyes she had

164

always adored. His hair was shorter but slightly longer on top.

"It's... nice to see you again." His words were sincere but serious.

She sat quietly and wouldn't lock his gaze. She didn't mean to be standoffish, but things were different now. All the affection and adoration she once felt for him was suddenly absent.

"Serene, you... really don't remember *anything*?"

"I —I just remember being attacked. I'm... really tired," she said, avoiding the subject. Her head was pounding, and she didn't feel like talking.

When he didn't budge from his position, she finally looked up at him but found it uncomfortable to hold his stare. It was as if his maturity and wisdom, along with his striking features and uniform, demanded her absolute attention while in his presence.

Alex looked down at his hands, "Serene, there's something I have to tell you."

"Okay?... What is it?"

"You're... pregnant."

"What?" She questioned as she searched his face for sincerity. If the pain wasn't enough to cause her to burst into tears, after this news, her eyes struggled to contain their tears. She swallowed, pushing down her emotions. "How... could this have happened?"

Clearly, she knew how it happened, but she had trouble making sense of the situation since now all those memories felt more like a dream than a reality. She was also only twenty-one with no job, no career, and no husband. She couldn't even fathom the idea of a baby.

Alex continued talking about the accuracy of the test but she couldn't hear him. A tear escaped as she wondered what she was going to do now, and how she could ever justify this to her family.

By law, she was a Light sector citizen, where sex before marriage was illegal. Would she be penalized? Stoned?

"Serene?" Alex tried to get her attention. "I wanted to give you more time but the cops, your mother, everyone is wondering.

Eventually you're going to have to explain what happened."

"Do they know?" Serene asked quickly, worried. "Alex, do they know!"

"About the pregnancy?" He studied her panicked face. "No. No! Of course not. You can decide when or if you're going to tell them."

Alex watched her fight back tears, but he didn't know how to console her. He had missed her, and it hurt him to see her like this.

"Leave, please." Serene's voice was muffled as she covered her face with her hands. She didn't want anyone, especially Alex, to see her cry.

Alex touched her leg over the blankets and did his best to comfort her.

"Serene. I'm *so* sorry."

He knew what this meant to her, and to her family. A pregnancy out of wedlock wasn't something they would approve of. He was, however, convinced that this had not been her fault. He knew Serene well, and there was no way she would have chosen this path willingly.

As he looked her over, he noticed she was still beautiful, but she had marks on her neck where someone had clearly strangled her. Her arms and body were bruised, and she had a bandaged wound on her shoulder that would surely leave a scar. He wanted to console her, perhaps by hugging her, but at the moment he had no idea what kind of relationship they had.

"Leave me." Serene said as she mopped up the tears with her hands.

Alex didn't want to leave but granted her request. When he exited the room, he told her parents to stay out and let her rest.

Serene lay crying, wishing she could disappear into nothingness. The pain was unbearable and the type of medication they gave her was limited because of her pregnancy.

After her family had left, Alex came in periodically to check up on her. A cop had come in sometime later, but she refused to talk to him and said she couldn't remember much.

Even though she remembered Tristan and their time together, the recent events seemed too insane to have been real. Even if she told anyone what she saw him become, they would never believe her.

Eventually, she gave the cops a name and a brief description of Tristan, hoping that would satisfy them and keep them from returning.

> ⪢ ⪡

Late, the following night, a nurse came into Serene's room and brought her a teddy bear.

"Hi. Serene right? How are you feeling?" the nurse asked softly but Serene didn't respond. "Look, I know you're pregnant and—"

Serene placed a single finger to her mouth signaling she didn't want anyone to know. "Oh. Okay. *Our secret*… I'm so sorry for what happened to you. I've been told you've been a bit… down, so I brought you a gift." The nurse set down a teddy bear and some chocolates on her bed. "May I ask how the baby is?"

Serene's eyes narrowed, confused by both the nurse's gift, questions, and demeanor. She looked like a pin-up girl in a nurse's outfit and her voice was sweet and high-pitched. Serene didn't want to talk but found it rude to ignore her.

"The baby is okay… we think. There's no spotting but it's too soon to hear a heartbeat."

"And how are you holding up?"

"I'm fine."

The nurse cocked her head and squinted her eyes, doubting her.

"They can't give me proper pain meds because of—" Serene glanced down at her midsection.

"Oh. I'm so sorry. I can't even begin to imagine what you've been through. Here," the nurse said fluffing her pillows.

"Thanks." Serene straightened herself up.

"If you ever need anything, I'll be checking in occasionally. My name is Lea. I don't work on this floor, but I'll still come in to see you." She smiled at Serene and walked out.

Serene looked down at her gifts and then back up at the open door perplexed by what had just happened.

3 a.m.

Serene awoke hungry and her chocolates were all gone.

She pressed the nurse's button and, in a flash, Alex came rushing through the door. His face expressing panic.

"Oh. I'm sorry I didn't know that was just for emergencies. I—"

"No, it's fine," he interrupted her, nearly out of breath. "Press it whenever you need something... What's wrong?"

"I'm... hungry?" she whispered, embarrassed.

He gave her a beatific smile.

His glee confused her. "What?" she asked him, unamused.

"Nothing. I'm just glad to see you're up and well, hungry." She didn't smile back. "What would you like? The Cafeteria is closed, but tell me what you'd like and I'll do my best to get it for you."

She thought for a moment. She was so hungry she suddenly wanted to eat everything. "Chocolate milk and a brownie," she said, realizing the small box of chocolates had just been a tease.

He chuckled and shook his head in disapproval. It wasn't exactly a nutritious food choice. "Well, I can probably find a chocolate cake. Is that okay?" She nodded and barely smiled, but it was enough for him to realize that she wouldn't be depressed forever.

A few minutes later he returned, setting down a chocolate cake and two types of milk, 1%, and whole, on the table with wheels, which he moved over to her bed.

"Guessing they didn't have chocolate milk?" she asked.

"Surprisingly, no." He sat on the bed to join her.

She tore open the plastic entrapping her spoon and ate the cake in only a few bites. It wasn't the best cake ever, but after barely eating for days, it was heaven.

Realizing how awkward she must have looked when she was gathering the last crumbs on her plate, she decided to break the silence.

"So… you're my doctor? That feels weird to say."

"No. You should know my focus is Oncology. Dr. Lee, he's your doctor. I just asked permission to see your file and look after you once in a while."

"You mean you found out I was here and you wanted to show off to our families?"

Alex gave her a guilty smile. They both laughed.

"So, *Doctor* Alexander Elbridge," Serene exaggerated the sounds.

"Yes Ma'am," he said giving her his million-dollar smile. He had not heard many people say it yet and wasn't used to the title. "I'm actually happy you're here. I practically live in this hospital, so it's nice to see a familiar face."

She looked down and he realized what he'd said. "I didn't mean it like that. Of course, I would rather you weren't in the hospital."

"I know. Is there a nurse here?" she changed the subject.

"Yes. Why? What do you need?" he said, eagerly.

Serene's cheeks became flushed. "I really need to go to the—" she broke off awkwardly. She didn't want him helping her go pee.

"Here. I'll help you." Alex got up and placed an arm behind her back and another under her legs, giving her no opportunity to object.

"No! I'd feel more comfortable if someone else—" She tried to push him away, but she was still weak.

Alex knew how modest and shy Serene was, but he was determined to be the one to help her.

"Don't worry, I'm not going to look," he assured her as he carried her out of bed. Serene did her best to cover the open back of her hospital gown as he lifted her. She had matured in the past couple of weeks, but it was finally obvious to her that she needed to be more assertive around men—it seemed they always had their way with her. She also wanted anyone else but Alex helping her. She had grown a grudge against him for leaving her that she desperately wanted to keep.

In the bathroom he placed her down gently. He then rolled the IV unit inside so she could have free rein and closed the door leaving only enough room for the cord.

"I'm not listening by the way," he said loudly as he walked away. "I'll be on the other side of the room."

Serene peeked through the door, to make sure he wasn't nearby.

When she was done, she washed her hands and gazed at herself in the mirror for the first time since arriving to the hospital. The view shocked her. Bloodshot eyes with deep circles under them were sunken in a pale bruised face surrounded by frizzy straw-like golden-brown hair. On her forehead was a large, rectangular bandage and bold, purple bruises covering her neck. When she pushed her hospital gown down to expose her shoulder she gasped when she finally saw the mark Tristan had left.

Even though the majority of the claw marks were covered by thick bandages, she could still see where the three large gashes started, right above her breast, over her shoulder and curved into her back.

Serene had never felt more embarrassed about her appearance. She shook her head and tried her best to not think about it as she fixed her hair into a ponytail and forced herself to hold back the tears that were forming in her eyes.

Serene wanted to be strong, but she had never felt so lost and hopeless. Alex was the last person she wanted seeing her this way. She wiped the tears that escaped her eyes, but they became waterfalls, and against her will, a loud sob escaped her mouth. The sobbing caused an acute pain in her chest and she collapsed in pain. She grabbed her chest and tried to breathe but it only made the pain worse.

Alex heard her crying and rushed to her aid. He walked into the bathroom uninvited, and she covered her face.

"Get out!" She yelled her voice hoarse and breaking.

"Serene, please… just let me help you."

"No! I don't want your help. I don't want you around. I don't want you as my doctor!" she yelled as she sobbed.

"Serene. You need to stop crying." He knelt down to where she had collapsed on the floor and tried to place an arm around her, but she pushed him away.

"Why don't you understand? I want anyone here but *you!*" Her hands shook and she couldn't stand up straight.

Alex went against protocol and held her against him. He knew her sobs were causing the pain to expand in her chest so he needed to do everything in his power to get her to stop crying. He sat against the bathroom wall and hugged her to him. Shushing her, holding her, and swaying gently.

Serene was meek, kind, and in his eyes helpless. She had a sweet disposition that made him feel bad for her, and therefore he always wanted to come to her rescue.

He caressed her hair as he hushed her. He knew Serene's family rarely showed affection, and right now she needed someone.

"It's okay, Serene," he said as he placed his head next to hers.

But all his kindness was too little and too late for Serene. She still hated him, and through the pain she finally broke and began to vent everything she had locked deep inside of her heart.

"You left me, Alex." Her cries got worse and her voice was shaking. "You left me, and you stopped —you stopped calling. You stopped loving me when all this time… all this time I had waited for you. I waited until I just couldn't—"

He closed his eyes. "Don't think about that now Serene, please."

"You promised, and you made *me* promise and now… now."

He knew what she wanted to say. That he'd abruptly stopped calling after they would talk almost daily. That he'd promised her and her family that he would return to marry her.

His heart broke. At some point he'd explain everything to her, but now wasn't the time. They both simply needed to move on.

"Serene, I am so sorry. It was never my intention to hurt you… I was young, we were young… Come."

He helped her up; the bathroom floor wasn't a comfortable place for them to continue talking. He picked her up again, laid her on the bed, and grabbed some tissues from a nearby table.

He sat by her side and she took the tissue box from him as she gathered herself, doing her best to stop crying.

"What am I going to tell everyone? How am I going to tell everyone that I'm pregnant?"

"I'm not sure. But they'll understand that this wasn't your fault."

"Yes, it was. It was Alex." She didn't want to, but she needed to vent to someone about it. "I didn't even know him and we went out on a date. I liked him a lot. Your sister… she was against it. He was actually very sweet at first. He took me to his place; I should have known better."

"Serene, don't defend him. Have you seen what he's done to you?"

"No, you don't understand. He wasn't like this when I met him. He turned into some sort of monster—!" She realized if she went any further, she would sound insane.

Alex got up and was fuming. He knew Serene well, her morals, her convictions, so he was absolutely sure someone had taken advantage of her.

"Serene, Listen to me. Be *very* careful what you say. You have just been through a very traumatic experience. Many people, they say things happened that didn't, and they end up blaming themselves. Whatever happened to you, whatever that Dark sector scum did to you, it wasn't your fault. You-"

"But it was! I told him-"

"No, it wasn't! You have to understand that, Serene. Whatever you think you caused or whatever he manipulated you into doing, it is *not* your fault."

Alex knew Light sector laws well. If there was any doubt in the community that she wasn't raped, she would be punished, penalized and her reputation would be ruined. He needed her to see through the fog and gather the courage to defend herself.

Serene remembered the monster she saw and how it all seemed more like a nightmare than reality. Was it possible that what she remembered wasn't true? Tristan had convinced her into sex, but after that she gladly gave into him several times, so she didn't feel blameless.

Yet now, she considered Alex's words and wondered if Tristan had, in fact, manipulated her. She remembered Kamilla and how angry she was at him for cheating on her. She also remembered the neighbor saying that he had a new girl every weekend. She wondered if this was what he usually did—find a target and get them to lay with him.

Had I been just a conquest all along? Did he drug me?

She remembered the pill Tristan gave her before they slept together. *Was he a demon? What actually happened?* She wondered.

"Alex, I think I'm going crazy."

"No Serene," he said as his anger receded. "You're not crazy. You've just been through a traumatic experience. It's just going to take you some time to mentally heal… If you want, I'll break the news to your family. I can only imagine how Clair will take it and I don't think you should be around her when she finds out."

"No, I'll—" She stopped for a moment. Even if she tried to explain her pregnancy to her mother, she wouldn't even know where to begin. She also didn't want to see her mother's face when those words were spoken. If there was one person Serene had always been terrified of, it was her mother. "I guess. If you don't mind. It's best if you tell them. They'll have too many questions anyways. Questions I don't have answers to."

"Okay. I'll explain what I can and figure this out for you."

Silence crept between them as he began to compile what he

planned on telling her parents.

Alex eventually got up and gave her a quick hug, "It's going to be okay, alright?" he whispered, still hugging her. "I'll take care of everything. Whatever happened to you, it's not important now. What's important is you getting better." He held her stare, "Understood?"

She nodded and slightly smiled at his tenderness. She felt lucky to have friends like him and Casey. Serene no longer questioned her relationship with Alex. It was clear to her that they were just friends. After all, she was pregnant, and he was a smart, successful, handsome man with a whole life ahead of him. She was just happy to know that after all these years he still cared about her.

FIFTEEN

PROTOCOL

"Good morning, handsome! Breakfast is on the table," Lea said as she entered the guest room where Tristan lay sleeping.

Tristan's eyes swung open, and when she left, he dressed.

Gazing down at his arms, Tristan remembered parts of last night. A man in an alley had attempted to stab his arm with a pocket knife as Tristan consumed him. Yet, not a single scratch or bruise was visible now.

That's odd.

Finding his toothbrush in his bag of clothes, he brushed his teeth. Tristan's face paled when he glanced in the mirror.

"Lea!" he screamed, terror rattling his voice.

Lea appeared in the bathroom with lightning-fast speed.

"What! What's wrong?" she asked, worried.

He covered his mouth, distorting his voice. So, even with her sensitive hearing, she couldn't make out the words. "I can't understand you!" Annoyed, Lea grabbed hold of his wrists, prying his hands out of the way. "Okay now, what were you saying?"

Tristan forced a smile, just enough to show off his teeth. They were all long, pointed and wolf-like, except sharper.

"Okay?" she said, realizing he must have not noticed before.

"Yeah, about those… I'll set up a dentist appointment soon. He'll fix your teeth to look more natural if you'd like. You can also make them come out more too. Look…" She opened her mouth and all of her teeth grew about a centimeter longer, especially her canines.

Tristan never noticed that she had two sets of canines right next to each other, both on her upper and lower jaw.

"See, they aren't as sharp anymore." She touched the tips of them with her finger. "But I'd keep a few of them. It helps break down bone."

He looked into the mirror and ran his tongue over each pointed fang, not expecting them to be sharp enough to cut him, seeing that a knife didn't penetrate his arm last night. The cut bled for only a second before it healed. He looked away to focus on other questions. They were racking up.

"Since I'm… dead." He shook his head in disbelief. "My skin looks… well, like I'm dead." He ran his fingers over the pale and grey-tinted skin on his arms. "But you look normal."

Lea opened the mirrored door to her medicine cabinet and pulled out a pill bottle.

"Here, take two. They regulate your skin's color and temperature. It will feel uncomfortable for a bit, like you're having a mild fever, but you'll get used to it." She put two of the large pink pills in his hand.

"How long do they last?"

"Eight to ten hours. They dissolve slowly."

Now that he thought about it, he did remember Kamilla taking the same medication in the morning, and a few others as well. He figured it was birth control.

"Take them and then eat your food. You will start training today," she said, walking out of the bathroom.

Tristan noticed a normal-looking omelet at the table. The omelet was good, but he didn't want to question the type of meat inside. Lea put a cup of blood on the table and he was instantly attracted to it, drinking it all in one swig. He felt the slight fever Lea mentioned and looked at his arms as his skin turned a normal color again. It wasn't the tan he originally had, but it was a more acceptable skin tone. The pills, however, didn't fully remove the dark circles under his eyes.

"So, we can eat eggs?" he asked when she passed by him.

"Not often. Normal food makes us sick and weak. But it's nice to feel human sometimes. I'm going to call your trainer now," Lea said as she left the living room.

He inhaled his food and was surprised to find it did nothing to satisfy his hunger.

On the table was Lea's laptop. He remembered what Lea had said about clearing out his accounts, and he logged into his bank account. All three of his accounts were zeroed out. He exhaled in relief, thinking Lea had done the work for him. He called Lea over and asked her about it.

"Oh… crap," she responded when she saw his accounts.

"Wait? What the hell do you mean '*Oh crap*'? This wasn't you?"

"Me? How would I have access to that?"

It hit him that only Kamilla had access. "So, Kam stole all my money?"

"Doubtful. Kami doesn't need to steal. She has plenty of money, but maybe she did it *for* you? You can ask her about it eventually."

"Eventually?" He got up. "No. I need to talk to her now!"

Tristan had grown up struggling, and was terrified at the idea of being broke again.

"I wouldn't do that if I were you. I just called her."

"Why! Why did you call her?"

"There is a lot you need to learn about Kamilla. You just need to trust me, I'll explain soon, but right now you need to train."

Lea's house was located in a town about thirty minutes from the city. She had one Krov neighbor across the street but none on either side of her. It was a quiet area and the backyard looked infinite as it led into acres of rolling hills.

Before they walked outside, Lea handed him a very dark pair of sunglasses.

He laughed. "Is this supposed to keep me from burning?"

"You're not going to burn silly. How does that even make sense?"

He thought about asking her if vampires were real. At this point, even Santa Claus was a possibility.

She opened the door and he instinctively covered his eyes. The light was blinding and his eyes stung.

"Put on the glasses and open your eyes slowly. All your senses are just magnified. Your vision is heightened and so is your sensitivity to light and sound. You can use the glasses until we get you contacts. You'll get used to all of this quicker than you think."

"So *that's* why your voice sounds higher pitched and more annoying than usual."

"Har, Har."

He put on his sunglasses and stepped outside into the blinding light past the shade the house provided. He covered the sun with his hands as if the sun would cause him physical harm.

Lea laughed at him.

When his eyes adjusted, he put on his usual cocky persona feigning a boastful confidence, even though he remained uncertain as to what he could and couldn't do.

"What are we doing?" he asked as she stared down the empty road.

"Waiting for your trainer."

They stood in silence for several minutes.

"Lea?"

"Yeah?" she answered sweetly.

"I need you to find Serene. Please, I'm—"

"It's okay. I'll find her today, while you're training." Tristan didn't look convinced. "Stop. I *will* find her. You need to trust me."

Tristan sighed and nodded.

Moments later, an African-American man in a red pickup truck pulled up in front of Lea's house. He was middle-aged and wore a simple white T-shirt and worn-out khakis. He looked a little past his prime.

Lea ran up to him and gave him a hug and a kiss on the cheek. It was obvious they knew each other, but the middle-aged man had a serious look on his face, which was a sharp contrast to Lea. Still, he smiled and gave her a kiss on the cheek in return. After the stranger and Lea talked amongst themselves, they approached Tristan.

"Hey Tristan, I'm Jason." He extended his hand. Tristan shook it.

"I'm assuming you have something to do with my training?" Tristan asked, cocking his head. The man didn't look like a trainer.

"Why, I have *everything* to do with your training." Jason smiled at him. Tristan smelled the air and was suddenly starving. He smelled his own hand—it smelled amazing.

"I was in contact with a human just now, which is triggering your senses. We'll go out back and get started. Today we'll—"

Lea stepped away from them and climbed into her car. Tristan politely put his hand up and stopped Jason to approach Lea's vehicle.

She brought down her window.

"If you find her, find out about the baby."

"What if she's—?"

He looked down and kicked the dirt as he pushed away the thought.

"She's not. I just know she's still alive. So please, don't stop until you find her."

Lea nodded.

He put his hands together and bowed to her as he playfully expressed how grateful he was for all her help.

Lea smiled at how silly and adorable Tristan could be.

Tristan approached Jason, "Is it normal to feel all this pain? My stomach is killing me."

"Yes, but don't fret. I'll have a human here shortly."

"A dead human… right?"

Jason chuckled, "I don't expect you to have any self-control yet, but you will have to become used to the hunger cramps and not let them control you."

"What are those for?" Tristan helped Jason pull out some heavy chains from the back of his truck.

"I'm going to have to chain you up to something. Perhaps a large tree in the back yard."

"Say what?"

Before long Jason had chained Tristan's wrists and ankles to a large tree.

"These shackles are massive. Is this really necessary?" Tristan stood frowning. Looking as non-threatening as possible.

"We'll find out soon enough. You're a Golden so it's probably not necessary, but better safe than sorry."

Jason drove off in his truck.

Tristan leaned against the tree and waited. "Well, this is fun…"

A squirrel crawled halfway down the tree then stopped to stare at him. "Sorry bud… didn't know this tree was taken."

After about thirty minutes, Jason pulled up behind the house.

In the tail bed of his truck was a steel cage that was covered with a bloody beige cloth. When the car stopped, Tristan smelled the living human and bent over in pain. Jason got out of the car.

"Okay, Tristan. First, close your eyes." Tristan did as instructed, "Now, focus on your breathing. Relax and breathe. Don't fight the pain." Tristan bent over and began seething, drooling, and clenching his jaw. He pulled on the chains and every muscle and vein in his body strained.

"I can't! It's like I can't control my body!" Tristan screamed then turned around and yanked on the chains, attempting to slip his hands through the iron shackles.

Jason's nervousness grew as Tristan lost control. "Tristan! Your body is acting on impulse! Focus on something else! Anything else! A childhood memory. Or someone you care about."

Memories of Serene flashed through his mind, her smell, her face. He screamed louder than before as he pulled up on the chains. Within seconds Tristan broke one chain then the next. "Stop! Tristan! Listen to me!"

Ugh! I'm trying to stop! Tristan wondered. *Why can't I stop! I'm going to kill him!*

Finally free, Tristan jumped into the back of the truck, took off the cloth, then punched and ripped a hole through the steel cage. He grabbed the man by the throat and dragged his body through the opening he'd created. Tristan bit into his chest, ignoring his screams and consumed him clothing and all. The pain he felt subsided as his body rewarded him for giving it what it needed.

Jason stood there, eyes wide watching him tear the flesh off the man like an animal.

"Okay then," Jason stood unamused. "Usually the chains hold a bit longer but Enjoy... I guess? I'll get you another human tomorrow." Tristan looked over and spit out a metal button, and it hit Jason in the face.

Late that evening Lea walked through the door. Tristan looked at her smiling face and knew she had good news. She sat next to him at the dining table.

"So... she's alive!" Lea said, overly cheerful as if Tristan was going to be excited by the news. He was relived, but not excited. He knew she was hurt.

"Tell me everything. Where is she? How is she? How's the baby?"

"First of all, I'm not going to tell you which hospital she's in, I'm not stupid, but she's alive. Though…"

"Though what?" Tristan's face turned pale with worry.

"She's in pretty bad shape."

Tristan put his head in his hands as she continued. "Fractured ribs, bandages on her head, her shoulder. And I can't tell how the baby is unless I talk to her."

Tristan got up and paced. The guilt he was feeling overwhelmed him. Even if Serene was alive, did she lose the baby? He ran his hands through his hair as he pictured her in that state.

"Lea, I know you're already doing so much, but I need you to do me one more favor."

"What?"

Tristan kneeled in front of her and held both of her hands, "I need you to be my eyes. Find a way to go to her every day. Ask her about the baby. I need to know every detail. Please. Be there for her because I can't–" Tristan's voice broke and his eyes became glossy.

"Oh Trist," Lea hugged him. "It's okay. We'll find a way."

Over the next few days, Tristan insisted Jason train with him every day from sunrise to sunset. He was learning to control his appetite and Krov protocols as well.

"Krovs have strict laws and protocols you must follow if you hope to survive."

"Should I be writing this stuff down?" Tristan joked as they walked together.

Jason ignored his playful banter, "First, food: Feedings have to be large, and Krovs get hungry often. A Krov's metabolism is much faster than a human's. To survive we must consume at least two humans a week, and regardless of any other food a Krov consumes, it only takes a full day of not eating human flesh and bone to become incredibly weak. In three to five days you would die.

Secondly, methods and protocol: There are no rules on *how* to end a human's life, but most Goldens avoid killing innocent humans as much as possible. We do our best to avoid human suffering."

"We? So, you're a Golden?"

"Isn't it obvious?"

Tristan had no idea. Jason's eyes were brown, but he was more focused on the discussion at hand. "What about Reds? How do they kill?"

"Reds enjoy capturing their prey, raping them and consuming them while they're still alive."

Tristan cringed. "Jesus Christ. Is this true about all of them?"

"Most. Especially the males. It's said a Red's empathy is reduced once they turn. Goldens seem to gain empathy, but, none of that has been proven."

In Lea's garage, Jason placed a large black duffel bag on the table next to a dead body. Jason showed him tools used to break down the body for consumption.

"What's this?" Tristan unsheathed an interesting looking black dagger. It was large and heavy, and one edge was jagged while the other was smooth.

"That's the only type of blade capable of cutting through us. It's forged with Alpha Krov DNA for durability along with other metals." Tristan gently ran his thumb against the blade and to his surprise, it cut him. "It's also highly expensive." Jason grabbed the dagger and put it inside his duffel bag so that it was no longer a distraction. "As I was saying, all Krovs must learn how to clean up after themselves. Losing control while hunting is no excuse, and if the cops track you down, you're usually on your own. We have people on the inside that help us, cops and judges who are Krovs, but they can't help all of us. Gloves are to be worn at all times, and hunting is an activity best done at night.

When bodies are brought home, they must be consumed quickly, and any remains must be destroyed or disposed of properly. Human body parts in the trash is never a good idea, so you kill and consume only what you need."

"So, what if a cop finds human remains in your fridge?" Tristan asked.

"Don't find reasons for a cop to look in your fridge."

"What kind of people do we kill?"

"I'll get to that."

Jason put on his gloves and began to disassemble the human on the table.

Later, in Lea's dining room, Jason pulled out a map and laid it on the table.

"Feeding grounds: Just as Dark and Light sector residents must be registered, so do Krovs. Of course, our systems are private. If a Krov is not registered, the person who turned them, as well as anyone else who knew them, would face severe consequences, including death. Krovs have hunting laws, and every Krov has to follow the rules given out by The Red Council."

"Yeah, but how would they know who turned who."

"You have Kamilla's DNA flowing through you. A quick test and they will know."

"When do I register?"

"You already have. For someone so close to her, you really underestimate Kamilla's organization skills."

Jason continued.

"To avoid over-consumption, each city is only allowed so many Reds and Goldens per precinct. Red Eyes are always given priority over hunting grounds and Golden Eyes have very little say as far as voting and the order of things. If any Krov kills without following protocol or hunts on forbidden grounds… they are quickly eliminated by the Council's Sentinels."

"I killed-" Tristan coughed, "a few people. I was unaware of the rules."

"I know. Kamilla informed us. She told us which precinct you were in and we took care of it. It seems as though she's got your back."

Tristan barely smiled.

SIXTEEN

JESSICA

Dawn had arrived, and the sun was just rising over the suburban landscape. After a long night at work, Alex was driving home to get some sleep. He knew Serene's parents were early risers, so he decided to pay them a visit first.

Serene's family had a beautiful but quaint colonial style home with a country garden. The house was just as he remembered it— white with blue shutters. But it wasn't exactly good memories that arose in him. He remembered bringing Serene home later than usual one day, when they were teenagers. They had gone out with a group of friends and as soon as they came to drop off Serene, Clair was waiting for her outside. Alex and his friends watched as Clair dragged her daughter inside by her hair. No one was able to see or talk to Serene for weeks after that night. Ever since then he made every effort to follow all the strict rules that came with dating their daughter, not because he was scared of Clair or respected her wishes, but because every time they broke a rule, it was Serene who endured the consequences.

Alex understood Serene's quiet and coy nature. Because of Clair, Serene lacked the ability to make her own choices. She had no control over any of her life decisions. Serene did as she was told, usually, which was why his family thought she'd make the perfect

Light sector wife. She was a logical choice, safe. But once they started dating, Alex soon found that she was more than just another bland and lifeless doll. She was very charismatic and when given the opportunity she had the ability to speak her mind, and challenge him. They could talk for hours. Serene also enjoyed teaching children and helping the less fortunate, all values he found endearing. Her kindness made it easy to fall in love with her.

Yet, his family wasn't interested in whether or not he found true love. They just worried on whether or not the woman he chose could be trusted with their fortune and Serene was zero threat. She was refined but never displayed any interested in their wealth.

Alex was in his normal clothing, which consisted of a polo shirt and khakis. He knocked on their door and Serene's father answered. Peter was dressed in his usual attire—black slacks, a tie, and a well-ironed dress shirt.

"Well good morning son! Come on in. We were just getting ready to go to a charity event. Is everything okay? How's my little angel doing?"

Alex walked in and suddenly felt like a teenager again. He looked up at the staircase and recalled how pride and excitement rushed through him every time he saw his girlfriend at the top of the steps.

"She's actually doing better. She woke up at two o'clock this morning hungry, and demanding I bring her some chocolate cake." Alex said playfully complaining, and they both laughed.

Moments later, he and Peter were sitting down at the kitchen table discussing Serene's health.

"I know you asked us not to pressure her at first," Peter said, then paused to take a sip of his coffee, "but she needs to tell us what happened. We're—"

"Actually," Alex said interrupting him, "she did finally talk to the police, but I was only able to pull minimal details. What happened to her was terrible though I'm sure." Peter looked at Alex worried then slightly turned in his chair to call for his wife.

"Clair? Clair! Alex is here!" he said yelling across the house. He then looked back at Alex, "Go on? So, what did she say?"

Alex was at a loss for words, and he nervously scratched his head. He honestly didn't know the whole story yet, but he felt obliged to protect Serene and her baby. What had happened wasn't important right now. He simply needed her family to understand this wasn't Serene's fault, and that they needed to give her some time to open up about the details.

"Well, she said she was lured by a Dark sector man who later attacked her and…" Alex thought it was best to get straight to the point. "Serene is pregnant now."

"She's what?" Peter's eyes narrowed, and after shook his head at the devastating news. "No. Are you sure?"

"Yes, I'm absolutely sure. It's still early but we were able to confirm it." Alex stopped talking as he noticed Peter had placed a hand to his chest and looked to be in pain.

"Peter, are you okay?" Alex asked worried. Peter got up and took a deep breath. Alex stood up as well and put a hand on Peter's back. "Peter do you need me to—"

"No. No, I'm fine," Peter assured him not wanting to make a scene. "I… just need some air." Peter walked away from him and stepped outside.

Just then, Clair walked into the kitchen with a big smile on her face. She was elegantly dressed in a simple white dress and a chunky turquoise beaded necklace. Her bleach blond hair was teased and well groomed. It was obvious she was dressed to impress. She greeted Alex with a hug and a kiss on the cheek.

"By the light of God, how are you my dear?" she said in a slight southern accent.

"I'm fine, but is Peter still having chest pains?"

"Oh, only sometimes, when he's stressed, but you know Peter. He hates doctors." She paused realizing what she had just said. "Well, except for you of course," she added nervously.

Only a few minutes had passed when Peter came back inside and saw them sitting at the table.

"Good morning Sweetie!" Clair greeted her husband with a bright smile. "I was just telling Alex about the charity event."

Peter's face was pale and his gaze was low.

"Clair. Alex has something he needs to tell you." They both looked at Alex.

"Oh? Is everything okay?... I don't understand. Last I saw her she was doing better." Clair stated.

Alex looked over at Peter and was upset he'd thrown him into the spotlight.

"Well? What happened?" Clair spat at both of them demanding answers.

Alex cleared his throat. "Serene is doing much better. She's actually eating now and is in less pain." He studied Clair's expression but she was unamused by the news.

"Well good. I'm glad," Clair said whilst fixing her dress to make sure everything was in its place. "Hopefully that means we can get some answers today."

Alex continued. "About that... Serene's memory's getting better. And we found out that she was, in fact, attacked by a man that... took advantage of her." The last words came out slower than he had intended. It took a moment for Clair to absorb what she had heard, but then her demeanor changed. Clair clenched her jaw and hit the table with her closed fist.

"So, I was right. That son of a bitch raped my daughter!" Alex was shocked by her language; he was convinced they never cursed.

Clair's facial muscles tensed and she bared her teeth as she looked up at Peter. "I knew it! I told you! We are going to personally find this bastard and he is going to rot in jail so help me God! He will not get away with this!"

Peter put his hands on his wife's shoulders.

"Honey, honey, calm down. The cops will—"

"Calm down, Peter? Calm down! Do you not understand what has happened? Our daughter was raped and nearly killed! Her life is ruined! Ruined! And you're telling me to calm down? You should be furious!"

"I'm angry too, Clair! But we need to focus on Serene now." He said, realizing that their focus needed to be on Serene's health and her pregnancy now.

Clair went into the hallway to grab her purse from the table. She was determined to get answers from her daughter. Anger and frustration towards Serene rose up in her. Clair felt she had been too lenient on her and these were the horrifying consequences. She was also mad at Peter for not backing her up. There was a reason she was strict with Serene. She knew how beautiful and naive her daughter was, and no one ever understood that everything she ever did was specifically to protect her.

Yet, protecting her daughter wasn't all Clair cared about. Her plans were also to use her daughter's purity and beauty to marry her into high society and therefore ensuring that she and her daughter could enjoy the life she had always wanted. Clair had made the mistake of marrying the man she loved. By doing so, she had sacrificed the comfortable life she had always yearned for. She didn't want that for her daughter. She wanted her daughter to have it all— money, status and love. Clair felt there was still a chance for Serene and Alex, despite everything. But she needed to talk to Serene, immediately, before she messed things up further.

"Clair, stop!" Peter demanded as he followed her outside but she continued walking.

"Clair, I order you to stop!" Clair's face went red and she stopped dead in her tracks. She looked around and noticed the neighbors watching them. By Light sector law, a wife had to obey her husband. "Come inside! We need to talk!"

Clair begrudgingly walked back to the porch where Peter was

standing and lowered her voice almost to a whisper, but she was still angry.

"Now we need to talk? I told you something like this would happen! This is your fault, Peter!"

"My fault?" Peter spat.

"Yes! Everything that is happening to our daughter is because we became too lenient on her. What was it you said? 'She's old enough to take care of herself?' Well look at what it has brought us, Peter! Look!" she said pointing at nothing in particular. "She went out once! Once! Without telling anyone where she was going and she nearly died!"

"Clair, whether she was twenty or twenty-five, did you really expect her to never go out on her own? You were way too protective of her instead of teaching her how to protect herself."

"Protect herself?" She laughed at him. "Like she stood a chance! Did you not see the state she was in? I wouldn't have had to protect her until she was twenty-five because she would have been safely married to him by then!" She pointed at the house and towards the kitchen where Alex was sitting, though Alex couldn't see them. She continued, "Then he would be the one protecting her."

Alex could barely hear them arguing but he understood what their conversation was about. He resented the fact that Clair wasn't this mad when Serene was brutally attacked and nearly killed, yet what seemed to have finally angered her was the fact that Serene's virginal status had been stripped from her. Alex wanted to go home but he realized this wasn't over, Clair still didn't know Serene was pregnant.

Alex opened the front door, determined to finish talking to Clair.

"Clair, I'm sorry but I have to leave soon, and I need to talk to you about something that's extremely urgent." Clair gathered herself, embarrassed that Alex had probably heard the whole thing.

"I'm sorry Alex. For a moment I had forgotten you were still here." She said, lying. Noticing a neighbor gawking, she realized it was better if they weren't outside anyways. Alex held the door open for them as they walked inside and into the living room. Alex followed.

Knowing how severe the situation was, Peter sat next to his wife on the couch and held her hand. Clair scrunched her eyes in confusion and knew just by how they were acting that Alex didn't have good news.

"What's going on?" she asked.

Alex sat across from them, "Clair, Serene is fine health-wise," Alex said calmly. "But she needs everyone's support right now. What happened wasn't her fault and there were… consequences."

"Well for goodness sake Alex you're scaring me," she said, placing a hand on her chest and slightly panicking. Peter and Alex looked at each other and frowned.

"Serene's pregnant," Alex finally said, trying hard to make his voice soft. He leaned forward and rubbed his face, worried as to what Clair's reaction would be.

Clair stared at Alex, puzzled.

"What? What do you mean pregnant?" She knew exactly what he meant, but she couldn't believe it.

"She's going to have a baby. We tested her twice to make sure. We were able to detect it early. There's no doubt Clair," Alex assured her.

She let go of Peter's hand, because from the way he was acting it was apparent to her that Peter already knew.

"Well," she said calmly. "That's just lovely… Thank you, Alex, for coming. I'm going to… get a glass of water," she said, faking a smile.

They both watched as she disappeared into the hallway. Peter and Alex looked at each other, amazed at how well she had taken the news.

Seconds later they heard a loud thump, and they both rushed into the hallway.

Clair had fainted.

> <

Alex walked into Serene's hospital room carrying some takeout. He knew just by looking at her that Clair had already spoken to her. She was staring out the window with the covers over her legs, and was holding her knees up to her face. He didn't try talking to her, but instead, set up the food on the table and rolled it over to her. He took a chair and pulled it up to the bed so that he could eat with her.

She didn't budge.

Eventually, he broke the silence. "So, the good news is your mom knows now and you're still alive," Alex said as he tried to joke around with her, but it wasn't helping. He started to eat and hoped she would eventually join him.

"Alex? We are friends, right?" she asked softly.

"Of course. We've known each other for a long time. Why do you ask?"

"My mom, she's… crazy. She thinks I ruined things with you because of the baby."

He chuckled nervously and smiled.

"Well you know our parents always wanted us together." He cleared his throat, "What else did she tell you?"

"Not much. Just that my life is ruined, and I have to face the consequences of my actions," she said, then covered her face.

"Yes, I can only imagine how that conversation went." He then cocked his head and moved her hands to examine her face. "She didn't—?" he asked, concerned that Clair had hurt her.

"No, no. I'm fine," she assured him.

"Serene. Look at me." He asked softly and she did. "Look me and swear to me that she didn't hurt you."

"She didn't touch me." Serene said holding his gaze.

Later that night Alex came back to her room with a chess set. He had always enjoyed playing that game with her because she was great at it, and he loved the challenge. For the next two days, he came to her room and kept her company on every break he had.

After thinking long and hard about his next move, he advanced his remaining rook forward. "So, a rare opportunity just came my way. A residency position at a cancer center out of state has opened up. It's ten times the size of the pediatric oncologist department here, and it's world renowned. I would start next week."

"But you just started here?" Serene said.

"I know, but I'd be working with the best of the best and their cancer treatments are ground breaking. Would you prefer I stay?" He looked up to gauge her reaction.

"No, no that's awesome Alex," she said giving him her best customer service smile. "You'd be an idiot not to take it."

"Well good thing I'm not an idiot."

"Well I beg to differ. You literally just lost."

"Again? How? How can you see that many moves ahead?"

Serene smiled as she showed him every possible step left in the game.

Moments later Lea walked into Serene's room carrying a small vase of flowers. She looked over and saw Alex sitting next to Serene in bed. They were smiling.

Feeling awkward, she turned and put the vase on the table.

Alex looked at his watch, "Well, I should probably head back to my adorable clients."

"The woman who's been hitting on you, or the six-year-old?" Serene smiled.

"Both," Alex winked at her and walked out.

Lea waited for him to leave and then spoke. "Your doctor is cute."

"He's... not really my doctor, he just comes to visit."

"Are you two...?"

Serene cocked her head, then understood that Lea had meant if they had some sort of romantic relationship.

"No. NO. Not at all."

"Oh, well that's good." Lea smiled as relief overcame her.

Her words confused Serene. "Good?... Oh, are you interested in him?" Serene's eyes lit up and she playfully pushed on Lea's arm when she sat on the bed.

"No. He's not my type. I'm very particular about men... I'm more into... girls."

Silence crept between them.

"Oh..." A realization hit Serene, "oh is that why you...?" She looked at the small bouquet of pink Gerber daisies and orange roses.

Lea stood up, "No. Oh God no. You're cute and all but that's not why—"

"Can I ask why then?" Serene felt bad asking. She then shook her head, "I'm sorry. Forgive me. You're just being kind and I'm—"

"No, it's okay." Lea sat on the edge of the bed, "I know the lady at the gift shop. She gives me a massive discount and... and the staff usually tell me if someone is particularly down. They say I have a very cheerful personality, so I try to help where I can." Lea was glad she had already thought of an answer to this, in case it came up.

Serene still found her answer hard to believe, but Lea was nice and she enjoyed her company.

Casey came to visit later that night.

"So it was the homeless psychopath," Casey's eyes widened as she sat on Serene's bed. "You promised me you wouldn't—!"

"I know, I know. But he was so kind at first. He took me to a club, and we had a great time. Everything was great until... he took me to his condo and..." Serene looked down as she played with her fingers nervously. "I'd, just, rather not..."

Casey didn't want to push Serene, she felt terrible for her, "It's okay. I do want the details, but only when you're ready. I do have a question though... You had called me at one point and you seemed so calm and happy, did he kidnap and threaten you to act that way?"

"He didn't exactly kidnap me… and I was allowed to talk to you guys until you all left a slew of voice mails. At that point he began to change."

"Did you ever hear them?"

"Hear what?"

"The messages?" Casey asked concerned.

"No, why?"

Casey stared at her, "Nothing. It was nothing… It was just us calling about Alex's return. By the way, why are you still wearing your gown? Where are your clothes?" Casey asked, eager to change the subject.

"Mom didn't bring me much and I didn't want to bother anyone."

"It would probably help your mood if you got dressed. How about this: Tomorrow I'll bring you some decent clothes and I'll help you get all dolled up again." Casey smiled.

"Eh, tomorrow's my last day here but sure."

Casey silently clapped and squealed. "Also. I meant to ask you. What's up with the nurse?"

"What nurse?"

"The cute one who came in and dropped off the flowers earlier."

"Oh yea Lea. She's a bit odd. Why do you ask."

"Nothing, she just always gives me weird looks and smiles."

Serene laughed, "That's funny. Maybe she likes you! She told me she's into girls. Particularly red heads."

Casey rolled her eyes.

The following morning Casey brought Serene some clothes, hair essentials and make-up. Serene lit up and was happy to feel like her old self again. Casey had to leave soon after, but they shared a hug and Serene thanked her for helping her feel like herself again.

An hour later, Alex walked into Serene's room and was instantly frozen in place.

The window's blinds were wide open and the sun was shining bright on Serene, who was bent over with her foot on a chair painting her nails.

The first thing he saw was her well-rounded rear end. She was wearing a pair of blue jean shorts that he felt were too short on her, and he couldn't help but turn his head slightly to get a better look. She became aware of his presence and turned to look at him.

Serene had on a tight, sleeveless black shirt which covered most of the scars on her collar bone area. The shirt plunged into a deep V-shape showing off her ample cleavage and her necklace. She had such a delicate body that the size of her breasts made them impossible to avoid looking at. Alex never thought they were large, just amazing on her.

Once he took a moment to appreciate her body, he finally looked up at her. Her golden-brown hair was loose, glossy and flipped to one side. He noticed the bruises on her neck and body were completely gone as if by magic. He wondered if she was wearing make-up to conceal them, but he couldn't see any apparent make-up that stood out.

This wasn't the Serene he remembered. He remembered her being angelic, and cute. This Serene was different, she had grown up and was drop dead gorgeous. The hospital gowns sure knew how to cover up a woman's curves.

She approached him after putting down the nail polish and gave him a friendly hug.

"Hey Alex," she said smiling brightly. "Casey came by *and* as you can tell I'm feeling better."

Alex didn't hug her back. He just stood there, holding his clipboard down by his side, shocked, as she embraced him. When she noticed he wasn't returning her hug she looked up at him. Her face was fresh and beautiful, with a slight glow. Her almond-shaped eyes finally gleamed that beautiful hazel color that shimmered in the light reflecting shades of green, browns, and yellows.

"What's wrong?" she asked, disappointed. She was hoping he would compliment her the moment he saw her, but he didn't say anything. Alex snapped out of his trance and forced himself back to reality.

"Huh? Nothing. Sorry," he said with an icy tone and stepped away from her, "I was just looking," he coughed. "I mean thinking! Thinking about something that I want to do… had to do!" He cleared his throat. "I'll be right back." Alex turned on his heels and left the room.

Serene stood perplexed by his reaction.

Alex walked down the hallway and looked at his arms, he had goosebumps. He quickly rubbed them with his hands. He couldn't explain why seeing Serene like that had affected him so much. He sat down on one of the many benches decorating the hallways. He rubbed his face with his hands and then he laughed slightly.

God she's beautiful, he thought to himself. He was surprised that his mind suddenly became flooded with the idea of embracing and kissing her. He shook the thought away. Serene was off-limits, especially now, and probably forever. He was used to pretty women now, sexy women even. But this was a different feeling and he couldn't make sense of it. That is, until he realized Serene had been the only girl he'd ever loved. He shook his head and convinced himself he was being ridiculous. She was just sweet innocent Serene, after all. Zero threat.

He walked into her room again and she was lying down on her stomach reading a magazine. The first thing he saw again was her cleavage. He instantly veered his eyes away.

"Sorry, I had to take care of something," he said, closing the door behind him.

"It's okay. You're working. I feel bad that I take up so much of your time."

He sat down on a chair. "It's no problem. I like hanging out with you on my breaks."

She smiled and sat up, positioning herself Indian-style on the bed. He tried really hard not to look between her legs, not because he felt he would see anything, but because he was struggling to keep his thoughts clean.

"So. When can I go home? I feel perfectly fine now."

"Now, if you'd like," he said, instantly regretting those words. He didn't want her to leave, especially now.

"Awesome, good. I am so sick of being in here," she said, pretending to look miserable. He didn't know why, but her words hurt him.

"Really? So, I didn't make your stay pleasurable?"

"Nope," she said, smiling playfully.

"Hmm. Odd, because I recall you laughing and enjoying yourself whenever I laid in bed with you." He arched an eyebrow. When he realized he was flirting his cheeks flushed pink.

She smiled. "Well, Doctor Elbridge, if you want me to stay longer, I'll have to go out and crack another rib or something."

"Ha! Please don't. I'm only here another week. So, I'll just check on a few things and I'll take you home," he said, getting up to leave the room.

"No. I'll call dad; he'll come pick me up," she said quickly. He pressed his lips together, secretly wishing she wasn't so eager to leave.

"Okay, good. I'll be back to say goodbye then." Alex opened the door and looked back at her. They both smiled.

For the first time since he began his internship, Alex found it hard to focus on work. He needed to check on a patient before his shift was over, and then he'd go back to Serene and say his final goodbyes.

When he was done making his final rounds, he headed towards Serene's building in haste. However, in the corridor, a lady made him pause when she spoke to him.

"Excuse me, you're a friend of Serene right?" the stranger asked him.

Alex stopped to look behind him, "Yes, and you are?" He squinted, confused as to what this woman could possibly want. She was interesting-looking—attractive if he was into the dark gothic type, which he wasn't.

"Jessica. Can we talk for a moment?" Kamilla lied about her name. She was a pro at spying on her targets, and there was something about Alex and the way he interacted with Serene that told her he was more than just part of the staff.

"What is this in regards to?"

"I promise it's important."

Alex hesitated but led her down the hallway to a bench and motioned for her to take a seat.

"And your name?" She asked him as he sat next to her.

"Dr. Elbridge."

"Dr. Elbridge, how long have you known Serene?"

Alex didn't look at her. "Since we were teens. Why do you ask?"

"Do you care about her?" she asked, devoid of emotion.

Alex and Kamilla locked eyes.

"Yes. I'm sorry who are you in relation to her again?" He was annoyed by her personal questions. Her dark style clothing and make-up also screamed Dark sector resident, yet neither his family nor Serene's had any connection to someone so rebellious looking, at least, not that he knew of.

"Serene doesn't know me. I know Tristan," she mentioned calmly.

"Tristan? The man who attacked Serene?" his eyes widened when he remembered the name his sister used to describe the attacker. "Do you know where he is? Can you help us find him?"

Kamilla shook her head. "No. I don't know where he is and I don't want to know. Tristan's dangerous. It's not even safe for me to be here. I just wanted to warn someone that he *will* come back for her. He's obsessed with her. I'd recommend she stay as far away from the city as possible."

"Why would he come back for her? The cops are looking for him."

She sighed. "The cops won't find Tristan until it's too late. Listen, all you need to know is that he's out of his mind. He *will* hurt her again and next time she won't be so lucky."

He looked down, trying to absorb everything this stranger was telling him. "How do you know him? And how do you know so much about him?"

"I used to be his girlfriend. Listen you must trust me. He's psychotic… he *will* kill her. He's done this before." Alex saw fear in her face, gauging just how serious she was.

"I'll let her family and the police know," Alex got up and Kamilla followed.

"Okay, but I'm warning you. The cops won't stop him in time. If he finds her it will be too late. You need to take her far away somewhere. A place no one knows about it. Don't leave any trails or clues behind. I'm sorry, but it's the only way to keep her safe." She touched his arm gently. "Please… don't take my warning lightly."

Alex nodded.

"Here's my card." Kamilla handed him a hand-written card with a phone number on it. "I only ask that you don't get me involved with the police investigation. If Tristan finds out I spoke to you, or the cops come to me, I'll be in danger too."

"Okay. Thank… you," Alex said looking up from the card but noticing she had already walked away.

Suddenly, Alex's mind was flooded with worry for Serene's well-being.

Alex walked into Serene's room and greeted Peter.

Serene now wore a thin sage sweater over her previous attire. The sage color made her hazel eyes shine brighter than before.

Looking at her again, it was obvious to Alex why someone would obsess over her. She was as kind as she was beautiful.

"Peter, can I talk to you in the hallway real quick?"

"Uh, sure," Peter said following him out.

Serene scrunched her eyebrows, wondering why everyone was having all these private conversations without her.

In the hallway, Alex whispered to her father, "Listen, I don't want to stress her out because of the state she's in, but I have reason to believe her attacker will return."

"You really think so?"

"I think it's better to be safe than sorry. Just keep her close for a few weeks. Don't let her go out on her own or anything."

"No, of course not," Peter stated. "I hope the cops find him quickly."

"I'm sure they will. Do me a favor will you, please call me if *anything* happens anything at all. I do still care about her."

It upset Peter that Alex no longer had an interest for his daughter, but was glad that he at least took good care of her while she was here.

"I'll let you know, son."

"Thank you. I'll say my goodbyes to Serene."

"Tell her I'll be bringing the car around to the front entrance."

Alex nodded.

Serene smiled as Alex reappeared. "Is everything okay?" she asked as she sat on the bed rubbing her arm.

"Yes, everything's fine. I was just saying goodbye to your father. He's bringing the car out front." Alex sat on the bed next to her.

They were silent for a moment and he looked over, trying to read her emotions, but couldn't.

"Thank you, Alex, for everything," she whispered while staring at the floor.

"No need... You were an easy patient."

Serene played with her hands and desperately wanted to say how much she would miss him. She thought to herself how, if things had been different, if she had never met Tristan, their reuniting might have led to something more.

Who am I kidding, she wondered, *Alex stopped having feelings for me a long time* ago. *Sure, he hurt me and never officially broke up with me but it's time I let go of this grudge towards him. It should have been clear after he stopped talking to me that we were over.*

Serene sighed, finally letting go of whatever ill feelings she still had against him.

"By the way Alex, you'll be an *amazing* doctor. I just wanted you to know that I am so proud of you," she said sweetly. He smirked. "No, really. I can tell you really love what you do. You're going to save so many lives and help so many kids beat cancer and that's—that's amazing… You did the right thing."

"The right *thing*?" he said, asking her to elaborate.

She wished she didn't have to explain what she had meant.

"You know, focusing on your career, and leaving everything behind to follow your dream," she said, giving him a fake smile.

"Thanks, I guess?… Anyway, it was nice spending the last few days with you." He placed a hand on her leg. "Please take care of yourself. Remember, someone else is counting on you now."

Serene looked down at his hand and she gently placed her hand over his. Just then, Alex's eyes veered down to the promise ring he'd given her. She had worn it this whole time, just like his sister had told him. His heart became heavy with guilt.

"I will. I promise," she assured him as she got up and grabbed her side bag. He stood up, and she came in for one last hug.

He didn't mean to, but he went inside her open sweater for the hug. Wrapping himself around her waist, hugging her tightly, holding her closer than she had expected. He set his head on top of hers. She fit so perfectly against him. He wanted to remember every part of this. Her body against his, the smell of her hair; he had missed her, but he couldn't find the words to say it. He wanted to kiss her one last time, but he couldn't just ask her for one random kiss, could he?

Serene had also longed for his embrace, for closure, so she returned the hug with just as much vigor. But before things got too awkward, they both pulled away slightly.

He looked down at her, hoping, begging for her to look up so he could steal a kiss. Just one.

And then, she did.

For three solid seconds, their eyes met. He looked at her lips but froze. He hated the fact that he never acted on impulse, and his window of opportunity closed as she fully stepped away.

She spoke to him with her head down. "Well, good luck, Alex, in everything you do. I'll see you around. Perhaps during the holidays." She tucked a lock of hair behind her ear.

He smiled at the familiar, submissive manner in which she stood, looking down, fragile and shy. It reminded him of the Serene he used to love.

Just grab her. Kiss her! he thought. It would have been so easy knowing she was never one to object, but instead the words, "Goodbye Serene," escaped his mouth.

"Goodbye, Alex."

Alex stood in the room as he watched her leave.

And just like that, she was gone.

SEVENTEEN

WHO'S KAMILLA?

Early in the morning, Tristan was out back at Lea's place timing his speed as he waited for Jason to arrive. He was sweating and exhausted from his morning workout, but it was exhilarating to test out his newfound strength, speed, enhanced senses, and agility.

Jason finally pulled up into the backyard in his red pickup truck. Tristan walked towards him greeting him with a bright smile.

"Ah. I see you got your teeth done. Looking good," Jason said smiling back at him.

Lea had convinced him to go with the option she had chosen of leaving only two sets of sharp canines on the top. They filled the rest down to look normal.

"And the contacts," Tristan said pointing at his eyes.

Jason acted unamused but smiled as he walked past him holding a brown paper bag.

"I have a question." Tristan said turning to walk next to him.

"Shoot."

Using a small towel to wipe the sweat on his brow Tristan asked, "Why are we training like this? I mean, I know we need to hunt but… this seems like a lot of work for just hunting humans. They are obviously weaker."

Jason walked past him and sat down on a bench as he pulled out an apple from his brown paper bag and bit into it. Tristan sat on the bench next to him. It was obvious to him that Jason was somehow enjoying his apple, so he waited patiently for an answer.

"You're right. Your training is… *different.*"

"Why?"

Jason sighed, "Lea… she told me you can be trusted. And most Goldens *are* trustworthy. However, I need you to promise me that what I'm about to tell you stays between us. Understood?" Tristan looked over at him, not understanding, but nodded.

Jason continued. "For one, you're a Golden. Goldens are small in numbers and we're unable to defend ourselves against the Reds. In a group, however, we stand a chance against one or two of them. As far as they are concerned, we should be eliminated. They believe Goldens are a mistake, but we're not. Whether you become a Golden or a Red has, I believe, more to do with your soul than anything else, and unfortunately good guys finish last. That's just how nature works, but that's not necessarily a bad thing."

Jason took another bite of his apple then looked over at Tristan as he continued. "Have you ever noticed how in the animal kingdom the fiercest animals are able to roam freely without worry? That's basically how Reds live among us. All the other species fear them, but somehow, the weak, manage to survive… Wait long enough and most of the time you'll notice the predators lower in numbers or become extinct. We Goldens are patient. We don't have numbers, or the strength, but we have… something else. I'm not sure what it is yet but good always defeats evil somehow. Nature finds a way. Dinosaurs die while the small survive. Strong empires collapse. Terrorists get defeated. 'Blessed are the meek, for they will inherit the earth.' You see, Tristan, the problem with having more strength and power is you become comfortable. You start believing you don't need anyone, and eventually you let your guard down. We Goldens on the other hand are always on the alert and ready. We have to be to survive."

"So, we train to survive attacks from Reds?"

Jason looked out into the distance. "No, Tristan. We train so that one day… we won't have to."

Tristan absorbed what Jason had explained. Every day he was learning more, and yet there was still so much he didn't understand. "Kamilla, who is she?"

Jason whistled, then chuckled. "I hear you're her love interest. Boy, she wants you." Tristan's face became flushed. He was annoyed that such private information got around. Jason continued. "I know Kamilla well. Good luck with that. That's one Krov you do not want to mess with."

"But who is she?" he asked again, realizing he knew nothing about her. The real her.

"I hate to break it to you but, Kamilla is Ignatius's daughter. *The* Ignatius."

Tristan studied Jason's face, searching for clues as to what or who this man was.

"I'm sorry, who's Ignatius?"

Jason laughed again. "Let's just say he's a very powerful man— completely untouchable. The strongest Red this world has ever known. He's their Alpha and their leader. If I were you, I wouldn't get on her bad side, not only for your sake, but for the sake of those around you. Anyway, have you eaten? I brought another apple."

Tristan shook his head at his ridiculous offer. *Why is he eating an apple anyway?* He wondered. "Kamilla, she had powers."

"What kind of powers?" Jason asked, as he put away the apple.

"She picked me up without touching me, and there was some sort of… red mist around her."

"Yes. She is a second-generation Alpha. I'm surprised she's not stronger than she is," Jason said getting up and ready to continue training, but Tristan needed to know more. He needed all the leverage he could get if he hoped to protect Serene from Kamilla. He walked with Jason.

"What's second generation Alpha?"

"Well, do you know what first generation Alpha is?" Tristan didn't respond as he didn't know the answer. Jason explained. "We, including the Reds, aren't the end result of what those scientists were trying to create. You do know our history?"

"Lea gave me a synopsis."

"Good. The first Krovs were fast, strong, and we had an appetite to destroy the enemy, but as soldiers, in the age of firearms and weapons, they needed something better, the end result being a solider with the ability to control objects through telekinesis. It was wishful thinking on behalf of the scientists and their superiors. They imagined a solider that could remove the enemy's weapon from a distance, stop flying bullets, missiles and the such. Of course, this seemed impossible, and the test subjects could barely levitate a single blade of grass." Jason kneeled down to pick up a blade of grass. He placed it in his open palm then levitated it. It was a neat trick but hardly functional.

"But Kamilla. She lifted me."

Jason allowed the grass to fall onto the ground. "Yes, as I was saying the scientists were trying to perfect this before the labs were destroyed. However, as time went on, eventually there was an Alpha, a perfect Krov. There have only been a few Alphas in our history. Red eyes are strong, but Ignatius's powers are far beyond anything you or I can imagine. To take control, he had to defeat the only two remaining Alpha Reds that existed, and that battle was intense. I still remember the news stations reporting the damage."

"So, Alphas are the end result of what those scientists were trying to create?"

"Yes. I'd go as far as to say that Ignatius would have exceeded their expectations." Jason said while he pulled out heavy chains from Lea's storage unit so that he could continue to train Tristan's self-control. But Tristan wanted Jason to finish answering his question.

"Second generation, how can that exist? I thought you guys weren't fertile."

"We aren't... Kamilla is the first second generation Alpha we know about. That apparently happens when an Alpha 'turns' one of their direct offspring. Honestly, I know little about it."

Tristan was lost in thought. He needed two things from Kamilla, his money and a way to keep Serene safe. Kamilla was too strong to control physically and had a powerful father. He'd have to find another way to manipulate or control her.

"Now, I know I tell you every time, but the point is to NOT to break the chains." Jason begged convinced he wasn't even trying. Goldens were never this strong so Tristan was obviously using significant force.

The next day, Lea pulled up to Jason's house, since he had texted her that they would be there today. She wondered why. Tristan was a Golden, and Jason only trained Reds at his house. She walked into his seemly normal house and then through the basement door that led to Jason's expansive underground training facility.

Lea had never been there.

When she reached the bottom of the steps, her jaw dropped at the sheer size of the place. The basement expanded far beyond the house above it. The walls and floor were made of thick reinforced concrete walls, similar to a bomb shelter, and it was well lit. There were rooms to either side of her that looked like cells with wide reinforced glass windows.

She stopped studying her surroundings when she noticed Jason several feet in front of her looking through the window of the largest room at the end.

Lea and Jason stood by the window observing Tristan.

She cocked her head when she saw the insane amount of chains on the wall attached to Tristan. It was excessive.

She watched as he painfully, and loudly, fought off his urge to attack the male human in the cage in front of him. Cries of utter agony escaped Tristan's mouth. His face, neck and arms showed his strain as he pulled on the chains. The walls and what seemed to be bulletproof glass did little to muffle his screams.

"This-this is torture! Why is he here and chained up like that?" Lea demanded answers.

"Well, as much as I love working outdoors, he kept breaking the chains and going through the steel cages. He even uprooted a tree."

"What?" Lea scrunched her eyes.

"I thought he simply lacked self-control, but I realized it wasn't that. He's simply too strong for the single chains, and he was easily breaking them. Also, last night when it was dark out, I noticed something."

Jason debated telling Lea what he saw. If his intuition was correct, it would be a dangerous situation for all three of them.

"What? What did you notice?" she asked.

Jason decided, both for Tristan's protection and for Lea's, to not say anything until he was sure.

"Nothing. Just that he's a bit stronger and lacks self-control. So, I brought him here, where I can control him."

Lea sighed in disappointment. Everyone knew Tristan struggled with self-control, especially when it came to sex and drugs. His past drug use was a habit Lea felt guilty for, since they always pushed it on trainees in their youth.

Lea and Jason stood there watching Tristan suffer in endless torture as tears and sweat streamed down his face. Jason bit his nails anxiously. It killed him to keep such an important find to himself.

"Okay. Well, I can't sit here and watch this. I will be upstairs. Let him know I'm here." Jason nodded and quickly waved her away. When he saw she was gone, he walked to the light switch to turn off all the lights. After a few minutes, in Tristan's cell, he saw it again. It only lasted a second but Tristan's eyes would shine a bright yellow light and then fade.

>≺

The following morning Tristan was sleeping on Lea's couch when he heard a knock on the door. He was shirtless and wearing only a pair of grey sweat pants when he stood up to open it.

"Kam?" His tired eyes focused.

She cocked her face as she studied his yellow eyes and his slighty bigger build. Being a Krov suited him.

Kamilla wore a short black dress with tall black boots and purple eye shadow. It was apparent she had done her best to look especially nice today. Not a single sleek black hair was out of place.

"Trist. I… know you're still mad but can I come in?" she asked sweetly and lowered her head. If she was a cat her ears would surely be down. But Tristan was still furious at her. He wanted to go off, demand her to leave and slam the door in her face, but now, he knew who she was, so he was careful not to anger her. He also needed her so, reluctantly, he stepped aside allowing her inside.

"So, how's your training going?" she asked as she glanced around at Lea's humble house with disgust.

"It's… way more difficult than I thought. The pain… it's unbearable… but I'm getting closer."

"Good. Look, I just came by to say I was sorry. I lost control; you understand how hard it is now that you're a Krov." She stood really close to him and continued talking to him in an overly sweet manner as she gently touched his chest and traced the lines and shadows that were there.

Repulsed by her touch, Tristan took a step back putting some distance between them.

"I got mad okay?… jealous." Kamilla said coldly, "I became obsessed with you while you were human. You're a Krov now, so you must know how hard it was for me. I'm also a Red. I lack the kind of empathy you or Lea have. It's not fair. I wasn't always like this."

Tristan looked away, "Please, Tristan. I need you to understand."

Tristan rubbed his closed eyes thinking, *keep it together and don't kill her.* Not that he thought he could.

"You're not still mad are you?" Her eyes became glossy and gentle.

"No Kam! I'm not mad," he spat, wanting to say, *I'm fucking furious!* But instead said, "I was way past mad several days ago."

"I know and I understand. You have every right to be angry. And I'm *so* sorry... I—I've missed you," she said trying to be as nice as possible, but the way she was acting confused him. She was *never* this meek around him. He was trying to start an argument and she wasn't taking the bait.

His body was stiff, and his expression was cold. She walked up to him but he moved back a step.

Tristan seemed scared of her now, and she hated seeing him act like this. She wanted the old Tristan back. The confident man she fell in love with.

"Why are you really here Kamilla? And why the fuck are my accounts zeroed out? I know you have something to do with it."

"Yes, I took care of them for you. I have your money," she said nervously, "... Here," she pulled out a credit card from her purse. "You can use this for now. I haven't stolen a penny, I promise! You'll get everything back in time. Once I clear your name, I'll transfer it." Tristan took the card. When he placed it in his back pocket Kamilla jumped and hugged him taking him by surprise. "You're turned now! I can finally hug you as *hard* as I want!" she said, overly cheerful. "It feels so good to not want to kill you."

Tristan locked his jaw thinking, *just go with it do not piss her off. You need to give her hope or else she'll kill Serene!*

But acting like he cared for her was extremely difficult now.

Tristan reluctantly placed an arm on her back, barely hugging her.

Just then, Lea came out of her bedroom and she gasped when

she saw Kamilla there. The women's eyes locked and Lea ran into the kitchen like a scared mouse.

Kamilla stayed for breakfast. Everyone was quiet at the table, which made the awkwardness worse. Kamilla tried to smile at them doing her best to cut the tension but it was hard to, especially when they were all munching on crunchy, ground pieces of human blood and bone, as if it was cereal. Lea burped loudly and Kamilla's eyes narrowed at her.

"What? It's my house."

The door opened and Jason walked in to pick up Tristan for training.

"Why, if it isn't little Kami. Wasn't expecting you to be here," Jason said walking over to her and kissing her hand as if she were royalty.

"I figured I could pay you in person," she said, pulling out a check from her purse and handing it to Jason.

Tristan now understood who was paying for all this. Had he known he wouldn't have accepted.

"J, would you like some breakfast? It's fresh!" Lea insisted, smiling.

"Sure," he said sitting on the only empty seat at the table.

"He's the best trainer around these parts." Kamilla looked over at Tristan. "I spared no expense. He usually trains Reds and sometimes Sentinels."

"If the pay is right," Jason smiled. "Kamilla how's your father?"

Kamilla was quiet as she looked at Tristan.

"Oh yea, Tristan knows now." Jason said filling his mouth with crunchy human-o's.

A few moments later Kamilla quickly and awkwardly asked Tristan, "So… what happened to the girl?"

Everyone stopped eating and understood that she was talking about Serene. He looked over at Lea nervously. It was hard for him to hide what he felt for Serene, but he did his best.

"Not sure. I think I killed her. I killed a lot of people that night."
He shrugged making it appear as if he didn't care, but Kamilla didn't
fall for it. She had seen Lea at the hospital basically coddling Serene.

"I'll find out... anyways good luck with your training." She
smiled and stood up to leave.

Kamilla walked out the front door and a few seconds later
Tristan followed her outside.

"Kam. Kam hold on," he said as he grabbed her arm. Kamilla
turned to look at him. Tristan knew Serene's life was in danger, so
he needed to convince her Serene was no longer a threat. "If you
want us to clear the air, I need to know something." Kamilla stood
quietly. "I swear I will never see that girl again, but I need you to be
honest. Did you intentionally leave me with her knowing I'd kill
her?" When she didn't respond, he grabbed her arm harder. "Tell
me!" he yelled, no longer holding back his anger.

"No, Trist! I told you I just lost control," she said tearing up. "I
swear to you. I would never intentionally kill anyone out of spite!
How dare you even accuse me of it?"

He searched her face for any glimpse of sincerity. Kamilla was a
lot of things, angry, jealous, and he could even understand how she
ended up killing him knowing she could bring him back but would
she kill an innocent life?

"You don't believe me." She wiped a tear, "I'm *sorry*. I swear it
was an accident. I was mad and—" She stopped to look at his hand
gripping her arm. "Trist you're... hurting me."

He let go of her arm. He could never hurt her before, but now
his grip was painful.

"Do you have *any* fucking idea how much pain I was in?"
Tristan paced, "Did you even care? Kamilla, I would have rather
died!" Tristan was seething.

Kamilla became increasingly nervous and combed a shaky hand
through her hair. "I know. I'm so sorry. But you have to understand
that it was also torture for me every single day to both care about you

and hold back my impulse to hurt you. Do you have any idea what that's like? What it's like to want to kill someone, eat them and yet love them at the same time!" Kamilla yelled as tears rolled down her face.

Tristan had never seen her cry this way. He knew exactly what Kamilla struggled with, and he unfortunately sympathized with her. Being a Golden had made him soft, and he hated it.

"Okay," he said, taking a deep breath and doing his best to contain his anger towards Kamilla. "I just... don't want anything bad happening to her just because you saw us together. I know how jealous you can get." He locked her gaze and narrowed his eyes. "But, I swear to God Kamilla, if *anything* happens to her I *will* find out and I'll know who was responsible."

Kamilla's eyes widened in disbelief. She thought it unfair to blame anything that happened to Serene on her.

"I'd *never* forgive you for it." He growled.

Kamilla wanted to be angry at him for the way he was talking to her. As a human who didn't know any better, she dealt with it, but it was obvious he knew who she was now. She did, however, like the fact he was no longer acting like a scared puppy around her. This was Tristan she knew; This was the man she loved.

"Trist..." She swallowed. "You should know I would never hurt an innocent on purpose. I was the one who worried she was too young for you." Tears ran down Kamilla's face again. "And I'm so sorry I hurt you. I never planned to turn you in that manner. You were supposed to feel no pain. You were supposed to be medicated through your transformation. Please." She held her head low, begging him to hold her. "I wish I could take it all back."

Tristan sighed. If there was one thing that calmed his anger, it was a woman in tears. He still didn't trust her, but he had to convince her that things were back to normal, for Serene's sake.

"Just... come here," he said trying to sound gentle. He hugged her and held her in his embrace as he spoke. "I will never see her again. Understood?" Kamilla nodded, "I nearly killed her so I won't risk it. The poor girl probably thinks I'm a monster now, anyway."

Kamilla had always appreciated Tristan's gentle nature and she had missed his embrace. Now that he was stronger, it felt even better. The truth was, she had expected Serene to be dead initially and therefore she was expecting Tristan to never give her another chance. In a way she was glad Serene's life was spared. Tristan would not have been as forgiving. Serene was still a threat, but she'd figure out a way to keep them apart. If Serene thought Tristan was a monster now, she'd find a way to make her absolutely terrified of him.

EIGHTEEN

THE MANSION

I t had been a few days since Serene left the hospital. Clair had been standoffish with her and they had barely exchanged a handful of words. Serene knew her mother was still mad for what had occurred, and it was uncomfortable waiting for the moment her mother would go off on her for running away and getting herself pregnant. She wished her mother would punish her and get it over with already so that the tension was out of the way. Oddly enough, it was the fact that she was pregnant that kept her safe.

For the first time in her life, Serene felt her mother had been right, about everything. Clair had always brainwashed her with religion and warned her about the dangers of men, the world outside, and the demons that lurked hidden in society, tempting people, causing them to sin. The counties became divided into sectors before Serene was born, but during history lessons, she had learned that these imaginary 'demon' sightings are what caused the tensions to build politically in the first place. Conservative Lights were convinced that the growing sin in society, such as drugs, sex, same-sex marriages, and divorce rates were allowing these monsters to manifest.

Yet, Liberal Darks became convinced it was all a hoax, or that there was some logical explanation for the sightings and the rise in murders. What was most disturbing for Serene was the fact that she had finally indulged in these behaviors, only to be face to face with the demons she once believed were a myth.

Serene didn't tell anyone what she had seen that night. Too afraid to know what it had all meant. Just thinking about the fact that she had probably fallen for and slept with a demon terrified her.

Many nights since the attack, Serene had begun to suffer from nightmares; some were about being attacked that night, others were about what her baby may look like. Serene loved kids, but naturally, she wondered if her baby would be normal.

As Serene slept she was startled by the loud noise of her window breaking. It was dark, and she couldn't see much so in a panic she lit the lamp located on her nightstand, but it wouldn't come on. The electricity was strategically shut off and the entire house was consumed by darkness.

Suddenly, Peter and Clair awoke to the sounds of screams echoing throughout the house.

"It's Serene!" Peter gasped and scurried out of bed to get to his daughter.

In Serene's room, a man grabbed her by the throat and lifted her out of bed. She tried to see who this person was, but in the faint moonlight all she could see was a man with dark shoulder-length hair who's height and body type resembled Tristan's. Except his eyes were glowing red! The monster then mercilessly flung her across the room.

On the floor and hurt, she struggled to get up.

"Tristan? Stop! Please! Why are you doing this? Please, don't hurt me!" She cried as she crawled out of her room, but the monster grabbed her legs and dragged her back inside as she hopelessly clawed at the wooden floor.

"HELP! NO, NO, NO!" She screamed, praying, hoping that this was all just another nightmare. Her screams were ignored as he pulled her up by her hair and grabbed the nape of her neck. The monster then attempted to shove her into the wall face first but part of her body hit a desk.

When he released her. She looked down at the location of the pain. The corner of the desk had hit her abdomen. She collapsed overwhelmed by the pain and just as Peter busted into her room, the monster vanished.

➤ ◄

Clair, Serene, and Peter were in the living room. The lights were back on, and Serene was sitting on the couch, wrapped in a blanket, crying.

After Peter hung up with the police, he called Alex, since he lived only four blocks away.

Alex arrived before the ambulance and he kneeled to examine her. She had bruises on her neck, and she was in pain all over again. Alex felt guilty for not doing more to warn others. It was obvious this man was disturbed and determined to kill her.

"Where does it hurt?... Serene?" He asked softly but Serene seemed confused, and wasn't responding to anyone's questions. Alex held her hands, trying desperately to make her feel safe again.

Serene looked down and lifted her pajama shirt slightly to reveal a large deep red and pink area on her abdomen. When Alex applied the slightest bit of pressure, Serene gasped and leaned forward in pain.

"I'm taking you to the hospital. We need to make sure you and the baby are okay."

"911 has already dispatched an ambulance," Peter said.

"I'm taking her myself. I know her history."

He placed an arm under her legs and another around her back lifting her in his arms. Serene continued to cry into his shoulder, lost in despair.

A tired Alex walked out of the emergency room and into the waiting area where Peter, Clair, Casey and Alex's mother, Lillian, sat in an isolated corner.

He sat in front of them, "Serene seems to be okay. I was worried she had hit her head again or that the hit to her abdomen had caused internal bleeding but she'll be able to go home in the morning."

"And the baby?" Casey asked.

"She's spotting, but there's hope everything will be okay."

"I don't know what we can do to keep her safe," Peter said with his hazel eyes full of tears. He felt helpless and needed to find a way to protect his daughter.

"We need to have an alarm, surveillance cameras—" Clair explained.

"No, that won't be enough." Alex said, remembering what the mystery woman told him, "He has no reason to hid his identity so cameras and alarms won't deter him. By the time any help comes it would be too late. We aren't dealing with an amateur. This man has done this before. In his state of mind, he won't stop until he gets what he wants."

"Wait. How do you know this?" Casey asked.

Alex sighed and leaned forward over his legs, resting his elbows on his knees. "A lady came up to me. She didn't want to be involved in the investigation, but she warned me that this man was mentally unstable and that he would come back for her."

"Alex!" Lillian gasped, upset at her son.

"You didn't think that was important for us to know?" Peter exclaimed.

"I know! Trust me I feel horrible for not telling everyone."

"What else did this lady tell you?" Casey scowled at him.

"She said our best bet is to take her somewhere far. Where only we know where she is."

Clair started mentioning family members that Serene could stay with when Casey interrupted the conversation.

"Wait! Alex! Can't you take her with you for a bit? You're leaving tomorrow. Can't she go with you?" Casey asked him, nearly begging.

"No, I don't think Peter and Clair would allow that. It's not proper for me to live alone with a woman. Plus... I'll be busy with work," Alex said, rebuking the idea.

Clair and Peter looked at each other. Peter nodded, agreeing with Alex.

They continued talking amongst themselves, but after a moment Clair thought about what Casey had suggested. She wondered if this could work in her and her daughters' favor. After all, Serene was already pregnant, so what was there to lose? In fact, they might end up falling for each other again. Clair knew Alex liked Serene, and she needed Serene married as soon as possible. Serene's pregnancy was still a secret to outsiders, so having Serene away during her pregnancy was also suddenly an *excellent* idea. If everyone kept their mouths shut, no one would be the wiser.

"I actually think Serene staying with Alex would be a great idea," Clair said calmly, interrupting their conversation. They all looked over at Clair surprised. They never allowed Serene a single night out with him after ten, let alone to live with him.

"I agree as well! You've already been taking superb care of her as it is Alex," Casey lit up at the possibility of them mending their relationship.

"I *really* don't think you guys would feel comfortable with me and Serene living together... by ourselves," he emphasized the last word.

"Oh, Alex don't be ridiculous!" Clair almost laughed. "Peter and I completely trust you. We've known you and your family since you were a kid! And you're almost like family now." Clair turned to look at her best friend Lillian. "Your son took such good care of her while she was in the hospital. We would be incredibly grateful if he did us this favor. So long as we kept this discreet."

Lillian nodded and placed a hand on Alex's arm. "If it's okay with you I have no objection," she whispered. "I've respected every decision you've made so far. So, this is up to you."

Alex felt the pressure, but after all the recent events it was the least he could do.

"Yeah. Okay," Alex rubbed his legs. "If it will keep her safe, I will take her with me for a month or so."

"Yes!" Casey whispered loudly.

Later that night, in the hospital, Serene expressed to her mother numerous times that she didn't want to go with Alex, but Clair had her *ways* to convince her.

The next morning, Serene was back at home packing her bags when Alex arrived to pick her up. His grandparents had passed away a few years previously, and he had planned to take on their home in Oregon. The house was about forty minutes from the Children's Angel Cancer Center, where he would be interning. Since he graduated Magna cum laude from a prestigious university, he had an array of hospitals open to having him intern.

Alex took it upon himself to go upstairs and help Serene with her luggage. Later she stood next to him as he loaded the car.

"You know, my mom has never let me sleep over at your parents with Casey. Even while you were away at college. You don't find it odd she's letting me go out of state with you?" Serene pointed out as he placed the last of her luggage in the trunk of his Bentley convertible. Serene knew what her mother was up to, but she wondered if he did.

"Odd why?" he said, offended. "Because I've done nothing to have them mistrust me? Because they've known me since I was a kid and our families are close? What's so odd about that? Plus," he said closing the trunk of his Bentley. "They don't have a choice."

Serene was convinced her family would have found another way if they really wanted to.

Several hours later, Serene stared out the window of the car when her stomach growled. She sat up in her seat.

"Can we stop for some food? Actual food?" Serene begged, tired of the gas station junk food they had consumed.

Alex looked at the clock in his car. "Might be too late for that." It was well after midnight. "My grandparents... they have a very large kitchen, last I recall. I'm sure you'll like it." Serene's lips barely curled. "Actually... I'm kind of glad you'll be with me for a while, I'll have my very own master chef." He smiled at her, but she was slightly peeved at the idea.

"Oh, so now I'm your cook?" she spat.

"Hey, I've lived off fast food and cereal for the last three years. I don't think I can handle another year like that."

She finally smiled brightly. It was nice to know that even someone as perfect as Alex had an Achilles heel. The man couldn't cook to save his life.

"Okay. I'll cook. But I refuse to be your maid. So, I'm not cleaning up after you," she said, crossing her arms.

"If you're not paying rent, damn right you will be!"

Her eyes opened wide in anger and she hit his shoulder, though not as hard as she had hoped.

"I'm just playing." he laughed.

Suddenly, she felt like a freeloader and realized she would have to get a job quickly. She didn't like the idea of not paying rent. In the meantime, it was only fair if she helped around the house.

"I'll have to cook dinner for myself every night, anyway. So, I'll oversee that and the housework, at least until I find a job."

"I was kidding… Plus you're *not* getting a job," he said in a demanding tone.

"Excuse me? I'll get a job if I want. I thought you didn't mind women working."

"I don't. I just have money, and I think you should focus on getting a degree in something. Something other than your religious studies."

"I don't think continuing college is a good idea for me right now," she said looking down at her stomach, realizing how her whole life and plans had changed so drastically in such a short period of time.

He glanced over to see her touch her abdomen.

"Serene, it's because of that baby that you have to go to college, now more than ever…" Serene was quiet. "Also, don't ever say what you said last night at the hospital."

She looked over at him, "Don't say what?"

"You told me you didn't want the baby… that you hoped you had miscarried when you saw the blood."

"I… I'm sorry. I wasn't thinking straight. It was a rough night." She looked down as she nervously played with her hands. She loved kids and always dreamed of having her own, but she never expected to be pregnant under these circumstances, and she was haunted by what the baby would be like.

"Serene," he breathed as he placed a hand on her leg the way Tristan had done on their first date. But with Alex, it felt right. "Your baby is a blessing. I *promise*, everything will be okay. You will love that child very much. And you'll be a great mother. I know you will." Alex's voice was sweet, and his words filled Serene with peace.

He knew he couldn't help her forever, but at that moment he made a commitment to be the person she needed for a while.

A few hours later, Alex was still driving and Serene had awoken from a long nap. The sun had just started to rise as they went down a winding, wooded road. The road looked wet like it had just rained. The trees, green and yellow-leaved, were a stark contrast to the blackened branches that held them. In the distance she saw majestic mountains.

Moments later, they came up to a large iron gate that had a rusty old chain with a lock on it. Alex got out of the car to unlock and remove the chains. He walked back to put a gate-code into a keypad and got into the car again. As the gates opened, Serene noticed the very tall walls that surrounded the property. She wondered why the property was so well protected.

As they drove up a long and narrow curvy path, Serene realized acres of land surrounded the house. They weren't even close to the house yet, but the building was so large Serene could see it in the distance. It had a very tall entrance and they decorated most of the exterior walls in large stones. It was hard to tell by just looking at it, if it was two or three stories tall. Serene looked over at Alex and wondered why he never mentioned that his grandparents owned a mansion.

When they exited the car, Serene heard a stream nearby but couldn't locate it.

Even though the mansion was impressive, she could tell from the unkempt gardens out front that no one had lived there for a very long time.

"This place is much larger than your parents' house, and your parents' house is huge." she said in awe.

"Yea... mom's not much for large, older homes anymore. They sort of creep her out," he said scratching his head trying to be humble. He then pulled out a pair of keys and walked up the stairs to the double doors.

The door creaked open, and they entered the house. Serene walked in behind Alex and looked up at the vaulted ceilings in awe.

Alex turned on the light switch, but no lights turned on.

"Weird. The electric should've been turned on by now. I'll call them."

"It's not the power company." Serene blurted. "The gates were working."

"Hmm. True. Must be another issue then. I'll call an electrician and the power company just in case." Alex walked back outside while dialing on his phone.

Inside, Serene smiled as she looked around. It was clear by the accumulated dust everywhere that the house had been abandoned and not cleaned in years. The foyer was enormous, with two separate sets of dark wooden stairs that met at the top. The marble floors were cream colored and the furniture was covered in haunting white sheets. Right in front of her and between both stairs was a table. She removed the covers over it to expose a glass table. She looked straight up, and a beautiful chandelier hung gracefully. The walls were decorated with elegant yet old wallpaper and molding. Serene couldn't wait to see the house lit up and cleaned.

Continuing to explore, she walked through the large living room and then made her way into the kitchen. As she approached the window by the sink, she saw an amazing view of the brook she had heard earlier.

"So, what do you think?" Alex said as he came up behind her.

Serene smiled. "It's nice… big, though it needs a lot of updating and fixing."

He looked around and placed his index finger on the counter, then he rubbed the dust off it with his thumb. "Yea, and cleaning," he pointed out.

"I was thinking, maybe, *if* you're up to it." He gave her a suggestive stare while the corner of his lip curled up into a sly smile.

"Oh no, Mr. You better help me. I'm not cleaning all of this up on my own," she said, walking away from him. She knew it would take a decent-sized staff just to dust the place.

"Not on your own, you're pregnant after all, but if you could be in charge of this, it would thrill mother. You can hire all the help you need."

"So, you're *not* going to help at all?"

He scratched his head. "I will... but I'll be pretty busy. I'll talk to mother about the budget. You can do whatever you want to the place." Serene looked at the view from the kitchen and took a deep breath, reluctantly accepting the job.

He walked up to her and pushed the side of her head into his lips kissing her head. "Thanks in advance... I'll go get our things."

She did have a few ideas for the place, and if she was able to hire help then it could be fun.

The following morning, Serene was in the kitchen cleaning out the fridge and cabinets. Alex walked in dressed professionally for work.

"What are you doing? No! Get something to eat first before you start this," he demanded as he did his tie.

"I'd love to, but how am I going to get into town while you're gone?"

"There is an old Mercedes in the garage. I'll see if it's working. By the way, I don't want you lifting anything heavy or exerting yourself. Walking and lifting light things is fine, but not too often. Don't use harmful chemicals and drink plenty of–"

"Alex! Stop!" She rinsed out a rag over the sink. "I know what I'm doing."

"Hey. I'm just looking out for you." Their eyes met. "And as your *doctor* that's an order, understood?" He winked at her.

This was the Alex she remembered. He had already let the title go to his head. "Yes sir, anything else?" She rolled her eyes.

"Get groceries. Healthy stuff." He pulled out a few hundred from his wallet and set it on the counter. "I'll check on that car for you."

Alex was kind, but it always bothered Serene that he acted like a sixty-year-old trapped in a young man's body.

NINETEEN

WOMAN OF GOD

A few days after moving into the house, Alex drove up and saw a few men trimming down bushes and mowing the lawn.

"Serene finally hired help," he said to himself.

Alex exited the car carrying a briefcase and wearing sky blue scrubs that enhanced his eyes. He had just finished a stressful 20-hour shift and was hoping to unwind.

As he opened the door, he saw workers putting up wallpaper in the foyer. He turned and saw Serene in the dining room on the right, giving directions to a man about where she wanted the chair railing on the wall. Serene's hair was up in a messy ponytail and she was wearing an oversized gray sweater with a pair of skin-tight black shorts. She looked confident and seemed to have done a great job orchestrating the whole project.

She glanced over and walked up to him. He caught a glimpse of some paint on her hands. He shook his head in disapproval.

"You're not painting, are you?" he said, ignoring her welcoming smile. "Serene, the fumes."

She rolled her eyes at him. "Alex. It's fine. I just accidentally touched some paint, and all the windows are open in the rooms they are painting in or putting carpet down. And trust me, I'm staying away from those rooms."

Alex doubted her. He looked around and sniffed, noticing a strong smell in the air, but couldn't identify if it was toxic.

"... this was a bad idea," Alex whispered shaking his head.

"Oh relax, will you? I know what I'm doing."

He frowned at her words. "Do you know whether the fumes in the paint they are using is safe for you?"

Serene pressed her lips together. She wasn't sure.

"Just... go wash your hands."

"Okay. So, how was work?" she smiled attempting to change the mood. "I thought that navy blue would go great in—"

"Now Serene!" he yelled, pointing towards the kitchen. His eyebrows low.

She jumped, startled by his words. "Fine... Geez."

As she walked away, he called out to her, "You also have paint on the back of your sweater."

Serene took off her sweater as she rushed to the kitchen sink to wash her hands. *Why's he so mad?* She wondered, hoping that once he'd seen what she had done to the place so far, he'd be filled with gratitude. She was mistaken.

Flustered, Alex went upstairs to shower.

Okay, I may have overreacted, Alex thought to himself in the steaming hot shower and sighed. *She's been through a lot. I should be more patient, but... she's just constantly getting in harm's way. I need her to understand that I'm just looking out for her.*

After his shower, he made his way down the stairs, determined to apologize but stopped short the moment he saw her.

Serene was standing at the top of a ladder, with two men holding the ladder at the bottom, and she appeared to be doing something to the chandelier. She was wearing a short white tank top, which looked more like a sports bra and the soft skin around her waist was taunt and exposed. Her spandex shorts might as well have been underwear.

To make matters worse, her pink bra was visible through the

thin material of her shirt. He watched as the two men holding the ladder checked her out and spoke to each other in another language. From the way they were smiling and looking up at her ass, he knew they were ogling Serene.

Alex rubbed his head.

"She's only been here four days, and she's already given me a headache," he whispered. If anything happened to her, everyone would hold him responsible. The thought bothered him. He came here to focus on work not be someone's babysitter.

As he watched her from a distance, he began to understand why Clair was so tough on Serene. He remembered Clair would constantly get on her case about her clothing. If anything was too revealing, they forced her to choose something different. Alex didn't want to be the bad guy, but she *was* his responsibility. So, he didn't care anymore if she became angry at him. He thought, if she continued to act like a child, he'd treat her as such.

Alex walked up to the men and ordered them away as he held the ladder for her. He didn't ask her to come down, instead he waited patiently until she was finished.

"Okay, done." she said once she had placed the last missing crystal on the chandelier. Alex looked away as she walked down the ladder.

"I need to talk to you for a moment, in private," he said once Serene was safely on the ground.

"Okay? Sure," she shrugged.

She followed him through the house filled with workers and they entered a set of double wooden doors that led to a large, dark office, with only a desk inside. She looked around and since there were no chairs, she sat on the only piece of furniture in the room.

Alex took a moment to admire her body, then veered his eyes away and paced for a few seconds as he figured out what he would say to her. He hated being strict with her, but he felt he had no choice.

"Oh great. What's wrong *now?*" she asked, annoyed. Whenever he rubbed his chin she knew it meant something was wrong.

"You just… don't get it do you? What part of, 'you're pregnant now, there's a life inside of you,' don't you understand?" His eyes narrowed.

"What? What did I do this time?"

"Serene you can't be doing—You can't be climbing ladders putting yourself at risk! Do you realize how many things have happened to you recently? Do you need a recap?"

"I *wasn't* putting myself at risk! I'm being safe about everything!"

"No, no, you're not! I will not be responsible for you ending up in the hospital again. No climbing ladders! No lifting! No drinking coffee. No having paint all over you! No—"

"Okay, whoa! First of all, Alex," she said holding up a single finger. "I don't know what's gotten into you but you *really* have to stop this."

"No! They left *me* with the responsibility of taking care of you. You—you've always been extremely careless! And that's probably why—!" He stopped himself before he said something he would regret.

"Why what?" she yelled, offended.

He looked up at her as if it was obvious. "Serene… Look at you."

She looked down and covered the scars that had healed on her shoulder blade.

He rolled his eyes. "That's not what I meant; I'm talking about your clothes. You can't be wearing *that* around other men, around… me. It's like you want—" He stopped himself again from saying that she did these things to get attention because he knew she didn't. "What exactly are you trying to do?"

"Okay, *first* the paint, and *now*—*now* you're getting on my case about my clothing? There is nothing wrong with what I'm wearing!"

"Yes, there is! You're a woman of God Serene. You can't be dressing like, like you're easy! That's—" He sighed, and he decided to just say it. "That's... that's probably why you were raped in the first place." His voice was almost a whisper.

Serene's jaw dropped. She couldn't believe that he'd gone as far as to blame her for what had happened. He had no authority to talk to her in such a manner. Her face went red and her eyes were nearly in tears. Serene had never stood up for herself, but Clair wasn't around, and she was desperate to give Alex a piece of her mind.

"You..." she stood up to walk towards him, "are NOT my father! You are not my mother or anybody to me! How dare you tell me what to wear? It's shorts and a tank top. Get over it! It's not like I'm prancing around in my underwear. You're the one who told me to take off my sweater in the first place! I was never allowed to wear what I wanted. Why?" Serene continued as tears began to escape her eyes. "Because of this stupid Light sector dress code? Even if I followed the code, I still wasn't allowed to wear a damn tank top in public. Everyone else could. But, no! I'm... I'm supposed to be some sort of saint right? Is that it? I'm supposed to be a perfect Light sector girl and die a virgin unless I got married! I mean, look at you! You went off and had your fun but no..." she started shaking as she paced, "it's okay for you right?" She sneered at him. "You're just *perfect* either way, in the eyes of everyone, in the eyes of God! I'm twenty-one and pregnant and suddenly I'm easy? Is that what you think of me?"

She realized now, more than ever, that she could never ever tell anyone the truth about her and Tristan. If this is what people thought about her now, they'd think the absolute worst of her then.

Alex realized he'd lost control over the situation. She had taken everything he'd said wrong, and he didn't mean to upset her to such a degree. Yet, he still needed her to understand what he had meant. Unfortunately, that meant revealing more than he'd hoped.

"No. Serene, I don't think that... I didn't mean to imply you were easy."

"Well, it sounded pretty clear to me," she said her face only inches from his.

He was hesitant to say what was on his mind, but Serene needed to hear it from someone. If he didn't explain to her how he felt, she would never understand.

"Serene… you're sweet, intelligent, and you're—you're beautiful."

She rolled her eyes and walked away from him. "And I know when you hear *beautiful,* you're imagining pretty but it's more than that. You're… *desirable*." He rubbed his forehead, embarrassed. "I don't want to be forward with you, or disrespect you, but it's the only way you'll understand why I'm upset, why your mom was so strict about what you wore, where you went. You compare yourself to other girls, but you're different in more ways than you know. A tank top on most girls is just a tank top. On you, it's a temptation. It's all we want to look at."

Looking down at the floor, she suddenly wished she had worn a different shirt underneath her sweater. She felt naked and uncomfortable in her own skin, and she hated him for making her feel that way.

"Whatever, Alex. It's probably just you that feels that way." Serene's cheeks flushed.

The corner of his lips curled as if it was adorable that she didn't understand how much of a bombshell she actually was.

"It's not just me Serene. First, you're here because a man is stalking you. Second, the men that were working here today kept staring at you, and I don't mean to sound rude, but if you keep dressing like this, looking the way you do and being the gentle girl you are, trust me, you're going to get attention you don't want. You may even end up hurt again. I just… don't want anything bad happening to you."

There was a long awkward silence between them.

"So, I guess, once again, I can't wear what I want here. Great!"

she said, disappointed that no matter where she went there was always someone telling her what to do.

"No. It's fine... " He crouched down to sit on the floor and rubbed his hands against his face. "I don't want things to be the way they were at your parents. You can wear whatever you want here. Just... take into consideration what I said and please, don't give me a heart-attack like you did earlier. Just try to be more careful, that's all. Whether you like it or not, I *am* someone to you; I'm your friend."

They were quiet for a moment and neither was looking at the other.

Whilst he sat, she took the opportunity to rush out of the room and go upstairs.

She changed her clothes and sat on the bed as tears escaped her eyes. She wasn't flattered by their conversation, she was embarrassed.

TWENTY

THE TEST

Four weeks into training, Tristan was still in Jason's underground facility, but was no longer chained.

In the room with him was a man.

The plump older man with silver hair was on the ground, chained to the floor by his ankles. His arms tied behind his back. He was alive and his mouth was covered with duct tape. Tristan was sitting on the floor shirtless just a few feet across from him.

"Alright! It's been two hours already can I eat him?" Tristan yelled at Jason who was standing at a safe distance inside the large cell.

"Not yet… You have to be *really* hungry," Jason said calmly.

"I am! I'm fucking starving!" Tristan growled, causing the man to shake.

"Alright! Then you have to be *starving* for *longer*. I'll be back in an hour," Jason made his way out of the room but turned at the doorway. "That man better be in one piece when I come back." He walked out of the room and closed the door behind him.

Inside, the human looked terrified to be left alone with Tristan, and began to give muffled screams once Jason was out of sight.

"Oh, shut up!" Tristan groaned. "You keep up with those annoying sounds again and I'm going to start on your legs, just for being a nuisance!"

The human screamed louder, but Tristan felt no sympathy. Jason had explained to him who this man was. Not every victim was a proven criminal, but this one was. He was the leader of a human trafficking ring. Specifically, he abducted young girls to sell to Krovs. Apparently some Krovs weren't just killers, they were also lazy.

At Lea's house, Tristan was on the couch e-mailing Serene, pretending to be Lea.

"Serene might think you're *into* her now." He smirked.

"Don't do that!" She smacked the back of his head as she walked by the couch, "You'll scare her away. She barely responds as it is."

"By the way you lied. There's nothing between her and that doctor anymore."

Lea rolled her eyes, "If that thought helps you sleep at night— Oh!" her eyes widened when she remembered something.

She ran to her room and came back to Tristan with a bright smile on her face.

"How much do you love me?" She swayed back and forth like a child while hiding something behind her back.

Tristan gave Lea a penetrating stare. After a moment she handed him a folded-up piece of paper. "It's Serene's address! I finally trust you won't go running over there now."

He took the paper from her hand and opened it. "You... shouldn't have given this to me," he said, setting the paper down on the table.

"I thought you could at least physically write to her instead of pretending to be me. You know... *try* and explain everything. Well, you can't do that but—"

"Yeah. I'll figure it out."

If Tristan wanted her address, he could have asked her for it via e-mail, but he thought maybe Lea was right. A hand-written letter would help. Serene hadn't heard from him directly in about a month, and even though he couldn't fully explain himself yet, he needed to let her know he still cared about her and would come for her soon.

➤ ◄

A few days later, after writing Serene a letter apologizing and ensuring her that he would return, Tristan went to Jason's house more determined than ever to complete his training.

When he arrived, Jason instructed him to go down first.

Tristan confidently walked downstairs and into the training facility, determined to get today over with.

When he entered the main cell, he was expecting to see a man chained to the floor, but there wasn't a man, there was a woman. She had spiky dark hair, piercings, and was attractive. The athletic woman was wearing a tight white tank top that had blood on it and a pair of ripped up jeans. She wasn't chained, the woman sat with her hands tied behind her back, and her legs bound together. She also *didn't* have duct tape over her mouth.

When she saw Tristan, she wasn't scared; she was a proud woman.

Tristan looked back at Jason.

"Well, are you going to go in?" Jason said.

Tristan's confidence dwindled, but he walked inside.

He kept his eyes veered away from her, and yet he couldn't shake her aroma.

Suddenly, a burning discomfort consumed his body as an overwhelming hunger overtook him. It felt as if he hadn't eaten in days, mixed with the need to ravage a woman sexually. It had been an extremely long time since he'd laid with a woman, and it was a feeling that resembled true starvation.

"It's very different, isn't it?" Jason said as he walked inside the room joining him. "What you feel right now." Tristan stood silently, eyes closed, shaking & sweating. He could smell her sweat, her strawberry lip gloss, her feminine wetness. "No, Tristan. You have to look at her; otherwise there is no point to this."

"Your methods are so fucked."

"You were complaining yesterday that things weren't progressing fast enough. You want to swim? In the cold water you go."

"I can do it if I don't look at her."

Tristan wanted desperately to be chained up. His body was shaking as he fought the impulse to go near her. He didn't know if he wanted to hurt her, rape her, or eat her. The truth was he wanted to do all of that simultaneously.

"You can't walk around with your eyes closed in the real world, Tristan."

He didn't want to breathe, because the smell was intoxicating, but his heart rate was speeding up, craving more oxygen. Men smelled and tasted like common food. Like rice, or bread. But a woman's smell was like a juicy, salty, sweet and fragrant steak cooking on a grill, but even that was a weak comparison.

"Everything about you that is primitive is enhanced. Humans have lost the ability to smell what you're smelling, the pheromones and hormones in her sweat, but it still exists in plenty of animals, though it probably doesn't make animals feel the way you do. No... your attraction to them is more intense.

Her chemistry is different. You don't even have to taste her and yet you know she tastes better than a male. As a Krov, sexual desire and appetite are intertwined. It's easy to understand when—"

"I know how it works." Tristan growled.

As he stood there with his eyes closed, he heard the door to the cell lock behind him.

His heart began to pound and he tried to exit the room. However, the door was locked. *Fuck*

"Don't you dare break my door," Jason mouthed on the other side of the glass.

238

Tristan paced, violently running his hands through his hair.

"Whoa. Calm down lover boy." The female spoke, "Not sure what exactly that Morgan Freeman wannabe was saying but... I've been raped by worse. I'd take you any day."

"Shut up." Tristan spat as he paced. *Seriously! Out of all the victims the girl he doesn't gag?*

"Just untie me and we'll have a little fun."

"I said shut up! You have no idea the amount of danger you're in!"

"Hahaha... your cute when your mad. I'm not—"

Without thinking, he opened his eyes and met her gaze.

As if in slow motion, he looked down to see her cherry lips open and close as she spoke.

Small glimpses of her soft wet tongue made his manhood harder than a nightstick. And, with every breath she took, he could almost see the sweet fragrance escape her lips.

"Stop!" Jason yelled suddenly inside the cell.

Breathing hard, Tristan looked down, his eyes wide open and his mouth salivating. He was holding her down on the floor by her neck and she was struggling to breathe. In the haze he released his grip just enough to allow her to live, but he couldn't control his body enough to release her.

She coughed, doing her best to breathe, his grip, still too tight.

"Back. Off. Close your eyes—", Jason spoke slowly, but Tristan blocked out his voice. Instead his ears were focused on everything that was happening inside the woman's body. Her heart rate was loud. Her blood gushed through her veins making a beautiful visceral sound. The sound of her swallowing reminded him of her warm throat. It was all too much for him to bare!

Without thinking he kissed her, but it was merciless. His tongue was bruising and overbearing and he bit each lip, causing her to bleed. Blood dripped down her chin as he licked down her neck. He pulled on the delicate fabric of her shirt and bra, ripping it off of her. Then, as if by reflex, he opened his mouth wide and bit into the soft fleshy upper part of her breast.

The woman gave a mind-numbing scream as he tore into her. The sound vibrated in his head. He tried to tune it out but he couldn't! An intense migraine-like pain followed a high-pitched ring flooded his brain. He immediately stepped back tearing her flesh away as he did. He wiped his mouth and savored the piece. He looked at the large red wound as blood drained down her body.

Her eyes were full of tears as her screams continued.

Struggling to regain control and ignoring the excruciating hunger pains in his gut, Tristan walked out of the room.

Unwilling to watch her suffer, Jason pulled out a knife, lifted her head, and slit her throat.

Tristan sat outside on Jason's porch and popped a beer. He had cleaned off most of the blood but he still had some on his white t-shirt.

He was severely disappointed in himself, and now he feared, more than ever, getting close to Serene again. He had always wanted kids and a family one day, but Serene and the baby's safety came first, and he knew it was best to stay away from them indefinitely.

Jason came outside to sit with him. He sat in his favorite rocking chair and lit a cigarette.

"Would you like one?" Jason calmly asked, and Tristan refused. "You did very well in there."

"Are you insane? I lost control. I don't think I'll ever be able to control this."

"Now, what makes you think that?" Jason asked.

"Because... I've had problems with addiction for years. Drugs, sex. I've never had any self-control."

"But you did manage to control both of them, right?"

Tristan was silent. Drugs no longer affected him the way he

needed them to, so he'd finally stopped. He also hadn't slept with anyone since Serene, and he realized he needed a woman, badly, but he only wanted her.

"I mean, you stopped doing drugs and you stopped having sex—"

"And how the hell would you know?" Tristan's eyes narrowed.

Jason laughed. "Tristan… I'm with you every day, in case you haven't noticed. I also know when a man's in love, and you my friend have it bad."

Tristan's expression softened. "That obvious?"

"Well, it definitely is now." Jason smiled and patted Tristan's leg. He then took a long drag of his cigarette. "I wasn't lying. You did well in there. Male Krovs, they often kill their first woman. You couldn't have done better in there today. I mean it."

"I shouldn't have hurt her."

"Why? Because she's a female?" Tristan didn't answer. "Well, you're going to have to get over that fact. Let's go eat and we'll train some more outside," Jason got up.

"I'll wait out here," Tristan said, not wanting to see him cut up the woman he'd just attacked.

What if that had been Serene? He worried. *If only I could forget you, halo.* His mind flooded with memories of her smiling in the sunlight, her soft skin, and her warmth. He squinted as he allowed the pain to consume him. A small price to pay for her memories. Memories that although innocent aroused him. "God, I need you."

The next morning Tristan was having breakfast with Lea at her place, but the food came with a side of guilt, and he was pensive. He dreaded going to Jason's again because he knew there would be another woman waiting for him.

However, Tristan now understood why Jason had surprised him with a female yesterday. The anticipation of being around a human female excited him and the mix of arousal with shame made his stomach churn. Even self-gratification wasn't helping.

After breakfast, Lea picked up their plates and placed them in the sink. Tristan stood up to leave, but stood still for a moment, observing her as she washed the dishes.

"What?" she smiled, sweetly.

"Is it... easier now, being around me?"

Lea chuckled and shook her head. "Way easier."

He took a step forward and placed a hand on the counter next to her.

"You act *different* around me now."

Lea laughed, "Different how?" He held her gaze. "Oh, you mean I don't want to jump you every two seconds? Yeah, sorry about that. Those pesky little Krov symptoms sure get to us."

"So, you're not... attracted to me anymore?" Tristan frowned.

Lea shut off the water. "Why does it matter?"

"Curious." He shrugged.

Lea dried her hands on her shorts. "No, Trist. I'm not attracted to you in the slightest. In fact, once you became a Krov, I was like— ugh, what did I ever see in him?"

Tristan smiled and shook his head. It was odd seeing her so composed around him, but he liked it. He was also good at noticing a woman's subtle cues. The fact she was wearing a thin pink tank top and no bra meant something.

Tristan debated acting on his urges. He only wanted Serene, but last night, he couldn't sleep. His mind and soul needed her, and he was seconds away from taking Lea's car and finding her. If he didn't curb his desperation soon, he would risk hurting Serene.

"You look cute today." He smirked

"What? This old thing?" She looked down at her pink tank top and black shorts.

"No, the messy ponytail thing on either side." He touched and grabbed a strand of her blonde hair from one of her pigtails.

She froze, and closed her eyes as he lifted her chin to meet his lips. She had lied, human or Krov it didn't matter, it was still torture being around him. She kept herself from begging him, knowing he was serious about Serene. However, she could never deny him.

His hands went under her pink tank top, and she surrendered to his touch, gasping when he pinched her nipple. It was nice to finally feel some force from him.

With no effort, he lifted her up and sat her on the granite counter top. He removed her tank top and placed his forehead against hers as he looked down and admired her curves for a moment. Lea wasn't thin but she didn't need to be, she was cute, and her softness and sweet nature reminded him of Serene. "Agh." He groaned as he closed his eyes and placed both hands on the counter. Images of Serene flashed through his head causing his chest to tighten and the pain to return.

Lea noticed his arms shaking, and she held his head up to look at her.

"It's okay... It's okay to think of her." She whispered. Tristan gazed into her eyes and noticed they were glossy with tears. It was clear she wanted him, but he couldn't do this to her nor to Serene.

"I'm sorry. I wasn't thinking. It's just, this *need*, it won't stop. No matter what I do." He clenched his jaw. "It hurts, and I can't stop thinking about going to her, about hurting her—"

"Then let me help you, Trist." She held his face. "I do want you, but I also want to help."

"No, I just need to endure, but I'm afraid. Afraid I will go to her before training is complete."

"I know, and this will help."

"How?" His eyes widened. "How will this help?"

"Your stomach is full, but your needs aren't being met. You need to solve both. It will... speed up your training."

He gazed up at her doubtful. Was she being honest? Or was she just using him? Lea was many things, she obsessed over him for years, but he never knew her to blatantly lie.

"Be honest. Have Krovs done this before and been successful?"

"Yes, and Jason knows. But he also knows how you feel about Serene."

No. He thought. *I just want Serene. I need to go to her now! It can't wait any longer!*

And you will kill her! Another voice inside him screamed. *You will kill both of them. Is that what you want? You're not ready, you know you're not ready!*

But she needs me and I—I need her.

"I don't want to hurt you." His voice broke.

"You won't. I'm a Krov."

"That's not what I meant. You've been amazing, but my thoughts will be with someone else. You don't deserve that."

"Please let *me* figure out what I deserve. I know what this is, and I know you care about her."

"I just... want to be allowed to think about her. To crave her." A tear escaped his eye.

"Then do so." She lifted his face and kissed him.

For the first time since his transformation he didn't fight the rush of memories. He was desperate to remember her face, her smile and their time together. Desperate to hold her and be lost inside of her.

A vision of the first time he saw her became so clear he swore he could touch her. Light surrounded her face as she tried to console him near the garden gate. With his eyes closed he pulled her in, kissing her,

"*Serene.*" He whispered as he allowed the pain and arousal to consume him. A tear ran down his cheek. He pushed his body in between her legs remembering her trembling body against the building on the school property.

"Serene," He moaned again, "Please, I need you." He said, his mind now lost in her memory and slowly entering a madness he couldn't escape.

He pulled Lea closer to him, crushing her and grinding against her, giving his body what he craved, desperate to sooth the pain he'd been feeling for weeks.

"Trist... please, your hurting me."

Trembling and breathing hard he stopped and placed his forehead against hers.

"I'm sorry. I didn't know I could hurt you." He caught his breath. "I'm frustrated, and it's hard to gauge what's too much pressure now. Please be patient."

Lea nodded nervously.

He lifted her, and with her legs wrapped around him he brought her into the bedroom closing the door behind him.

Moments later the house shook, and the sound of broken furniture, falling picture frames and Lea's moans filled the house.

Tristan sat on the side of the bed, the pain completely gone. But instead of feeling relieved, he was overwhelmed with guilt.

"Are you okay?" Lea sat up in bed as he put on his jeans. He was brooding and clearly unhappy. "Trist? If you're worried you hurt me, I'll be okay."

"I'll be in the car." He said walking out.

"You'll thank me later," she called out, feeling his guilt as well her own.

Tristan regretted failing Serene. But, for the first time ever, he had a successful day at training. The blonde female survived three hours in the cell unscathed. Jason congratulated him and was confused that he wasn't happy about his accomplishment, but Tristan knew this had been a short-lived solution. One he would never repeat.

TWENTY-ONE

THE BET

T he house was beginning to feel like home to Serene. Renovations weren't complete but the house was clean, dust free, and was freshly painted.

Alex was sitting at the dinner table eating a delicious meal of roasted lemon chicken and homemade mash potatoes with gravy.

Serene set a bowl of seasoned green beans on the table. Alex immediately dug into his plate and moaned, amazed that the food tasted better than it looked. With his mouth still full he said a few words.

"This… is amazing."

Serene was wearing a light blue vintage style dress and a modest pearl necklace. A common outfit for the proper Light sector women. This was the Serene Alex remembered. To him she looked noble and dignified, and he felt comfortable with this side of her.

"Thanks, glad you like it. You forgot to say grace."

They held hands and gave grace.

Serene served him the vegetables. "Did you get the information?"

"Oh."

Alex pulled out some papers and a pamphlet from his black briefcase and handed them to her.

"Volunteer orientation at the hospital is on Monday."

"That'll work."

Serene looked at the pamphlet for a local college as she ate. She was going to be volunteering at the hospital while possibly going to school for nursing.

"You might want to enroll soon; the next semester starts in a few weeks. But, why a nurse? Why not a doctor? Don't limit yourself. I think you'd enjoy being a Pediatrician."

"No. I think I'll just stick to nursing. I'm not nearly as smart or as composed as you. Plus, that's a lot of school to pay for."

"Between being smart and being dedicated, only one is necessary to succeed, Serene. And you've always been both." He was bothered by the fact that Serene thought of herself as lacking in intelligence. He knew she had scored high on her SATs.

Alex sighed when there was no more chicken on his plate.

"I'll decide later… I have to call father about tuition. So, I'm not even sure we can afford this school." She got up and gathered their plates.

When she placed them in the sink, Alex walked up to stand beside her.

"I already called him for you."

"Oh? How's he doing?" she asked while rinsing off the plates.

"I told him I'm paying for your college," he said, ignoring her question.

Serene stopped what she was doing and placed her hands on the counter. This was too much; she didn't want to feel like she owed him more than she already did.

"Alex, no. My parents will pay for it."

"It's already done. I knew you would object, so I made an account in Clair's name."

Serene glared at him.

She wasn't as upset at Alex as she was with her mother. How dare she take advantage of him that way! She opened her mouth to protest when Alex's phone rang. It was Serene's father.

"Hello?" Alex said answering, "Yea she's in front of me…" He walked away from her so she couldn't hear the conversation.

Serene carefully followed, hiding behind a wall as he spoke and paced in the foyer.

"Yea, I think so too. What do they say?" After a moment Alex continued. "Do the cops have any leads yet? Okay. I have something to protect us. Sure. You may also want to delete my phone number from your phone, and any history on it just in case. Can't be too careful. I wouldn't keep calling until he's found… Well he can steal your phone, check the—yea exactly. Yes. Correct. Watch anything you say on the internet too. Okay, I'll tell her. Alright."

Serene walked into the foyer. "What were you guys talking about?"

Alex sighed. "That man… he sent a few letters to your parents' house—no return address. He… seemed to know a lot about you."

Serene's heart skipped a beat. "A few? What did the letters say?" Serene worried that Tristan had revealed something about their time together.

"They didn't give me all the details. All they told me was that the letters mentioned he was sorry for hurting you. That he had to stay away for a while, but that he hasn't forgotten about you and loves you or something along those lines. He's insane, obviously, but why send it if he knows you're not there anymore? I mean, if he was stalking the house wouldn't he realize you weren't living there anymore?"

"Maybe he's not stalking?" her eyes were wide and her heart began to race.

"Or maybe he knew they'd contact you about it?… Who knows. With men like that, you can't expect their actions to make any sense. By the way, don't tell anybody where you are located. No one. Not even family members or friends. Okay?"

"Of course," Serene nodded nervously.

Even though he turned into a monster, part of her wanted to know what those letters actually said.

Saturday afternoon, Alex didn't have to go into work, but he decided to check on a special patient. It was a young, intelligent, and cheerful young girl who was fighting cancer. Luckily, she was on her last round of chemo, but her health was very weak. She was improving but his intuition forced him to check on her, so he decided to go to the hospital on his day off.

Once Alex left, Serene jumped at the opportunity to indulge in a big cup of coffee and a pair of delicious pastries she had hidden from him. Alex had become very critical of what she ate for the sake of the baby.

With her giant coffee mug in one hand and a plate of illicit goodies in the other, she went outside to sit at the table by the pool.

It was the end of spring so they had fixed the pool and she was very excited that it had a heater. Alex wouldn't be home for hours, so she checked the temperature of the water with her foot.

Feeling it was perfect, she ran inside to get into her two-piece red bathing suit. It was time for a tan.

Alex was on his way to the hospital when his phone rang.

"Alex here."

"Hi, Dr. Elbridge?"

"Yes?"

"Hey, Dr. Edwards told me to inform you about Sarah. She passed away last night."

"What?" Alex's car came to a screeching halt and he pulled over. "How? What happened?"

"It looks like her heart gave out. They won't know anything for sure until later."

"Can you check to see if she received the slow release potassium last night? I asked Beatrice to administer it before I left."

There was silence on the phone for a minute.

"She did receive a small dose last night."

"No, I specifically said slow drip over several hours! Not a—" Alex closed his eyes and composed himself. "Sorry. Thanks for letting me know."

Alex hit the steering wheel. He always kept his emotions in check but he was angry and heartbroken. Sarah had become very special to him in such a short period of time. He didn't understand how it was possible that she had died when she was showing signs of improvement. This was the first patient to die under his care, but Sarah was a vibrant twelve-year-old girl with her whole life ahead of her.

He expected moments like these in his career, but deaths were never easy.

He turned off the car and got out to mourn his loss and ponder over what had gone wrong. The potassium was supposed to help her heart and organs cope.

If I had stayed... If I had just ensured the nurse did as I asked perhaps... He wondered while staring at the tranquil landscape. *I'm so sorry Sarah.*

Logic told him her odds wouldn't have been much better either way. Her body was weak, and the potassium would have barely helped her heart, but in this field of work, the slightest decision meant life or death.

Alex walked into the house with his eyes downcast and his shoulders slumped. He didn't care to look for or talk to Serene. He just wanted to be alone, so he went straight up into his bedroom.

Once there, he took off his belt and unbuttoned his shirt. He stopped when he heard a splash.

The master bedroom's balcony was located above the pool, and he opened the glass double doors that led out onto the balcony. When he looked over the ledge, he saw Serene, and, not wanting to be seen, he moved back to stay out of sight.

After a few minutes, she got out of the pool and sensually squeezed the water from her hair.

Alex had never seen her like this. Even for someone as picky as he was, her body was absolute perfection. *Well, if it wasn't for the scars on her shoulders caused by that psychopath.*

He walked back into the bedroom, doing his best to avoid the temptation that Serene constantly caused. As he undressed, he stopped for a moment to debate whether he should join her.

Serene lay sun-tanning when she was startled by a loud splash. She instinctively covered herself with the towel and watched the pool, hoping and praying that the person who was ascending was Alex.

To her relief, it was.

"What happened?" she called out. "I thought you were going to work?"

"Patient canceled on me," he said, calmly wiping the water from his face.

She lifted an eyebrow. Serene knew about Sarah and didn't understand what he meant by 'canceled.'

"Do you… want to talk about it?" she asked concerned.

"Not really. You coming in or what?" he forced a smile.

"No, I think I'll just head inside now. It's actually kind of cold out," Serene knew going into the pool meant he would see her bathing suit.

"Come on, I just got here," he begged her. "I could really use the company." He then splashed water her way.

Serene found it refreshing to finally see Alex in such a playful mood. She looked under her towel and wondered how she would get into the pool without revealing herself. Alex sure knew how to make her feel exposed when she was fully dressed before, so now she was blushing in embarrassment.

Covering herself with the towel, she reluctantly walked into the pool. She made sure to cover as much of her body as she could.

He laughed at how ridiculous she was being because, eventually, she was going to have to lose the towel. He noticed her flushed cheeks and, in a sense, felt proud. *Serves her right for wearing such a garment.*

After her body was mostly in the water, she put the towel near the edge of the pool. When Serene noticed he was staring, she coyly covered the top of her chest with one hand and submerged herself underwater to swim towards him.

She met him at the center of the pool.

"The water's perfect isn't it?" he said, trying to start conversation and get her mind off of what she was wearing.

"Yes. Glad I convinced you to fix the pool?" Serene fixed her drenched hair and pushed the strands away from her face.

"Well, it didn't need fixing per se but yes, it's nice. Are you feeling better today?" he asked, worried about the nightmares she'd been experiencing.

"I'm okay. Actually, I was very nauseous this morning, but I had some food and felt better."

"Oh, what did you have? I'm starving."

She hesitated telling him since she knew he would object, but she decided to annoy him instead. "Coffee!" she said, defiantly.

He gave her a playful look of horror but then said, "Well one cup isn't bad."

"No, I had two cups. Two very large cups." She lied and showed him with her hands an exaggerated example of the size of the cup. "And I'm going to have some *more* later."

"You *wouldn't*," he said, playfully.

"Yup. And I had a pastry and I might just have wine later too! While I'm at it, smoking looks fun," she joked.

He laughed and splashed water in her face. She splashed back, and they continued until they both had to back away.

"Hey. Do you remember how you would always beat me at holding your breath?" She asked, and he nodded. "Well, I've been practicing for the past few years and… I bet I can beat you now."

Alex scoffed, "I'm still undefeated."

"Hey, don't be so cocky! I bet I can win now."

"Okay… So, what do you want to bet on?"

She thought about it for a moment.

"If I win, I'm allowed to do whatever I want for a month! And you can't get on my case about anything," she said proudly.

He frowned. Serene had a knack for doing things that annoyed him. It wasn't her personality that bothered him, it was her carelessness that kept him on edge. "No. Absolutely not!"

"Come on!" Serene said.

"No, Serene! Knowing you, you'd go… skydiving, or do something just as audacious!"

"Okay, okay. One week? Come on, you can't survive seven days?" She looked at him sweetly then said, "Please? I promise no skydiving. No dangerous sports."

He began to think of terms he could offer her in return. He knew Serene was the type of girl that, given an ounce of freedom, would do something crazy in an instant. He found small bits of her free-spirited nature amusing, but he also enjoyed knowing he could bring her back to where she belonged. To where she was safe.

She pushed again to convince him once more. "You can't handle one little itty-bitty week without being all crazy controlling and over-protective?"

He rolled his eyes. "You mean responsible and cautious?"

"No! I meant crazy ninety-year-old trapped in a young man's body who wouldn't know how to have fun if his life depended on it."

He frowned. Is that really how she perceived him?

"Fine, but no climbing ladders, no drinking alcohol, no coffee! Your feet stay on solid ground at all times. Anything you can possibly fall off is completely off-limits, and actually… anything, where you can get easily hurt, is off-limits. Also, if I win you become my maid, and you will do anything and everything I ask you to do, without complaint."

Serene squinted at him. "No. If I win drinks are allowed unless it's alcohol. But fine, no ladders or high places. But I can easily get hurt cutting a potato or something so no to that rule as well!"

He laughed then held his head back in frustration, knowing that if she won, he'd somehow regret it.

"Fine… fine! I'll agree to those terms. One week. You won't win anyway." he said with confidence.

"Yay!" She stood in front of him, preparing herself for the challenge.

"Okay, ready?" she asked him, and he nodded back agreeing. "Okay, on the count of three. One, two… three!" They both took a deep breath and jumped up then into the water, but she instantly ascended, cheating.

Laughing quietly for a moment she then took a deep breath and went under. A few seconds later he extended his hand to ensure that she was still underwater with him. They both eventually let out the air in their lungs and sank to the bottom. She held still, determined to win because freedom was something she desperately wanted.

After about forty seconds his body began to panic. He extended his hand once more to pat the top of her head. Surrendering, he came up gasping for air. He was disappointed at himself but knew it had been years since he'd practiced.

Alex looked down at her underwater, and after a few seconds passed, he began to panic. He wondered if this could have an ill effect on her and the development of her baby. He wasn't sure, and he didn't want to find out, so he quickly went down to pull her up.

With haste, Alex wrapped his arms around her waist and lifted her out of the water.

As she surfaced, she gasped loudly for air, choking in the process.

He held her, "Geeze, Serene! Are you trying to kill yourself?"

After she had caught her breath, she smiled and put her hands up in triumph.

"I won!" she screamed and her smile couldn't have been bigger. She had a contagious smile and he was happy for her. "Now I get to do what I want."

"Hm Maybe..." he said calmly, standing in front of her.

"No maybe!" She poked at his chest. "A bet's a bet."

He smiled. "You got lucky. I was going to have you clean the house every day in a tight maid's outfit." His voice was almost flirty.

Serene giggled.

She then looked down and realized that his hands were on her hips. Her face turned red, and she took a step back but Alex gently brought her back to him, pulling her to him by her waist.

Serene covered her chest with her arms and kept her gaze low. Her heart was racing. She didn't fear Alex, but it had been a while since he'd touched her.

The way she looked right now, tested Alex. Looking down at her, he tried to pull away but couldn't let her go. *I should never have touched you*, he thought, but now, it was too late. He craved her comfort, her skin against his, if only for a moment. Alex held his head low, next to hers. His hug gentle but binding. Without thinking he kissed her shoulder, holding his lips against her wet skin for a moment.

They both closed their eyes and individually fought with themselves to find a way to stop where this was going, but neither of them wanted to move away. After what felt like an eternity, Serene finally spoke.

"I'm... going to... go inside now," she whispered.

"Okay." he whispered back.

She waited for him to release her, but he didn't. He kept his head down and his hands behind her waist. Serene pulled back, staring up at his eyes, made a bright blue because of the pool's reflection. He veered his eyes towards her lips since he had desperately wanted to kiss her for weeks. He felt that if he kissed her once, just once, that he would satisfy that curiosity and never kiss her again. It was an excuse he kept telling himself, but knew it wasn't true. The moment he kissed her he knew it would lead to more. Still, to allow himself this moment of bliss, he convinced himself that he would kiss her, apologize, and then promise to never repeat his actions. He just desperately needed this one, single, individual kiss.

His chest rose and fell as his breath quickened. He lowered his head down to hover his mouth right above hers. She pulled her head back and was about to speak but just as her lips parted; he kissed her.

Serene closed her eyes and didn't fight as he made his way inside. Their kiss was slow and intimate. He wanted to remember everything about the kiss, how she tasted, how she trembled nervously, and how her lips and tongue felt as they gently caressed his.

His mind was consumed with thoughts of finally having her to himself. He became aroused and ready as he allowed himself to yearn for her. He pulled her in as close as he could, embracing her as if they would be parted again by fate.

Serene surrendered to his kiss and wrapped both arms around his neck. She had missed him and for a while thought he no longer wanted her. She was wrong.

Alex knew these actions were leading them into dangerous territory. His thoughts were flooded with having her, right here in the pool. He wanted to allow himself to abandon all reason and lose himself in this moment of spontaneous carelessness. He remembered all the years of frustration while dating her and dreaming of the day he would finally make her his. However, this time, there was no one around, and he was the only person holding himself back.

Despite hoping it wouldn't happen, the kiss intensified his feelings for her and he was helpless to stop it. He wanted to touch her, see her, to finally see what she looked like topless, but the voice inside of him warned him about the consequences. The two women he'd slept with in college were methodically planned encounters, chosen knowing he felt nothing for them. They were mindless sex and nothing more. He had never let himself get lost in a moment of carelessness, but this was Serene, his childhood girlfriend, and he was blindsided by her.

Ignoring the nagging voice in his head, he untied the front of her top. When she realized what he'd done, her eyes immediately opened and she tried to look down but he continued kissing her, forcing her to focus on their kiss as he brought up his hand up to caress her naked breast.

Memories of Tristan rushed through her mind and she clearly heard his voice say, *Stop. You're mine!*

"Stop!" she screamed, and he pulled away.

Alex was taken aback by how loud her scream had been.

Serene held her bathing suit top against her body with both her hands then quickly walked over to grab her towel.

"Serene," Alex called out, but she got out of the pool and ran inside.

Alex stood in the pool, regretting what he'd done. He felt foolish and reckless for acting before weighing out the consequences. He wanted to run after her and apologize, but he needed a moment for his arousal to settle.

Once inside her room, Serene went into the bathroom to shower. She didn't know why, but she felt guilty for what had just happened. She didn't want Alex to think badly of her, and at that very moment, she made a promise to herself to *never* wear anything like that again for as long as she lived with him.

Serene, now freshly showered, put on an over-sized black turtleneck shirt and black stretch pants.

Sitting in bed Serene worried that things between them would be awkward now. She felt embarrassed, easy, and unsure of herself, something she realized she had never felt with Tristan. Tristan made her feel beautiful, clean, and comfortable in her own skin whenever he touched her, and suddenly she deeply missed him. Or at least the version of him before he became a monster.

Those two weeks with him had been the only time she had ever truly felt free, and Serene longed to feel that way again. Yet Tristan was her past; it was a lost moment in time of intense passion and complete abandonment of everything that she felt she stood for.

But what exactly did those letters say? she wondered. *Is it possible they explain why he attacked me? Was there a valid explanation for everything? I'm not crazy. I know what I saw, but what does it all mean?*

She sat with her eyes closed going over all the details of both attacks, something she had avoided for weeks. It was easier on her psyche to avoid and forget, but now she had grown the courage to relive those moments.

That woman... she attacked him, then something happened to his body. He was... changing and in a lot of pain.

She cringed as she remembered his tearful face and the blood and teeth that dripped from his mouth.

Then he attacked me. But why? There was anger, and desperation in his eyes, but when he loosened his grip, softness and sadness... as if he was able to recognize me again.

But, in my bedroom, Tristan had red eyes, before they were yellow. Why had they changed?... and his hair was longer and thinner than before... He also didn't smell the same. Tristan always smelled like Sandalwood, Juniper, smoke and soap.

A vision came back to her. The only time a part of his body had hit the moonlight in her bedroom. "He had no tattoos on his arm," Her eyes sprung open. "That wasn't Tristan." She flinched, startled by a knock on her door.

"Yes?" she yelled, frightened.

"Serene, can we talk?"

She wanted to be alone to figure this out some more, but knew it was best for them to tackle the issue quickly, to eliminate any awkwardness.

She opened the door and sat in bed again.

"Glad to see… you're all dressed up," he arched an eyebrow at her choice of attire.

"Yes. Hey, I'm sorry. I didn't know you would be home so soon. If I had known I wouldn't have worn–"

"No, it's fine." He said confused as to why she's the one apologizing. "You did nothing wrong."

"I feel I did. I just don't want things to be awkward now. Let's just pretend this never happened. Please?" Her glossy eyes looked up at his.

Alex sat on the corner of the bed feeling downhearted. He had come in to have a very different conversation. He had meant to apologize to her, but also to tell her he was developing romantic feelings towards her again. He also wanted to reveal to her what had happened when she went missing. But a question entered his mind, and he had to know the answer.

"Serene, why did you scream like that?"

"What do you mean?"

"In the pool, you looked terrified. Did you think I was going to—?"

"No, I… I don't know why I screamed," she nervously rubbed the tip of her index finger.

He laughed softly, but it was out of sadness. She shouldn't have felt fear. Nervousness, embarrassment, even bashfulness would've been the appropriate response, but not fear.

"There is no reason to fear me, Serene. You know I have always respected you." It was obvious now that Serene had been severely damaged.

"I know. I'm sorry," she whispered. "I didn't mean to react that way."

In the pool, when Alex touched her, Serene realized she no longer saw Alex the way she used to. She used to dream about being Alexander Eldridge's wife. He was handsome, smart, rich, but now she had matured, and she didn't always like how she felt when she was around him. She wondered if they would argue more than they would enjoy their time together. And yet, when he wasn't being controlling or overly serious, he was kind, gentle and she wanted to melt in the safety of his arms.

She watched him nervously play with her blanket.

"You used to not be so…" He sighed. Serene, never feared his touch. In fact, she used to yearn for it, beg even. "Anyway, I'm the one who's sorry," He got up to leave the room. "I was in a bad head space today. It won't happen again. Please, don't feel awkward around me. We'll just act like it never happened."

She nodded and sat quietly as he walked away.

Alex stood right outside her door and placed the back of his head against it. Once again, he was frustrated that he couldn't say what was on his mind. He struggled to admit that when he saw her that day in the hospital, looking her best, he'd instantly fallen in love with her all over again.

TWENTY-TWO

THE CEREMONY

It was dark out, and Tristan was blindfolded inside Jason's red truck. They pulled up to a bar located outside the city. It was almost closing time, and Jason could see a few people inside, one of which was their carefully selected victim.

After Jason made sure no attractive females were around or visible inside the bar, he instructed Tristan to remove his blindfold. The windows were up but their sense of smell was so acute they could almost taste the humans nearby. Tristan took a deep breath.

"Smells like thanksgiving doesn't it?" Jason pointed out.

"I smell a female." Tristan's eyes wildly searched the area.

"I've been to this bar plenty of times. Trust me when I say you've nothing to worry about."

Tristan grabbed the thick folder that was lying in between them on the seat.

"So, this is your grocery list for the month?" Tristan made light of the situation.

"More like *our* grocery list for the next two weeks."

Tristan opened the folder. Inside were criminal background checks and details on potential prey, as well as photos. He looked at the picture of the man they were planning to take.

"Randal Jessie Jefferson," Tristan said as he continued reading.

"It looks like he just roughed up a few people. Hardly justifies us killing him."

Jason laughed. "You'll soon learn that sometimes you just want an easy meal. We Goldens do our best to avoid killing innocent people, but when you have strict precincts and you need to eat, you become less picky. It's better than losing control and killing a hard-working Mother of two or a nun for instance." Jason lowered his window and lit a cigarette, then continued. "By the way, if you continue reading, you'll see that in the list of people he assaulted, one of them was his daughter, and two of them were his ex-wives. His recent partner also went missing."

"Doesn't mean he killed her."

"True."

They were silent for a moment and a few people left the bar. After several minutes, Tristan asked him a question that had been on his mind for a while.

"You said, when I first started training, that whether we become a Red eye or a Golden eye has everything to do with our *soul*? What does that mean exactly?"

"Well, are you a spiritual person?"

"No. I think it's absolutely absurd to believe in something that you can't prove exists."

"Hmm," Jason sat pensive. "Well, I believe contrary forces are necessary for the universe to maintain balance." Jason took another drag of his cigarette then continued. "Light and darkness, positive protons, negative electrons, predator and prey, and the battle against good and evil—things cannot exist or maintain balance without the other. There is no shadow without light. Tell me, have you ever met anyone who you knew was downright evil?"

"I think there is good and evil in everybody. You can't label them as one or the other," Tristan said preparing to disagree with all of his theories.

"Yes. But, most of the time, the scales tip. Maribel and Serene, you talk about them a lot. Tell me, did you see evil in them?"

Tristan thought about it for a moment, and in the past, he was never able to find anything but selflessness and good in his mother. Serene also had a kind disposition.

"So, you're saying if my mother or Serene were Krovs, they'd be a Golden? A rare Golden?"

"From what you tell me, it's very likely."

Tristan laughed at Jason's theory. "Well, I hate to break it to you, but I am living proof your theory is completely and utterly flawed."

"You think you're evil?"

"I think I'm a lousy person, yes. I mean, look at me," Tristan waved over his body. "There is nothing good about who I am or what I've done. I'm an atheist; I wasn't as good to my mother as I should have been. I was a drug addict. Heck, I even sold drugs to underage kids when I was hard on money, got caught, and went to jail. I hurt various women who cared about me, I failed Serene, slept with Lea recently and all of that is just the tip of the iceberg."

"You slept with Lea?" Jason held back a smile and it infuriated Tristan.

"Serene was worth waiting for. My need to go find her became too much, and I knew if I went, I'd kill her. I became impatient, and there's just no excuse for that. So, again, your theory is flawed."

"Tristan, these aren't typical circumstances! There's also nothing in what you just told me that makes you a bad person. So what? You've made mistakes! We've *all* made mistakes. I've done my share too! What matters are your intentions, your need to make things right, and whether or not you felt remorse. What eventually makes you a good person is learning from your mistakes, and your subconscious innate desire to be a better person."

Tristan shook his head.

Jason sighed, and after a moment he spoke again. "Cheryl… Her name was Cheryl. We were… in love, engaged. I thought I was ready. I waited four weeks; we had made wedding plans. I couldn't make her believe I had just left her. Back then, here in the states, there weren't many trainers. I went to her, everything was okay for a moment, until it wasn't."

"What happened?"

"I hurt her…" Jason became emotional. "That's… all I will say on the matter. The guilt consumes me every day, and it's a cross I must bear. You haven't failed Serene Tristan… not yet. For you at least, there's hope."

Tristan studied Jason's sorrowful expression, trying to gauge what had happened. Had he raped her? Wounded her? Was it possible Jason murdered the love of his life? The thought terrified him.

Their victim stepped out of the bar.

Jason turned on the car. "Ready?"

Tristan motioned to Jason with his hand, waving him onward.

It took Tristan eight weeks to fully control his urges, which was sooner than anyone had expected. Late at night, Lea was preparing to take him into the city for a ceremonial welcoming party. It would be his first time going back into the city and he was nervous.

Tristan sat on the bed putting on his boots. Lea sat next to him.

"Are you sure you're ready for this?" she asked softly. "This usually isn't done until the fourth month."

"I think I'll be fine." He then stopped what he was doing. "I ate plenty tonight, I'm stuffed. It shouldn't be too hard."

There was a knock at the door and Lea got up to open it. Lea had invited a few of her friends to help escort Tristan into town. Kamilla, naturally, invited herself. They told Tristan no one would wear their contacts that night, and he came out of his room to greet them.

At the door was Kamilla and two other Red-eyed Krov women. He knew them all, because he'd dated them before.

Saya was a proud looking, short pixie-like African American female with red eyes. She was into steam punk and the side of her head was shaved.

Kira was an attractive, voluptuous, red-headed pale woman, and she was also a Red.

"He's a Golden? You're kidding, right?" Saya said to Lea in shock.

"Yup! Surprise!" Lea held her hands up.

"Guessing Lea nor Kamilla told anyone." He said hugging Saya and staring at Kamilla.

"Well, well, well. It's nice to finally see you again, Trist." Kira studied him from head to toe. "You're looking good."

That relationship didn't end well, so he quickly changed the subject, "What are the chains for?"

Kira was holding four chains that were attached to a steel belt. It looked like an instrument intended for bondage.

Lea explained, "So, all four of us will be attached to you. It's only a precautionary measure since your only two months into training." Saya placed the steel belt around his waist and under his shirt. Each side of the belt had two chains that led to their own cuff. Saya then cuffed herself to him and Kira followed. Kamilla walked up to Tristan and greeted him with a tap-kiss, then cuffed herself.

Tristan walked up to one of his clubs leading the four beautiful women attached to him. He understood why Krovs hid under this kind of lifestyle. What they were displaying didn't seem so out of place here.

Tristan walked past the line of spectators and up to the well-built bald bouncer who was surprised to see him.

"Been a long time Boss. Good to see you," he said nervously and not looking directly at Tristan as he opened the door. "Kamilla," he said acknowledging his manager. She nodded but didn't look at him.

When they walked inside, the mix of industrial rock music was louder than usual, but Tristan had learned how to tune his senses. Some spectators thought nothing of their display; while others watched and stared as Tristan emitted a sense of power and dominance. He also noticed the various attractive women looking at him. Some didn't affect his lust for them, which made him wonder if they were also Krovs but then, he saw a brunette in the crowd.

As if in slow motion she turned and smiled at him, her flowing hair moving graciously through the air.

Tristan stopped and put his head down. His body tightened, his muscles seized, and pain emanated from his bones as he tried to tune out the image he just saw. Placing a hand to his chest he tried to look up again but the chaotic display of human skin was everywhere. His mouth was salivating and he became aroused. He kept his eyes closed as he attempted to stay focused.

"Trist? If we need to leave, just let us know," Kamilla said looking at her nails, acting as if she expected this result.

"We have sedatives. Should we use them now?" Saya said studying Tristan but asking the others.

"Bring him into the closet. I'll take one for the team, Kira winked at him."

"Over my dead body." Kamilla hissed.

"No!" He said breathing hard through his teeth. "No. I'm fine." He was used to being in pain every single day, but this was new. "I'm fine now." He lied, feeling as if his body would explode. He stood up straight and he forcefully regulated his breathing.

"Let's get moving then. The faster we get away from the crowd, the better," Saya insisted. Tristan nodded and flexed his fist as he continued walking, the pain of holding back his impulses was making him angry.

When they reached their destination, a large private event room with crimson walls, there was a gathering of Krovs waiting for them. They were all sitting on red couches and stopped talking as soon as they noticed his presence. This wasn't the type of party Tristan had expected. To him it felt like a dream or an intervention as he saw all his ex-girlfriends and lovers staring at him with bright red eyes.

A few men were also present. It was obvious Krovs only selected fit and attractive candidates.

A woman closed the double doors behind them, which helped muffle the music, but there was a ledge with a window where they could see over and into the club. He focused on the chatter that was happening around him. They all seemed excited that he was turned, but shocked and disappointed that he was a Golden.

"I knew he would be."

"Shut up, no you didn't"

"I would have never guessed."

"Yes, another Golden!" said a rare Golden-eyed female in the back to her Golden-eyed partner.

Kira unchained him from the others, and they removed their cuffs. Kamilla handed him a glass of blood red Champagne and everyone else was holding the same type of drink.

Kamilla greeted a few friends and then turned around to begin her speech.

"So, as you all know, today we welcome Tristan to our clan. He has been our *favorite* trainee for quite some time," A few people laughed, "and a beloved friend, but today we can finally call him family." Everyone clapped and a few of the guys hollered something in the back. They were old high school buddies. "I would also like to announce that we have appointed him a position on the Red Council. I think we could all agree that though he is new, he will do well to represent us." The many voices in the room expressed a sense of confusion.

"But, Kami, he's not a Red," Raven spat.

"Thanks for your perceptive observation, Raven." she mocked, "We are all well aware of that. *However*, this time The Council has voted to make an exception. He will be given the same privileges and feeding ground priorities all Reds enjoy."

Tristan looked over at Kamilla, confused and upset. She hadn't discussed any of this with him, and it became clear that others were upset.

"To Tristan!" Kamilla waited for him to drink. He did, and everyone quickly drank and stood up to clap for him.

Saya came up to them with a small object on a black pillow. It was a sinister-looking crow pin that seemed to be forged in gold and black Damascus metals. There was a circle around the crow, and in place of its eye was a bright red jewel. He looked around and noticed everyone else had on the same pin, but theirs were silver or black with a red or yellow jewel as the eye. Kamilla had on the same type of pin she was now putting on him.

She then whispered to him as she attached it to his jacket, "It's mandatory to wear this during meetings or gatherings, but you can also wear it out if you want other Krovs to know what your status is among them." Kamilla smiled.

"I see there was a purpose to our business ventures," his forehead creased.

"What do you mean?"

"Hell of convenient to have places around town to hold your little gatherings. Was it *ever* about helping me?"

"You own these clubs."

"Do I? Because last I recall I'm a fugitive without a cent to my name." His eyes narrowed.

Abruptly, a woman who was slightly older than the others came up to hug him. "Tristan! So big now."

"Rebecca?" Tristan asked the graceful brunette woman.

"Yes. It's about time," she said in a Russian accent. "I'm the one praised for recruiting you."

And you're still hot, Tristan thought as he studied her. She definitely aged well, and didn't look a day over twenty-five, but attraction felt different now. Krov women didn't excite him, because surely Rebecca would have brought back those feelings. However, he could still appreciate their beauty, and personality was more of a factor, now more than ever.

Rebecca had been his first. He was fourteen and freshman, while she was his friends much older sister. She had also been the first woman to break his heart.

"Well congratulations Tristan, if they didn't keep you, surely we would have rioted." She laughed and joked.

As the night went on, Tristan tried to enjoy himself. After all, they had all gathered to celebrate him. Ever since his mother's death he had kept to himself, but it felt nice to catch up with friends and put aside all the stress and pain he'd been going through. The red champagne they were drinking also helped relax him. It seemed to be different somehow, since he could feel a buzz.

"Matt?" Tristan's eyes widened as soon as he spotted him. Matt was an old friend of his back in high school and he rivaled Tristan's beauty. He had shoulder-length blond hair and used to have blue eyes, but was now a Golden, the only other male Golden in the room. In a room of about forty-five Krovs, Tristan had only spotted four other Goldens.

"Glad they chose to keep you bud." Matt smiled and gave him a half hug.

"Seriously? I could punch you right now! I could take all the girls lying to me, but you?"

"Listen man, I was in the same boat as you until recently. Lea turned me only two years ago so that I had a better chance of being drafted."

"Yeah, I heard you play professionally now," Tristan said, pointing out his football career.

"Yes, I play for Wisconsin as of a month ago."

"Man, this is so weird, but it all makes sense now. Us basically dating the same girls."

"Well, we were part of the same clique in school."

Tristan always wondered how he became part of the most popular and exclusive group in high school. Matt and a few other guy friends even discussed methods they'd used to overcome the chill and pain that came with sex. At times, being part of the group felt like a cult. They were all close and cared for one another but no one was allowed to date outside of the group; if they did, the girls became fiercely jealous.

"So, have you... slept with a human yet?" the corner of Matt's lips curled into a sly grin.

"No. Not yet. Though I've heard it's something."

"It's definitely something all right. Just be careful, it can become an addiction, fast."

Tristan wanted more details. However, he felt it was best if he avoided those conversations.

After talking to more exes than he ever wanted to in one sitting, Tristan sat alone with Lea.

"Well, you look like you're having fun for once."

Tristan's smiled faded. "I'm going to find Serene this week."

"Really? Don't you think you should try to be around other attractive females first."

"That may be more dangerous than meeting up with her."

She laughed at him. "How so?"

Tristan lowered his gaze. To him, none of this was a joke.

"I care about her too much to hurt her. When I first turned and sensed she was pregnant, I stopped. It was painful, but I was able to do it then, I know I can do it now." Lea shook her head. "Just trust me, what I feel for her will help me get through it."

"Are you trying to convince me, or yourself, Trist?... You know I'm not stopping you."

Tristan leaned back on the couch, lost in thought. He wasn't sure he could handle himself, but he wanted to return to her soon, regardless.

Lea watched his mood shift. He'd been happy for only a

moment before reverting back to being reclusive. Even in a room full of Krovs who still wanted him, regardless of the fact that he was no longer a delicious sexy human, he still couldn't get Serene off of his mind.

TWENTY-THREE

THE DATE

It was Serene's first week volunteering at the Children's Angel Hospital, the same hospital Alex worked in.

A friendly girl named Stephanie, with curly brown hair and a Spanish accent, was training her, and they both wore blue jackets to represent their roles as volunteers. Serene learned that staff members would occasionally sneak into a random child's room and cheer them up by emerging from the foot of their bed with a playful puppet show. Regardless of how sad a child was feeling, they always made an effort to make them laugh and it was the highlight of Serene's day.

It was lunch time, and Serene waited patiently for the elevator when a young man stood next to her to do the same. He was very buff, especially next to Serene, and had spiky blond hair. They always seemed to meet up at the elevator at the same time for lunch, but never spoke.

Once inside the elevator they both stood in silence.

She cut the tension and spoke. "Hi."

"Hey"

They stood quietly.

"So… I'm new here."

"So am I." He smiled.

"So, what's—"

"—Surgeon." He cleared his throat. "Surgical resident."

"Cool… I meant to ask, *what's your name?*"

"Oh. Chris," he said, finally smiling.

"Serene."

Chris nodded, and the elevator opened. They stepped out.

When they reached their destination, they both got their food, and he went to sit with his friends as usual.

Serene sat alone.

After a few minutes he walked over to her with his slice of carrot cake.

"Mind if I sit?"

"You're good," Serene said smiling, and he sat across from her.

"So. You said you were new in town. Right?"

"Yup." She perked up.

"I was wondering… If you were free… would you perhaps like to—?"

"I'd love to."

He smiled. "I wasn't finished asking, but thanks. I was just trying to think of something more original than dinner and a movie."

Serene looked out the window. She had won the bet, and other than eating and drinking what she wanted she wasn't exactly taking full advantage of her free week.

"You know what I'd *really* like to do… Chris?"

He lifted an eyebrow.

"I'd like to go dancing. You know… actual dancing." She locked his gaze and pointed her fork at him. "Like in the movie Dirty Dancing."

Chris almost laughed but then noticed her awkward seriousness.

"Okay?" He cleared his throat. "Sure. I'll… see what I can do."

She gave him a smile that lasted only a second then continued eating.

It was Saturday morning.

Alex had lost the bet, and ever since then Serene continued to annoy him with her new-found freedom. She wore what she wanted when she wanted, and ate what she pleased. Last night she had even gone out with Stephanie to a birthday party and didn't make it back home until after midnight.

Alex had stayed up waiting for her, and ever since that argument their relationship felt strained and awkward.

Serene went into the kitchen where he was, and made herself an exaggerated amount of coffee. She was using the biggest cup she could find, and she grabbed a hidden pastry from her secret stash in the cupboard.

In contrast, Alex was making himself a vegetable smoothie, and from the corner of his eye he saw her pull out junk food from the cupboard.

"I really wish you wouldn't do that." Alex called out to her as he poured his green slush into a cup.

"Oh, that reminds me." She balanced her coffee and pastry in her arms and grabbed a chocolate bar from her stash.

He knew she was doing this to annoy him.

Furrow browed he walked up to her, and she sipped her coffee loudly on purpose.

"As of tomorrow, our deal is over. No more coffee, no more junk food, no more coming home after midnight, and I will personally be making sure you take your vitamins every day." Never losing eye contact he pulled out a vitamin bottle from the cupboard and slammed it on the counter next to her.

Serene got in his face as if she was about to say something but instead took a large, exaggerated, ungraceful bite of her pastry and walked away.

M. LEE WOE

Alex squeezed the bottle but then took a deep breath and put it away calmly. It was only one more day, he could deal.

Unbeknownst to him, the coffee was decaf now and she had a bottle of pre-natal vitamins in her bathroom that she took religiously. However, annoying Alex was just too much fun, and perhaps there was still some grudge left after all.

Later that night, Serene got ready for her date with Chris. Yesterday at the birthday party, he informed her that he'd set up professional dance lessons for them! Serene was excited. She wasn't extremely interested in Chris, but he was nice and Alex never took her anywhere.

Serene felt some guilt about angering Alex further. He was still unaware of their plans, but she promised herself she would be home before midnight and text him from Chris's phone all night so that he wouldn't worry. Well, not too much at least.

She took a shower and did her hair, choosing to wear a red sleeveless dress, dark thigh-high stockings and black high heels. A lot of her secret attire was bought with the help of Casey and their secret on-line shopping.

She gazed at herself in the mirror with pride.

Even though she looked irresistible, and slightly inappropriate, she wasn't trying to look provocative. Serene was just trying desperately to have fun. She was never allowed to play dress up or experiment so, she overcompensated, choosing to also wear dark make-up and bright red lipstick. It was her last night being allowed to do whatever she wanted, so she thought *why not?* it was likely she wouldn't have this opportunity again.

Serene had given Chris the gate code. She had asked him yesterday to call the main phone when he arrived and wait for her to come outside.

Unfortunately, he didn't. Chris came up to the door and rang the bell.

When she heard the doorbell, she quickly grabbed her purse and ran downstairs, trying desperately to get to the door before Alex could. But by the time she reached the stairs, it was too late.

As he opened the door, Alex was surprised to see a well-dressed, buff blond man standing there. "Can I help you? Wait how did you get past the gate?"

"Um, I'm here to see Serene?"

"Ummm," Alex mocked him. "I think you have the *wrong* house. Try next door." He then rudely and loudly slammed the door on him.

Serene ran down and tried repeatedly to open the door but Alex stopped her each time.

"Are you insane?" he said, as he pressed a hand against the door keeping it closed. "Wait. What the *hell* are you wearing?"

"Alex, stop! He's a nice guy!"

"Nice guy? Are you *crazy*? That guy will break you! He looks like he can take on both of us!"

Desperate to think of something Serene bit his arm. Alex screamed, removing his hand from the door.

Serene quickly opened it.

"Chris!" she yelled, waving wildly. Chris saw her just as he was getting in his car. Alex grabbed her and pulled her back inside.

"We just moved here! There is no way you know this guy. He could be a murderer or *worse!*" Alex's face flushed.

Serene lifted an eyebrow, wondering exactly what was worse than a murder?

This was the final straw. Alex had dealt with her little annoyances all week. He understood her thirst for freedom, but he felt this was too much. He would not gamble her safety with a stranger the size of a bear!

"Well, he did tell me he enjoys cutting people open," she joked. Alex's eyes widened. "Relax!" she laughed. "He's a surgeon at the hospital. That's where I met him. Here, ask him." Serene fully opened the door and motioned at Chris to come in and he did.

Alex put on a calm and collected face, and they all stood in a triangle, but no one spoke a word.

Serene saw them staring at each other and broke the tension.

"Ahem. Chris, this is my *brother*, Alex. Remember I told you about him? He's a bit of an over-protective jerk." Serene's eyes pierced right through Alex.

He looked at her with equal scorn but did his best to hold back his anger. Chris extended his hand to greet him, but Alex ignored his declaration of peace and began asking questions.

"So, you're a surgeon?"

"Yes. She told me you're a Resident Physician there? I haven't seen you around."

"Funny. I haven't seen *you* around either," Alex glanced over at Serene.

There was an awkward silence.

"But you know Doctor Edwards, right?" Serene asked Chris. "That's who Alex is working with."

"Ah yes. Troy Edwards. I hear he's a bit of a stiff," Chris pointed out.

"A stiff?" Alex asked.

Chris continued, "Yea, he's very hard on the interns, quizzing them on things they obviously wouldn't know yet. But he's the best at what he does, so I guess he's worth learning from."

From that information alone, Alex realized that Chris probably did work at the hospital, but that didn't mean anything. He still didn't know him.

"Alrighty. Well I'll see you later, Alex." Serene took one step before Alex quickly grabbed her by the arm and looked at Chris.

"It was nice meeting you Chris, but Serene can't go out tonight."

"Yes. I. can," she said through her teeth at Alex.

"No. You. can't," Alex said through his teeth right back at her.

She managed to release herself from his grip, but he circled her waist from behind with his arms. Chris raised an eyebrow as he watched the two of them argue.

"Maybe I should go?" Chris asked, not wanting to cause any trouble.

"No! I'm going!" Serene fought Alex's grip on her. "Just... give me one second." She turned around in Alex's arms and looked up at him. They were so close she could almost kiss him. "Let me go, Alex, or I swear I will bite you again," she whispered, but Alex ignored her and spoke to Chris.

"I bet she didn't tell you she was pregnant, right? Cuz she is. She's what..." Alex looked down at her. "Two months pregnant now?" Chris glared at the two of them completely baffled.

"Stop it, Alex!" She cried out.

"Um, no she did not," Chris said squinting his eyes.

"Tell him Serene... Or are you going to deny the *innocent little being inside of you*," he said, changing his voice to further irritate her.

"Hold on, Chris. I am pregnant... but... Alex he's... he's insane," Serene said out of breath from struggling and barely able to speak.

"By the way, Chris, the baby's mine. So no, you can't take Serene out because, because..." Alex pretended to cry hysterically, "because I'm in love with my baby sister!"

Chris's eyes widened, bewildered by what was happening. He didn't want to take part in whatever was going on with this family.

"I'm going to go now Serene. Sorry." Chris stormed out.

"No, hold on. Chris!" Serene screamed still in Alex's arms.

"Ugh! Damnit, Alex! I won the bet!" her body was shaking in anger.

"I don't care. The bet's over!"

She continued to fight him off, but he didn't release her until he heard the car leave. Once he knew it was safe, he let go.

Serene's face was red with fury. "What the hell is wrong with you Alexander? That's enough! I'm leaving! I'm calling dad!" she yelled as she made her way to the house phone.

"And what exactly are you going to tell them anyways? That you dressed up all sultry-like and I stopped you from getting hurt again. Oh, *please do*!"

Ignoring him, she dialed her parents' number. Serene was done with Alex. She was going to go back home immediately!

TWENTY-FOUR

THE CHURCH

On a Sunday afternoon, after a large meal, Tristan left to go find Serene. He only had Kamilla's credit card, but he had pulled out daily cash advances until he could purchase a used black Honda. He needed a vehicle to consistently see Serene.

Tristan arrived at a Light sector border, where his car was checked for weapons and contraband. It was an annoying step that bothered Tristan so much he rarely left the city. Kamilla had given him a fake ID with a picture of his new look. To be safe, he'd cut his hair a bit shorter and wore blue contacts. There was still a chance he could be caught, but as a Krov he could fight his way through if he had to.

"You're clear," the officer said after inspecting his license and the vehicle. Tristan drove through.

Having lived in the dark and damp city his whole life, the fake cookie cutter homes, flourishing gardens and bright pastel colors bothered his eyes. After about an hour he reached Serene's community. Most houses had white picket fences like Serene's home did.

He rang the doorbell and stood squinting and fidgeting with his jacket and hair. He was nervous but well fed and was confident he wouldn't hurt her.

He stood waiting, reciting things he wanted to say to her in his head.

He was first going to apologize profusely for all the pain he caused, and then he would explain everything to her. Every last detail. Even if it was against Krov law to reveal it. He was more worried about Serene being mad at him for attacking her, and for being gone so long.

Tristan knocked on the door a third time and concluded that either no one was home, or they were ignoring him. A neighbor who was watering his garden, called out to him.

"They aren't home!"

"Excuse me?" Tristan said and they both got closer to each other. Tristan didn't need to get closer to hear him, but wanted to speak to him.

"It's Sunday. They are at the church right now." The gentlemen in a pink sweater informed him.

"Do you know what time they'll be back?"

"Late. They're usually there all day."

Tristan asked him for directions to the church and left.

Walking up to the tall white church felt odd for Tristan. This kind of clean and bright atmosphere just didn't feel natural. He walked inside and found himself in a long hallway. To his left he saw an open door where everyone in the chapel appeared to be in assembly.

When he walked in several faces in the sea of people turned to look at him. His attire and demeanor brought unwanted attention. He wore all black while everyone was wearing white. Apparently, there was a dress code.

He sat at the very back of the church. A few teenage girls giggled amongst themselves as they looked back to study him. He took off his studded jacket hoping it would help. Unfortunately, his fitted white T-shirt exposed his defined and tattooed biceps and he was now inadvertently entertaining them.

"Not better," he whispered.

Ignoring them he tried to spot Serene and saw a girl who he believed was her. He thought it was best to wait until the assembly was over.

After a final prayer, the crowd began leaving the building, most of whom looked at him in a judgmental manner, especially the older ones. But a lot of the younger women smiled at him flirtatiously.

His heart began to race when he saw Serene. She stood up and he made his way through the crowd towards her. The feeling growing inside of him was worse than anticipated. The right thing to do was to wait until she walked past him, but something was driving him towards her. Memories of her flashed through his mind, causing him intense migraine-like pain. The stabbing feeling in his chest and brain became so great that he had to stop to catch his breath and close his eyes. He gently held onto the corner of a pew, trying to control himself but he was nearly crushing the wood with his hands.

She began to walk towards him, but he didn't look directly at her.

Just then, as if by reflex, he grabbed her wrist. They both stood still for a moment as he built up the courage to look at her. *Please God, don't let me kill her.*

"Ow!" she screamed while he was lost in his own pain.

She was angry and shook her hand trying to release his crushing grip on her.

Once he looked up at her, he let her go and ran outside to catch his breath. He bent over in pain, the veins on his arms and neck were strained and he placed his hand over his chest, trying desperately to relieve the tension.

"That wasn't Serene." He closed his eyes and forced himself to relax.

After his heart no longer felt like it was leaping from his chest, he scanned the crowd. There were tens of women all with similar hair and wearing white dresses. Finding her would be tougher that he thought.

An old woman walked past him, and he placed a hand on her shoulder as gently as you would touch a butterfly.

"Excuse me. Would you happen to know of a girl named Serene? She has long golden-brown hair, hazel eyes—"

"Yes, we all know Serene. Why?"

"I really need to talk to her. Would you happen to know where she might be?" he asked her kindly.

"We haven't seen her for a while… but ask Peter."

"Peter?"

"Serene is Pastor Brook's daughter." The lady pointed to a man near the door wearing a white suit and standing next to him was a very snobbish blonde lady. They were shaking hands as people were leaving.

The old lady walked away.

"You've got to be *fucking* kidding me," Tristan whispered, upset that Serene never once mentioned her father was a Light sector minister. "Well, this explains everything."

Tristan looked down at his attire. If he'd known what her parents did for a living, he would have worn something more appropriate than the dark jeans, jewelry, and the printed black T-shirt he usually wore.

After Tristan took a moment to absorb what he was up against, he decided to introduce himself.

Peter and Clair's eyes widened when he approached them, but tried to look indifferent as they shook his hand and welcomed him to the church.

"Welcome son. May the light of God shine upon you." Peter said.

"Thank you."

"You must be new here."

"Yes. Actually, I was wondering if you could tell me where Serene is."

"Serene?" Peter looked over at his wife then back at Tristan. "Do you know her?"

"Yes actually. I was, am... I'm her boyfriend." He immediately regretted his words and wished he would have said 'friend' instead.

Clair grabbed Peters' arm. "I'm sorry we didn't catch your name?"

"Tristan."

Clair's jaw dropped.

Serene's father's face became red with anger. Clair kept her cool and walked away. Once she was behind a post, she pulled out her cell phone, and dialed the police. Tristan noticed what she was doing and knew it was time to explain himself.

"Listen, I know Serene was hurt. It was an acci—"

"You have *some* nerve showing up here after what you did!" Peter said outraged.

"Sir. I promise you it was all an accident. I can explain—"

"If you even think about going near my daughter again, I swear I—!" Peter yelled in outrage but then placed a hand on his chest as the stress of finally facing his daughter's attacker caused his chest to tighten.

As he fell to the floor, bystanders and Clair rushed to his aid.

Tristan immediately vanished.

Tristan drove a safe distance away before frustration overtook him. He lifted his hand to hit his steering wheel but stopped himself, knowing it would shatter into a million pieces if he did.

"Argh! Damnit!" He jerked his cellphone from his pocket and dialed Lea's number.

"Hello?" Lea answered.

"Lea, I need you to come to me now."

"What? Why? What happened?"

"I'm not sure. Serene's parents fucking hate me! They know I'm the one who attacked her. I also think her father just had a heart attack. I need you to find out if he's okay and bring Serene to me."

"Okay where?"

"I'll text you the address. Listen, I passed a park on my way here. I'll text you that address too. Find Serene and bring her to me."

Tristan paced at the park for over two hours when his phone finally rang.

Fucking finally Lea, "Yeah."

"Her father is okay. An ambulance was called but he wasn't taken. I followed them to their house, but I don't see Serene with them. I even snuck a peek inside through the windows, but it's just them. I'd go up and ask them about her, but I don't think it's smart after what just happened."

"No. Don't do that just—" Tristan sat on a bench and put the phone to his forehead nearly crushing it. "Just… go home. We'll try something later."

He hung up.

I can't take this anymore. His hands became fists as his frustration and need for her grew. *She's not replying to the e-mails. I have no other way of contacting her, and she's not with family!*

Where the fuck is she!

Annoyed that nothing hard enough was nearby, he forcefully punched the concrete sidewalk underneath him.

A strong gust of air hit his body.

The mind-numbing sound temporarily left him deaf.

Car alarms began going off in the distance and a cloud of dust and debris surrounded him.

When the dust settled, he looked down and realized there was a twenty-foot sized crater beneath him.

He looked at his hand. Not a single scratch was visible. His eyes studied his surroundings. All around and above him were pieces of rubble in all shapes and sizes suspended in mid-air. When he closed his eyes, they finally came crashing down around him.

He climbed out of the crater and walked away. A few bystanders looked at him with their jaws dropped or their hands over their mouths.

Tristan had fought Jason's insistence.

Jason spent hours training him to levitate blades of grass, convinced that there was something special about him. When Tristan learned to levitate grass, Tristan thought it was nothing major. But Jason explained that it had taken him decades to learn levitation. In only weeks Tristan's control of his powers increased, and eventually Jason's theories were confirmed.

Tristan was an Alpha.

TWENTY-FIVE

THE PICTURES

The Day Before (Saturday)

Serene struggled with the phone.

Alex and her had just argued about her going on a date with Chris and she was calling her father to tell him she was coming home.

"And what exactly are you going to tell them anyways?" Alex yelled. "That you dressed up all the sultry-like and I stopped you from getting hurt again. Oh, *please do*!"

Ignoring him, she held the phone to her ear as it rang.

Alex secretly pulled out his cell phone and snapped a few pictures of her and her skimpy outfit as proof, should any questions arise. Her dress was so low it was nearly falling off her, and her hair and make-up was messy from having just wrestled out of his arms.

Serene's eyes widened when she noticed what he was doing.

Leaving the phone off the hook she ran after him, taking off her high heels in the process.

"Give me the phone, Alex!"

"No."

"I am not kidding. I will kill you unless you give me that phone right now!"

Alex ignored her and continued walking into the living room.

"ALEX!" She screamed trying to sound as threatening as possible, but Alex calmly put the phone in his pocket and sat in his favorite chair.

Desperate, Serene kneeled on the floor in front of him. "Okay. If you want me to say, I'm sorry, I will... I'm sorry, okay!"

He was emotionless as he grabbed the laptop from the table next to him and opened it.

"I've been a pain, and—and I've been disrespectful but please. I'm asking as your friend, delete the pictures."

Alex didn't flinch.

"Ugh! I swear if you don't delete them right now, I will hate you forever!"

He smiled inwardly; he felt he was great at this game because there was nothing she could do or say that would faze him. More than likely he wouldn't show her parents the pictures. He hated seeing her in trouble with them, but she had been annoying him all week and this was payback.

Controlling her antics would also be a breeze now that he had leverage.

After a few minutes, Serene was still on the floor groveling at his feet.

Alex rolled his eyes, "Serene, just stop it already! I am never giving you the phone. You should've known better. You can't just go out with men you barely know! You *know* a mentally deranged man is after you, and yet you don't even seem to care! It's mind-boggling!"

He closed the laptop to look down at her. "If you don't care about yourself, at least have the decency to care about me. If something happened to you, it would be *my* head! I made Peter and Clair a promise to keep you safe. A promise that I have regretted every single day since then. So, no, I'm not giving you the phone. And the next time you pull a stunt like that, I'm posting them online. End of story."

"Oh, whatever, Alex." she replied with scorn and stood up.

"Stop pretending to be this old grumpy man around me. I see right through it. Your twenty-four! I know you had a lot of fun partying in college, getting drunk, and going home with random girls! And now that you've had your fun, you won't let anyone else do it—"

"You think I partied? Do you seriously think I would have graduated as fast as I did, with the GPA I finished with, if I was off getting drunk every night?" He pointed towards the window. "I'm *sorry* that I act like a grumpy old man just because I'm focused on my career and my future. I wish for the sake of your child, you'd do the same!"

"Oh my god, stop lying!" she rolled her eyes, "I saw the pictures!"

"What pictures?"

"Tom's page!" Serene said, referring to the social media page his pictures had shown up on. "Spring break."

"Tom Wilcox?" He rubbed his forehead, "Serene, that was a rare occasion."

"See! You admit it! While I was basically stuck in a convent that dared to call themselves a college, you were out having fun, drinking, partying and... Ugh! You're such a hypocrite, I hate you!" Serene plopped herself on the couch with her arms crossed.

Alex looked over at her, feeling remorse. He had no idea that Serene knew Tom or followed him on social media. He sighed dejectedly. "I'm sorry I didn't know you—"

Serene rudely turned on the TV and put up the volume.

He glanced over wishing she would go up and change her attire, but he knew she wouldn't, simply because it was what he wanted her to do.

As she watched TV, Serene was thinking of ways to beat him at his game. She knew as long as he had those pictures, he'd constantly threaten her with them. She could wait until he fell asleep and then steal his phone. But, knowing Alex, his phone had a password and he would likely transfer the pictures somewhere on his laptop before

289

the night was over.

Alex was smart, but he could be beaten. It was apparent whenever they played chess.

Suddenly, she had an idea. It was going to be awkward, but it was probably the only way.

She went to the bathroom and fixed her hair and make-up. She stared in the mirror, pumping herself up while she conversed with herself.

Okay girl you can do this. Ugh, there has got to be another way. She said slamming her hand on the counter. *Just do it well and do it now. He's probably transferring the pictures right now!*

Serene rushed into the living room and was glad he was still working on his laptop. She took a deep breath and gathered herself before she approached him.

"Alex?" She whispered sweetly while looking down and playing with her hands. "I'm honestly sorry for how I've been lately."

When he didn't respond, she took a step forward and ran a finger up the arm chair. "Can I make it up to you?" She bent over to kiss his cheek softly, holding her lips against his warm skin long enough to give him the hint.

"Serene, I know what you're doing," he said harshly as he continued to do work on his laptop. "You're trying to get your phone back."

"And yet, you're not stopping me..." Serene unbuttoned his shirt just enough to slide her hand in. His chest was smooth and warm. Alex closed his laptop and sighed, looking up at her through narrow, serious blue eyes.

She bit her bottom lip. "I know why what I do makes you so mad."

He thought he'd made it clear why her antics upset him, but he was curious. "Why do I get mad Serene?"

She locked his gaze, "Because... you want me." He looked away and tried to act unaffected. She then whispered in his ear,

"Because… you still think about me. About our kiss… I'll tell you a secret. I think about it too."

Alex knew she was acting, but her words reluctantly brought a chill up his spine. "Serene…" He tried to find words to stop this but couldn't get himself to. She placed her hand under his chin forcing him to look up at her.

Her eyes looked straight into his soul. His deep blue serious eyes melted. They were soft, partly closed, and yearning. He looked at her lips as she slowly bent down to kiss him.

His mind fought his feelings for her, but her kiss was no match for him. He closed his eyes and was surprised at the way she teased his lips, biting and sucking them individually. He'd never known her to kiss that way. Tired of her teasing, he dug his hands into her hair pushing her towards him allowing him to slip his warm tongue into her mouth. The way she circled his tongue, bit and teased made it obvious that she was trying to arouse him.

When did she learn this? He wondered, entranced by her seduction, but he wasn't going to let her win so easily. Those pictures were worth more than a kiss, and the price of her annoyance lately was steep.

As they kissed, he put one hand over his pocket to protect the phone and placed the laptop on the table with the other. She noticed that regardless of how passionate their kiss was, he was still guarding his pocket. Distracting Alex wasn't going to be easy.

Putting both hands on the chair's arms, she carefully straddled him. As she had hoped, he moved his arms up to make space for her knees. She lifted her dress up to press her body down against his hardness.

Jesus, Alex internally gasped as he focused on the sensation of her pressed against his manhood.

Serene was still as she straddled him, her face lowered and her cheeks flushed in embarrassment. Alex had never seen a woman be sexier than Serene was at that precise moment. Her red lips were slightly parted, her hair fell in perfect cascades of glossy brown waves around them, and her breasts were barely contained in her red dress. He looked at her gold cross necklace, and for a moment, envied its location.

He loved what she was wearing, but only in this context, alone, with him. He was finally admitting that he wanted her and over time subconsciously became more possessive. If anyone ever saw just how sexy she actually was he would surely seethe with jealousy.

When she had stopped moving, he knew he was gambling. At any moment she could decide that her plan wasn't working and give up. Every second that passed the stakes were rising. He needed to communicate that her efforts were not in vain.

"You can do better..." His voice was low and she looked up at him. *Your move Serene.*

Unsure of what to do next, she leaned forward to place her head next to his. She gently kissed his neck, trailing down to his collar bone and then up to his earlobe, gently biting it. He moved his face towards her leading her to kiss him and she did. Serene placed her arms around his neck and their kiss deepened, causing her to become aroused. She wasn't expecting to feel this way. Alex was awakening something she hadn't felt in months.

Noticing she was trembling, he caressed her thighs and then her back, soothing her, letting her know she was safe. She parted from his kiss and with her eyes closed and her head down, she began to grind against him, making cute moaning sounds, allowing him to hear how good his hardness felt against her opening.

He was officially aroused, and his body began to ache for her, but when he tried to kiss her, Serene pulled back.

She had a plan; If he wanted to kiss her, he would have to use his hands. In the meantime, she teased him and hovered her mouth over his, pulling away every time he tried to kiss her. It was sweet torture for him.

She closed her eyes, and as if she were overwhelmed with lust she moaned his name.

"Alex." her eyes scrunched closed. "Oh, Alex." Her acting was on point.

The beautiful sound of his name on her lips instantly caused him to dig his hands into her hair and pull her to him so that he could lose himself in her warm mouth. She sped up their kiss, forcing him to focus on her. Their breathing was heavy and her moans became louder. He caressed her back and then tried to unzip her dress. She leaned forward to assist him in his endeavor.

As he unzipped her, she used the opportunity to slide her hands on either side of him and then, as planned, she moaned softly into his ear, "Please Alex," she moaned, "Make love to me. I'm begging you."

Alex's eyes sprung open as she slipped her hand into his pocket and grabbed his phone.

With as much speed as she could muster, she ran out of the living room. Barely making it to the stairs when he caught up with her. He grabbed her arm pulling her to him.

"No, Alex. Please!" she screamed. "Just let me delete the pictures. Please!"

He looked at her worried face perplexed. It wasn't the cell phone he was after.

"Make out with me." He said calmly. "Agree to make out with me and I'll let you delete the pictures."

She looked up at him confused.

"Go ahead. Delete them!" Alex yelled letting her go.

"Okay!" Serene looked at the phone, flustered. "I—I need the password."

"Oh my god. Here, I'll do it!" Alex put the password in and handed her the phone. Serene sat on the staircase nervously fumbling through the photos.

After she was sure the pictures were deleted, she spoke, but her voice was shaky.

"Okay, I got them," she said, out of breath. "They're gone."

"Good."

She got up and handed him the phone. "In case you backed them up, this also means you can never threaten me with them again."

"I won't." he said softly and took back the phone.

She fixed her hair and wondered if he would seriously force her to make out with him. He put the phone away and kept his gaze low.

She began to walk up the steps, and after a moment he followed her. Her dress was halfway unzipped, and his eyes were burning a hole in her back. When she reached the second floor she began to walk towards her room.

Alex caught up with her and she turned around as a familiar fear took over her. His arm encircled her waist as he brought her in for a kiss. As they kissed, he noticed she was shaking. He stopped immediately.

"Serene, why are you shaking?" He caressed her face. "Are you scared of me?"

"No. Yes. I mean, I'm worried what this may lead to."

"I promise. If you want to stop, I'll stop."

She lowered her head. "That hasn't worked before. It never works."

He lifted her head to look at him. "Serene, you know me... I would *never* hurt you," he said again, reassuring her. "I've always respected you. So, if you don't want this, I won't force you. But please," He placed his forehead against hers, "I need you."

She closed her eyes as his last words echoed in her head like a memory. She wasn't sure if those words caused fear or passion in her. Right now, they made her remember Tristan, and the bittersweet ecstasy, the pain mixed with pleasure, the fear and the adrenaline that raced through her body when he claimed her and made her his.

Alex kissed her cheek and then trailed down her neck. "Serene... My Serene." His words hypnotized her as she remembered how she used to yearn for him. She also used to trust him, but she wondered if she could trust him now. She wanted to be held, caressed, and kissed, but feared it would lead to more, like it had with Tristan. She had wanted sex with Tristan that night, she was sure, but right now she wasn't sure what she wanted from Alex. All she knew was her body was yearning to be touched, caressed, and loved.

"Okay." she whispered surrendering.

He searched her face, making sure this was what she wanted. "Okay?" he nodded. She nodded in return.

Kissing her, he lifted her into his arms and brought her into the master bedroom.

Gently, Alex sat her on his bed and took off his shirt. His body didn't hold a candle to Tristan's, but Alex's toned body and long torso could have easily landed him a job as a trendy all-American jean model.

Alex grabbed her hand, and by lifting it he requested her to stand up. She stood up and he gazed into her eyes as he finished what he had started on her zipper. He then pushed her dress down, over her hips, and allowed it to fall to the ground.

Alex looked down and was shocked when he noticed she was wearing sexy, black lingerie-style underwear. He was taken aback by how amazing she looked, but was also angry that she would wear it out on a first date.

He scrunched his brows. "Did Clair buy this for you?" he asked concerned, nearly killing the mood.

"No…" Her cheeks flushed. "Casey and I figured out how to order stuff online through a third party and have it come to the school."

"Oh…" he forced himself to hold back his disapproval, "Well, it looks good on you."

He knew she looked better than 'good.' She was breathtaking. Unfortunately, Alex was never great with words. Digging his hands into her hair he kissed and held onto her waist until he coaxed her into bed.

Serene's body relaxed as he slowly kissed down her chest.

He placed a hand on her waist and began to pull down her underwear.

"Wait—" she gasped.

"We are *not* having sex," he said, looking up at her. "I just want to please you."

"The underwear stays on," she warned. "I'm serious, you said, 'make out'."

He looked down, dejected. He had learned how to pleasure a woman and was desperate to show her.

"Can I at least touch you?"

"No, Alex. You can kiss me or we're stoppi—" Alex muffled her words with his mouth and settled himself in between her legs. She was lucky he had an *incredible* amount of self-control, because he wanted to persuade her into letting him please her, but he'd have to find another way.

She put her arms around his neck, and she lifted her hips to grind against him. She was proud of the fact that Dr. Alexander Elbridge, with his good looks and high standards, was rock hard for her.

He studied her face, watching her enjoy his hardness, but seeing her getting pleasure caused the frustration in him to grow. His pants didn't allow him to feel much.

"I missed you, Serene," he said burying his face in her neck. "God I've missed you."

"Harder," she begged him and he obliged, rubbing against her with intense force pushing the gates of her womanhood, threatening to break inside. She lifted her arms, searching aimlessly for something to hold, remembering Tristan's bed frame.

Alex tried to slide his hand under her bra to touch her, but she slapped his hand away.

Irritated, he bit her bottom lip, and she yelped.

Suddenly, she began to feel the tension building. It had been months since she had orgasmed and she yearned for it. Her moans turned into small screams.

"You're so perfect, Serene. You've always been perfect," he said as she kissed down his neck.

"Harder." She breathed, her word nearly a cry.

Alex worried about hurting her, but Serene was used to a rougher foreplay. Hesitating, he did as she requested. He rubbed against her until he was nearly bruising her.

"I'm going to come," she said, covering her face in embarrassment.

"It's okay… come." he pried her hands away from her face and kissed her.

She moaned into his mouth as the tension inside her built up and came crashing down, leaving only ripples of pleasure that pulsated throughout her body. He studied her face carefully, wanting to remember how she looked as she came for him beautifully. He had fantasied about this moment for years.

He slowed down and finally stopped. "*Good* girl," he said, proud of her.

Serene found the phrase odd.

He lay beside her and trailed the back of his finger down her body to her thigh. He was still yearning for her and would have given nearly anything to have her at that very moment. He knew now, more than ever, that he wanted her, all to himself.

Suddenly, she laughed.

"What?" he said smiling propping his head up with his arm.

"Nothing… I just, never knew I could come like that. Without—"

"Without having anything go in? It doesn't have to."

"Yea but if so… why didn't we do this years ago?" she asked, almost angry at the fact that they hadn't.

He laughed, "We probably should have." He slid his arm behind her neck and pulled her against him. "See… I told you. You can trust me. We always said we would wait until marriage anyways."

"You didn't!" she said, upset at the fact he obviously slept with plenty of women in the last few years.

He became serious again, "Serene, you must know they meant nothing and… I plan to wait until marriage from now on."

"Same here," she agreed. She didn't plan on marrying him or anyone anytime soon.

He continued to trail the back of his finger down her body and then stopped at her navel. He noticed she wasn't showing yet.

"I think we should probably have the wedding next month or sooner, before you start showing," he said, reminding her of the inevitable.

"What?" She sat up to look at him, confused. "Um, no." She rushed out of bed and picked up her dress.

He got up as well and wondered why she was upset.

"What? Would you rather do the courthouse thing? I'm not sure Clair or mother would like that."

She gasped and looked at him wide-eyed.

"Alex, I'm not marrying you. Are you crazy?" she scolded him as she used the dress's fabric to cover herself.

He scrunched his eyebrows. "What exactly is crazy about what I said?"

"What's crazy? I can't believe you're being serious—we haven't even dated! We aren't even a couple. You haven't bought me a ring and… Wow you—you're such a jerk sometimes." she said, closing her eyes and rubbing her forehead.

"I'll get you a ring! We'll go out tomorrow for it if you want. And why am I a jerk exactly?" he asked, genuinely confused. "I've been nothing but—"

"Why are you a jerk?" She laughed, baffled by his question. "Hmm, where do I start? You're conceited, you're controlling and… No. You know what? Just forget it," she said, not wanting to go into the many reasons Alex annoyed her.

She left the room and he went after her.

"Why are you suddenly so upset?" he asked. "We were just having a moment!"

She stopped in the hallway. "Why am I upset?" She put a hand in the air, exhausted by how smart, yet clueless Alex could be sometimes. "Because this isn't what I want Alex! To just rush into marriage. And honestly, what makes you think that for a *second* I'd marry you?"

"Because you just said it in there!" he said through his teeth, frustrated and pointing at the bedroom.

"No, I did not! I said I'd *wait* until marriage. Not that I would marry *you*! If I was going to marry you, you'd..." She sighed. "You would have to do *a lot* better than what you just did in there! We'd also have to at least date each other for a while. And forgive me for, I don't know, wanting to be in *love* before I get engaged!"

"Yea well, you think I wanted this?" he yelled. "Dammit, Serene, I want that too! I'd love to be able to take you out on exotic vacations and date for a while, but you went out and got yourself pregnant! Because of your *carelessness* I have no choice now but to rush everything for the sake of you, your family, and the baby!"

Serene's jaw dropped.

She was surprised at how insensitive Alex could truly be.

He was partly right; she had gone out with Tristan on her own accord, and she *was* to blame for the pregnancy, but, as far as Alex knew, she had been attacked and raped. So, what he has said was way out of line and only proved to Serene how much of a jerk he could be.

She ran off into her bedroom and locked the door behind her. She then threw herself on the bed and hid her head into the pillows so that he wouldn't hear her cry.

Alex stood shirtless in the hallway, with his hands on his waist, knowing he'd, yet again, upset Serene. He figured he'd have to get used to her tantrums. He walked up to her door and tried opening it, but it was locked. He pulled the keys out of his pocket and looked for the right one. As he moved the key towards the lock, he realized it would only irritate her further to know he could open her door at any moment. He knocked instead.

"Serene. Can we talk?" he requested, but she didn't answer. He sighed. "I didn't mean what I said to come out that way."

He stood there for a moment and played back the conversation, noting all the parts that had upset her.

"I know what happened to you wasn't your fault. I... It's just that in the process of dating you, I know I would find myself being a father and having all the responsibilities of a husband anyways. It's a lot sooner than I had expected, but I want to do things right with you... *for* you."

She still didn't answer. He was irritated that she wouldn't respond, and he added this to the list of things he needed her to stop doing. He *hated* being ignored.

As he walked away, he relaxed, and understood why he agreed with Light sector laws, now more than ever. Things would be a lot easier if she were his wife. With her bound to him he could protect her better, and she would have to obey him. He felt that all this freedom wasn't doing a person like Serene any good. She needed rules and guidance.

Serene lay crying.

She had heard what Alex had said, but she was absolutely sure that she didn't want to marry him. At least not like this—not this fast. She cared about him, and some days she even liked him, but she didn't love him. She had felt love before, though short lived, she remembered a bond that wasn't binding, but liberating. Tristan had made her feel free and yet safe in his embrace and she yearned for someone to make her feel that way again.

The next morning Serene went to a local church with Alex.

She kept to herself and barely spoke to him.

Later in the day, Clair called Alex and spoke to him about Tristan showing up at the church. Alex decided it was best not to upset Serene further, since her father was okay, despite the scare.

TWENTY-SIX

VERMILLION

A few days after the church incident, Tristan drove into the city and parked in front of a large black corporate building. He wore a thin grey shirt under a casual black sport coat, and because of the time of day he was sporting dark sunglasses. His attire wasn't exactly professional, but it was more appropriate for visiting Kamilla at her job.

Kamilla had sent various texts which forced him to come visit her. He was annoyed because he was awaiting news about Serene from Lea and didn't want to go.

> Kamilla: *Tristan! You're not replying!*
> *You need to be at the Vermillion building at 11 a.m., It's urgent.*
> Tristan: *How urgent?*
> Kamilla: *Life and death! Read your other texts. I'll come get you.*
> Tristan: *No! Fine. I'll be there.*

Tristan had picked up Kamilla from her job before, but he'd never stepped inside. When he walked into the building's vast lobby, he was greeted with a hologram. It was twice his size and depicted a red spinning world. The words "Vermillion Enterprises" floating above it. As far as Tristan knew, Ignatius had established one of the wealthiest, most successful corporate empires in the world, but he had no idea what they did.

Various screens surrounded the lobby. The only thing Tristan could gather from the videos is that their business dealt with science and technological innovations. He went through security, and on his way up the elevator he took off his glasses.

His phone rang.

"Yeah."

"It's true," Lea sighed. "Her parents weren't lying. She no longer lives there. I scoured the house after they left. She's gone."

Lea had asked Serene's parents about her whereabouts yesterday, but they only mentioned she was off at college. They wouldn't mention what college.

"Then just find someone else! Family, friends, anyone! Someone must know where she is!" Tristan scolded while pacing in the elevator.

Lea hung up, fed up with the way he'd been treating her lately.

Trist took a deep breath and tried his best to relax. He called her back.

"Lea, I'm sorry. I didn't mean—I'll do things myself from now on. Thanks for everything." He hung up the phone and looked up at the ceiling sighing. "Where are you, halo?"

The elevator stopped, and he exited.

Leaning over the reception desk he spoke to a pretty blonde, "Hey, I'm here to see Kamilla."

She barely met his glance when she coyly lowered her head and smiled. "I'll let her know you're here. Please, take a seat."

He sat to wait for Kamilla in the ultra-modern, white, and almost clinical waiting area. He wasn't sure what she did exactly, but knew she was an administrative officer for her father's corporation.

After a few minutes, Kamilla emerged from a hallway wearing red stilettos, a black leather pencil skirt, and a black lace bodice. Her attire was corporate worthy, but still very Dark.

As she approached him, he got up from his seat to greet her.

Kamilla surprised him with a quick kiss on the lips before greeting him.

"Why are you ignoring my calls?" she frowned, "I thought you weren't mad anymore?" Kamilla's voice was soft and her body was uncomfortably close.

"I haven't, I've just been... adjusting." Kamilla kissed him again, but this time she slipped her tongue in forcing him to fully kiss her. He pretended to be into it but immediately felt uncomfortable when he noticed the blonde girl at the reception desk staring at them. He gently pushed Kamilla away.

"Ugh. I miss how you used to taste." She sighed dejectedly.

"Kami, about my accounts..."

"Is the card not working?" She cocked her head, pretending to not understand what the problem was.

"It is... but I need to re-establish everything under my new identity now."

"About that. I've been busy making you a free man. You won't need your new identity soon," the corner of her lips curled, "I'll talk to you about that later. But first, my father wants to see you."

Before he could object she grabbed his hand and dragged him into the elevator.

Once inside she pressed the button for the one-hundredth floor. She then moved in front of him and placed her head against his chest. Tristan knew it meant that she wanted a hug so he sighed and held her.

"Trist, I... really miss you."

"Me too," he said, spaced out and thinking about how to find Serene.

She looked up at him. "My father, he thinks we are a couple. I know you said you needed time but—"

"Kamilla about that—"

"I love you." She looked up at him through glossy eyes. Tristan was shocked. Sometimes those words were thrown around, but he could tell by her expression that she meant it.

"I do, very much. I thought that maybe this feeling would cease once you were a Krov, but... It's just different now. I don't care anymore how long it takes for you to love me back. I just want to be near you again," she said, hugging him tightly.

He looked up at the ceiling and sighed, knowing the situation was getting worse. He needed to put a firm stop to her advances, but how? And what would happen if he did? Would she get angry and wonder if he still had feelings for Serene? Was he willing to risk Serene's safety? No, he needed to pacify her and make her believe everything was okay... at least until he knew more about her, her father, and whether Serene was safe.

When they reached the top floor, the doors opened. Tristan noticed the heightened level of security. There were three men on either side of them, wearing full bullet-proof attire. It wasn't the fact that the men were armed to the teeth that made Tristan feel uncomfortable, but the fact that they each had on the bronze-colored crow pin that identified them as Sentinels. Jason had explained how powerful and well-trained Sentinels were.

Tristan and Kamilla walked past them, and into a hallway that wasn't lit. Only very large illuminated fish tanks that extended the length of the hallway lit the way. The black floors had a long, blood-red carpet going down the center, which almost glowed under the fluorescent lights of the fish tanks.

As they reached the end of the hallway, there were four more Sentinels guarding a pair of very large, tall, and red leather-bound doors.

"I'll wait here," Kamilla said calmly as she took a seat on a nearby bench.

"Gee thanks." Tristan said, feeling forced to enter the lion's den alone.

Tristan wasn't intimidated by powerful figures, but from what he'd heard, Ignatius wasn't just powerful in status and money, he was an Alpha, and apparently the most powerful one to date. He took a deep breath and grabbed the door handle.

"Wait, why do I have to see him?"

"Because he's my father?" Kamilla cocked her head.

"I just don't think we are at the 'meet the parents', point in our relationship yet." he jested.

Kamilla laughed. "Just go. You'll be fine."

"What does he want with me?" His voice was serious.

Kamilla shrugged.

Ignatius's office was everything Tristan had expected; Ridiculously large, and lavish. The wall of windows were curved into a C-shape, but darkly tinted. Decorating the walls were a few open metal shelves with various decorative objects. The floor was a silver metal that had lines leading to the center of the room where Ignatius's desk sat prominently. The statues, shelves, lamps, and even his desk looked like they were made of a very strong metal, perhaps titanium. It was apparent that everything around Ignatius had to be exceptionally durable, as if at any moment he could lose control and break something by accident.

Ignatius's large metal chair was turned facing the window. The windows in front of him doubled as a screen, displaying various statistical financial reports and data. In the center of the screen was the streaming video of a man he was having a meeting with. Tristan walked closer, but by doing so made his presence known to the man in the video. When the man on the screen looked up at Tristan, Ignatius automatically ended their conversation and the stream ended.

"Tristan, I presume," Ignatius said softly not turning around in his chair. "Do not wear cologne around me. I find it rather... annoying."

Ignatius's sense of smell was even more acute than that of a normal Red.

306

Tristan sniffed his sleeve and was puzzled since he hadn't put cologne on that day.

Ignatius stood up and walked towards the window with his back to Tristan.

His silver hair made a small V-shape on his back, and the length of his hair fell barely below the line of his very broad shoulders. It wasn't silver due to old age, it was metallic, similar to the color of the furniture in the room. Ignatius was also wearing a well-tailored, sleek, and seemingly expensive black suit. He was fairly thin and about as tall as Tristan. At first glance, he didn't appear physically powerful, which surprised Tristan.

After a moment, Ignatius spoke again in a slow and careful manner.

"So… you're one of their trained gigolos? Hmm…. How does that work exactly? Do they, perhaps, pay you for your services?"

"No," Tristan stated coldly. He knew that Ignatius was trying to offend him, and unfortunately it was working. He'd dated, a lot, but he refused to be known as some sort of halfwit Krov sex toy.

"Shame. From the information given to me, by now you could have made a fortune. But I gather you're not very bright. Any financial success you think you've had is all due to Kamilla."

Tristan clenched his jaw. Picking a fight with him would not be the best idea, so he bit his tongue.

Ignatius turned to look at him.

Tristan's scrunched his eyebrows surprised at how young this man looked. He didn't look a day over thirty. For whatever reason, he didn't age as other Krovs did. His skin was pale, and his eyes were a deep purple, the same color as his tie. His dress shirt was silver, like his hair, and he had an evil smirk on his face.

"I'm not sure what you've heard, but I promise you, I'm *far* from being some idiot playboy. Do you think Kamilla would be interested if that's all I had to offer?"

"Hm. Kamilla isn't the only one who keeps pretty things around just for fun."

Tristan clenched his fist, doing his best to contain his anger.

Ignatius studied Tristan while holding a closed hand over his mouth. "Honestly, I don't see what the fuss is about. Even if sex was the only thing you offered, I'm sure you're hardly worthy of her. But alas," he said, sighing in disappointment, "You're right. The silly thing says she loves you."

Ignatius walked towards him. "You do understand how that could happen. Krov women often have trouble finding a mate, so you must know she settled." Ignatius stopped to stand right in front of him.

Tristan kept his look stoic, hiding any sign of intimidation. He wanted to tell him off, but fighting him, and possibly dying, wasn't on his to-do list that day.

After they stared at each other for a moment, Ignatius walked off to pour himself and Tristan a drink that looked like scotch.

"Tell me Tris-*tan*... have you tasted a beautiful woman yet?" Ignatius asked, referring to a human.

"During training," Tristan said, as he begrudgingly accepted the drink.

"Fascinating isn't it? To fuck your food and consume her simultaneously, having her body nourish you in every way possible. It beats the hell out of normal sex, doesn't it?"

Tristan never did what he was describing, and found the idea incredibly disturbing. Tristan downed the drink, knowing it wouldn't do anything to him.

Ignatius smirked and very slowly sipped his drink.

"You know... we don't usually allow Goldens in our species, let alone on the council. We worry they might... dilute our kind further." Ignatius took the empty cup from Tristan's hand.

When Ignatius set the cups down, he turned to look at Tristan.

"Tristan, I'll do you a favor... but it's not because I like you. I will tolerate your sorry existence for the time being, for the sake of Kamilla." His eyes began to glow a bright purple. "But I warn you, if you *ever* hurt her in any way, trust that I won't hesitate to give you a slow, painful, and agonizing death."

Tristan looked around and noticed that all the small objects on the shelves were suspended in mid-air and slowly moving towards him. Tristan kept his cool but took a step back as Ignatius continued. "Once Kamilla's *ridiculous* obsession with you is over, be assured that you *will* be off the council and if you're lucky I may choose to let you live but…" Ignatius rubbed his chin and shrugged his shoulders, "not likely."

They glared at each other.

Suddenly, Tristan began to lose his balance. He closed his eyes and put a hand on a nearby table.

Feeling dizzy, Tristan stormed out.

Kamilla followed him down the hall.

"Trist, what happened?" she asked, calling out to him, but he didn't say a word and they both rushed towards to the elevator. "Nothing. I just need you to come with me and get my finances in order," he said coughing and feeling vertigo.

"There's a council meeting in five minutes."

"So?" Tristan said with a hoarse voice.

"So? You're part of the council. I sent you several texts."

"I never wanted to be part of any goddamn council Kam!" he yelled, angry that he ever got involved with her in the first place.

They entered the elevator and he balanced himself by holding onto the wall. Kamilla quickly pressed the number twenty-four.

"Fine!" she said, nostrils flared. "If you didn't want to be part of the council, you had days to tell me! I tried to call you. I fought to give you that position. I was trying to do something nice! You won't return my calls—"

Tristan took a deep breath and knew he was screwed. He had to keep her happy until he found a safe way out of this mess.

"Ugh! Goddamnit, fine!" he said, not wanting to make her angry.

His world began to spin, and he became progressively dizzier. "What the hell did he give me?"

"Who?"

"Your father! He gave me a drink."

"Oh…" Kamilla said, finally realizing what had happened. "Yea. My father, he's developing goods for the Krov population in the near future."

"What?" Tristan asked furrow-browed.

"He just gave you a strong drink. It gives Krovs an effect similar to being drunk. So, you're fine," she said smiling, but Tristan was wasted.

The council meeting was being held in a very spacious room, with black walls and only dim glowing yellow sconces for lighting. Tristan sat around a large steel oval table, along with the other council members. Kamilla sat next to him but he was leaning to his side, and rubbing his forehead in an effort to alleviate the feeling of vertigo. Tristan knew what being wasted felt like, and this was much more intense.

On a large screen in front of them, various maps were displayed with sections and major cities flooded with the color red, and smaller portions colored yellow. The rest of the map was a neutral color.

Around the table were at least twenty council members, each wearing their gold damascus pin.

"How long's the meeting?" Tristan asked Kamilla.

"About an hour, give or take. The effects of the drink should wear off by then. Also, you do know that anything that goes on during these meetings is confidential, right? And that any leak of information is punishable by death?"

"No, Kam. I didn't see that on the *fucking* agenda this morning." He whispered.

Minutes later, Kamilla held his hand under the table. Tristan noticed some of the council members sneered when they looked at him. It was obvious that no one other than Kamilla wanted him there.

When Ignatius walked in, everyone stopped talking as if they were terrified, which was odd to Tristan since all the council members seemed devious and powerful by their own accord.

Ignatius sat farthest from the screen and very loudly placed his feet on the metal table.

A man by the name of Armador stood by the screen talking. He was tall, had short dark hair and his uniform looked like he belonged to a military strategist team. Tristan was initially not interested in what the man had to say, but after a few minutes in he couldn't help but pay attention.

"As far as recruitment goes, feeding grounds in the cities are exhausted. We can no longer recruit without alarming the government, police force, and citizens. Even if we continue to blame the missing humans on the ever-increasing crime, we are risking a lot if we continue this way." Armador explained to the council members.

"So, we simply move on to more rural areas and Light sectors," said a council member who Tristan noticed was wearing glasses, though Tristan didn't understand why, since Krovs had excellent vision.

"No. At the rate we are recruiting, those feeding grounds will be exhausted within a year," said another council member with a foreign accent.

"Ignatius," Amador said, "we thought we could postpone the second phase, but our food needs are growing, and even our people within the police force can't continue to cover up the damage."

"We should just eliminate the Goldens, it will buy us time!" yelled another random council member. "We can't—"

"What's phase two?" Tristan whispered to Kamilla.

Kamilla whispered back, "Once recruitment quotas are met,

phase two means organizing to take over major government branches. But we're at least a year away from quota—"

Kamilla caught her father's glance and she stopped talking to Tristan. He then spoke in his usual slow, and soft tone of voice. "Eliminating the Goldens... would only buy us a few months at best," Ignatius said as he played with a small marble-like glowing sphere on the table. His speech was slurred. It was barely noticeable, but Tristan could tell that the drink had affected him too, though not as strongly. "Goldens are weaker... but we may still need them. We must simply ask them to give up their feeding grounds. They will have to move outward. Was the order to halt Krov registration outside of recruitment placed last week?" Ignatius asked Armador.

"The order goes out tonight your eminence," Amador lowered his head substantially to where it was almost a bow.

"Tonight?" Ignatius narrowed his eyes and cocked his head.

"Um, many pleaded with us to give them time to register family members and recently turned Krovs sir," Armador nervously bowed again. The other council members didn't look surprised and lowered their gaze as if they were also guilty for not following through.

"We needed just a bit more time, to turn and register those closest to us. After tonight, I assure you, no registrations will be allowed with recruitment or otherwise. Anyone caught turning a human will immediately be eliminated. We are sorry for the delay." They all waited for Ignatius's reaction, but he simply continued to play with his marble sphere.

Armador continued. "So..." he coughed, clearly relieved that Ignatius didn't react harshly, "We will continue to grow recruitment without turning, to prevent any further feeding ground issues. Once the farms are ready for the picking, we will continue with phase three."

The screen then changed to images of the many ranks they had created. "We are hiring the best men from many branches. They will be joining our ranks as we continue to build."

312

Various profile pictures showed up on the screen and Armador continued. "But, it's difficult to continue to grow our man-power as we have without turning them. Or telling them who and what we are—"

Kamilla spoke, "Originally, father, it was easy to recruit simply by turning them. Many recruits were thankful for their powers and were usually on board for a Krov take over. However, feeding grounds are tight now. We can no longer afford to turn them so how do we—?"

"Wet their appetites," Ignatius said interrupting. "Offer to pay them well if they join our cause. Make it... worth their while. Run the selected human candidates through training and then explain to them the benefits of staying on board. Show them who we are and the power that they can one day hold. After all... *Everyone wants to be a Krov*," Ignatius said, extending his arm outward.

"With all due respect Master, how much more do you wish to offer them?" Armador asked kindly.

"Does it matter? As much as you want. Lie to them!" Ignatius yelled as he unintentionally slammed his hand on the metal table that was bolted to the ground. Everyone, including Tristan, was startled for a moment.

Ignatius then spread his palm on the table and calmly lifted his hand away from it. With everyone stunned, and their eyes wide open, Ignatius continued in his soft voice. "Just... explain to them what will become of the humans. Join us or become human cattle. Only a fool would object. Offer them however much it takes, then lower their pay after a month, just enough to survive. And then recruit more."

"And if they object to the pay cut?" the council member with the glasses asked.

"Do the same when someone objects to joining us. Kill them."

Ignatius lacked any emotion.

Tristan, although drunk, was appalled at everything he was

hearing. Human cattle? Farms? What was happening?

The rest of the meeting was a blur. Finally, all of the members stood up to leave. Tristan sat, lost in thought.

"Come on, Trist, let's grab some lunch," Kamilla helped him up and placed her arm around his waist to make it easier for him to walk.

They walked out and into the elevator.

"So, what will happen to...?" Tristan asked Kamilla as he tried to find a way to phrase the question.

"What will happen to what?"

"Humanity?" Tristan said loudly, looking dumbfounded. He was pissed that she seemed so unaffected.

"I thought you didn't have family?" She asked confused as to why he was so upset. "If there is anyone you want to turn, you'll have to do it tonight."

"Seriously, Kam? I'm talking about people in general! Human farms? Is this currently happening?"

She noticed his disapproval and knew he was reacting on pure emotion, "Ugh I hate that you're a Golden. Don't worry, Father's working on a project so that they will all be brain dead. Humans won't suffer or see it coming."

Kamilla left the elevator and looked back at his sorrowful face. "They're just food, silly! Come on, I'll get us some Thai," she said, giving Tristan an eerie smile.

Tristan was glad he was drunk and out of it, otherwise, the fact that human farming was currently happening would have affected him harder.

TWENTY-SEVEN

THE CANCELLED PROPOSAL

Alex had left the house without telling Serene where he was going. He had mentioned marriage to her a few days ago, but she had not yet accepted. However, he was confident she'd come around and had taken note of everything that had upset her. One of those reasons was the way in which he had brought up marriage. So, he needed to buy a ring. The next time he'd mentioned it, he'd be prepared.

As he drove, he dialed his phone.

"Morning Clair, how's Peter doing?"

Clair and Peter were currently in their car and on their way to a charity event.

"Oh, he's doing perfectly fine Alex, thank you. I'm just worried the psycho will return. The nerve of him showing up at our place of worship! I can't even sleep at night. What did Serene say when you told her?"

"I... actually haven't had a chance to. I don't think it's a good idea to worry her in her condition. I do, however, have some good news," Alex said, smiling, and he kept quiet for a moment to work up the suspense.

"Well, what is it?"

"I wanted you... to be the first to know that I... am in fact, going to marry Serene. I asked her last week."

Clair's eyes opened wide in excitement. She held the phone to her chest and in complete silence motioned with her mouth, "*Thank god!*" She turned to Peter who was driving.

"Peter! Alex asked Serene to marry him! And she said yes!" Clair exclaimed as she grabbed and shook Peter's arm with enthusiasm.

Alex heard what she had said to Peter, and he decided to clarify.

"Well," he cleared his throat, "she didn't exactly say *yes*."

"What? What do you mean?" Clair's excitement turned into worry as she wondered if her daughter might have, once again, messed up a good thing.

"I think she had initially said yes? But we still have a few things to work out. I did, however, tell her she might start showing soon and that I wanted to make the wedding next month or earlier and I—"

"—No I completely agree with you. The wedding should be soon!"

"Good, but that scared her off a bit. She thinks it's too soon. Would you mind talking to her? Just let her know I didn't want to rush the wedding either, but due to the circumstances—"

"No, no Alex. No need to explain dear. I'll call her today."

"Thanks. Oh, and Clair, please continue to keep everything else that happened a secret for the time being. I don't think—"

"No worries son."

"Hey sweetie! How's my little angel, or should I say, *angels,* doing?" Clair's child-like voice spewed through the phone. Serene rolled her eyes and knew something was up. Her mother never spoke in that tone unless they were offering her something in return.

Serene was on the phone in the kitchen, baking, and wondering where Alex had gone since it was his day off as well.

"Angels?" Serene questioned.

"Well yes, you and the baby."

"Oh. We are doing well," Serene said while filling up a muffin pan with a blueberry mix. "Wait, I thought Alex said you guys couldn't call here?"

"Well yes, but he told us about the good news! I am so happy for the two of you!"

Serene rolled her eyes and was immediately disgusted at the whole situation.

She scoffed silently, "What did he tell you?"

"Well, just that he proposed! Your father and I are—"

"No, Mom, that's not what happened! He asked us to—" She stopped and realized that she may not want to tell her mom the whole story. "I mean, he spoke to me *about* marriage. That's all. He never actually proposed."

"Well, he just asked us for your hand in marriage! So, if he hasn't proposed yet, he's doing it soon!" Serene rubbed her head as the whole situation was being blown way out of proportion.

"Mom, listen. I'm not marrying Alex. We haven't been getting along. I don't know why he thinks I'm going to marry him."

Clair attempted to keep her cool. "I don't understand. I thought you guys liked each other?"

"We did. We do, but we *just* started to like each other again. Don't you think it's a horrible idea to get married in haste?"

Clair was silent for a moment. She knew demanding her wouldn't work, not with the distance between them. Clair also knew if she put too much force on Serene she would rebel against her. Serene had been *different* ever since she ran away, and Clair hated it.

"I understand, sweetie. Just know, Alex really cares about you. We couldn't say anything to you at the hospital because of the circumstances, and Alex had asked us to keep quiet, but the very first day Alex came back into town he told us he'd come back to be with you—"

"Wait what?"

"We tried calling the last number you called us from, but you weren't answering...." Clair continued talking. Serene was shocked at the information her mother was giving her. She officially had a headache and her world began to spin.

"Wait, Stop! He did what?" Serene pleaded with her mom to stop talking so that she could fully understand.

"Alex will kill us if we told you more, but Serene you have to understand what that poor man has been through. The humiliation!"

"Mom! Just tell me!"

"Okay. So, he invited us to dinner at Lillian's, and he and Casey were planning a party. No one was allowed to tell you he was back. Vivian was going to meet up with you at your dorm room and ride with you to the airport, except the cab was going to take you to a party at the Grand Hotel instead. The whole congregation was there. Alex was going to propose as soon as you walked in. Except the day of the engagement party Vivian couldn't find you!"

"No, no, no." Serene put a hand on her pounding chest and closed her eyes. "I was packing to visit a college out of state! Vivian had plane tickets!"

"You, Casey, me, and Alex were going to go to Paris for a few days right after. Casey had bought you the most beautiful dress for you to change into at the party right after the proposal. There was a hair and make-up stylist too. Serene it—"

"No, mom, stop!" Serene began to shake, "What about the college? And the colleges I spent hours researching!"

Clair was silent.

"Sweety... There was no college. I wouldn't have let you go and live in a college out-of-state by yourself. That's *insane,*" she laughed, "We were just using that as an excuse to..."

As her mother trailed on Serene was speechless and couldn't breathe. She had been counting down the days when she would finally have her freedom. And now she was learning it had all been a lie.

A sob escaped her, and she collapsed on the floor with her back against the kitchen cabinet. A whirlwind of emotions overtook her. Anger, sadness, guilt.

"Serene, I know it sounds fast," Clair said, breaking the silence. "He wanted to take things slow with you after everything you've been through, but he cares about you enough to hurry the wedding and protect you."

"Protect me from what?" Serene spat through tears.

"You know… rumors. Light sector penalties. A child out of wedlock is a serious matter in our sector. I mean, we'd defend your case, and pay the penalty if we had to, but if you have the wedding next month, it'll work out perfectly because no one else here knows you're pregnant. After the wedding, you both won't come down until another year or so. We'll even change the baby's birth date…"

Clair continued talking, and Serene shook her head in disbelief. She was so mad that her family continued to take over such critical life decisions. She didn't care about rumors or the law; she had planned to move out of the Light sectors once she had a job. And now, once again, she felt trapped. The fact that she never felt strong enough to defend herself infuriated her.

But she was done acting like a frail little girl with no voice. Clair wasn't there to hurt her, and she was determined to give her a piece of her mind.

"Is that why you allowed Alex to bring me up here, mom? To avoid rumors? Because you're ashamed of me?" Serene looked up as tears streamed down her face. "Well mom, I'm sorry to break this to you, but I'm not marrying Alex. I don't love him!" Her voice shook, "I've done everything you've ever asked of me, mom, because I *know* how important your image is to you. I'll stay up here and hide if you want me to so that you and dad can continue to make the church and the world believe that our family is perfect! But I am not marrying Alex, not now and perhaps even ever."

There was a long, intense silence between them. Serene squinted her tearful eyes as she expected her mother's wrath.

"Serene… we only want the best for you. Just keep in mind that your child needs a father. God may have let something terrible happen to you, but he always makes things right. He let this happen so you can realize that there's a man who adores. A man who loves you regardless of anything and is willing to love you and that child the way you both deserve. Think about it, honey. I know you're a smart girl and that you'll do the right thing for your baby. Goodbye. We love you."

Serene took a deep breath and wiped her tears as she let her anger subside. She was shocked but glad her mother had reacted that way. "I love you too, Mom," her voice squeaked.

Serene knew her mother had just given her the illusion of a choice. Yet she was determined to find a way out of it. She gently rubbed her stomach as she cried.

"I'll finish school little one. I promise. I'll find a job and move to a Free sector. You won't have much, but you'll never go without. If you're a girl, I can't let you live this way, not here."

Serene sat there thinking things over. Before Tristan came along, she loved Alex. She wondered what her response would have been had she gone to the party they had made for her. Would she have agreed to a life of obedience? The truth was obvious. She would have said yes to Alex. Regardless of his indifference and the nights she spent awake crying over him, she wouldn't have embarrassed him at the party, and she would have forgiven him eventually. She wondered if Tristan ruined her chance at happiness for giving her a taste of freedom, or, could he possibly have saved her from a life she never truly wanted?

Months Ago, Tristan's condo

Tristan had just woken up when curiosity led him to check Serene's new phone. They were absorbed with each other, but her family and friends wouldn't stop calling or texting, so they agreed to keep her phone on silent.

As he unlocked her phone, he saw it had blown up with phone calls from many unknown numbers, and the voicemail had several messages. While Serene was in the shower, he checked the messages.

The first few were from Clair, and a girl named Casey asking where she was; he quickly deleted them. Then he heard a few more messages:

"Serene! Where are you? I'm not supposed to tell you, but Alex is back in town! Call me and your father immediately! It was supposed to be a surprise, but he is dying to see you! When you see how handsome he is now you're going to faint!"

"Hey, it's Casey. Thanks for giving me a way to contact you but… they are asking me who this friend of yours is. I don't know what you want me to tell them. Your mom said she already mentioned my brother's back. He really wants to talk to you. He wanted to surprise you with…. something."

"Hey, it's… been a while… It's me, Alex… They said you've been gone for over a week now and no one knows where you are. I'm not sure why you are doing this. I hope you aren't doing it to spite me. If you are, I understand. I transferred, and I'm doing my residency at the local hospital. I—"

"Sorry. Machine cut me off. I just wanted to let you know… I've really missed you. I kept my distance because it was torture to talk to you. Anyway, I want to spend some time with you. Catch up where we left off. I asked my sister every time we talked if you still wore the ring I gave you. Please call… everyone's worried sick about you. And Serene… I still love you."

Tristan scoffed. He didn't want to listen to any more messages since they had overwhelmed him with jealousy. He had no idea who this Alex guy was, but he didn't want anything getting between him and Serene, so he deleted all the messages and placed parental controls on her phone in order to block the numbers and keep her from calling them.

A man, possibly her boyfriend, is back and is saying he loves her? Where does that leave me? Why hasn't she mentioned him!? He wondered.

Serene got out of the shower and came into the bedroom wearing only a towel. As she walked by him, he grabbed her hand and looked at her ring. She wore it like a wedding ring, and it looked expensive. Was she engaged? Serene didn't think anything of him examining it and she dropped the towel on purpose so that she was naked in front of him. He instantly looked up as her body was the perfect distraction, but he needed to know what he was up against. He was enthralled with Serene, and possessive of her. He pulled her towards him on the bed and made her straddle him while fully naked.

"Who gave you that ring?" he asked as his eyes narrowed and focused on hers.

"What?"

"You look at it a lot; you play with it all the time. Who is he?"

Serene squinted her eyes confused, but then she looked at the ring. Her eyes softened. "He's... the only other guy I've ever dated. We dated for years. My parents... they like him. No, actually they *worship* him, so they allowed us to date. He's very religious and uptight, which is why my parents trust him. Anyway, he went off to become some big shot cancer doctor or something." She shrugged it off and pretended it didn't matter anymore. "He hasn't spoken to me in about a year. I thought we were in love." She said with longing as she gazed at the ring lovingly.

Tristan's jaw clenched, and he closed his eyes trying to control the jealousy he felt. He noticed she would play with the ring and be lost in thought periodically, and now he knew why. Serene still had feelings for this man.

"Does he mean anything to you now?"

"Why all the questions?" she asked annoyed and tried to get off of him, but he forcefully kept her in place.

"Why are you avoiding my questions?"

"Because... it's not important! He—" She took a deep breath. "Before he left, he gave me this ring and made me promise that I'd remain a virgin until he returned to marry me. He said he loved me but needed to finish school. Said he needed to stay away and focus on school for us. For our future. I need to put clothes on." She tried to shuffle off of him.

"Since when?" he asked irritated while holding her in place. "What if he came back? What if he asked you to marry him? What would you say?"

"Alex?" Serene searched his eyes, trying to understand where Tristan's insecurities were coming from. "I... I don't know. He stopped talking to me a long time ago."

"What do you mean you *don't know*?" Tristan scrunched his eyebrows, angry that she couldn't reassure him that her heart belonged to him now.

"Why are you acting so weird?" she squinted her eyes.

"I just..." He looked away. He never worried about a girl leaving him before. "I need to know, if your ex ever came back, what I'm up against."

"*Tristan*," Serene smiled and gently cupped his face and kissed him, "you are insanely jealous. You have nothing to worry about. He's not coming back."

"Then say you belong to me."

Serene searched his eyes and couldn't understand why a man as caring and as handsome as Tristan was so unsure of himself. She had loved Alex, but Tristan was her reality and she had fallen madly in love with him. So much so that her feelings for him scared her. Yet, she hadn't fully let go of her feelings for Alex.

"Serene?" he asked her again.

She was looking away from him and debating her answer.

"I'm... I'm yours, Tristan," she eventually said coming back to meet his gaze. "Plus, my promise is broken now, don't you think?"

she smiled brightly. "Quite a few times, actually."

The corner of his lips curled, and he kissed her hand, the one with the ring. But he wasn't satisfied with what Serene had just told him. He needed proof that Alex wasn't a threat, and he knew exactly how to make her prove to him that he wasn't. While still holding her hand, he gave her an ultimatum.

"If this... man doesn't mean anything to you... take off the ring. Throw it away. I'll buy you a new one."

"What? No! It was a gift." Against her wishes, he began to take it off. "No, Tristan, stop it!"

When he'd managed to remove the ring, he placed it in between the mattresses. She tried to retrieve it, but he pinned her down on the bed holding her wrists above her head as he hovered over her.

"If you take the ring out from where I put it, it means you still have feelings for him. So don't touch it. Understood?" His face was almost touching hers as he gazed deep into her eyes. She laughed for a moment but then noticed he wasn't smiling.

"Jeez. okay. I won't touch it."

"Good. I trust you."

He softly tap kissed her but pulled away for a moment to study her face, outlining it with the back of his finger, remembering every curve and detail in case he ever lost her. She didn't know it yet, but he was already madly in love with her.

Now, knowing he could lose her with just a mere phone call, he yearned to be inside her more than ever. Her body was home, warm, loving, soft. "Serene," he whispered as he made his way inside her, taking what was rightfully his. She rarely protested, always allowing him to find comfort and safety in her warmth.

The next day Tristan saw her in the living room cleaning. She was wearing a tight set of stretch shorts and a tiny white tank top. He leaned against the doorjamb.

He loved watching her, wondering how anyone could look so

angelic and sweet, and yet so sexy. Just then, he noticed the ring. The damn thing was back on her finger.

The peace he felt escaped him. It was now clear. If she ever found out Alex was back in town he could lose her. They had a history; he did not, not yet. But he planned on keeping her distracted and enthralled with him for as long as he could. Erasing any feelings she had for the man that left her. Tristan felt Dr. Boy had his chance. Serene was a rare gem and he shouldn't have left something of such value out for the taking.

Serene looked up at him and smiled. The corner of his lip curled. His sole mission now was to get her to voluntarily lose the ring. He walked up to her, grabbed her waist and lifted her as he kissed her. Her legs wrapping tightly around him.

For once, he actually wanted a girl to have that dark consuming obsession with him because that's how he felt about her. He needed her to crave him, live for him, worship him because he already felt that way about her.

When her feet were back on solid ground, the mood changed as he pulled on her hair forcing her to look up at him. Serene made a sound expressing her discomfort. He spoke in a low, passive-aggressive tone.

"You took the ring." She looked up at him, unapologetic. "How do I make you understand that you belong to me now?" She noticed his anger, but simply looked away from him. He grabbed her face so that she was forced to focus on him again. "I *will* possess your heart, body, and mind, because that's what you've done to me, Serene."

"Trist—" She tried to speak, but he placed his hand over her mouth.

"You *lied* to me. You told me you had no feelings for him," His eyes narrowed, "So, now I'm going to edge you until you cry and beg for release and I won't stop until you've fully convinced me that you live and breathe only for me, and Serene…"

His gaze pierced through her wide eyes like a knife. "You *will* cry for me."

She searched his face, trying to understand his anger, and then she screamed as he pulled on her hair again, but he quickly muffled her scream with his kiss.

If she was going to keep the ring, she had to prove her devotion another way.

Later, in the dim light of Tristan's living room floor, Serene laid naked in front of his electric fireplace, sweating, with her hands tied behind her back. He gently untied the intricate rope pattern. She was breathing hard and her eyes were slightly swollen. She had come for Tristan more times than she could keep track of.

Once her hands were released, Tristan held her limp body against his own, comforting her. His fluids seeping out of her and his sweat dripping over her.

"You're mine, Serene. You will never belong to anyone else," he whispered gently like a chant.

"I will only belong to you, Tristan." Serene recited. As if she had been forced to memorize it.

"You will never think of any other man."

"I will only think of you, Tristan."

"You will live for me and me alone."

"I will only live for you, Tristan."

"I love you, Serene."

"I love you, Tristan."

"Forever?"

"Forever."

The present

It had been only a few hours since Serene had hung up the phone with her mother.

Alex had returned, and he was whistling as he walked through the front door. It was clear to Serene that he was in a good mood, which was rare.

As he walked through the foyer, he saw Serene staring at him from the living room, legs and arms crossed. He walked up to where she was sitting and bent down to give her a kiss on the cheek.

He was smiling, but she was impassive.

"Sit," she demanded.

He looked at her, puzzled. He didn't enjoy taking orders from his soon-to-be fiancé, but he obliged and sat right next to her on the couch.

"Not here... there," she said, pointing at his favorite chair. He scrunched his eyebrows confused and upset she was treating him this way, especially since he'd just gone out and bought a ring worth half as much as her parents' house.

Again, Alex did as he was told.

After a brief moment of silence, she finally spoke.

"Mother called. I'm sure you know why."

"Yes. I asked for your hand in marriage. Just in case," Alex shrugged.

"*Just in case,*" she said calmly and smirked. She knew both Alex and Clair were absolutely convinced she would follow through with their wishes. Serene was determined to prove them wrong, but first she needed to address something that was irking her. "By the way, she finally told me how you had invited them over to dinner to discuss my future."

Alex sighed and leaned forward over his legs, resting his elbows on his knees. He had specifically asked Clair not to say anything for a reason.

"Okay, fine. Yes. I moved back and had a talk with your parents about being serious about you, and perhaps maybe even marrying you," Alex said nervously.

"So, you asked them for my hand in marriage *then* and now *again*?" Serene mentioned, finding it odd as to why he had to do it twice.

"I guess, sort of. And why exactly are you mad about this?" he said, lifting an eyebrow. When he knew the odds of knowing the whole truth were likely he came clean. "Casey wanted to throw a party for us. Everyone we knew was there and—" Alex stopped himself from mentioning that it was an engagement party.

"So, you moved back into town and spoke to my parents about marriage, and you didn't even think for one moment to maybe, I don't know," she laughed and raised her hands, "maybe see if I was okay with it? God, Alex! You hadn't spoken to me in over a year! I hadn't seen you since the previous Christmas!"

"I'm sorry! Everyone thought it was a great idea." Alex rubbed his face, annoyed because it felt like no matter what he did to make her happy she was always mad at him. "Again, why are you *so* mad? I'm sorry I didn't ask you first. I'm sorry I stopped talking to you. What more do you want from me?"

Alex could understand a variety of complex thoughts and ideas, but he was horrible at understanding the logic behind a woman's emotions.

"Why am I mad?" she yelled as she stood up and put her hands through her hair. She wasn't mad; she was furious! "I'm mad because you always assume I'm just going to fall into your lap again! What makes you think it's just okay to ignore me and not see me for over a year, then come back and assume I will marry you!? You needed to come to me! You needed to address the fact that I spent weeks and months crying over you! You needed to make sure I forgave you for that and not just assume an engagement party would fix it! You are so conceited sometimes it's—it's ridiculous!"

"I'm ridiculous? I'm ridiculous!?..." Alex got up and grabbed her hand to show her the ring she still wore. "You're the one still wearing the damn ring I got you!" He ungracefully let go of her hand and then continued. "Every single time I called Casey, she told me you always wore it! That you cherished it! That you still loved me! That you worshiped the ground I walked on! Why did I assume you would agree to marry me? Because that's what we had promised each other!" His face was red with fury. "So, forgive me for coming through on my promise to you. I never thought it would come back to bite me!"

"Oh, so it's not that you love me then, it's that you feel obligated because of the promise you made?"

Alex paced in front of her, "I set goals, I reach them. I make promises, I keep them! I promised everyone and you I would come ba—"

Serene took off the ring and handed it to him as her eyes began to water. "Here, take it! You're no longer under any obligation! I release you of your damn promise!" She tried hard to contain her tears, but they escaped.

He looked at her and wouldn't take the ring.

She lost patience and grabbed his hand, forcing him to take it.

"Serene, stop."

"No!"

He grabbed the ring and placed both his hands on her shoulders. He calmed down and spoke to her softly. "Serene, it's not about feeling obligated. I do love you. I have *always* loved you. I knew you were waiting for me, and I knew you'd never stop loving me. I felt alone often and wanted to pick up the phone or contact you, but it became hard to even speak to you. Every time I did I wanted to rush home. Every time Clair hurt you I wanted to drop everything and…" He stopped. "I'm so sorry and I did have people try to fill the void, but they meant nothing Serene. My main priority was to finish med school quickly so that I could run back and protect you."

Serene was barely touched by his words. Not everything Alex was saying was a lie, but he'd left out the important fact that he did enjoy his time as a bachelor.

Alex went to hug her, but she quickly moved away.

"Then why didn't you tell me all this in the hospital; when I broke down? Why didn't you tell me you loved me and came back for me? Why didn't anyone tell me any of this! It's been months since you came back!" Serene scolded through tears. This was the moment Alex was dreading. He had no idea how to answer this.

He took a deep breath. "Serene… you were gone for weeks. No one knew where you were. Then you arrived at the hospital nearly dying. It was a lot to take in." He hesitated to continue, but he hoped she would understand. "You were attacked, raped, and with child. I loved you *very* much but those are life-changing events. I had to rethink everything. I didn't know if you were emotionally traumatized, or if you had lost your memory. Anything could have happened, and… I simply wanted to wait for your sake, we all did."

Serene hadn't expected that answer. She shook her head in disappointment because nothing he had told her was a good enough excuse.

"Is this why you insisted on bringing me up here with you? To sort out whether I was traumatized or not? To test me? To keep me around until you decided whether to kick me to the curb or marry me?!"

"No! Clair insisted you come and live with me for a bit, so did Casey!"

Serene's eyes widened. She had suddenly realized something. She became red in anger and made fists with her hands but held them by her sides. "My mom and Casey were the ones who insisted on me coming up here with you?

Alex saw the gears turning in her head and ran his hand through his hair. "No, Serene, wait—"

"You are so full of it, Alex!" She walked away and into the foyer.

"Serene, let me explain—"

She turned to face him. "You did come back for me Alex! You threw a party and even wanted to marry me but the *very* moment you realized I was attacked and pregnant you changed your mind entirely! You didn't want *time* to sort things out. You found out I was damaged goods and you ran for the hills! You immediately didn't want me anymore!"

"No, Serene, it wasn't like that!"

"YES, it was! Why else would you feel so strongly about me that you were willing to propose to me on the spot but then the moment I'm lying in the hospital, you suddenly plan on moving? You told me you were moving within two days of me being in the hospital. You almost left town again without even telling me why you even came back in the first place!"

Alex felt cornered.

He turned away from her and placed his hands behind his head.

Finding out she was pregnant *had* changed his mind. He thought he was coming back to a virgin, something beautiful something pure, but the first time he'd seen her at the hospital, her shoulders had large open wounds, and she was bruised and badly beaten. He had found no beauty in her.

However, it was the fact that she was pregnant that had finally made him question everything. Alex lived his life on a schedule. Clear deadlines and dates. When he'd graduate, when he'd marry, when he'd have a child. He knew not everything could be planned but, for him, this had been too much.

He was quiet, and eventually whispered, "I had no problem bringing you up here with me... and look, it was what I needed to sort out my feelings for you."

"Yes, but you weren't planning on it! Had it not been for Casey or my mom, you would have left me and never looked back."

Her tears flowed like waterfalls. "Tell me I'm wrong, Alex? Tell me!"

Alex stood quiet, unable to look at her, realizing there was nothing he could say.

Serene ran upstairs to her room.

Alex was devastated. His eyes finally shed a tear as the guilt ate away at his heart. Opening the front door, he went outside to cool off.

It was a breezy afternoon, and he sat on the steps. What Serene had accused him of was exactly how he'd felt. He didn't want another man's child. He wanted to come back to Serene and have it be just the two of them for a while before children became a strain on their marriage. He had also wanted to be the first and only man to have ever touched her. He was enraged that someone had taken from her what was meant for him.

But, regardless of everything, Alex's feelings had now changed. He loved her, wanted her and her baby. He just needed her to understand that, but first, he took a moment to analyze for himself *why* his feelings had changed.

Alex knocked on her bedroom door, but she didn't answer.

He took out his keys as he knew knocking was useless and opened the door.

Serene shook her head and scoffed, angry that he had a key to her bedroom all along.

"Get. Out," she said as she closed a suitcase on her bed.

"Where are you going?"

"Anywhere neither you nor Mom will find me."

Alex looked at her suitcase and quickly left the room.

Fear and despair suddenly overtook him. His brain raced with every possible scenario that could evolve from this. The worst being her getting hurt or going missing.

He ran downstairs to grab all the car keys and stashed them away. Then he went to the house phone and tore the base out from the wall, destroying it. He took his cell phone, shut it off and hid it away in his office above the bookshelf. He noticed the computer and he took the modem with him, stashing it away as well. He looked around trying to figure out if he'd missed anything. He knew there was no one within a fifteen-minute drive. Yet, just in case she planned on walking, he changed the gate code and rushed to the cars to pull out the sensors that opened the gates. Finally, after he felt confident that he'd covered all his bases, he went back upstairs hoping what he had just done wasn't necessary. Whatever the outcome of their conversation, he was now sure Serene wasn't going anywhere.

He prepped himself before he walked back into her bedroom.

"Serene. I'm so sorry, you're right about everything," he said, surrendering to her. She was out of breath and had finished packing her last suitcase.

"Okay, everything is packed now." She said as she went over the plans in her head. Her collection of jewelry, clothes, bags and shoes was worth at least ten grand. Not much but it was enough to get her established somewhere.

He laughed slightly. "And how exactly do you plan on carrying that?" Her suitcases were huge.

"I don't know. If you won't help me, I'll figure it out."

"Serene, you're being ridiculous. You're safe here. You don't have to go. I wish you could just hear me out—"

"I've heard enough! Why don't you understand that I don't want to hear anything you have to say?" Serene said, glaring at him, and then went back to scouring the room to assure she had grabbed everything.

He tried to get her attention, but she rudely stopped him each time.

If she was going to be his wife, he had to learn how to control her tantrums.

"Serene, Stop!" He gently grabbed her arm. "You *will* listen to me!"

"Oh, *shut* up," she rolled her eyes and easily escaped his grasp. "I said, I don't want to hear it!"

"Fine," he said, holding on to his pride, and calmly walked out of the room. He had never begged, and he wasn't going to bring himself down to that level with her, or with anyone, ever.

Several minutes later, Serene walked into the foyer and noticed all of the keys on the key holder were missing. She tried not to panic.

"That's fine, I'll call a cab."

She made her way towards the phone and saw the empty space on the table. When she realized the phone base was gone, her heart began to race. She walked into the foyer and was startled when she heard Alex's loud echoing voice from above the stairs.

"I just want to talk," he said loudly but calm. "Is that okay? Or do you still want me to *shut up*?"

"Alex..." she said her body tense, and her hand over her heart, "you're... scaring me."

He rolled his eyes. "I'm not *trying* to scare you. When have I ever done anything to hurt you?" He waited for an answer. "Oh, that's right, never."

"Alex, I just want to go," she said, softly looking up at him from the foyer.

"And you can... once you've calmed down and allowed me to speak."

He walked away, towards his bedroom.

She looked around, trying to figure out a way to leave, but knowing Alex he'd probably thought this through. She went into the office and saw his open laptop, but there was no internet connection. Serene slowly sat down in his chair and remembered that the house was surrounded by acres of land and they weren't near any other houses.

Before she was angry, now she was beyond that—she was scared of Alex. And for the first time in her life, she wondered what he was capable of.

After a few minutes, she realized she had no choice. She would have to confront him, and pretend everything was okay until she had access to the phone or cars again.

Serene went upstairs, and then cautiously walked into his bedroom.

Once inside, she noticed he wasn't in the room, but the sheer white curtains were flowing in the breeze. She got closer and saw one of the doors to the balcony was open. She walked out onto the large balcony and saw him sitting at the table where they would often play chess together.

Alex was very carefully arranging the gold and silver chess pieces on the decorated board. The weather was surprisingly nice, and, if it wasn't for the fact that they were in this very concerning circumstance, she'd probably spend the day outside hiking.

They didn't say anything to each other, and she eventually sat down across from him. When he made sure every game piece was absolutely perfect and aligned, he made his first move. He then motioned to her with his hand that it was her turn. They played chess in awkward silence for a few minutes.

Eventually, he spoke. "I... need you to know, above all things, that I'm not perfect."

"Well there's a shocker," she spat.

He arched an eyebrow at her comment. "Are you *ever* going to be respectful when I talk to you? Or are you *always* going to act like a rebellious teenager?" he said scolding her as if she were his daughter.

She badly wanted to tell him off but knew he currently had the upper hand so she was silent.

He continued. "I made a mistake... two mistakes."

She opened her mouth to say 'a few more than that!' but she bit her tongue.

"The first one was leaving you alone, for too long," he said acknowledging the fact that she was very pretty with an endearing disposition, and it was foolish of him to leave her unattended knowing somebody would eventually attempt to lure her in. "So, nothing that has happened to you is your fault, you see? It's mine. Had I never left you, or, if I hadn't lost contact last year, we would have been happily engaged by now. So, for that... I am sorry."

She moved her Bishop to threaten his Queen and he moved his queen out of the line of fire.

"My second mistake was thinking I could live without you when

I found out you were pregnant. Which again is my fault. Had I been with you, or had I kept contact, it would never have happened.

I'll admit I fought my feelings for you, even while I was away at school but… that's the annoying thing about love, isn't it? You can't control it. Trust me, I tried. So, my second and biggest mistake was thinking, even for a second that I could stop loving you simply because you were pregnant."

She looked at the board for a moment and then strategically captured his Queen.

Yet Alex was completely unaffected by her move and continued talking. "But see there is one thing neither of us realized. I didn't even see it myself until recently. While I was busy fighting off my feelings for you, I had accidentally fallen in love with the very thing that caused me to fight my feelings for you in the first place."

She stopped and looked up as he finally had her King cornered. She absorbed his last words, and her heart was pounding. He grabbed his Rook to finally checkmate her King, winning the game, but instead, he used the rook to knock over his own King in surrender.

Serene was shocked since Alex rarely beat her at chess.

"So, you see… I have a serious problem now. I can't stand to lose you. Not only because I love you, but because I realized I am in love with that child. I found myself protective of him or her in the same way I am with you."

They looked into each other's eyes and for a moment she saw the sincerity in them. He wasn't angry, or upset, or demanding. He was… emotional.

Since day one he was protecting the baby inside her. Even when she didn't care, when she was careless. He cared even when she was hoping she had miscarried. It was him who convinced her it was a blessing. Alex had cared for and protected the life inside of her even when she got mad at him for it.

"Serene, I fought my feelings for you, and I ran because I was afraid. I was afraid I could never love your child, afraid I would never feel that parental attachment but somehow... I already do." She looked down and placed a hand over her stomach.

He got up, and he knelt in front of her.

She watched as he gently grabbed both of her hands.

"Stay... *Please*," he whispered softly. His words caught her off guard and she didn't know what to say.

Just then he pulled out the engagement ring. It was gorgeous, flawless, five carat emerald-cut diamond with an elegant design surrounding it, and it shined brighter than anything she had ever seen before.

"I love you, Serene. I love everything about you. I want to protect and take care of both you and the baby forever. You *both* are my everything. I couldn't bear anything happening to either of you. Please, be my wife. Please give me the honor of being the father of your child."

He kissed her hand as he nervously waited for her to decide.

She was speechless, and for a moment she had forgotten how to breathe. She hated herself for her forgiving heart. Just a few minutes ago she was convinced she hated him. She had no idea how he did it, but her hate was gone as if it had never existed in the first place, and it was replaced with tenderness, and an immense amount of appreciation for him.

"I... I want to," she breathed. "I really do but," her eyes watered, "I'm just not in love with you yet, and... I'm not sure if I can be the submissive wife you want me to be." She didn't want to lie to him, and she feared not being able to successfully fill the role of being Dr. Elbridge's Light sector wife.

"I know. I know you fell out of love with me. And that's my fault. But I'll win your love, respect, and affection again. I promise you; I will work at it every day until... until you're absolutely crazy about me again," he said, smiling as tears escaped his eyes.

They both laughed quietly at the fact that they were both crying. He placed the ring on her finger and then kissed her hand, placing his cheek on it shortly after.

His tearful eyes met hers and he caressed her face. "I love you Serene, and I care about you both. My priority will always be to make sure you're taken care of, and that your—*our* baby," he said correcting himself, "is born into a marriage with loving parents."

Against her will, his words melted her heart and she couldn't stop the tears that escaped her eyes. She didn't love him but felt that she could learn to love and appreciate this side of Alex one day. She brought up her hands to touch his face, wiping his tears away.

He came up to kiss her, and as he did, he lifted her by her waist, spinning her around in celebration.

"Is that a yes?" He said as he lowered her to place his face right next to hers.

Serene smiled and nodded.

He kissed her as if she had just saved his life.

TWENTY-EIGHT

THE SURPRISE

Early in the morning, and a few days after Serene had accepted his proposal, Alex snuck into Serene's room to wake her up with a kiss.

"I have a surprise for you." He whispered as he sat on the bed.

"Oh no. Did you try to make breakfast again?" She rubbed her eyes.

Alex laughed. "After yesterday, I promise I'll never put you through that misery again." She smiled. "Come. Get dolled up and we'll go."

After a decently long drive they arrived.

Serene watched in awe. The building they parked in front of was breathtaking, built with white stone and had rows of tall roman columns at the entrance.

Alex got out and gave the valet his keys. He escorted Serene out of his car and held her hand as he gently pulled her up the steps.

Inside, a blonde lady with a bun stood ready to greet them. She extended her hand to Serene, wanting to welcome her, but Alex, being full of excitement, rushed past her.

"We'll be right back." He told the lady. "I need to show her something."

The lady smiled and nodded, giving him permission.

Alex dragged Serene further into the building. They were both smiling, and Serene struggled to keep up in her heels.

As they walked through the immense building, Serene looked up at the cathedral-like ceilings that were adorned with glistening gold paint and angelic paintings.

The walls and floors were a creamy glossy marble, and their footsteps echoed loudly in the gigantic emptiness of what she could only describe as a roman marble palace.

Alex opened a pair of very large double doors and led her outside.

Serene gasped when she saw acres of highly manicured gardens.

Alex walked her down the steps and past a large fountain, then eventually down the center path between two large hedge mazes.

"Where in the world are you taking me?" Serene said out of breath.

"Just a little further."

Moments later, they made it to a large open area. In front of them was a small circular structure with steps that led up to a flat marble-floored platform. A row of roman columns adorned the back in a half-circle and the whole structure was open and decorated with hints of ivy. Up above them, the columns held a long-curved marble slab that spelled something in original Latin.

Serene caught her breath as she read, "And they shall become one."

"Close. It actually reads, 'and *he* will become one'. Eh, they tried."

Serene and Alex laughed.

He took her up the few steps and she looked around as the view from there was even better. She could see the sun shining on the large Roman-style building, and a few scattered cherry trees were blooming, beautifully adorning the large open areas.

"Do you like it?" he asked, standing behind her.

"I've… never seen anything like it," she said in awe.

"There are beautifully sculpted gardens as far as the eye can see," he said watching Serene absorb the beauty that surrounded them. He walked up to her and hugged her from behind. "It's booked and reserved, exactly two weeks from today."

Serene choked.

"That's… too soon, Alex. Sooner than we talked about," she said, turning around and placing a hand over her quickly beating heart. This didn't feel like her life anymore. *What is happening?*

"I know. We were aiming for a month from now but the only couple that agreed to give up their reservation for the amount we offered had this date."

Serene's eyes widened. "How much did you pay them? We could have had it at Dad's church."

Alex hesitated to tell her that her attacker had shown up there and it wasn't safe.

"Serene, it's done and paid for… You'll be three months pregnant in two weeks." He got closer to her and lifted her face to meet his gaze. "*Please.* I'd like to have you… *soon.*" He kissed her softly.

Serene's body began to shake and her world began to spin. She felt undeserving of this, and of his love, but most of all she felt this was all too much, too soon. Happiness escaped her. Her feelings went past that and now she was on the verge of fainting.

Clair was in charge of the wedding, and when Clair was in charge of something, she was like a drill sergeant: cold, determined and ruthless. Serene felt elated to have others handle the wedding plans. The morning sickness was taking a toll on her body and she never felt comfortable giving orders.

Over the next few days, everything around her felt like a blur, or a dream, where everything was moving fast, and all she could see were smears of colors caused by the various people in motion.

Serene and Alex barely had any time to themselves. He was working, and she was being dragged around town by Casey and Clair. Whenever they did have a moment together, Alex mostly just told her how excited he was about the wedding, particularly their wedding night. He knew it was best if he stayed away from her. Which wasn't hard to do when Serene had her mother staying temporarily in the house. They were forced to be on their best behavior.

At the Roman marble palace, Serene emerged from the dressing room in a large elegant wedding gown. Serene thought it too much, but Casey, Clair, and Lillian had persuaded her last week that she looked stunning in it.

Serene, on the other hand, had never felt so embarrassed in so much fabric. The train was immense, and the gown was heavy and hard to walk in. She looked in the mirror, and where there should have been a smiling, glowing bride, there was a woman with sad eyes and a half-smile. It seemed everyone was so happy and focused on the wedding that no one ever took the time to notice her despair. She tried to make it obvious that she was struggling, hoping someone would come to her rescue or ask her if something was wrong… but no one ever did.

The wedding was only an hour away, and Serene was in the bathroom dry heaving. Apart from her parents and Alex's family, no one knew she was pregnant. Serene was miserable, and she had never felt so helpless.

Three months ago, she swore she was in love with a man she had had only spent two weeks with, and then suddenly Alex came back into her life, and now she was marrying him? She wondered how so much had happened in such a short period of time. Had her and Alex waited a few months, perhaps it wouldn't feel like her world was spinning out of control.

Her wedding dress fanned the bathroom floor as she kneeled with her head over the toilet, feeling ill. A tear escaped her eye, and when it hit the water, it caused an echo in the emptiness.

She wiped the tears that followed as if drying them would prevent further tears from coming, but they soon came pouring out. A terrible feeling of despair came over her as she realized that no matter how hard she fought to gain control of her life, it all seemed useless.

She felt like a helpless passenger in the back seat of a car where Alex was driving and Clair was at his side, and the car was speeding faster and faster toward a brick wall. No matter how hard she screamed, no one was listening, but soon the inevitable was coming and the tension was unbearable.

Her mother knocked on the bathroom door. "Hurry up Serene! You have photos to take."

Serene placed a hand on her chest, trying to control the tension building there. She tried to get up but fell when she felt the floor shifting underneath her. She knew how she was feeling for days, even weeks. She also knew she should have found a way to stop the wedding days ago, but she had also hoped her feelings would change by now.

Every kind gesture, every kiss, every smile Alex gave her filled her with hope. And when she had doubts, she'd shake them away, feeling like she was being stupid and selfish. He would tell her he loved her and when she wouldn't say it back, he'd hold her and promised he'd be patient.

But, on the day of her wedding, several thoughts crossed her mind. *What if I never fall in love with him? What if he spends his entire life trying to get me to love him in vain, only for my heart to remain sealed?*

She had loved Alex before, but then she had felt something more with Tristan. Those weeks had changed her views on love. She never felt pressured to be anything but herself. She remembered how it felt to be in his arms. Remembered her cheeks hurting from laughing and smiling so much. She could be anything she wanted to be, and he adored her regardless. It was a feeling she knew now she would always long for.

Serene exited the bathroom and ran downstairs to find Alex.

The dress was tight and heavy, and she struggled to breathe. She felt dizzy as she ran down the main staircase and nearly fell. Once downstairs, she realized that she couldn't even begin to fathom where to find him.

As she ran frantically, she ungracefully tripped over her dress and fell to her knees. One of the groomsmen saw her fall and alerted Alex, who was standing near the doors that led to the courtyard.

Alex saw his bride for the first time in days. He was mesmerized. She looked elegant and as angelic as ever. It took him a moment to snap back to reality and realize that she had fallen.

He ran to help her.

"My dear, what are you doing?" he asked her as he helped her up. "Are you hurt?"

She was breathing heavily, and she tried to speak but her words weren't clear. "I… need to speak to you… Please, Alex. In private." Breathing deep in her dress was difficult.

Alex saw the look of desperation in her face and instantly knew what this was about, yet he refused to let anyone see them this way. He grabbed her arm and with haste led her down a hallway and into a private room. He closed the doors behind them.

Alex made the perfect groom. Not a hair of his sun-touched brown hair was out of place. The black and white suit fit him like a glove. His handsome good looks would rival any of those Disney princes she grew up watching. So, she did her best to not look at him directly.

344

Serene turned away from him ashamed and took a deep breath.

"Alex, I'm sorry. I'm so sorry. I... don't know how to put this." She put her fingers through her hair nervously, messing up her perfect up-do.

Alex was already upset. A bride never acted this way unless she had cold feet, but he decided to hear her out.

"I can't... marry you. You deserve someone better. Someone who's head over heels in love with you. There are tons of women who would happily take my place and be the kind of wife you're looking for. The kind who would gladly submit to being your Light sector wife. It just isn't me though. I should have said something sooner, and I tried. I promise you, I tried... I'm not getting married today. I'm *so* sorry."

Alex stood there, stoic.

"You're allowed to be angry. I will take all the blame," she whispered as her body tensed up.

He looked away from her and took a deep breath in disappointment. He *was* angry, but he couldn't let her see it. He needed to find a way to solve this matter because he was convinced that there was *no way in hell* he was going to allow her to make a fool out of him, *again,* in front of all of his friends, his family, his colleagues, everyone!

He was tired of convincing her. He wanted her regardless of her impurity, regardless of the fact she was having another man's child, that she wasn't well educated. He had slept with more attractive and more educated women who'd blow up his phone. All wanting a chance to date him. He wondered how it was possible she didn't want him? Alex was a logical person and something was off.

He had always respected her, always treated her very well, give or take a few arguments. He also knew he was handsome, rich, educated, and treated cancer children for Christ's sake. It made no sense to him as to why she would deny him. He took a moment to think before his mind went to a place he really didn't want it to go to. Because right now, he felt like hurting her.

He spoke slowly, forcing kindness into his words.

"Serene, it's normal to have cold feet. You're neither the first nor the last bride to feel this way. Let's just get through today. I beg you."

"No, Alex, this isn't cold feet," she turned to look at him. "I know what I'm supposed to feel right now. Trust me, I'm embarrassed and ashamed at how I feel. I can't even repay you or your family for everything that they've done. And I fully accept your family never speaking to me again, but understand... I would be lying to you if I married you. I will be hurting you in the end. I realize this now."

Alex rubbed his temples as he paced.

Serene wanted him to say something, anything.

He stopped and looked at her.

"Serene, answer with simply a yes, or a no.... Do you love me?"

"What?" Serene squinted, confused. She hadn't said those words to him in years and she had already told him that she didn't.

"I said do you LOVE me? Do you care about me? Dammit, Serene it's a simple question!" he said, finally losing his temper.

She stood there looking down as she struggled to sort out her emotions. She tried hard to concentrate and to define what she felt for him.

He saw her struggling to answer and so placed his hands on her shoulders. "Serene. Try this. Just answer quickly with how you feel. What words come to mind when you think about me?—The good things that come to mind." He added, knowing she could think of a tens of negative things about him, but he had to force her to think positively.

"You've done a lot for me. More than anyone ever has. We've known each other for a long time. You were by my side at the hospital, you were always there when I had nightmares... I know you love me, and the baby. I care about you, *very* much. I appreciate you and adore you, but I don't…" She looked up at him and saw the worry in his gorgeous blue eyes as he prepared himself to hear the words he was dreading.

That she didn't love him, that she'd never love him again.

But just then, as she studied his face, she realized she couldn't say that either. She couldn't say it because she did care about him. Yet she wondered if that would always be enough.

"No…" She looked over, finally sorting her emotions. "I do… I do love you, Alex… just not the way I'm supposed to. Nor do I feel like I could ever truly be in love with you the way I should, and that's the problem."

Alex sighed and held her hands.

"Serene, listen. You will, you will love me the way you're supposed to. It's just that things are moving fast for us. I understand that. Like I said before, we would have dated a while. I would have done things to make sure you fell in love with me again and I will, I will still do those things."

"Yes, but—"

"You find me attractive, don't you?"

"I—" Of course he was attractive, he was gorgeous.

"And you just admitted you love me, right? That you care about me a lot?"

She knew where he was going with his words, but she would not let herself be convinced into marrying him on the off-chance that one day, she *might* fall in love with him.

"Yes, but we fight. Constantly. You're this well-organized, smart, serious, and mature guy who follows Light sector laws to a fault, and I'm nothing like you. I'm messy, rebellious, childish, I've always struggled with Light sector rules. We have nothing in common. Nothing! We are miserable living together most of the time. I mean, how could you possibly be in love with me when you're always irritated at me? If I don't embody the qualities of that Light sector wife you desire then—"

"Because Serene! Love is not logical!" he said, finally going off on her. "It's not! Trust me. I've tried to find a logical reason as to why I am absolutely crazy about you and none of my answers can fully explain why I feel the way I do about you!... It's an annoying entity in my head and in my heart that cannot be reasoned with. And it's frustrating because it's free to bond with whoever the hell it wants regardless of what I want or who I feel is a good match for me!" He pointed at his chest, "I've tried to forget about you. Twice already! But I can't! So, you're right, we fight! And quite frankly you get on my nerves half the time, with your rebellious antics and your immaturity. Do you *really* think I don't know how hard it will be to control you as my wife? God Serene I'd have better luck with a wild horse!" His face was now hovering hers, "But, I would rather spend my life fighting and arguing with you than a lifetime without you." Alex grabbed her pulling her to him and kissed her out of sheer frustration. She tried to pull away but he held her against him until she gave in to his kiss.

Afterward, he gently held her face and through glossy eyes he spoke to her again. "Serene, all I need... is for you to envision loving me someday. Can you see it?" he searched her eyes for answers.

Suddenly, there was a frantic knock at the door. Alex reluctantly walked away from Serene and opened the door before Clair had a chance to bust through it.

"Serene? Alex? Why are you guys in here?" Clair asked completely baffled.

"We aren't... sure about this yet. The wedding," Serene said nervously, unable to look at her mom directly.

Alex hated what he was about to do. But he truly believed it was for the best, and with so little time left, he was desperate.

"No, actually. Unlike Serene here, I am very sure about the wedding, but it seems like she's the one with cold feet." He narrowed his eyes at Serene.

"Is that true?" Clair asked her, barely hiding her frustration.

"No Mom, I mean... I'm confused, and I'm worried about where my feelings are right now. It just... doesn't feel right," Serene began to shake. There was no one she feared more than her mother.

"Alex, could you please give us a moment," Clair asked him as she glared at Serene.

"Absolutely," he agreed.

He walked up to Serene and caressed her face as she looked up at him through tearful and worried eyes. "My love, everything will be okay. You'll see." He kissed her hand and though she held it tightly, begging him to stay, he let her go.

As he passed Clair, he whispered through his teeth in frustration. "Please, I beg you, reason with her. She's nervous and scared and I don't want her making a scene."

"Don't worry about a thing, Alex. I promise you, I have this under control," she whispered to where only he could hear and patted his arm. They looked at each other with a mutual understanding that Clair would get Serene through this wedding by any means necessary.

Alex took one final look at his bride and was hesitant to leave her, but knew it was the only way to get through today.

Once Alex had closed the door, Clair looked at Serene, her face red and her eyebrows furrowed.

"What the hell do you think you're doing?" Clair's hands became fists.

"Mom... please... " Serene cried as her mom got closer, but she tried to stay strong. "I'm sorry! But there is nothing you can do to change my mind. I don't love Alex! And it's my choi—"

Serene felt a familiar sting burn her cheek. Clair had slapped her. Serene regained her balance, and as her face flushed in anger she gave her mother a face of utter hatred. But Serene's expression only angered Clair further and she hit her again, this time louder and harder than the last. The blow caused Serene to fall to the ground.

Serene placed a hand over her cheek to soothe the burning pain.

Through tearful eyes, she looked up at her mother in horror. "Hit me all you want Mom. I'm not doing it!"

"You stupid, unappreciative bitch!" Clair scolded.

When Serene realized she was about to kick her she turned around and got into the fetal position shielding her stomach. Clair kicked her back with relentless force. Occasionally digging her heels into her ribs. "How dare you do this to Alex! After everything he's done for you!"

Alex stood by the door listening. Her sobs and screams were too much for him to bear, and he placed a hand on the doorknob determined to go in and stop Clair from further hurting the woman he loved.

But just then, he carefully thought things through, and he stopped himself. He looked up in tears and ashamed at himself for allowing this to continue, but he couldn't get himself to go in and to save her. He wanted Serene too much to let her slip away.

He wiped his tears and walked away.

Inside the room, Serene could barely talk between her mother's kicks.

"I don't... love him Mother!" she sobbed.

"Love? You wouldn't know the first thing about love. The way Alex takes care of you. The way he offers you the world. The way he desperately wants to marry you regardless of the fact you're carrying another man's child. That's love! You don't know how stupid you are to not realize what you are so close to losing!"

It wasn't the first time Clair had hurt her this way, and Serene knew from experience that even in a building surrounded by guests, she was capable of so much more. Serene never won a battle against her mother, but this situation was different. There was too much on the line.

Before, Serene was hopeful that at least one day she would leave and obtain her freedom, so she suffered through it, but now, marrying Alex meant living her whole life forced to conform to someone else's vision of perfection. Clair was a temporary hell, but marrying Alex was a lifelong sentence without parole. Light sectors didn't believe in divorce; even if she moved, she would always be married to Alex, and by law be forced to do as he commanded.

Clair was sick and tired of seeing Serene wrinkle her dress on the floor so she grabbed her by the hair and lifted her up against the wall.

"Alex is handsome, rich, successful, and from a wonderful family. He's kind and willing to give you anything your heart desires. All he asks from you is that you let him love you! And you're so useless you can't even do that!" She slammed her head against the wall.

Serene attempted to pull her mother's hands out of her hair as she screamed in pain. To mute her screams, Clair used her other hand to squeeze her throat tightly nearly suffocating her. "Now you listen to me very carefully. You will marry Alex today or I swear to you, Serene, that baby will *never* see the light of day! I will NOT allow a child out of wedlock! Do you understand?"

Serene's eyes widened and her fighting stopped. She was willing to deal with anything her mother threw at her that day, but her motherly instincts kicked in. She took Clair's threat seriously because Serene knew she had meant every word. Clair's image in her community meant everything to her, and Serene bore the scars to prove it. Whether it was paying someone to perform an illegal abortion, drugging her, or stealing her child. Clair's ruthlessness knew no bounds and Serene wasn't going to gamble with her child's life.

Turning blue, and through tears, Serene did her best to nod and express her surrender.

Clair finally loosened her grip and Serene fell to the floor, coughing, and heaving as she struggled to breathe again.

"Now, go get your makeup and hair re-done. Once again, you've ruined someone else's hard work."

Clair adjusted her dress to make sure everything was in its place and walked out of the room.

She saw Alex nervously watching from a distance. Clair nodded and Alex faked a smile.

Alex felt horrible for what had happened, but he found an ounce of comfort in the fact that soon she would be his wife, and he'd never allow Clair to hurt her again. He would demand obedience from her, but it wouldn't be as bad as it was with Clair, so he was thoroughly convinced he was also marrying Serene to protect her and provide her with the safety and stability she needed for her and her baby. He gave himself those reasons as an excuse for what he'd just allowed, but the reality was he always achieved his goals, no matter the cost.

Serene's mom never left her side. Assuring everything happened as it should. Without a single question, the paid make-up artist swiftly fixed Serene's face, hiding any evidence of the beating she had just endured.

Eventually, a smiling Clair handed over her daughter to Peter, who instantly began to cry when he saw how amazing his little princess looked.

Serene tried to smile but it was impossible to do. So instead she kept her gaze low and did what she could to fight back the tears as she walked down the aisle with her father.

The garden was overly decorated, and though she never looked up, she felt the warm stare of the crowd. The sounds they made reminded her of hungry wolves. Her heart began to race and her breathing made it hard to hear the music. The gown's train was heavy, like chains clasped tightly around her waist. The sound of her dress dragging across the floor irritated her and her tiara was like a crown of thorns, itching at her scalp. The veil hiding her face, intended to symbolize her innocence, was successfully lying to everyone. The heavy bouquet felt as heavy as a cross and, regardless of her efforts, the tears of sadness and despair started to seep through her eyes. The long walk towards Alex felt like an eternity, but she'd welcome an eternity if it meant never reaching the altar.

Her father removed the veil to show off her beautiful but sad face, and tears were flowing down her cheeks.

Unfortunately, her tears were mistaken for tears of joy and she heard the crowd 'awe' as they were overtaken by emotional admiration.

Alex was awestruck by her simple beauty, and when he looked at Peter, he finally smiled and nodded in proud accomplishment.

Serene never cared to look around at all the decor, but she knew it was lavish and unnecessarily expensive. The smell of the lilies made her sick to her stomach. She was convinced that she was about to throw up, so she began to sweat and tremble.

Alex noticed her shaking and grabbed her hand to massage her palm as her father walked up to the altar to read from the book.

Serene had zoned out until a specific part in her father's speech.

"Wives… submit to your husbands, as unto the Lord, for the husband is the head of his wife even as God is the head of the church. Now as the church submits to God, so also should wives submit in everything to their husbands.

Husbands, love your wives, as Christ loved the church and gave himself up for her, that he might sanctify her, having cleansed her by the washing of water with the word, so that he might present the church to himself in splendor, without spot or wrinkle or any such thing, that she might be holy and without blemish… "

Serene tried to block out everything that was happening and began to focus more on not throwing up.

"Do you Alex, promise to have and to hold Serene from this day forward, for richer or for poorer, in sickness and in health, to love and to cherish, till death do you part, in according to God's holy ordinance, and the eternal laws of the Light?"

"I do," Alex said with absolute certainty.

"Do you Serene, promise to have and to hold Alex from this day forward, for richer for poorer, in sickness and in health, to love, cherish, and to obey your husband, submitting to him in everything, till death do you part, in according to God's holy ordinance, and the eternal laws of the Light?"

There was a long silence. Alex and Peter looked at Serene anxiously awaiting her answer.

TWENTY-NINE

THE FIGHT

T he secret Krov Assembly was being held inside Vermillion Enterprise's Headquarters after Midnight.

Tristan was sitting next to Lea in a dark, packed conference room full of thousands of other Krovs. He placed a piece of paper with an address on Lea's lap.

"What's this?" Lea whispered.

"I broke into Serene's house today. Found out her friend's last name is Elbridge... I later did some research and found her address."

"Serene's address?" Lea asked, hopeful.

"No, Casey's. She's Serene's best friend. I need you to go to that address, talk to her, and make her tell you where Serene is. You told me you spoke to her at the hospital. She'll recognize you."

Lea ignored Tristan for a moment and paid attention to the important announcements being made at the Krov Assembly.

"...and as of this moment, turning humans is strictly forbidden," Armador's voice through the microphone felt like thunder. The crowd's chatter grew exponentially at the news. "Registration is closed, and anyone caught turning a human will be swiftly eliminated..."

"Lea?" Tristan said, trying to get her attention. Her eyes were stoic. Something was worrying her.

"Okay," Lea replied. "I'll go see her tomorrow. I just… have something I have to take care of first."

"Damnit, Kamilla! I need my money," Tristan sat on the side of his bed, in Lea's guest room. He was shirtless and Kamilla was trying really hard to seduce him. Luckily, she no longer aroused him for several reasons.

"I said I will. Don't you trust me?" she said as she came up behind him and kissed his neck. She was in her underwear and begging him to finally take her.

Tristan looked away. "How can I when you haven't done a single thing to return *my* money to me, and there is a tight limit on that card."

"It's not that tight, Trist. You were able to buy a car, and like I said, I will return everything to you soon." She then sensually laid back in bed. "Might even be sooner if you come back here and… finish what we started." she patted the space on the bed beside her.

Tristan's frustration and annoyance grew. He knew that she was toying with him, and he refused to let Kamilla continue to treat him like a trained sexual pet.

He stood up and put his shirt back on.

"Where are you going?"

"…Out."

"Out where?" she said in an angry tone.

He ignored her and left the room.

Kamilla made a fist and hit the mattress. If he was human, she would have killed him instantly, but he was much too strong now.

Tristan walked out the front door but stopped dead in his tracks when he saw Lea struggling to carry an athletic young man inside.

The stranger had short blond hair and his eyes were red. His white T-shirt and jeans were soaked in blood and he was acting rabid. It was clear he'd just been turned.

"Help me!" Lea said breathless and in a panic. "I thought I could handle him." Her arms were scratched up and her clothing was covered in blood.

"Bring him inside so I can feed him!" she begged.

"What the hell did you do Lea!?"

"He's my brother! I... I couldn't leave him behind!" Lea knew that once the new order of things began, her brother would live a miserable existence in a human concentration camp where they would be turned into mindless cattle and reproduced for food. Lea hoped that by quickly turning him that somehow, she could get away with it. She knew it was risky, which is why she hadn't informed Tristan and went ahead alone.

Tristan begrudgingly wrapped his arms around the stranger's waist from behind, then dragged him inside.

Once inside, he lowered himself to hold him steady on the floor as Lea gathered food in the kitchen.

"You couldn't bring him here before turning him?" Tristan yelled.

"I tried! But he wasn't listening! So, I killed him. I had food in the car but apparently it wasn't enough, and he escaped!"

A fully dressed Kamilla walked out into the living room but hid away from view once she saw the chaos.

Lea put a giant bowl of human flesh on the floor in front of her brother, and he immediately took to it.

"Wait. Is this James?" Tristan shook his head. "Did you not listen to a damn thing that was said in assembly?" Tristan wasn't upset at Lea for trying to save his life. He was upset that Lea would risk her life over a man who was a known troublemaker and often mistreated her.

"No one will find out! I promise!" she exclaimed nervously, but what she had done had put everyone around her at risk.

357

"Did he attack anyone?" he asked.

Lea placed her hands on the counter and lowered her head. "One. He killed a man. In another car."

"Jesus fucking Christ, Lea! They are going to find out!" Tristan tried to hold back his anger and was also trying his best to hold James but the bowl was empty and he was trying to run off.

Lea began to throw stuff out of the freezer and onto the floor as she spoke. "Stop yelling at me! I couldn't just leave him! If... if it was Serene you would have done the same!" Tristan looked at her for a moment thinking it was unfair that she would compare someone like Serene to her deadbeat brother.

"That's different!" Tristan expressed vehemently through his teeth.

"How is that different? You love Serene, don't you?" Lea's eyes watered.

"Argh! Just-Just fucking feed him for christ's sake!" James kept screaming whenever Tristan applied force to restrain him.

As Lea and Tristan struggled to feed James frozen meat, Tristan looked up to see the door close. He realized that Kamilla had likely heard everything.

The next morning Jason walked up to Lea's house and knocked on the door. Lea had messaged him about the possibility of training James, but she was too busy arguing with her brother in the bedroom to hear Jason's knock.

James was angry at Lea for turning him. The painful transformation made him resent her further, and he was trying to get Lea to take him back into the city, but as a new Krov, understandably Lea was against it.

Tristan was eating a bowl of crunchy human bones, doing his

best not get involved, when he opened the door for Jason.

"Where is he?" Jason looked up at Tristan with tight, worried eyes.

"Lea's bedroom."

Jason walked over to her bedroom and knocked on the door.

"Lea? It's me, Jason."

Lea wiped a tear from her eye and opened the door. Her face was red and her eyes were swollen. Behind her stood her out-of-control brother. Lea exited the room and slammed the door behind her.

"I don't have much money for training, and you know he can't be registered."

"Yes. I know. Which is why I cannot train him."

"I know, but can you make an exception?" Lea looked at Jason with tear-stained eyes. "Please, Jason. Just this once, I need your help."

Jason kept quiet.

"Fine! If you want money, I'll—I'll find a way to pay you!"

"It's not about money." He put his hand on her shoulder. "You know why I can't train him. Plus, he's a Red."

"Oh, so if he was a Golden you'd help him, huh?" Her face scrunched, and the tears began to flow. She waited for a response, but he stood silent.

"You know what, forget it!" Lea said, going back into the room with her brother.

Jason and Tristan glanced at each other. Jason then motioned for Tristan to follow him into the backyard.

Once they were at a safe distance from the house they spoke in private.

"Tristan, you know if I could help I would, but—"

"I know. I don't know what the hell she was thinking, but I don't want to see any harm come to her, so if you know of a way to avoid getting in trouble with The Council, I need to know."

Jason paced for a moment as he tried to think of a solution.

Tristan had an idea. "What if I talk to Kamilla and convince her to help us?"

"I know that you've known Kamilla for a long time, but I've known her for longer. So, trust me when I say, she can't be trusted."

"She helped me."

"James is not you. Kamilla may have done a lot for you because she sees you as a potential partner, but otherwise she would have killed you a long time ago."

"So, what the hell are our options then?" Tristan exclaimed as he put his hands on his waist.

After a moment Jason finally spoke. "Run."

Jason walked up to stand right in front of him. "Run. Leave now... go where no one will find you and do it quickly."

Tristan squinted in confusion when suddenly, they heard Lea screaming at the top of her lungs. They ran inside hoping James hadn't hurt her. When Tristan walked through the door, he saw her brother lying headless on the ground in the middle of the living room with three Sentinels around him.

A fourth Sentinel was grabbing Lea by the neck, choking her. Tristan charged at him, causing him to release Lea. The force with which Tristan tackled him was so strong; they both crashed through the wall and into a nearby bedroom.

In the living room, Lea was on the floor, bent over and coughing, when the three remaining Sentinels aimed their guns. One at Lea, one at Jason, and another pointed at Tristan.

They all put their hands up surrendering when a Sentinel prematurely fired at Lea's head.

As if in slow motion, Tristan saw the bullet enter her skull and explode out the back.

"Nooo!" Tristan yelled; his eyes glowing bright. The Sentinels' were blown back by an invisible force while their weapons were suspended in midair. Simultaneously Tristan rushed at them, face red and seething as their weapons were flung through the window.

Shards of glass showered the living room.

Jason watched Tristan fight the three remaining sentinels and used it as an opportunity to run through the open front door. Lucky for him his truck was right in front of the house. He opened the passenger door, unzipped his duffle bag and found his prized possession. Jason unsheathed his large obsidian dagger and took it in with him.

Trying not to be seen, Jason used his speed to find the first "dead" Sentinel, who was lifeless on the floor of the bedroom. Jason attempted to sever his head, knowing they could regenerate.

Through the gaping hole in the wall a Sentinel took notice and went after him. Jason did his best to hold his own, mostly avoiding the hits, but regardless of his efforts to evade, he was punched in the abdomen and thrown into a wall. Jason fell to his knees in pain but staggered up, knowing if he stayed down, he'd die.

Something inside Tristan snapped the moment he started fighting, and his punches were a lot stronger than either of the two Sentinels expected. With incredible force, Tristan struck one of the Sentinels in the face, causing him to double over in pain as his bottom jaw had flown off of him.

The second Sentinel ran up behind Tristan, ready to attack, but Tristan turned around and grabbed him by his midsection, lifted him and slammed him into the floor.

To finish him off, Tristan stepped on his head with such force his skull shattered, leaving a puddle of blood and mush in the small crater.

Tristan had eliminated two Sentinels single-handed; now two remained. One was jaw-less and doubled over in pain, and the other was attacking Jason. Dust and debris was everywhere as Lea's house struggled to stay erect.

Tristan's eyes glowed bright yellow again as he approached the Sentinel attacking Jason.

"What the fuck?" the Sentinel said.

Just as Tristan approached him, the Sentinel with the missing jaw thought he'd sneak up behind him, but Tristan noticed. In the blink of an eye Tristan was behind him and punched his lower abdomen with such force it caused the Sentinel to fly through the house, past the hallway, and into the wall at the end.

The Sentinel that had been attacking Jason was shocked by Tristan's power, and he quickly made a run for it through the front door.

As the last Sentinel ran, Tristan bent down to help Jason up.

"You... have to get him, he'll... warn..." Jason breathed, trying to speak through the pain. Tristan didn't wait until he finished explaining, and with unimaginable speed he went outside, jumped in the air and landed right behind the runaway Sentinel swiftly snapping his neck.

When Tristan went back to the house, he noticed Jason was removing the head off the second Sentinel at the end of the hallway. Tristan searched frantically through the rubble trying to find Lea. When he finally found her, she was lying underneath a bookcase, with a trail of blood coming out of her mouth and her hair doused in blood. Tristan levitated the bookcase off and away from her and then knelt to lift her into his arms gently.

Jason had just finished beheading the third Sentinel and then walked out into the living room.

"Is she...?" Tristan looked up at Jason through tear glossed eyes.

Jason examined her while she lay in Tristan's arms. She had an exit wound in the back of her skull caused by the bullet. He placed two fingers on her neck searching for a pulse.

"She's gone," Jason said calmly. "If she was a Red she'd make it back but she's a Golden."

Tristan looked at Lea's face as he fought back tears. "So? Are you telling me she won't regenerate?"

"She's intact... if the damage isn't extensive, she may come back. To be honest, I've never seen one come back from something like this.

Tristan held her tenderly against his chest as he gently laid her on the couch. Jason went outside to find the fourth and final Sentinel. The Sentinel had just started moving on the ground when Jason grabbed him by his hair, exposing his neck and began the grueling task of beheading him.

Inside, Tristan knelt in front of the couch holding Lea's hand when Jason returned.

"It must have been Kamilla," Tristan wiped a stray tear. "I should have stopped them sooner. I should have disarmed them as soon as I saw them! I should have stopped that bullet."

"Don't blame yourself, Trist." Jason sat down on a nearby chair as he placed his hand over his hurt abdomen. "You did well. We wouldn't have stood a chance without you."

Moments later, Tristan placed Lea's lifeless body in the back seat of his car. He had wrapped her in a thin blanket. After they loaded their cars with any necessary items, Jason got in his truck and led the way.

Nightfall came, and after several hours they drove up to a hotel. Once Jason checked in, Tristan carefully brought Lea inside and into the bathroom. He sat her lifeless body next to the tub.

"What are you doing?" Jason stood by the door to the bathroom.

"There's blood in her hair and she's—"

"Tristan, she may not even—"

"Just Stop!" He caught himself. "Sorry. I know the odd's, but I can't leave her looking like this."

Jason walked away.

Tristan turned on the warm water and Jason returned with a plastic cup so that Tristan could wash her hair.

Tristan laid with Lea in bed. If she woke up, he wanted to be there for her.

Around 3 a.m. Tristan woke up.

He sat up against the headboard and turned on the lamp. He glanced over at Lea who was suddenly shaking, sobbing and rubbing her head.

"Thank God," he whispered.

On the table next to him were two very large pills and a glass of water, set there by Jason in case Lea woke up in pain.

"Here, take these," Tristan said, handing her the water and pills.

Disoriented and crying, Lea did her best to do as he instructed. She continued to cry as Tristan held her.

He exhaled and kissed her hand. "We thought you were gone."

"What... happened?" Lea whispered, looking around. "Where are we?"

Tristan shushed Lea as he looked over at Jason, who was sound asleep. He spoke softly, "Sentinels came. They attacked us."

Lea pulled away from him and laid on her back, placing a hand over her throbbing head.

"Just go to sleep. We'll talk in the morning,"

"No ugh. I'm... fine. Wait." She sat up and her eyes searched the room, "Where's James?"

Tristan looked down at his hands. "...I'm Sorry."

"No." Lea covered her mouth with her hand and cried, "No please no... please."

Tristan pulled her to him, "I'm so sorry Lea." He shed a tear, "I should have been there." He caressed her hair as she cried on his lap.

After a few minutes, she wiped her tears. "How did we-I mean-How are we here?"

"We had to leave in case more Sentinels showed up."

"That's not what I meant." She sat up, trying to make sense of things. "There were three. No, four of them."

"I know."

"Did you," she squinted at Tristan, "kill them?"

He didn't respond.

"But how?... They're Red Sentinels and you're a... Unless you're?" she said, awestruck and searching his soft but tired golden eyes.

"Not just any Golden?"

"Do you have any idea what this means?"

"Yes. You need to sleep Lea. You're still healing." He turned off the lights and as he laid down she cuddled next to him.

"Thank you, Trist. I... owe you my life," she whispered.

Yet he didn't feel he deserved a thank you, especially since he'd failed to save her brother and she had almost died.

The next day Tristan woke up and didn't see Lea next to him. He ran outside and noticed Jason's truck was missing, but Jason was still inside.

THIRTY

TRISTAN, SERENE & ALEX

I
t could have been the fact that everyone was so cheerful, or the
fact that she was forced to continuously smile for the cameras
that caused Serene to feel better. Mostly, she was just relieved
to have gotten through the vows without embarrassing herself or
letting her nausea and nerves get the best of her.

Amongst the synchronized chaos within the palace's beautiful
marble walls, Alex would occasionally rip her away from someone
she was talking to and kiss her passionately. He'd never looked so
handsome, but his charming smile only made it a little easier for
Serene to pretend.

Serene acted as if everything was wonderful, successfully playing
the role of Mrs. Elbridge, the happiest women in the world. But
today she wasn't acting for an audience, nor to protect her mother.
No, today she was doing it for her own sanity. If she didn't, her
emotions would spiral out of control. Perhaps if she tried hard
enough to believe this was her *happily ever after*, somehow, even she'd
be convince of it. After all, things could be worse. Now at least she'd
never have to live with her mother.

In the ballroom, several large sparkling chandeliers hung
gracefully from the ceiling and tall roman columns separated the
dance floor from the dinner tables.

The tables were dressed with white linen, gold silk, and an overabundance of candles and exotic flowers flowing out of the tall vases.

Serene was taking pictures with her new sister, Casey when Alex decided to steal her away to have their first dance.

She couldn't help but notice how happy Alex was. His smile was contagious, and her cheeks were now hurting for more reasons than one.

Maybe I did panic. Maybe it was cold feet. Perhaps I can love Alex one day. She hoped. They slow danced as the lights dimmed above them.

"Alex, I'm... sorry about earlier. I didn't mean to..."

"Don't worry too much about it. We got through it." He gave her a spin.

"No, I... owe you an apology," she said sincerely, gazing into his eyes. "I *am*... falling for you."

"Oh? Well, that's a relief," he joked. "I guess," he placed his head right next to hers, "that may make tonight better."

They laughed and she lowered her gaze.

"Are you looking forward to it?" he said as he gently brought her face up to look at him.

Serene felt naked in a room full of spectators as they exchanged this very intimate conversation. She simply gave him a slight smile.

Alex kissed her and then sensually trailed kisses down her neck.

"Alex, people are watching," she whispered coyly.

"Oh, I don't care if they watch the whole thing."

When she noticed they had an audience she turned red and pushed him away. She wasn't rough about it but Alex glared at her and clenched her waist, pulling her tightly against him.

"Don't." He whispered loudly before she could object. They studied the crowd carefully from the corner of their eyes. "You're my wife now, so you will do as I say."

"Ale—"

"Especially tonight. Understood? You *will* be punished for the way you treated me."

Serene's face went pale, and the music around them disappeared until all she could hear was her heart racing. She was unable to believe this was the same Alex from just moments ago.

Just then, Peter came up to them.

"Alex! She may be yours now, but this angel owes her father one last dance."

"Of course," Alex said, still glaring at Serene. He then kissed her cheek and whispered, "I do hope my love is well rested."

Alex walked away as Peter stepped in to dance with Serene. He was beaming with joy, but Serene was still reeling over what Alex had just told her. Alex would never hurt her, she was convinced of that, but a part of her now feared what the future held.

As Serene danced with her father, Peter gave her an earful of marriage advice and began to cry. It was hard to absorb that he was losing his only daughter.

Suddenly, his face went pale.

"Dad? Dad, are you okay?" she asked.

"Yes, just… a little dizzy from the dancing," he said, barely able to breathe.

Peter wiped his tears and tried his best to regain his composure.

"Perhaps you should sit down?"

"It's just indigestion. I get it all the time," he hugged her tight. "I'm going to go out for some fresh air. I love you."

"I love you too, Daddy," she said as she saw him walk away.

Serene stood there worried when, just then, Casey's new boyfriend Brandon approached her.

"Mind if we dance?" he asked.

"Um." Before she could object, Brandon pulled her onto the dance floor.

Serene had never met him before. Casey's parents had set them up a few weeks ago, but he seemed like a nice guy.

As they finished dancing, the surrounding crowd began to migrate to the large patio outside. Alex was called on by a few people and Serene followed behind him.

Everyone was in chaos and gathered densely around something, or someone.

She then heard someone mention the name "Peter" and she pushed her way through the crowd to get a closer look. When she finally saw them, Alex was kneeling over Peter, checking his pulse. The shock of seeing her father on the floor caused the world around her to go silent.

His eyes were open, and his body lay motionless on the floor.

A Week after the Wedding

Serene felt like she was living in a fog. She felt lost in her own darkness and overtaken by a deep sadness.

She was refusing to talk to anybody, even Alex. They barely spoke, both before and after the funeral, and Serene insisted on staying in separate bedrooms for the time being.

Serene was in bad shape; her nightmares had returned, and the nausea had become unbearable. She had stopped eating and was spotting again. Alex took her to a specialist where they informed her that she was at risk of losing the baby, and that her chronic nausea had turned into hyperemesis. As she cried in the clinic, he held her close.

Like a routine, every morning since the funeral, Alex went into the bathroom to console her. And every night, Alex held her as she cried herself to sleep. He felt guilty somehow, and angry for various reasons. He was never angry at her, but was furious at the universe for what his wife was going through.

Lying next to him, Serene was so close, yet she had never felt further away. As she began to fall asleep, her back was pressed up against him, and he couldn't help but hold her closer and caress her thigh. He cautiously trailed his hand up her leg and under her silk nightgown. His caress dangerously close to her sex.

"Serene, I love you," he whispered sweetly in her ear, then kissed her shoulder. "Have I done enough to prove that to you?" Serene gently pushed his hand away and he sighed in frustration. She was his wife now and she had yet to fulfill her duty but he wouldn't force her into it, not under the current circumstance. Still, it had been about two weeks since her father passed, and though he felt terrible for asking he needed to know.

"Serene?... When?"

"I... don't know," she whispered.

"Serene. Love. I need to know... I'm your husband now, and you don't know what this is doing to me. Tell me anything. Will it be weeks? Months? I can be patient if I know what I'm up against."

She thought about it for a moment. The last thing on her mind was sex, and it annoyed her that he could even think about sex at a time like this. She knew it would be at least a few months, but she was already starting to show, and by then she'd be even bigger. Not to mention how sick and exhausted she'd feel. She felt bad asking him to wait, but thought it was unfair to also keep him hoping that every night he laid with her, there was a chance.

"I promise... after the baby," she said, closing her eyes and clenching the pillow.

He dropped his forehead on her arm dejectedly. He needed it to be sooner, a lot sooner. He kissed her, passionately, and his need for her grew. Ripping away from her lips, he decided to leave the room before he forced her into something he'd later regret.

Lea rang the doorbell at Casey's parents' house.

She had left the hotel without warning because she knew Tristan and Jason would object to her leaving. They were about to leave town, and she had promised Tristan that she'd visit Casey. Luckily, they had grabbed her purse when they left the scene, so she had Casey's address.

Lea knew how much finding Serene meant to Tristan, and knowing she had placed a target on their backs it was the least she could do.

Casey answered the door. She was wearing a green cardigan that enhanced the beauty of her pale skin and glossy red hair.

"Lea?" Casey couldn't believe who she was seeing.

"Yeah, um. Hi," Lea said looking around and squinting at the sunlight that always felt brighter in Light sectors.

Casey smiled. "Come in."

They both stood in the foyer, nervous and unable to look at each other directly. Lea had changed her clothes but her eyes were still swollen from grieving over her brother.

Lea cleared her throat. "I'll cut to the chase. I'm here to talk about Serene."

"Yeah. We've all been so sad."

"Sad?"

"Yes, didn't you hear? Her father died during her wedding reception."

"Serene's wedding?" Lea cocked her head, searching Casey's face for approval.

"Yes, the poor girl can't catch a break."

Lea absorbed the shocking news and thought of ways to use this new information to find Serene.

"Yes, *Serene's* wedding. Well, that's actually what I'm here for. We've kept in touch after the hospital, and she told me about the wedding, but I never heard from her since then. I wanted to send her a wedding gift."

"I hear you," Casey said, placing a lock of her red hair behind her ear. "She hasn't spoken to anyone since the incident."

Lea noticed something odd about Casey. She was acting weird,

371

coyer than at the hospital.

"Well, I was wondering if you had her address? I was unaware her father died. I should probably send her some flowers."

"Sure. Um. One sec." Casey walked away.

Lea studied the house for a moment and she whistled quietly at how big and expensive it was. Casey finally returned with a folded-up piece of paper.

"That's her address and phone number." Lea took the note and put it in her pocket. "And my phone number... too."

Lea slowly lifted her head to look at her. Casey kept her gaze low and played with her hands nervously. Lea wasn't used to Light sector girls, but she felt Casey might be flirting with her.

"Thanks... um. It was nice to see you again," Lea said, smiling. "I'll text you."

"Sure. Okay."

Casey opened the door for her. Lea passed through and turned around to hug her. "Bye."

"Bye," Casey whispered as she closed the door.

Lea had always been overly cheery, but after all the recent events she felt like she would never smile again. However, after speaking to Casey, she couldn't keep her lips from curling up into a smile as she drove off.

On the way back to the hotel, Lea called Jason's phone from Tristan's cell phone.

"Lea?" Tristan exclaimed worried.

"Hey."

"Where the hell are you? You took my phone? From now on don't ever leave without—"

"I know where Serene is," she said, interrupting his rant. "I have her address in my hand." Tristan froze for a minute and didn't know what to say. "She's a few states away, but you can make it there in half a day."

"Hold on…"

"Trist. I'm only a few minutes away… Trist?" she tried to get his attention, but he had put down the phone to find something to write with.

"Okay what's the address?" he asked her nervously.

"I'll be there in just a few—"

"Just give me the goddamn address."

Lea quickly gave him the address and telephone number.

"Thank you so much, Lea. I'm leaving now." He hung up.

"Tristan, wait. Trist!" Lea yelled into the phone, but he was gone. She tried calling again, but it was busy. She debated whether to tell him about Serene's wedding.

After calling again and hearing it was busy, she realized it wouldn't stop him from going to see Serene. She was, after all, carrying his child. She also didn't want to be the one to give him the bad news.

"Hello?" Serene said, answering the phone.

Tristan pulled his head back in relief. The sound was music to his ears. He closed his eyes and focused on her soft voice as he paced outside of the hotel.

"Hello? Is anyone there?" Serene repeated. Her voice was just as he remembered it, gentle and sad.

Serene didn't recognize Jason's number and hung up.

Tristan looked at the phone. He felt that the address he had was likely accurate since the number had worked, so he got in his car and drove off.

"Hey, hey wait!" Jason yelled as he ran after him thinking Lea and Tristan had left him stranded at the hotel.

Ten Hours Later

7pm

Alex was busy in his office when he heard the doorbell and frantic knocking at the front door. It was raining, and he rushed to open it. "I said I'm coming!"

When he opened the door, he found a very tall, well-built man with bright green eyes glaring at him. He was sporting a black leather jacket and his hair was dripping wet. Alex squinted and cocked his head as he wondered, yet again, how people kept getting past the gate.

"Can I help you?"

"Serene. Where is she?" Tristan growled.

Alex stood silent for a moment, analyzing the situation.

"How did you get past the gate?"

Tristan was annoyed at his pointless question. He didn't mean to be rude, but his heart was racing since her scent was overwhelming. His body was also reeling in pain since his hunger and desire for her was increasing.

"The fuck does it matter? I climbed!" he said, as if it were obvious. "Just tell me where is she?" Tristan was so hungry it took a lot of effort to avoid killing the man standing in the way of his objective.

After Alex refused to respond, Tristan walked past him and into the house.

Fumbling, Alex pulled out his phone to call the cops.

Without hiding his speed and agility, Tristan took the phone from him and crushed it with his hand as if it were a cracker.

He let the pieces fall on the ground.

Alex's eyes widened in shock.

Tristan's anticipation had grown exponentially on his way there, he also hadn't eaten, so he was tired, hungry and slowly losing control.

"I. Just. Want. The girl," Tristan assured him making it clear he didn't want any trouble.

The storm was getting worse and it was now thundering loudly.

Alex suddenly made the connection and knew who this man was. His face then became red in anger and he didn't care how quick or how strong this man was. He was trespassing! And likely came with the intention of hurting his wife.

"Get out!" Alex yelled. "She's not here!"

Tristan knew he was lying. Her scent was everywhere and he even began to salivate.

Ignoring him and with super speed he searched around the bottom floor, breaking doors open and calling out her name. Alex stood dumbfounded. He had never seen a person move so quickly, or open locked doors with such minimal effort.

Tristan held a hand to his chest as the painful desire and anticipation of finally seeing her was causing a familiar pain to build up in his chest. But he shook his head and did his best to gather himself.

After searching the bottom floor, Tristan came back to the staircase where Alex was.

"Listen asshole, I said, she's not here!"

"I KNOW she's here!" Tristan growled in his face. Alex took a step back but showed no fear. Tristan then made his way upstairs.

"Serene! Serene, please. I need to talk to you."

Alex went into his office and nervously opened a locked drawer to retrieve a gun. He then ran upstairs.

Tristan followed the scent and found her bedroom. He opened it and as her fragrance hit him a voice screamed in his head; *you're going to kill her!*

Tristan wasn't ready, but now it was too late, his body made his way inside as if by impulse and he was powerless to stop it.

When he noticed the room was empty, he heard a gun click behind him.

"I said she's not home."

Three Hours Earlier

4pm

Alex was exhausted. He had tried just about everything to cheer

Serene up but she had refused to even leave the house.

In a final attempt he called Stephanie, her friend from the hospital, and asked her to come over. Alex knew they had started to become close friends.

"What's this?" Serene said, walking into the foyer. Alex and Stephanie were standing there.

"Um, Alex here thought it would be nice to take you shopping." Stephanie smiled.

"Oh? I'm sorry, Stephanie. I can't I've just been—"

"Please? I haven't heard from you since the wedding and Alex promised me I could... *spend some cash for myself girl,*" she hinted, talking through her teeth. "And girl you *know* damn well I need some shoes."

Serene almost smiled. "All right. Give me a minute to freshen up."

Moments later, Stephanie got behind the wheel of Serene's new luxury SUV. Serene wasn't up to driving.

"Don't wreck her," Alex joked through the driver's side window.

"Oh, I'll definitely try not to."

Alex walked over to the passenger side where Serene was getting in.

"How much?" Serene asked as she looked at the heavy credit card that now bore her new name: *Serene Elbridge*

"As much as you want, sweetie. Have fun." He kissed her forehead and put the seat belt on her.

"No, Alex. Give me a number."

He held the door open and sighed.

"Two, three... thousand?" He squinted, trying his best to come up with a number.

"One thousand," she stated, then looked away from him.

He wondered why she had asked if she already had a number in mind.

"Okay then. One thousand and not a penny more!" he joked

with her and they both smiled.

Alex was relieved to finally see a glimpse of a happier wife, and he was filled with hope. Soon, they would finally have their happily ever after.

>― ―<

Tristan halted and turned around. He then glared at Alex and fearlessly walked up to him backing Alex into the hallway. Alex kept his gun aimed but was shaking. "I swear to God, if you hurt her again, I will stop at nothing to kill you!"

Tristan looked away and smiled, trying hard not to laugh at his pathetic threat.

"I didn't mean to hurt her." Tristan said calmly while his eyes burned a hole through Alex. "It was an accident."

"You're so full of it!" Alex fired the gun, but Tristan moved too quickly and twisted Alex's hand, nearly crushing it. The pain caused Alex to drop the gun and it slid under the railing to the bottom floor.

"I'm going to ask you one last time." Tristan walked up to him. "Where... is... Serene?"

Alex swung at his face but Tristan dodged it. "You are NOT raping my wife!" He swung again but Tristan grabbed his fist in mid-air, then cocked his head.

"Your wife? Rape?" His eyes narrowed.

Alex stood in front of him seething and out of breath. Tristan released his hand.

"Alex, is it?" Tristan asked, vaguely remembering him from the phone messages.

Alex walked up to him, red faced, and swiftly kicked him in the groin. Once again this did nothing and all Alex could do was hop in place, his foot reeling in pain.

Tristan rolled his eyes, "I'm not sure if you've noticed yet... but you can't hurt me."

Regardless of his warning, Alex swung at Tristan again. Tristan gave up, allowing him to hit him in the face.

His fist hit Tristan's face loudly but had no effect. Alex looked down at his now broken and bloody hand.

"What the hell!?" Alex cried out leaning against the wall, holding his bloody hand. Punching his face felt like punching a brick wall.

"Are you guys married?" Tristan asked him calmly, but when Alex refused to answer his anger grew again. "I said, are you guys fucking married!?"

Alex studied his broken hand and was about to pass out from the pain, but he did his best to not faint or cry.

"Yes," Alex finally responded.

"When?"

After a few moments Tristan lost patience and walked up to him, grabbed his collar, and dragged him up the wall. Tristan didn't mean to lose control, but images of Serene were flashing through his mind and the anticipation was killing him. He was desperate and needed her. "When! When did you marry her?"

Alex's voice shook. "About—about two weeks ago."

Tristan looked down, shook his head and laughed. He then let him go, causing Alex to collapse on the floor.

Tristan paced, running a hand through his hair, and then stopped to look up at the ceiling. His eyes were closed as he feared the answer to his next question.

"Did you sleep with her?"

"That is none of your—"

"Just tell me if you fucking slept with her before I break your other hand!"

"...Yes," Alex said, lying. "Of course."

"I don't believe you," Tristan said, convinced that Serene and him had a bond that wasn't easily broken. Yet he also knew over three months had passed.

"You really think I wouldn't sleep with my wife?" Alex yelled, noticing his disappointment and seeing it as a form of surrender on Tristan's part.

"No." Tristan shook his head, "You're lying!"

"Why the hell would I lie? She's also pregnant with my child! And we are *very* happy."

Tristan knew the child wasn't Alex's.

"She's not happy! Not in Light sectors. She can't be!" Tristan paced as he held his aching head. He refused to believe Serene had completely forgotten about him and their time together. He also knew what marriage in Light sectors meant for Serene. The Serene he knew wouldn't have chosen that lifestyle. Serene wanted to be free.

"I don't care what you believe. Get out of my house!"

Mentally and emotionally exhausted, Tristan sat down across from Alex in the hallway.

Alex stood starring at him, puzzled.

After a few minutes Tristan finally spoke, "Do you love her?" His voice was soft.

"Why do you care?"

"Listen, asshole! I'm not sure what you heard, or who you think I am, but I care about Serene. I didn't mean to hurt her. It was an accident!"

"AN ACCIDENT?" Alex laughed and cried while holding his hand. "I guess if you call raping and assaulting her to the point she's fighting for her life an accident!"

"Just answer the goddamn question."

There was a deep silence and Alex joined him by sitting on the floor across from him, blood still dripping from his hand.

"Yes… I love her. More than life itself," Alex said sincerely. "I'd do anything to protect her. And if you actually cared about her, you'd do the same, but obviously you don't."

Tristan scoffed. "Don't *pretend* to know me. I've been through hell and back just to be here. Contrary to what you've heard, Serene was willing for me, multiple times... I never—" Tristan stopped himself. He knew he wasn't completely innocent.

Alex scrunched his already red face. "You're a fucking liar. I saw the bruises! The slashes! Who are you trying to fool?"

Tristan knew it was useless explaining himself to this *man child*.

Alex continued. "Do you know what it's like to wake up to nightmares of you hurting her? Because that's her life right now! That's the life of the women you hurt because God only knows how many times you did these detestable acts."

Tristan got up as he tried to control his temper.

"For the last time... I didn't rape her!"

"Then why is she terrified of you? Huh? Do you have any idea the kind of strain you have placed on her and the baby? The kind of strain you will put on her if she sees you again? She almost lost the baby. Twice already. The last thing Serene needs right now is YOU."

Tristan was silent as he kept his back to Alex. He didn't believe a word this man was saying... but then, on a nearby table in the hallway, he saw a framed photo of Serene smiling in her wedding dress next to Alex. He walked over and picked it up. It was true. Serene was married.

No, no, no, it didn't make any sense.

Tristan studied her smiling face. He was filled with painful desire for her and the context of the picture simultaneously also caused an intense feeling of loss in him. Had he waited too long? Did he lose Serene forever?

"Please," Alex said, "I beg you... leave us alone. Serene can't handle this."

Tristan was devastated. It had also never crossed his mind how stressful and dangerous the whole situation might be. If she was really that afraid of him, even if he did manage to control his appetite, he wondered if it was worth the risk, given her possible health issues.

"Is she really having nightmares?" Tristan asked with deep

concern as he continued to look at her photo.

"Yes, and her father just died two weeks ago. Please. She doesn't need any more stress. She's been through enough, and I can't stand to see her go through anymore grief."

Tristan gently put down the photo. He didn't want to let her go again. He wanted to at least see her once. To see her smiling angelic face looking up at him. To feel her fragile body against his, and hear heart beating next to the sound of his unborn child's heart.

He didn't want to believe Alex, even with the evidence right in front of him he wanted to talk to her and ask her personally if she was truly happy. But, until he learned more about her health, he needed to be cautious. When he had stepped into her room, he had also realized what he had tried desperately to ignore... he wasn't ready.

Jason ended up hurting the love of his life, all because he'd lost patience. Tristan would not make the same mistake. He was determined to keep them safe, even if it meant waiting.

"You mentioned she almost lost the baby twice. You're a doctor, what state is Serene and the baby in?"

Alex's eyes narrowed, wondering how he knew about his profession. "She's... not well. She's lost a lot of weight and all the stress has caused further issues. We are doing everything we can: progesterone treatment, bed rest. She had contractions last week and spotting. She just started feeling better again. Should anything go wrong, the baby's too underdeveloped to survive." Alex noticed a change in him. Tristan no longer felt like a threat. For whatever reason, and for only a moment, they both bonded over their love for Serene and the baby.

"You're right," Tristan whispered.

"About?"

"Serene, and the baby. They cannot afford any more stress. Please, take good care of her. Love her and live peacefully."

"So, you're going to leave us alone?" Alex asked doubtful.

Tristan made his way towards the stairs but turned to look at Alex, leaving him with a warning.

"For a time, you have my word, but I'll be watching. If you've truly won her love, you'll never see me again. But if she's not happy, married or not, once *my* child is born, I will be back for them."

The following morning at the house, Alex and Serene held hands while talking to the employees of a security company. Alex's broken hand was bandaged and severely damaged, but in time doctors assured him he'd recover.

When Alex explained what he wanted done to secure the house more, the employees began their work.

"I'm amazed the burglar didn't steal anything," Serene said to Alex, "and that you managed to scare him off."

"Yes, I'm glad you and Stephanie weren't around. God only knows what would've happened." He lifted her hand and kissed it softly.

Serene hugged his arm and consoled him.

EPILOGUE

B efore heading out to work, Alex kissed his smiling wife in the kitchen of their new home. Once he left, Serene drank her orange juice while sorting the mail.

A large yellow envelope that read *Serene* in bold marker, grabbed her attention, but there was no postage.

Serene opened it on the kitchen counter. In it, was a three-page hand-written letter and a picture of her and Tristan laying together and smiling brightly.

Along with the letter was a CD with a list of songs written on it; It was the illicit music she had once requested from him. She scanned the letter and was shocked to see Lea's name mentioned and her familiar email at the end. A baby's coo echoed through the house.

Spotify Playlist: Krovs - Into Darkness

ALSO BY M. LEE WOE

M. Lee Woe is not afraid to push the boundaries of romance with her dark and thrilling novels. If your looking for fresh, intriguing, dark and twisted romance, she is working towards building her brand. Keep updated at_www.m-lee.us

KROVS: Blinding Light

Keep a look out for book two as the Krov saga continues. -M. Lee Woe

Blue - A Dark Fantasy Romance

A young girl named Valia lives in the poverty-riddled sectors near the outskirts of Arcadia city. Here her family is far from the Overlord's tyranny but not immune to its effects. After hearing about the many wonders and magic that take place within the Main Palace, Valia becomes obsessed with finding a way inside. Eventually, her dedication pays off. Unfortunately for her, it is the worst and greatest mistake she will ever make. She will be welcomed into a world of wonder and awakened with a new name.

-M. Lee Woe

Made in the USA
Coppell, TX
01 August 2020

32206034R00229